A LANE

MW01505571

THE HINDENBURG SPY

L.A. CHANDLAR

OLIVERHEBERBOOKS

Cover art by Kim Killion

Published by Oliver-Heber Books

0 9 8 7 6 5 4 3 2 1

Praise for The Hindenburg Spy

"L.A. Chandlar delivers a thriller both historically rich and breathlessly tense, making the Hindenburg disaster feel new. *The Hindenburg Spy* takes readers behind the iconic image of the burning airship into a world of espionage, pre-war glamour, and danger. Daring mayoral aide Lane Sanders navigates smoky clubs and international intrigue alongside Josephine Baker, Churchill, and FDR—a dazzling who's who of the era. Chandlar's prose is crisp, vital, and full of wit—fiction that doesn't just revisit the past but lets us feel its heat and momentum."

—John Copenhaver, award-winning author of **Hall of Mirrors**

"By opening the pages of L. A. Chandlar's *The Hindenburg Spy*, readers allow the author to transport them to a meticulously recreated historical setting, populated with all the expected diversity, while never losing sight of the fact that the topics under discussion are as timely as ever. The art deco ambiance of NYC envelopes the reader in comfort, before the extended set-piece aboard the Hindenburg itself becomes a white-knuckle ride for Lane Sanders, Daphne Franco, and for the readers themselves."

—Kristopher Zgorski, award winning author

Praise for The Hindenburg Spy

"*The Hindenburg Spy* is everything a historical mystery should be. It's set in a place and period you think you know, but it brings startling revelations. There's a wealth of delicious historical detail, but oh so lightly delivered that the story never takes second place. And the treatment of sombre themes is genuinely thought-provoking. What a treat!"

—Catriona McPherson, multi-award-winning author
of **The Edinburgh Murders**

"L.A. Chandlar's latest Lane Sanders Mystery, The Hindenburg Spy is a historical thriller packed with sleuthing, secrets, suspense, sinister plots, and all that jazz!

The elements for amazing storytelling are all here. A feisty, smart and daring protagonist, evocative writing, a rip-roaring pace, celebrity cameos (Fio LaGuardia, Josephine Baker, even an up-and-coming Winston Churchill make appearances), and nuggets of history that shine on the page. I am, for instance, indebted to Chandlar for introducing me to Eunice Carter, NYC's first Black woman prosecutor. Who knew? *The Hindenburg Spy*'s authentic backdrop makes it not just a satisfying read, but a resonant one. Do yourself a favor and pick up this book!"

—Cheryl Head, author, **Time's Undoing** and the
Charlie Mack Motown Mysteries

"L.A. Chandlar's latest historical thriller—featuring the indomitable Lane Sanders—shakes a heady cocktail of a heroine with moxie with the dangerous gangs of Fiorello LaGuardia's New York, adding a splash of witty banter, and a dash of romance. Featuring a race against the clock (and Lane against her nemesis) to save the Hindenburg, it's the absolute bee's knees crossed with the cat's pajamas!"

—Susan Elia MacNeal, **New York Times**-
bestselling author of the Maggie Hope series

"*The Hindenburg Spy* has it all—deliciously dark secrets, a cast of characters that leap off the page, jazz music, and historical context that lends authenticity to this thrilling ride of a book. Readers are in for a real treat."

–Wanda M. Morris, award-winning author
of ***Anywhere You Run***

Praise for National Bestselling Author L. A. Chandlar's Art Deco Mystery series

"Chandlar's lush historical novel follows Mayor LaGuardia in 1936 as his political future stalls under the weight of a missing persons case. Chandlar sets out to capture the complexities of the 1930s, a time of great art and culture as well as a time of great suffering."

—Crime Reads

"Chandlar has an eye for detail so New York City in the 1930s—the clothes, the nightclubs, the food—are all quite vivid and tangible."

—Historical Novel Society

"From the colorful and well-researched backdrops that make you feel as if you are definitely part of the 1936 realm; to the vibrant characters who must fight both good and evil in themselves to see justice done, Chandlar has done a fantastic job creating a suspense that you'll wish to read again."

—Suspense Magazine

"Readers will love The Gold Pawn for its compelling plot, rich historical details, action, and mystery, as well as the likable main characters... Chandlar has found a way to blend accurate historical facts with a more contemporary mind-set...Readers will eagerly await the next book. Highly recommended."

—Mystery Scene

"Colorful characters and rich historical flavor buoy Chandlar's frothy second Art Deco mystery…the complex central puzzle will keep readers turning the pages."

—Publishers Weekly

"Engaging, vivid, and intriguing, this historical mystery is not only a fascinating behind-the-scenes of Fiorello La Guardia's New York, but an action-packed adventure with quirky characters, snappy dialogue, a hint of romance—and starring one of the pluckiest, most entertaining heroines ever."

—Hank Phillippi Ryan, national bestselling author
of **Trust Me**, on **The Gold Pawn**

"[*The Silver Gun*] was just phenomenal… I absolutely loved this book and HIGHLY recommend it to anyone who is a mystery lover."

—Valerie's Musings, 5 stars

"It's easy to get lost in the myriad plot threads of this gleefully rendered story with its colorful characters, both real and fictional."

—Publishers Weekly

"Action packed and filled with 1930s charm."

—*Kirkus Reviews*

"L.A. Chandlar is a terrific new voice in mystery—an author you are going to love!"

—Charles Todd, *New York Times* bestselling author of THE BLACK ASCOT

THE PEARL DAGGER, L. A. Chandlar's latest Lane Sanders adventure, is an action-packed romp through 1930s New York's dance clubs, hotels, and halls of power. Lane is a heroine with charm, brains, and guts. Working on special assignment for her boss, Mayor Fiorello LaGuardia, she pursues a criminal syndicate with long-buried ties to her own late parents.

Chandlar's research is impressive, from lovingly detailed architectural descriptions to transatlantic crossings and swank 1930s New York nightlife. But it's Lane herself, the engaging star of this series, who will delight readers most.

Cameos by Orson Welles, Winston Churchill, J. R. R. Tolkien, C. S. Lewis, and others round out a strong cast of cops, gangsters, reporters, and street urchins.

As fun and exciting as a toboggan ride in snowy Central Park, one of the many treats you'll find in THE PEARL DAGGER.

—James W. Ziskin, Author of the Anthony and Macavity award-winning Ellie Stone mysteries

"L.A. Chandlar writes with an exuberance that brings her characters and settings fully to life. Whether it's doing the latest dance steps at one of New York's hottest jazz clubs, or battling bad guys on a dark city street or a deserted theater, The Pearl Dagger will have you breathless at every turn!"

—Alyssa Maxwell Author of *The Gilded Newport Mysteries A Lady and Lady's Maid Mysteries*

"With her third Art Deco mystery, Agatha-nominated author LA Chandlar showcases a masterful display of history--whether it's New York's storied past or main character Lane Sanders personal backstory and chance encounters with some of the most well-known names of her era. The result is like an intricate dance that seamlessly moves from slow and deliberate to heart pounding and fast paced. You never know which direction you'll be led next. The Pearl Dagger is a must for both history buffs and mystery lovers alike."

— Kellye Garrett, Agatha, Anthony and Lefty
award-winning author of Missing White Woman

"Dangerous villains and gangsters in 1930s NYC, with humor, history, vintage cocktails, and art as a backbone…"

—Jen J. Danna

"*The Silver Gun* has humor, excitement, mystery, danger, romance, lots of great characters, and more! I highly recommend *The Silver Gun*, especially to those who live, work, or vacation in the Big Apple, and to cozy readers who like their mystery mixed with history." —*Jane Reads*, 5 Stars

—*Jane Reads*, 5 Stars

Prologue

It was the voice I'd remember most. The flames violently tore through the behemoth like a demonic hand had swiped its talons through a carcass of molten metal and fire. A roiling ball of hellish colors engulfed half the ship. The flames viciously charged upward and outward, a fiery maw devouring the ship, the people, the airfield. Thirty seconds from start to scorched finish.

Explosions, people running and screaming, heat that seemed to have a face, then an impossible leap. Yet what was etched into my mind and my soul forever after was the reporter live on the radio exclaiming to the world a heartbreaking and guttural, "Oh, the humanity!"

Chapter 1

I had a nemesis. A mortal enemy, if you will. As an influential aide to the mayor of New York City—especially Mayor Fiorello LaGuardia—it shouldn't be surprising that I might have a few adversarial characters in my life. But with Daphne Franco? Well, now. She's in an entirely different category. Moll and mobster, mixed with a sleazy Glenda the Good Witch from the book *The Wizard of Oz*—and don't forget to throw in a dash of insanity. More than a dash.

I tapped the file on Daphne neatly on my desk, the last tap with a little more forceful sass than strictly necessary. I opened the hefty packet and ruffled through the well-worn pages. How did one describe Daphne? There was something of a carnival specter in her. She orchestrated her unpredictable powerplays with a sexy, macabre nonchalance because it just plain brought her pleasure.

Did she make her criminal home base in a lunatic asylum? Yes. Yes, she did.

Did she create contingency on top of contingency plan for routing out enemies, making millions of dollars, all with flair-filled escape scenarios? Absolutely.

Did she hunt me down as a child and try to kill me? Yep.

Did I hate her? Oh yes.

She killed my parents and chasing her down had been as wild as riding the Cyclone at Coney Island. On fire. We were an odd match warring against each other, and no one to date had thwarted her except me. Everything was about to come to a head. And if I couldn't handle it? This time, the stakes were higher than I'd ever faced. Not only was the city I deeply cared about in danger, but I was also starting to get the feeling that we were at the precipice of global disaster.

In New York City, the gangsters were at war. Fighting for territory that developed during Prohibition, and Daphne had her hands in all of it. Everyone wanted the power that had grown exponentially throughout organized crime networks from the illegal sale of liquor.

Standing between the city and chaos was a band of my chosen family including a reporter, a group of street urchins, fellow secretaries, and a hot detective who was quickly becoming very important to me. It was a group led by my boss, all five foot two of him. He was a double minority as half-Jewish and half-Italian, first generation. He was a loudmouth and rude, but also humorous, kind, and a romantic art lover who fought for his city every day. While bellowing at everyone. With his black hair shining beneath a fedora, he seemed seven feet tall from his fearless stand against powerful gangsters.

Our team loved working together to protect New York and I'd learned to trust not only my own intuition, but to trust others so we could all save each other. On my most recent trip to London, I'd had the joy of performing a spectacular rescue of the aforementioned hot detective, my boyfriend Finn Brodie. It was glorious, I thought to myself with a smirk.

With a throng of mobsters vying for territory, Daphne Franco had lately been uncannily silent. Which meant she was either in the middle of it, or she was going to be. I was not about to let Daphne or any other gangster harm my city and my family of friends who fought together against the escalating threats these past several months. Though a part of me admired Daphne's skills and panache, I knew we could not keep going round and round. One of us was going to have to bow out one way or another. So I'd wait for her to come out of hiding and make a move.

The day began like every workday, with the usual energy, passion, and humor. But by nightfall, a few critical dominos had fallen, setting off a chain of events that would reshape the city, my own life, and the world. Even though in the end, most would never know what really happened.

———

CITY HALL WAS HOPPING with messengers, aides, and reporters scurrying about, plus the daily line of people who needed help and had nowhere to turn but our office. The mayor saw every single person, every single day. "Fio"—a dear family friend as well as my boss—moved through the crowd of petitioners with the speed of a Cord 812 Cabriolet, my current favorite car. I especially liked the navy-blue convertible model. With a price tag around $3000, it was catastrophically out of my league. But a girl could dream.

Fio was willing to work with the seamy side of the city as well as the power players. Speaking over seven languages and fighting for the little guy, he was loved by the people and often hated by many of the power brokers. He was small, but mighty. He kept the press running after him and never disappointed when it came to a good story. Fio was impervious to the typical ways—I'm talking bribes here—that the privileged were used to getting what they wanted in politics. And he was unafraid of making a scene, in fact he adored a good publicity stunt, such as pounding confiscated slot machines with a sledge hammer. His ability to be everywhere at once, loud, and unable to be persuaded with money… made him a venerable, powerful man indeed.

Having jumped into my work immediately this morning, I thanked my friend Roxy as she thoughtfully brought in a cup of coffee for me.

"I got the feeling you wouldn't get a chance to get a cup with the big lineup today. Seems longer than usual," she said, her baby-blue eyes smiling as Fiorello stepped over the tiger skin rug in his office, rubbing his hands together in great anticipation of a productive day.

"Good call. Thank you," I said as she set the cup down on my desk and turned quickly to dive into her daily pile of typing. "Hey, do you and Val want to go to lunch today?"

"I can, but Val's taking the day off," said Roxy.

"Again? That's three days this month. When we talked on the phone, she just made it sound like it was a bad cold. I don't ever remember her taking off three days in a whole year. Maybe I'll go check on her after work," I said, taking a sip of the hot, creamy coffee.

With a concerned tilt to her curly blonde head, Roxy smoothed the edge of her heather-gray cashmere sweater that fit snuggly to her perfect figure. It was an anxious gesture, clearly apprehensive. "Something isn't right lately, Lane. Valerie seems happy with Raff, so it's not that. But something is off."

I rolled my eyes. Raff, Val's recent new boyfriend, was the right-hand man of a notorious and strangely complicated gangster, Uncle Louie. But Valerie really did seem happy. Raff and his mob boss actually helped us on our last case. We stopped a horrible incident from happening that would have been incendiary for the city and our tenuous civil rights. Raff was helpful and he'd been nothing but courteous to Val. I was trying to convince myself that it would all turn out okay, but things were obviously complicated.

"Lane! Time to get through this line," barked my boss, interrupting our conversation.

"Yes, sir," I yelled back. To Roxy I added, "Let's swing by her place tonight." She gave a conspiratorial nod and went back to her desk.

After a couple of hours of work, plugging through press packets, notes, and agenda items, Fio bolted out of his office. I jumped to my feet. I did that about a dozen times a day, heart racing from his yelling, as I braced for handling anything from an impromptu press conference to a mad dash downtown to a relief station where he'd heard the staff were not treating his citizens with respect. Mrs. Zhao, a spindly Chinese woman wearing a white hat with a decrepit pink rose clinging for dear life to its rim, stood behind him, wringing her hands. She haltingly followed Fio from the office. Her eyes were filled with worry and fear, tears about to brim over making me want to put an arm around her.

"Lane!" he bellowed. "Call Ray, we need to get up to Harlem Prison. Now. On the double."

I grabbed the black receiver off the phone to call his driver, the cord almost knocking my coffee over. Fio ran back and forth, gathering his coat and Mrs. Zhao's, then barking orders at the office staff about what needed to get done while we were gone. In a flurry of action, the three of us raced down the stairs and jumped into the waiting sedan. Fio filled us in as he slammed the door.

"There's been a murder! And two *children* are locked up at Harlem Prison and need our help!"

Chapter 2

Ray drove like he was Bernd Rosemeyer, the latest Grand Prix champion who was on the Nazi Germany team. Fio spurred Ray on the entire way up to 121st Street between Lexington and Third, resulting in an unglamorous arrival. I had a queasy stomach from every muscle clenching on the high-speed journey in an effort to keep from banging into the door, the front seat, or Mrs. Zhao.

Despite the rambunctious drive, Mrs. Zhao managed to fill us in on why she came to the mayor's office. Late last night, she'd heard through the grapevine that there had been a murder, and two kids were being kept in Harlem prison but hadn't been arrested. One was a boy she knew from making her rounds as a well-known midwife in Chinatown. No one had seen him since yesterday and he missed some work that he'd been promised—a sure sign to her that something was wrong—so she began asking questions.

I appreciated not only her concern for the children, but her moxie. The friends and store owners she talked with in her neighborhood were too afraid to rock the boat, but she knew if she didn't speak up, no one would. She knew the police were of no help regarding two boys from Chinatown. Who would stand up for some unknown street urchins in a dubious situation? So she came to City Hall hoping that the mayor with the apropos bust of

Napoleon peering down from his office bookshelves might care enough. Well, he sure did.

Fio pulled his fedora rakishly over one eye and nodded curtly to me, making me grin. We were going into battle. Two other squad cars pulled up with reinforcements as Fio looked back at his sedan, probably wishing it had been a white steed he could have rode in on to save the day. I squared my shoulders, ready for the rude awakening the prison staff would receive—courtesy of Fio.

The terracotta and brownstone structure looked like it belonged in the past, a piece of history that used to be the corner-stone of the Village of Harlem in its earlier days. Its five-story center tower had several gables at the top with two clocks looking down upon us with a Victorian gothic glare.

Fio routinely shook down establishments that he discovered were not up to par, especially when it concerned his citizens. He burst through the front doors with the force of a linebacker, eyes darting everywhere at once, ready to pounce.

The four rather large policemen whom we had summoned filed in after us. One was Scott, a policeman who happened to always to be on hand to witness my more theatrical escapades. Finn and I had become quite the spectacle as of late. At least we were as successful in solving crime together as we were enter-taining.

A stunned audience of three inmates and one lackadaisical guard faced us, none too quick to move. The guard shifted in surprise then fell back into his chair with a loud crash and a few choice words. The three inmates didn't budge. I assumed it was from being in the presence of my famous boss, a true authority figure, which made the guard in the chair look all the more like a bumbling fool.

We stormed past them and into the adjoining dining hall, no official prison cook in sight. Fio rapidly located the cook asleep on the floor in the back of the kitchen, shook him awake by the collar, then promptly fired him. Fury at such negligence fairly radiated from the top of his head. He'd be bellowing soon.

The inmates were a scraggly and heartbreaking crowd. It

reminded me of when Finn told me about the routine that the NYPD detectives used to decide who to indict and who to release. They gathered up all the arrests of the day and with a microphone in the middle of the room, on display, the perpetrators would make their case. The detectives would decide what to do depending on that time at the mic. Only a few savvy, more intelligent guys would make the detectives laugh, knowing they'd go lighter on them if they curried a little favor. But most were just like the men I was seeing right now: undernourished, stunted in growth and intelligence, a vacant look in the eyes.

Fio shot me a knowing glare and I nodded. Without the basic needs of food, shelter, clothing, and education, why would we expect people to end up anywhere but here? Fio and I had a regular conversation along these lines, and he emitted a *grrrrr* as the scene of hopelessness riled him up further. And if the dining hall was in such disarray—a lone inmate dishing up food with no prison staff in sight—what on earth would the situation be for the two young children?

"Lane!" barked Fio. "We have work to do. I'm going to ransack the place."

Scott cracked his knuckles with an anticipatory grin. I went with Scott and another officer in one direction with the guard who was back on his feet. Fio and the other two cops went with the warden who finally showed up.

We basically ran through the place trying to scare the devil out of everyone, making the guards know that they were being watched, and they'd better shape up. Fio felt that every citizen deserved their government's best and the prisoners were citizens too. After quickly going through the forty cells, sprawling hallways, and the courtrooms, Scott and I suddenly heard a bellowing that sounded like a wild animal in both volume and ferocity. But just a bit screechy.

Scott and I turned to each other and simultaneously said, "Fio!"

Fiorello had discovered something, and by the noise he was making, he was not happy about it. We ran in the direction of the howling and flew down the incongruously beautiful iron and marble stairway that wound from the top tower down to the entryway.

"What's going on?" I called as I tried to get my breath back.

Fio was indeed raging at full volume. He was protectively holding the hand of a scrawny, ten-year-old boy, who in turn held the hand of another boy. They were dirty, needed a good meal, and obviously scared. But they clearly liked Fio. With each bellow, they inched a tiny bit closer to their hero. I honestly couldn't understand what Fio was going on about. He was so angry, his words all rushed together.

"Mr. LaGuardia," I said kindly but firmly and pierced him with my best impression of my Aunt Evelyn's glare. "Take a breath. What is going on?"

He and his two new little friends all took a bracing breath, their shoulders rising and falling together.

Fio cleared his throat and said, "Thank you, Lane. I'm so livid, I can hardly see straight. Mrs. Zhao was right. These two boys were in a dark cell. By themselves. In the ward with all the adults." His teeth gritted together in stormy outrage. But when he looked down at the two boys, his face was gentle and kind.

Scott, in an incredulous voice, asked, "Why? Why aren't they with the Child Society?"

"I asked the same," said Fio, reddening from the chin up all over again. "Supposedly, they'd been locked up for lack of twenty-five-thousand-dollars bail as material witnesses in a murder case."

I sputtered, "Twenty-five—that's more than a year's wage of twelve or fourteen people! You can't incarcerate witnesses. They're…they're *little kids*."

"I know. It's often the typical practice because it's so easy to lose witnesses, but not with children," said Fio with a grim look. "I will be taking them to the Child Society *myself*." He was not about to let go of that little hand. Aunt Evelyn would have fits about the whole thing. I wanted to ask the boys a few questions, but they needed food and a bath first.

"Come on," I said. "Let's take them to my place before the Child Society. They can get a good bath and a very good meal with us. We need to know more about this, and they need some extra care." I smiled down at them and they returned it with slightly wary, thin smiles.

"Good idea, Lane."

I didn't recognize the boys from Morgan's crew, a teen who had helped us immensely with a couple cases. She was the captain of her urchin gang, our very own group of Irregulars.

With an encouraging smile, I said, "Okay, kiddos. What are your names?"

The scrawny one on the left with dark red hair and green eyes murmured softly, "Patrick." The one on the right was smaller than Patrick, with black eyes that looked like they smiled easily and frequently. Since he looked like he was probably Chinese, he was most likely Mrs. Zhao's little friend from Chinatown.

Fio turned to him and asked, "And what's your name?"

He looked up at Fio with adoration and said loud and clear, "Frank."

The stout response tugged a smile from Fio's lips, and he said, "Nice to meet you, Patrick and Frank. Now let's go take a ride in my car and I'm going to get you to a more suitable situation. Are you okay with that?"

"Yes, sir," exclaimed Frank while Patrick nodded shyly.

When we got the kids out of the prison building, Mrs. Zhao greeted the boys with tender firmness, and Frank's eyes lit up with a genuine smile.

"Hello, Frank. I'm so glad you're all right. Why did they bring you here? Is it true what they said about a murder?" she quickly asked.

The boys looked like they would fold in on themselves, their joy at being rescued from that horrible place suddenly snuffed out. I was about to reach out to them and tell them they didn't have to talk about it yet.

But before I could, Frank blurted, "Yeah, we saw the murder, all right. We were there when it happened."

"Did you see the killer?" I asked.

The boys looked at each other in alarm and then both of them crossed their arms and shook their heads. After that, they refused to utter one word.

Chapter 3

Back home, Aunt Evelyn and Mr. Kirkland flew into action to take care of Frank and Patrick. Their kind and safe presence began to loosen the boys' tongues as they looked around our colorful and homey townhouse. Patrick was nervous about Ripley, our giant German Shepherd, even though Ripley was on his very best behavior. Frank, however, needed to be deterred from attempting to ride Ripley like a horse.

I smelled the hearty chicken noodle soup simmering on the stove as soon as we opened our front door. It was just what the boys needed—after a good scrubbing from Aunt Evelyn, of course.

Mr. Kirkland, Fio, and I all waited in the kitchen as we discussed the murder. At the prison, we had to get the boys out as soon as possible, so this was our first chance to talk about the details. The shooting was of note because the victim was a wealthy businessman. However, something seemed fishy to me, because Fiorello hadn't heard about it until Mrs. Zhao came along. Usually, he was on top of every major event that happened in the city from fires to burglaries, to car crashes from listening to his police radios that he had installed at the office, his home, and even his car.

Aunt Evelyn quickly got the boys in tip-top shape, and we

heard their orderly descent from the bathroom upstairs before we could see them. In walked two much cleaner little boys. The grime had been scrubbed away, hair had been washed and combed neatly, and they even wore a set of new clothes. My aunt believed in being prepared for all circumstances, so she had clean clothes of most sizes packed carefully up in our attic. Just in case.

Evelyn set them up at the kitchen table while giving them a lesson on etiquette, complete with instructions on putting their napkins in their laps and using the soup spoon instead of tipping the bowl to their mouths. We were all dying to dive into questioning them, but we needed to make sure they felt comfortable, otherwise they'd clam up again like they did in the car.

Meanwhile, I had called both Roarke and Morgan to ask them to come over, along with Finn. Morgan, head of our Irregulars, had been working lately with Mary Shanley, also known as Dead Shot Mary, one of our first women detectives in the NYPD, so I was able to locate Morgan quite quickly. Finn was out on a call, but Roarke picked up Morgan on his way over and they let themselves in, greeting a deliriously happy Ripley at the door.

"We're in the kitchen, come on back!" I yelled to them.

"Hey there! Looks like you're having a little party," said Roarke, taking in our domestic scene. Roarke was my dear friend and sleuthing partner as well as a devoted investigative journalist. We'd gotten into a lot of scrapes as we followed leads together. His intuition for a good news story and my own, well, nosiness, not to mention intense love for New York, compelled us to often *help out* the local police in running down clues. Especially when my own boss was threatened, or when I found myself in the crosshairs. Which, *ahem*, had been happening regularly as of late.

"I think I've seen you before," said Morgan to the boys. "Patrick and…is it Fred?"

"Frank," said Frank, after he slurped up a thick noodle then dabbed his mouth with his napkin, making eye contact with Aunt Evelyn as he did so. "Nice to meet you."

Morgan's had to hide a smile with his precocious greeting and I winked at her in amusement when she caught my eye. "And you as well, Mr. Frank," she returned. He merely nodded as if he expected nothing less than her genteel offering of conversation.

Mr. Kirkland, my grandfather figure and unspoken household manager, bit back a laugh, then asked the boys if they'd like another helping—and of course they did. You learned early on the streets to get what meals you could whenever they were available. Knowing this, he murmured to them they could have as much as they liked and that they didn't have to hurry, which produced a contented sigh from Patrick.

After the boys cleaned their bowls for a third time, we cleared the dishes and all took a seat again. Fio clasped his hands and set his elbows on the scrubbed pine table. He kindly looked at the boys and said, "We appreciate your help as witnesses, boys. Is there anything you can tell us about the shooter? Even something small or obvious? Such as, was it a man or a woman? Tall or short?"

Frank and Patrick exchanged a desperate look. Despite their rather gregarious nature now that they knew they were among friends, they abruptly retreated into themselves. Patrick shook his head minutely. Frank blanched and his eyes shifted side to side, then he looked down at his shoes.

I caught Morgan's eye and tilted my head toward the boys, gesturing for her to try to address them.

"Say, boys," she began. "Just so you know, you're not in trouble at all. You didn't do anything wrong."

"Yeah, we know," said Patrick softly.

"Well, how about you just tell us about that day and what *led up* to that time. Can you do that?" Morgan asked with a gentle tone.

They shared another look and Frank nodded. "Okay. We can tell you that," he said with a wary voice that told us he would not be divulging all his information.

Fiorello asked, "So what day was it?"

"It was just yesterday, Tuesday. I always help the newspaper guy on Tuesdays at four. The one on Lexington at 42nd Street," answered Patrick. The room took a collective sigh of relief.

Thankfully, the kids hadn't been in the slammer very long. The kitchen lights made Patrick's deep red hair that had looked practically brunette before his thorough washing, glisten with cinnamon tones. Despite being street urchins, they looked reasonably healthy so they must have some people looking after them. Probably Mrs. Zhao, which made me like her even more.

"Yeah," agreed Frank. "Usually we're downtown in Chinatown. But Patrick got that job, so we both go uptown on Tuesdays. I help out a shoe shiner outside Grand Central. He gives me a penny for every customer I get." I figured Frank was an outstanding salesman, so he would fare pretty well.

"So we finished our job kind of late. The daylight is getting longer, so we can work more. We decided to splurge on a knish from the cart at 44th."

"On Lexington?" asked Roarke, taking notes.

"Yes. The cart owner will give us two for a penny at the end of the day, sometimes for free. So we got our knishes, and then we decided to sit against the wall and have our dinner."

"Right there where the cart is? So up against the wall of the Chrysler Building?" I asked.

"Uh huh. It was a sunny day, so the walls were warm."

"And then a few money men came out. You know, top hat, a cane, and gold watches. Loaded."

Frank's eyes were huge, probably thinking of all the money it cost to wear things like that. Those men might as well have been from Mars they were from such different worlds as the boys. "Remember that tall one had a pocket watch with a big diamond on it?" he asked wistfully.

Patrick nodded with glistening eyes. "Sure do." Then those shining eyes clouded over. "But that's when *they* showed up," he whispered.

Frank swallowed hard.

"Who?" asked Aunt Evelyn. "Who showed up?"

Frank shook his head. Patrick sucked in his lips, refusing to speak.

"Well, what happened after that?" asked Roarke.

A little shudder went through Frank, making him look like he was a very little boy indeed. His voice went lower, and we all bent our heads closer. He said, just above a whisper, "The rich guys all separated and two of them crossed the street toward Grand Central. Then three men came up to the one with the diamond watch and top hat who was still standing there. It looked like they were just going to talk. They weren't threatening him that I could see. But something was off. I could feel the hairs on my neck go up."

When Frank's pause lasted longer than he could take, Fio prodded, "What happened next?"

"The leader of those men had asked a few questions, and by the look on his face, he wasn't happy with the answers. Then he turned in our direction and we heard him tell the other guy to finish it. That's when one of the guys pulled out a gun and shot him. Right there on the sidewalk. Right in the chest."

Mr. Kirkland placed a reassuring hand on Frank's shoulder.

Frank looked strengthened by that big hand and said, "Then all hell broke loose. Everyone was screaming, the three bad guys raced away."

"Did they take anything from the man that was shot? His wallet? That diamond watch?" asked Morgan.

"No. Then there were policemen on the scene. But the guy was dead already."

"You could tell?" asked Morgan.

"Yeah. That gun was huge. Way bigger than the cops' guns. There was a lot of blood. All over the sidewalk."

Patrick turned his head to the side and squinted his eyes. "Patrick," I said, "you look like you remembered something."

"Yeah," he said, putting his elbow on the table, giving it some thought. "Frank, didn't one of the guys say something else? Like *we'll do it*…or something like that?"

Patrick crinkled his brow. "He might have. I'll have to think about it."

"And they talked funny," said Frank with a quizzical look.

"How do you mean?" asked Evelyn.

"Not a lisp or anything. But I'm not sure. Just funny."

"Did you recognize any of those men?" asked Evelyn casually.

Patrick sucked in his lips again, and Frank became bolder, saying, "No. No way."

After a few moments of silence, I said, "I have an idea. Morgan, why don't you take the boys and Ripley to the back patio to look around. I think they'd like a break, and I bet they'd love looking at Mr. Kirkland's maple tree with all the lights." I winked at her.

"Got it. Come on boys. You'll love it." She led them outside and when she closed the door, we all looked at each other. I wondered what they were hiding that was worse than witnessing the actual crime, because they were able to talk about that pretty easily. I picked up a lovely old deck of cards on the side table and tapped them as I gave it some thought. The sound of the *tap tap* made me think of the file on Daphne from early that morning. I kept waiting for her to make a move, was this it? But the rich men didn't seem to be involved with the gangsters, at least they sure didn't fit the typical description.

"Morgan will get it out of them," said Roarke confidently.

"I don't doubt it," said Aunt Evelyn. "We can have them stay here with us for as long as you like, Fio."

"Thank you, Evelyn," said Fio. "Child Society will help, but it might be nice to give them some peace for a couple of days. They've been through a lot. I think Mrs. Zhao would like to visit them, too. I'll give her your number and address."

"I'd love to meet her," said Aunt Evelyn. She genuinely loved people. With her eccentric upbringing in Europe being Egyptian and French, not to mention her artistic nature, she was a gatherer. She connected with people of all kinds, uptown and downtown, street urchin to the first lady, Black, White, Indian, Chinese, Jewish, Mexican, you name it. They all loved her. "I have a couple of artist friends coming over later. I'll show the boys my studio and let them paint. We'll have a lovely time!"

"I have a feeling you better make an extra-large dinner, Mr. Kirkland," said Fio with a chuckle. "They have a mighty appetite for such little guys."

Despite that chuckle, he looked perplexed and unsettled.

I asked, "What did you think of, Fio? You look distracted."

He nodded. "I want to know why I didn't know about this. I'd heard about a shooting on the police radio, but the high profile nature of it hadn't reached me. And I certainly didn't catch that children were witnesses."

He was right. It didn't make sense and my unease began to grow. Outside in the sunshine, Morgan had been leading the boys and Ripley in a romp around the little yard. We didn't have our summer furnishings out yet, but the overarching maple tree held its sturdy winter lanterns and lights strung about, and Mr. Kirkland had planted yellow and blue pansies all around, giving us a taste of spring and summer colors coming. This time of year, I always felt desperate for color. I missed the green of the trees and the flowers all over the city.

After they ran off their big lunch, the boys collapsed on the wooden chairs outside, breathing heavily. I watched as Morgan used her street smarts and her charm to get them to confide in her.

Just then, I heard the front door open and a familiar voice ring out. "Lane? Kirkland?"

"Hey, Finn! Back here!" I yelled. I went to greet him halfway and came to a halt a foot in front of him. Concern etched his face and a sense of urgency radiated from his stance.

"What's wrong?" I asked, as our eyes locked.

Finn was a prominent detective and we first met when he'd been working undercover for Fio. We felt the chemistry between us before we even said two words. He had a dangerous job and he'd worried that the secrets of his past back in England, not to mention his daily employment on the streets of New York City, might bring me harm. But honestly, I could say the same thing. In fact, he quickly discovered that my job was even more dangerous than his at times. So we decided we worked best together. I could find his eyes in any crowd easily and could distinguish his walk among hundreds.

"We have a problem. There was a murder yesterday," he said.

"We might know something about that."

"Oh no." He wiped his face with an invisible washcloth. "Of course you do."

"But wait, you're on homicide cases all the time. Why is this one different?"

"Because we happen to be friends with the NYPD's main suspect."

"*Oh no* is right," I said rather queasily. "You'd better come with me."

Chapter 4

"Hey, Val, let me carry that bag for you. You look like you could use a little help," said Raff, trying for a convincing smile that belied the concern he felt.

She gave him a quick but scrutinizing look and said, "That's okay. I think I've got it."

Valerie switched hands and tried to act nonchalant—something at which she was not accomplished. He noticed she had on another new blouse with a high neck. She favored those, and this one, with its dark green swirls and tie in the front with a big bow, made her light green eyes shine. He loved it when she wore green. Her tiny freckles sprinkled over her nose and light dustings all over her arms and shoulders mirrored her youthful spirit.

"So after work, do you want to go see a show?" he asked. "*Shall We Dance* is playing, and I love a good romantic comedy. Especially with Fred and Ginger. Or maybe the Marx Brothers? *A Day at the Races*? What do you think?"

"Actually, Raff, I'm not feeling quite up to it. I think I might be coming down with something."

"Did you miss work again today?" he asked. She rarely missed a day at her job that she loved. She had been rather quiet, and now that she mentioned it, she did look paler than usual.

"Yeah, I called in sick."

"I thought you were going to go visit your family last night. Were you able to go?"

She cleared her throat and looked around. He got the impression she was trying very hard to look casual but failing miserably. "Yes, I went last night. Just a quick visit. I had some clothes to take to my brothers and some groceries. Actually, I need a couple of things, let's go in here for a second." She turned into the little neighborhood deli near her place. It had a good selection of groceries that might be needed at a moment's notice, and it was easy to get in and out quickly. No big lines, just people grabbing a few essentials. He followed her in, and they chitchatted about what she wanted to make for dinner. They'd been spending more and more time together over the last couple of months.

On Second Avenue, between 76th and 77th, there were all sorts of little restaurants, delis, hardware stores, bakeries and every other enterprise to make money. Raff had always admired New Yorkers' sense of industry. None of this plain-old begging like he'd seen in other cities. Even beggars had a tune or a compelling story. Everyone had an approach. Sure, you felt scammed sometimes, like the time he saw the same guy with no legs—honest-to-God—give a kiss goodbye to a pretty well-off looking lady who had been pushing his wheel chair, then he sort of jumped out of his wheelchair and got on the subway with a cup to start hobbling down the aisle of the cars to ask for money. Raff had heard his sob story about a dozen times, and one day he watched the guy collect almost twelve dollars. Raff had watched him for a half hour, then he hopped out of the car to that nicely dressed woman with a big grin who had his wheelchair all set for him. The next day, the same story all over again. So, sure, Raff felt a little conned because he'd given him fifty cents, but *damn*. He had to give the guy a nod for his industrial spirit.

Raff found a couple of apples that looked perfectly firm and tasty, so he picked those up, then went over to where Val stood below a shelf of jarred tomatoes. She was a tall gal, just under six feet, and he loved it that they looked almost eye to eye. When they danced, she just felt right in his arms. She reached up to the top shelf and as she lifted the heavy glass, she yelped. The jar slipped from her grasp and crashed onto the floor. A few other patrons jumped from the noise, and Raff ran over.

"Are you okay? Did you cut yourself?"

"No. I'm okay," she said softly. But she cradled her arm to her chest and winced. "I think I just pulled a muscle or something."

"Here, be careful of all the glass. Step over here," he directed as a worker rushed out with a mop and dustpan and began to carefully pick up the large shards while cooing not to mind at all, accidents happened. Raff looked gratefully at the man as he deftly cleaned the messy spill.

"Miss Valerie, hurt your shoulder again? I keep telling you to let me help you with those high shelves," he said not unkindly with a soft chuckle. *Hurt her shoulder again?*

A blush swept over Val's face as she looked embarrassed but also a little put-out with the worker. She was distinctly trying to avoid looking Raff in the eye.

"Val…" he began.

"I don't want to talk about it," she said in a clipped voice. She quickly took the unbroken jar of tomatoes that the manager held out to her and grabbed a loaf of fresh bread and zoomed to the checkout. Practically throwing money at the cashier, she went to grasp the bag of groceries with her good arm.

"I'll take care of it," said Raff as he swooped in and lifted the bag.

They walked back to her place in silence, and he wondered if she was trying to come up with a story that he'd believe about her seemingly recurring shoulder issues. The problem for her was going to be that in his line of work, his main job was reading people and situations to intuit danger, lies or subterfuge. And he knew she was not a good liar, her blushes and those honest eyes of hers betrayed any smoke screen, bluff or straight-up lie. Even when they played a game of cards, she had tells that he could read almost instantly. It was adorable. But this… This was no game. And he had a distinct feeling that it did not bode well for her. It was a serious matter, and what was worse was that he felt the same prickle of apprehension he always did when he and his formidable boss knew danger was lurking nearby.

Raff was still nursing his concern about Val's shoulder as he followed her up the three flights to her apartment. Red bricks flanked the stairway as they wound their way upward. The building had nice curves and little nooks that gave it a cozy feeling, not to mention the creative tenants who filled those spaces and their small landings with flowers here and there or even a couple of colorful paintings. The apartments sat above stores and restaurants, the doors leading up to the apartments tucked between the store fronts, almost invisible unless you knew to look for them.

Raff had grown up in a tight and overcrowded tenement. He and his folks had come from Portofino, just outside Genoa, for a better life when Raff was about five. He remembered Portofino with fleeting bits of scenes and senses from his early childhood. In fact, it was those memories that flooded the poems that he sought to write in the wee hours of the night. There was something special about late night, when morning hadn't yet begun to gray the skies, when he'd had his fill of good wine, the city was twinkling with its effervescent lights, and perhaps he'd been to a small club downtown where the music of a bass, violin, and guitar trio tinkered with the hearts of the little crowd. He just *had* to write the words and lines that came to him. And in those moments, warm memories of rocky cliffs, a seaside village, and aquamarine waters would lap at his thoughts. He'd love to take Valerie back there. To show her the colors, to feel the hot Italian sun on their browned bodies, to smell the scents of spices, salty ocean, wine, and flowers all mixed together.

He shook himself out of his reverie as it occurred to him that climbing the stairs was proving very hard for Val. She moved slowly and carefully. She usually flew up the stairs at the same pace as his. They finally came to her door. She carefully unlocked it, and they entered. Raff put the bag of groceries down and helped Valerie with her coat. She still cradled her arm, and it was difficult to get the coat off without hurting her more.

"Val," he whispered. "Here, sit down. Let me get some ice."

She sat, heedful of not jarring her arm. Raff watched her efforts, knowing she must be in a good deal of pain to be that cautious. He went to the ice box and took out a hunk of ice, carefully chipping off pieces with the nearby ice pick into the sink to make an ice pack with a towel. Then he went to the little bathroom and retrieved a couple of aspirin and brought a glass of water and the ice pack to Val.

As he walked toward her at the dining table meant for two, he said, "You know, Val, maybe we should have a doctor take a look at that—"

He'd been about to say that at least they could have Aunt Evelyn take a quick look at it, she'd had a bit of medical experience and might be able to say if it was something serious or not. But when he'd uttered the word *doctor*, Val's eyes shot up to him, wide with terror. That fear had made her suddenly careless of a jerky movement which brought forth a whole new round of pain. She winced but couldn't take her eyes off of him.

"No doctors. You have to promise me," she said through clenched teeth.

"Val, what is going on? You're never like this. What happened?"

Fear and anger raced through her eyes and then defeat made her face crumple as one tear slid down her cheek. "Oh, Val," he said, his hand cupping her chin with his thumb smoothing away the tear. "You can tell me."

Then a thought struck him a significant blow, making his stomach drop. He struggled to contain his anger, because what came to mind made his blood absolutely boil. She looked down, studying her glass of water, unwilling to meet his eyes.

Barely containing the tremor that he knew would be in his voice, he asked carefully, "You said you went home to see your family yesterday. What. Happened?"

"Not what you think," she said quickly.

"I don't believe you. In fact…" He stopped and softened his voice even further. "In fact, really Val, you need to let me look at your shoulder."

Her eyes never lost that haunted look, but it was a testament to her pain that she sighed and then solemnly nodded. He sat down in the chair next to her and gently shuffled closer. He looked at the bow of her blouse that had a loose tie and asked, "Do you want me to…?"

She nodded. "I don't think I can."

"Okay." He slowly eased the bow out of its knot. Then he carefully unbuttoned the top silk-covered button. Then the next one. And on down. A little shiver went through her. "Did I hurt you?" he asked.

"No," she whispered.

"Okay, I'm going to ease this off, first your left shoulder, then your right. Try not to tense up."

He carefully eased the blouse off one side, then the next.

"Oh, Val," he said, his heart breaking in one second, then a fury that he'd never felt in his entire life hit him hard. "Who did this?"

"No. I fell, Raff."

"No, you did not. Don't lie to me, Valerie. These are not bruises from a fall. Tell me. You are safe with me." His voice was soft like a whisper but solid and as reassuring as land in sight after a long sea voyage. "You know I never fly off the handle; I will listen carefully. And I want to help you." Inside, he struggled to keep his voice gentle. With every word, he wanted to throw someone out the window for harming a kind, vibrant soul like Valerie.

She shook her head in misery.

There were red marks on her neck like someone had his hands there, and dark bruises around her right shoulder especially. There was also a bruise on her rib cage. He gently put one finger there, and she gasped. He carefully felt around the area but there were no bulges. He thought of her laborious climb up the stairs. "Val, can you take a deep breath?"

"No."

"You have a broken rib. *Jesus*." He rubbed his face with both hands then got up and brought back the bourbon and two tumblers. He poured a good two fingers in each. "Here. Drink this. We are going to have a long talk. Please."

She watched him carefully as she picked up her glass. She nodded slightly and let her shoulders lower, like she'd finally found a place to set her burdens down. He felt his own shoulders relax. She would let him help her. *Thank God.*

Chapter 5

I brought Finn back to the kitchen and my insides warmed when I saw him look outside at Morgan, Ripley, and the boys romping around. A slow smile grew across his face. He was a good-looking man, I didn't mind saying, with his dark brown hair and deep gray-green eyes. But it was the kindness that I'd seen in him, shown at moments when he didn't know anyone was looking, that took my breath away. I'd been around plenty of people who put their pretended nobility on display for others, which always negated their actions entirely.

Everyone greeted Finn while Mr. Kirkland ladled some soup for him.

"So, it sounds like you've had a busy day, as usual," said Finn with a droll voice.

Mr. Kirkland rolled his eyes in appreciation since Finn's comment was a colossal understatement. We filled him in on finding the boys in Harlem Prison. Finn's eyes grew to a dangerous black when he heard that, as they were prone to do when he was incensed—and at other more enjoyable times. *Ahem*.

"I want to know which officers decided to do that," he said in an ominous voice.

"As do I," said Fiorello. I was sure he would find out who signed off on that move and there'd be hell to pay. Fio knew first-hand the plight of the little guy. He was not only little himself at five-foot-two, but more importantly, as a first-generation immigrant, double minority, he'd fought hard to be taken seriously his whole life, even as a fighter pilot in the war. So it was in his make up to not only care, but to fight for those who couldn't fight for themselves. Patrick and Frank's ordeal was fodder for that fire.

Just then, Morgan and the boys came in. They'd worn out Ripley, his tongue hung out and he was panting like a racehorse. Dragging himself to his water bowl, the dog drank with abandon, then collapsed.

By the smug grin on Morgan's face, it seemed she had found what she was hunting for. However, the fact that she looked both satisfied and a little peaked gave me concern.

Aunt Evelyn hid her amusement by pursing her lips and said, "All right, boys. I want to show you my studio, and I have a project for you. I'll be *right back down*." She gave us all her best steely gaze, and I took that to mean we were not to discuss anything until she returned.

Morgan was quiet as I gave her a glass of water, and we all talked about the Detroit Red Wings' win against the New York Rangers last week to win the Stanley Cup in three games to two. We were New Yorkers first, but the Wings were special to us, since I was born in Detroit. So, in this case, we were pretty happy.

After a burst of laughter and a few firm directives from upstairs, the *tap-tap* of Aunt Evelyn's shoes on the stairs alerted us that she was on her way back down.

"Oh, those boys! They have a lot of energy. What a delight." She sashayed in and, after seating herself back at the table, said, "Okay, Morgan, what did you find out?"

"Well, I let them relax outside and I used some tactics Mary taught me about questioning suspects. Not that they're suspects, but Mary says there's an art in getting people to give you information. So I asked in a voice that tried to sound casual but didn't hide that I cared. They really clammed up for a while, but then I got a few helpful tidbits. First, they saw the three money men come from the elevator. So they had to be colleagues, not just a random grouping. They'd met up in one of the offices, I guess."

"Or the Cloud Club," said Mr. Kirkland.

"What's that?" asked Morgan.

"It's a club where businessmen have their big meetings over a meal or drinks. Very high end, posh. I hear it's pretty swanky," he said.

I made a rude noise which made Finn laugh.

"What?" asked Morgan.

"Lane doesn't appreciate the Cloud Club," answered Finn.

"Why not?"

"Because they don't allow women."

"Oh. Yeah, I don't like that either," she said. "But you're right, those men were dressed up enough to be coming from up there. In fact, I bet you're right, because Patrick thought one of them looked a little soused. He wasn't outright drunk, but he said it was how people walk when they're drunk but trying hard to look like they're not."

Fiorello said, "I don't think there are any other restaurants or bars in there. Of course, the man could've had some drinks ahead of time."

"Then the more the boys thought about it, the more they were sure one of the guys said something about doing it *his way*. And here's the kicker: they recognized who the leader was, the one who gave the order to finish it."

And by the look on her face, it was someone we knew.

"And that's why I'm here," said Finn. "We have a prime suspect too."

"Well, out with it!" I exclaimed to Morgan.

"It was Uncle Louie. Louie Venetti."

Chapter 6

Louie Venetti was the leading crime boss in New York City. But he was complicated. On more than one occasion, he'd actually helped us out and even saved my hide. I had a constant inner battle between loathing him and his business, yet liking the guy. He wasn't like other mobsters who were vacant and soulless. He was learned and at times he was gentle and kind. Yet, his power was palpable. He could be ruthless and violent in his dealings, I'd heard, yet he lacked outright cruelty, especially to innocent bystanders. I was still flummoxed about it. I ran into him once around Book Mile and I knew right away he was a book lover, which was a significant bond. Booklovers can be any age, uptown or downtown, different religions or skin colors, yet when they discover a love of books, they're instantly off and running about their favorite authors and writing down each other's suggestions.

The strangest thing on top of all that? I found out that Venetti was friends with my mom when they were kids. Grew up in the same neighborhood. My parents died when I was only ten, and I recently discovered they were murdered by Daphne Franco as a consequence of their intelligence work during the war. Which was a very different story than I'd grown up with. I had a sneaking suspicion that Venetti cared deeply for my mom and her death had been very painful for him. *So what on earth am I supposed to do with all that?*

I must've looked vexed because Finn eased his hand under the table and gently rubbed my knee. I placed my hand over his, our fingers intertwining.

I looked around the table at the wide variety of reactions from Morgan's discovery. Finn and Roarke both had a grim set to their mouths. Kirkland and Fiorello looked like Mount Vesuvius directly before eruption, and Evelyn had her chin resting in her hand thoughtfully and even peacefully curious. A look that did not get past Kirkland.

"Evelyn. How can you sit there looking so placid? Unbelievable!"

Her brows went up, but she ignored his outcry completely. Turning to Fiorello, she said, "Fio, dear, you and Kirkland better take a deep breath. You look positively thunderous."

Kirkland sputtered, as if his thunderous expression had just been insulted. He stalked into the kitchen and banged some pots around the sink as if he were washing them. Loudly.

Fio did as he was told and took a deep breath, gripping the edge of the table.

I asked Morgan, "So do you think it really was him? I mean, most people in the city generally know what Venetti looks like, but it's his name more than anything that can cause an entire room to fly into a panic."

"Yeah, I think so. They seemed positive and even mentioned his large salt and pepper brows. But of course, it's possible they got it wrong."

"Well, that's why I came by," said Finn. "He's our number one suspect and that's on top of the kids fingering him for it."

"Really?" I asked. "I can't see him doing it."

"Lane!" barked Kirkland, roused far more than keeping his hands busy at the sink could manage. "I've told you, you cannot trust him." He gave up on the dishes, having gotten some of his angst out on the soup pot, and came back over to sit at the table with a huff.

"I know and you're right," I replied calmly, which put a damper on the approaching tantrum.

"Oh."

Fio snorted.

God, I loved this group. I replied, "I meant that he's much more careful than that. I admit, I have moments where I like him and I've appreciated his help, but I know he's dangerous. But come on, Lexington and 42nd? You'd have to be crazy to commit murder right there, midafternoon, no less. Especially someone as notable as he is. If he did do it, he'd have to be consumed with rage to act with such indiscretion. Which is also not like him and not what the boys saw."

"Well. I'll give you that," grumbled Kirkland. "He's not one to react foolishly. He's certainly not stupid and if it wasn't an act of passion, they'd planned it. Besides, what reason would he possibly have to do it himself? He'd have one of his men take care of it."

Finn interjected, "But the NYPD might not care."

"What do you mean? Oh. I get it," I quickly amended. "They've wanted to nab him for a long time but never had enough evidence. And now we have eyewitnesses."

"Exactly. True or not, the prosecutors might take their chances. I don't know. Maybe that's why the police kept it somewhat hush hush yesterday, so they could gather evidence before the press storm," said Finn, his Irish accent getting stronger by the second as he sat back in his chair and crossed his ankle over his knee.

I looked at my boss, the mayor. He'd been watching our discussion back and forth holding his chin contemplatively. He looked as torn as I felt.

Fio cleared his throat, then said, "I see the sides of both arguments. Lane, I want to take him down any way I can. However, I won't do it dishonestly. Besides, the real killer would still be out there and we'd waste resources on a trial. We'll need to investigate and confirm if Louie has an alibi."

"I agree with that." I thought about it for a moment then said, "I *am* still curious about his relationship with my mother—"

Kirkland interrupted with a *grrrrr*, prompting Aunt Evelyn to put a consoling hand on his shoulder.

Morgan had been quiet; she was often the silent, brooding type. I learned early on she thought deeply about things and would often add an interesting insight into our cases. I looked to her and asked, "Any thoughts, Morgan?"

"There's something odd about the meeting with the wealthy men possibly coming out of the Cloud Club. Street kids can see three kinds of people on the street a mile away: Cops, gangsters, and social workers. If Frank and Patrick think it was Uncle Louie, I'd put my money on them."

"Finn, what do we know about the victim and his friends that were with him?" asked Fio.

"The victim was Sherman Troppington. His personality was just as likeable as his name, meaning he was arrogant and generally tolerated by those around him because of his money. Wall Street man, one of the few who survived the stock market crash, saw an opportunity even in the midst of disaster. He lost some of his own fortune, of course, but had been more careful than those he gave guidance to with their money. Which also makes him disliked. Made money acquiring businesses that were in dire straits, stripping them down and selling them off in bits. But other than being despicably greedy, Troppington seems pretty clean and has no known dealings with underground crime. We located the two other men who were with him, but they weren't of any help. Lane, you look like there's something on your mind."

I'd been tapping my foot, impatiently thinking. "There is. Troppington...something about the diamond on his watch. Something is niggling my mind about it, but I can't figure it out."

"Well wait until you hear the name of one of the other men: Craig Severance."

Mr. Kirkland and I both said almost at the same time, "The architect?" Then we both looked at each other, grinning.

Aunt Evelyn interjected, "These two spent all of 1930 and 1931 going to look—pretty much every single day, mind you—at the Chrysler Building and the Empire State Building as they went up in record time. I couldn't get Lane to talk about anything else but those buildings."

"Well, when I wasn't busy doing all my college work, it was a nice reprieve," I exclaimed with mock indignation. I'd loved watching the builders bring life back into the city. I tried to visit both of those beauties as often as I could. In fact, the *Hindenburg* was scheduled to make its trip back from Frankfurt in just a couple of weeks. I decided I should try to plan a trip to the top of Empire State Building right when it was passing. It was amazing watching it float above us in all of its enormous grandeur, it would be sensational from the viewing decks at the 86th and 102nd floors.

"It's kind of odd that Severance was at the Chrysler Building, Finn," said Mr. Kirkland.

"Why is that?"

"Well, he was the main architect when it was Senator Reynolds who owned the land and the building plans. But after Chrysler bought him out, Severance decided to go work for the planning and building of 40 Wall Street. There was a big race between the Chrysler Building and 40 Wall Street for the tallest building. Got pretty heated too."

"Until the Empire State Building beat them both, hands down," I said.

"Who was the third man?" I asked.

"A Mr. Francis Suthers. Younger fellow, working as a banker downtown. Earnest guy, green around the gills, but poised and ready to play with the big boys," said Finn.

"How did they know Troppington?" asked Fio.

"Just business contacts from the Cloud Club. It's where all the bigwigs go to make connections and deals. But really, I can't find any ties with Uncle Louie. Something isn't adding up."

Finn was right: nothing about this was cut and dry. There was usually a clear motive in a serious and high-risk crime such as this, but all of the evidence was insubstantial. Why not take the victim's valuable jewelry and watch? Why attempt the murder in broad daylight? Why did the boys feel so strongly it was Louie but everything about it wasn't his style?

And when things didn't add up, I couldn't help but think of Daphne. Could she be behind this and to what end? I was glad that Finn felt things were fishy, too. It wasn't just my odd little friendship with Uncle Louie that was making me biased.

Feeling that we had taken the conversation as far as we could go, we began to clear the table and clean the kitchen. I mulled over the details, looking at the clues from different angles. Everyone was quiet, probably moving the puzzle pieces of the mystery around in their minds like I was. It was why I loved helping in these kinds of cases. I enjoyed a good puzzle, not to mention the adventure. It was also why I loved my job. I cared about my city and the people. At times it was a thankless job, but in the end, extremely satisfying.

I took my coffee cup to the sink and glanced at Roarke in his signature pinstripe suit and sandy blond hair. He wiped down the table and handed me a couple of glasses. Roarke Channing, my sleuthing partner extraordinaire and investigative reporter, wasn't usually quiet—unlike Morgan. At the beginning of the evening, he'd added to the conversation plenty. But for the entire discussion about the men outside the Chrysler Building, he hadn't offered a thought, a sarcastic reply, or even a derisive chuckle. His dimples weren't even showing. Which told me he was clearly up to something.

"Hiya, Roarke," I said, coming up behind him at the sink.

He yipped and gave a startled jump. "Oh! Hi, Lane."

"You're a little tightly wound. You okay? You were pretty quiet at the table."

In an overplayed, *oh pshaw* sort of voice, he said, "Oh, I'm fine. Just, you know, preoccupied with some work deadlines. You know how it is. We've got a lot going on next month with the coronation. Everyone loves the royals!"

I did know how it was, but he was acting a little sketchy himself, though his excuse of the coronation of King George VI on May 12th was valid. There was a lot of news interest when Edward VIII abdicated the throne so he could marry the American socialite, Wallis Simpson. She was divorced from her first husband, and the royal family were not allowed to marry divorced persons. So Roarke would indeed be busy with that, but his voice was tinged with a forced feeling of being over-merry, which made me suspicious.

I was a little disappointed, too, because I wanted a partner for an idea I had. Finn had the bearing of a detective—so he wouldn't do. I'd try again tomorrow, and if Roarke wouldn't come along, I'd go by myself. Which actually sounded intriguing too.

Chapter 7

"Hi, Roarke," I said cheerfully.

"*Yikes*! God, Lane. You scared me."

I'd been lying in wait just outside Room 9, the press room where reporters stood ready and waiting for my boss to make news. He rarely disappointed. I bribed one of Roarke's buddies with a bottle of bourbon to let me in so I could pounce—I mean casually wait—outside the office where Roarke camped out.

Taking full advantage of catching my prey off guard, I stalked slowly toward Roarke with a smirk and a knowing squint, piercing his golden-brown eyes with my glare. Not having a brother of my own to tease, I thoroughly enjoyed razzing Roarke. I poked him in the chest, his dark brown suit offset by a charming caramel-colored pocket square. I gave him a little jab with each word. "You. Know. Something."

His dimples came out in full, and even though he turned a lovely shade of rose, he accepted his defeat with good grace. "You got me. I knew I should have handled last night differently. *Damn*."

I was all set to banter, but he pulled an imaginary zipper across his lips. It was clearly a matter that he couldn't let me in on.

"Sorry, Lane. Mum's the word for now. But I promise you'll be the first to know when I can say something."

He patted me lightly on the shoulder as he swept past. Two of his friends watched our exchange with undisguised interest, and they ambled over to me as I crossed my arms and studied Roarke's form racing down the hall.

"Oh, I know that look, Benny," said the shifty one with a thin black mustache. "She's not taking no for an answer."

"I told ya, we need to keep an eye on this little dynamo just as much as her boss," said the other one with his camera slung around his neck.

"Yeah, yeah, yeah." I rolled my eyes. "Get back to work."

I left Room 9 and headed back to the office. With all the hubbub of yesterday, I didn't get a chance to stop at Val's. Roxy said she went by, but no one answered. I went over this morning, yet there was still no response. Was she staying with her parents? She rarely did that. She helped them a lot but preferred her own apartment. She was gone again today, which made it about a week since she'd last been in. She'd called and left a message with someone at the office unlikely to grill her—not me or Roxy. I was starting to get really concerned.

I didn't know exactly where her parents' house was. After all this time, we'd given them plenty of groceries and clothes to help with their kids and her father's unemployment, but I'd never actually been there. It was pretty far out in Brooklyn, not an easy commute, and I didn't have a car. So searching for her there was out of the question.

Pretty soon, I'd have to hit up Uncle Louie to ask if Raff knew where she was. Fio would just kill me. That was, if Finn didn't get to me first.

We had a normal, bustling day. Pondering yesterday's events, I started formulating my plan as I did a few menial tasks. I had thought about involving Roarke, but after some consideration, I decided I'd be better off on my own. And for once, my sleuthing would be at quite a ritzy place, instead of the Meatpacking District, Chinatown, or dangling off a bridge.

I adjusted my outfit before leaving work, taking off my earrings and colorful silk scarf and changing my shoes. I chose my understated black heels—which had wider heels than I'd usually wear—to go with my black pantsuit and white button-up blouse. My hair was styled in a marcel wave that I pinned up in the back, and I placed my favorite fedora at a saucy angle. I still received some frowns when I wore trousers, but if Marlene Dietrich and Carole Lombard could do it, so could I.

I took the train up from City Hall to Grand Central, exiting out to Lexington Avenue. I'd aimed to arrive at around six-thirty. The after-work drinking crowd was in full swing, but it wasn't yet late enough that my quarry might be on his way home to his wife.

In New York, if you didn't belong somewhere, the trick was to act as if you did, with the bold nonchalance of royalty. And I certainly didn't belong where I was headed.

I swept into my favorite building and immediately sought out the beautiful brass elevator doors. They were famous Art Deco masterpieces. I would bet that in one hundred years, people will still love them. The palm fronds design was fashioned with exotic woods that used warm oranges, deep russet browns, and silver and black. Art Deco mixed natural elements with modern: woods with metals, bold lines mixed with flowing petals. It was the segue between precious and timeless materials mixed with our industrial society. We were at the cusp ourselves, the doorway between two eras, and you could feel it in the air. In one small decade, women were suddenly cropping hair that had been long for centuries. Our hemlines went up, and I still marveled in the summertime that we could wear shorts—when less than twenty years earlier, women were arrested for indecency if their ankles, or God forbid their calves, showed in swimsuits or shorter skirts.

Yet it was a time that was broken from the war and from the stock market crash. The Depression still hung on with its relentless grip, but we remained standing. There was a push-and-pull tension. It was a time of soup lines, yet also a time of cocktails. Shantytowns as well as glamorous nights for Society at the El Morocco. Tedious unemployment lines, and yet music that could make us all dance right through the night. The Depression brought so many people down into despair, but this very building —and so many beloved new wonders—went up after the crash, *despite* it: the Chrysler Building, the Empire State Building, Rockefeller Center, to name a few. That resilience spoke to me; this building was the very symbol of it all. And now, I was about to wrangle my way upstairs.

I got on the elevator and selected the sixty-seventh floor. Even though the elevators were fast, it still took a while to get so far up. I kept my hands at my sides and tilted my head down. A few men got on the elevator after me, but they were too absorbed in their own discussion to pay much attention to me. With my heels, I was just as tall as the shortest one, and I decided to try to look like I was part of their group.

We arrived at the proper floor, and with a *ding*, the doors—just as lovely on the inside as on the outside—opened like a grand gesture of welcome. My pretend group of chums and I strolled into the Chrysler's Building's famous Cloud Club.

Chapter 8

I wasn't exactly sure what the Cloud Club would do once they discovered I didn't have the male equipment that allowed me into the establishment. Usher me out quietly? Make a big fuss? Call the cops? Women had been arrested for less…

I walked over to the bar, casual but determined. I mimicked a more masculine way of walking, moving with my shoulders and less with my hips. Yes, I wanted an excuse to infiltrate this place of male dominance simply because it deserved infiltration, but my main goal was to find Craig Severance. I had looked up his photograph in our newspaper archives, so I knew what he looked like. I had a few questions for him, and I wanted to see his actions and reactions firsthand.

I sat at the bar, trying to keep my shoulders squared and what I deemed manly. A few men in the bar still had their hats still on, so I blended in without trouble. If I'd entered the formal dining area, I would've had to take it off. As the bartender came near, I nonchalantly looked away from the bar toward the coat room, lowered my voice, and ordered a bourbon on the rocks. The bartender paused for a second, then moved away and made my drink. I really hadn't thought I'd get this far, so I was pretty pleased with myself. I'd actually practiced lowering my voice without sounding stupid or like a hoarse whisper. And I wasn't exactly chesty, so with a bulkier blazer that had some good shoulder pads, I cut a lean, not-too-curvy figure.

I scanned the room as well as I could. The hum of conversation was deeper than usual with the lack of feminine voices. The bartender shifted my drink toward me. I took a decent sip and carefully placed the tumbler back on the bar.

In a low voice, the bartender said, "That went down easier than I thought it might."

Lifting my eyes to meet his, knowing I'd been made, I said, "I like a good drink."

"You're okay for the moment, but I'd be careful. They'll make a ruckus if they suspect."

"Damn."

He tried to hide a smile and since he wasn't making a fuss, I decided to try to enlist his help. "Do you know a Craig Severance?"

He nodded. "Sure. Comes in here quite a bit. In fact, I think I saw him come in today. Why?"

"I'm with the mayor's office and I have a couple of questions for him about a murder he witnessed." My direct statement shocked the bartender a bit, I'm sure he was expecting something more feminine, like a jilted lover situation.

He may have been shocked, but he was pleased to help. "Okay then. How about I find him and give him a discreet message to come to the bar?"

"Deal. And uh… How about you fill me up again?" I asked, motioning to my glass.

"Got it," he said, grinning. He topped off my drink, then headed over to the dining room.

I studied my bourbon, hoping to be somewhat invisible. I saw out of my peripheral vision another bartender come around the corner, bar towel in hand, as he collected a few empty glasses.

"Well, love, you blend in. But in my honest opinion, you're a little too adorable."

Astonishment flooded through me as I looked up into the glittering, amused eyes of Finn. I couldn't get a word out, my mouth opening and closing like a stupid fish. He gave a small laugh and winked at me. Finally finding my voice, I asked, "How did you know?"

He looked around to make sure no one was paying us too much attention, then leaned onto the bar top with one arm. He lowered his voice and said, "As soon as the words Cloud Club were spoken at our council of war, I knew you'd try to infiltrate this place. And I knew that the first day you wore your trouser suit to work, that would probably be the day you'd go. Today was the day, so I followed you."

"You are such a rascal!" I whispered, wrinkling my nose at feeling beat at my own game, yet absolutely delighted at the hilarity of my predicament. I wished I could have magically produced the film of Finn following me through the city. What a pair we were. "Do you know the bartender or something? Or is this a new career path for ya?" I asked with a smirk, swirling my hand at his ensemble.

"Oh career path. For sure. I do make a lot of good tips," he quipped.

"Well you do look dashing," I purred, eyeing the tuxedo-style jacket and formal vest of his bartender's uniform.

"Careful, love, you're still supposed to be a man at the moment," he whispered, barely containing a laugh.

"Dammit, you're right," I said with a small snort laugh, sad to have to conclude our flirting.

Just then, the other bartender returned with a guy on his heels who looked curious and not at all skittish. Which already told me a lot.

Finn started filling orders from other patrons, I turned to the far side of the bar before Severance could get a good look at me. Then he sidled up next to me as the bartender poured him a couple fingers of bourbon. I gestured that it was on me.

"You were looking for me?" he asked, happily taking a sip of his free drink.

"So why does the architect leave the Chrysler team to build 40 Wall Street, yet enjoys the Cloud Club?" I asked, hoping my voice was low enough.

"Oh, I love both buildings. How could I not love this?" he asked.

"Makes sense. They're both spectacular," I said. "Let me be direct, unofficially, just looking for more information. Do you have any other insights about why Troppington was targeted when you and Suthers were leaving the Cloud Club with him Tuesday?"

He slowly swiveled to look at me better. This could get dicey. He looked up at the bartender who hadn't gone far and could hear everything we said, not to mention Finn, also within hearing distance and frequently darting his eyes toward us. The bartender nodded at him giving him a kind of *okay* signal. "Well, well!" he said not unkindly. "It isn't every day a beautiful woman dressed as a man asks me such important questions." Finn's stance flexed, ready to pounce.

"Didn't I have you going at all?" I asked exasperatedly.

"All right a little. A tiny bit," he said with his thumb and index finger an inch apart, demonstrating just how tiny.

I had to give a small laugh, and with that, Finn set his shoulders down. "Well, thanks for not calling me out. Really, I'm with the mayor's office and the crime isn't making any sense. We can't find a good motive; the three of you aren't known to be regular friends with a regular schedule…"

"You're right. I feel bad about Troppington. Even though he wasn't anyone's favorite—too smug, you know? But he didn't deserve that. We only saw each other up here. Suthers too. Just happened to walk out at the same time that day. Say, did you really come here and do all this just to ask if we'd known each other well?"

I gave a little cough. "Well, mostly. Thanks for clearing up that you simply enjoy this place despite having left the team who built it, so no hard feelings. But also…" I leaned closer to him and whispered, "I just wanted to see if I could infiltrate this bastion of men." I gave him a wink of my own and finished my drink with a flourish.

Just then, I sensed a presence at the end of the bar—a hushed conversation. I darted my gaze over to two gentlemen who were scowling at me as they whispered to an overbearing man with a haughty look in his eyes standing beside them. That *gentleman*, if I could use the word sarcastically, made his way over, strutting with an exaggerated swagger as if he owned the place. *Such an ass.* Finn's stance went right back to taught and ready.

The gentleman cleared his throat in introduction. Enthusiastic to make a big show of humiliating me, he said overly loudly, "We do not allow your kind in this establishment."

The volume in the room went down a few decibels. Severance eyed me, I could tell that he and the bartender were looking forward to the showdown. Finn, not so much. "Huh. A four-syllable word from a guy like you. Wonders never cease."

Not disappointed, Severance snorted into his tumbler of bourbon.

"Why, you little—"

"That's enough," said a surprisingly pleasant voice behind me. But the pleasant tone held a note of warning. And not to me. "I think that the notable aide of the mayor of New York deserves a bit of respect."

"But we do *not* allow women here," growled the large man. His friends at the other end were looking none too pleased themselves.

"Yes. Regrettably, this is true. Miss Sanders? Would you like to join me at The Algonquin Blue Room? I prefer the clientele there anyway."

"Yes, that would be lovely. Thank you." I smiled at the original bartender as I set a handsome tip on the bar.

I almost laughed when I heard him mumble under his breath, "Best tip I got all day." Finn slapped a towel onto the bar, wiping it down with a grin on his face and shaking his head in good humor.

Turning to Severance, I said, "Thanks a lot for your time."

"Definitely my pleasure," he said, raising his glass to me.

I received several glares as I walked what should have been a bit of a shameful march to the elevator. However, I had infiltrated the inner sanctum of the male business elite, so I didn't feel one iota of shame. And the maître d' looked somewhat aghast that the man escorting me out made a point of announcing to everyone that he preferred the Algonquin. I was pleased that my job earned me a measure of respect, but I was annoyed to no end that I myself wasn't enough to deserve it. Women had to work twice as hard for the same job and still got paid a third to half as much as men. I hoped the future would treat us better, but this inequality was centuries in the making, so I had my doubts.

We entered the elevator and I looked back at Finn, our eyes catching each other. I sent him a miniscule air kiss. The whole adventure had been even more fun than I'd expected.

As the elevator doors closed, I turned to my suave, tightly coiled friend, who sported a black mustache—part John Gilbert, part Clark Gable. He had a tight part through his pomaded hair with a black, piercing gaze to match.

"Well thank you for making my exit a bit more stylish, Mr. Dewey." It was none other than Thomas Dewey, our prominent district attorney.

Chapter 9

District Attorney Thomas Dewey and Fiorello were a powerful duo. Both were relentless in their efforts to dethrone the gangsters. Most recently, he'd taken down Lucky Luciano on forced prostitution. Which was a major trial because, up until that point, no prosecutor had been able to nab a gangster on anything more than tax evasion. Lucky got a thirty- to fifty-year prison sentence.

"Certainly, Miss Sanders. I have to say, I was a bit surprised to see high heels walking into the Cloud Club. But well-done on blending in otherwise." His one-sided smirk told me he was amused just as much as he was confounded. I got that a lot.

"Well, now I can look a little more like myself," I said, as I held my hat in one hand while loosening the back of my hairdo in the other. "But I have to say, I'm a fan of the pant suit."

"You are?" he asked.

"I like the pockets. Plus, you're never worried about a gust of wind or who's behind you on the subway stairs like you do in a dress or skirt. So would you really like to go to the Algonquin, or was that a parting jab to the Cloud Club?"

"Oh, I think our meeting is quite fortuitous, so I definitely meant it. On top of the jab. Are you aware of the shooting that made the papers and our high-profile suspect?"

I rolled my eyes. *I sure am.*

Just past twilight was one of my favorite times of the day, and the streetlamps, glowing windows, and headlights had blinked on like so many urban fireflies.

"Patience and Fortitude look pretty nifty," I said, nodding toward the lions flanking the main branch of the public library. Fio had named them in honor of what it took to build and guide a city. The lions were wreathed in spring flowers and greens, and a tourist posed next to them while her partner took a picture with his trusty Brownie camera.

"That they do. But did you deflect my question?" asked Mr. Dewey.

"I wonder if the Algonquin will be busy."

"You did it again."

"I know," I said, chuckling. "Yes, I know who the main suspect is. But the story doesn't add up. On top of breaking into the Cloud Club, I wanted to see if I could get any information out of Severance. I wanted to corroborate that he, Troppington, and Suthers weren't usually seen together as a group, and that their leaving the club was only coincidental. With no motive for killing Troppington, no theft, and their group of three not even a consistent gathering, it all seems very odd and very random. Even though the main suspect is capable of murder, it's just not his—"

"Style," he supplied.

"Exactly. Which means, someone is setting him up."

"And…how do we know that the *someone* isn't even more lethal to the city and our citizens?"

"Right. I thought about Daphne Franco," I said, slanting him a knowing side eye.

He let out a puff of air. "Yes, I'm sure you did."

On top of murdering my parents years ago, Daphne was the heir apparent and leader of a gang we'd been fighting the past year. Slippery, conniving, and demented—a winning combination. I never knew if she worked her insanity, or if it worked her.

"Do you know her whereabouts since our last run-in with her?" I asked.

"No. Which is more than worrisome," he said as we turned the corner.

There had been several gangsters vying for territory. Daphne orchestrated a coup against Rex's appointed heir and took over the gang. Finn and I recently followed her to Europe where she bolstered her position as the new leader but didn't attempt a reawakening of the underground crime network, focusing her efforts in the States.

I had some information about her that made me a target. Daphne hadn't just helped arrange the hit on my parents and tried to kill me as a little girl—I'd recently recovered a memory from that time in the hospital: I'd seen her injecting her own husband with a lethal dose of morphine. The infamous Rex Ruby treated people like his personal puppets. He'd groomed Daphne as his lover and heir to his crime network, but in the end chose his own son, Rutherford—Daphne's husband. So she got him out the way too. My knowledge of that murder could still ruin her. If anyone else learned Rex's son had been meant to inherit, it would destabilize her new leadership. For now, we kept it quiet; better to know who was in charge and keep an eye on her. But Daphne would always know I had something on her, which was a deadly position to be in.

I got the feeling Daphne and I both loathed and respected each other. She gave me the willies, though. She even had an office/hideout in one of our lunatic asylums. She would never stop. And I doubted her efforts to join forces with the gangsters in Europe were finished. She was like the mythological Hydra. Every time I thought I got rid of her, she'd show up with more heads.

"Why exactly are you going through all this with me instead of Fiorello?" I'd been having a marvelous time talking with Mr. Dewey like an equal, which made me wonder what he was up to. "Spit it out, mister."

He chuckled and said, "Well, I will be talking about it with him. But I have a friend I want you to meet, and I think that together we can really make sense of this. And maybe get some justice. Let's get a drink and have a chat."

Intrigued, I followed him the last block in near silence. He opened the door, and my first view of the Algonquin was a tableau of gracefully tall green palms against shiny black lacquer, glorious Art Deco columns, gold-edged sconces, and a perky ginger cat perched on top of the front desk, looking at me in judgment as if I were a little late for our appointment. We walked through the famed restaurant in the lobby, past the oval table of Dorothy Parker's Vicious Circle, and through the door to the Blue Room.

We both ordered martinis, and he started to tell me his story.

"See, I have a colleague who felt certain that there was more to the Lucky Luciano case—that we could bring him down for more than tax evasion. I admit that I didn't have much hope for it. However, after a long investigation in which my colleague hunted down informants, executed search warrants, followed up with a great deal of evidence, it was more than apparent that we had plenty to indict, arrest, and convict Lucky, as you know."

I nodded, taking another sip of the salty martini. I allowed a slow grin because I knew exactly who he was talking about, but I wanted to see what else he had to say.

"I don't think my colleague got enough acclaim with all of it. I don't know if the story will ever be as big as it should be. My name tends to take up a lot of space in the papers, and with my political ambitions, I am pleased with that part. But this person has a lot of intuition about organized crime and might be able to give us some insight about the Venetti issue. I'd like to set up an appointment with you. But uh…it might be advantageous to have it at a more unique venue."

This piqued my curiosity even further. "Sure. Just let me know where and when."

"I'll let you know as soon as possible, but the where will most certainly be at The Savoy."

"The jazz and dance club?" I yelped. That one surprised me.

He grinned back at me.

Chapter 10

The Savoy was one of my favorite places. Despite incredible racial tensions around the country and in New York, this place was a tribute to how art brought people together. It was created by a White entrepreneur, a Jewish businessman, and a Black real estate businessman as the manager. A ten-thousand-square-foot ballroom that could hold four thousand people, with dual stages at either end so the music never had to stop, complete with spring-loaded dance floor. The Savoy was elegant with its marble staircase and crystal chandeliers, served only beer and wine—no hard liquor—and no matter your skin color, bank account, or religion, the only thing that mattered was if you could dance.

Having been brought up by my artistic, philanthropic, and endlessly irreverent Aunt Evelyn, I craved places like The Savoy. Our home had always been full of every kind of person—from beggars to Eleanor Roosevelt. From the first Black NYPD officer to a scientist named Albert Einstein, from grubby street urchins to a comedian named Leslie Hope and the artist Diego Rivera. Any and all might be in our house on any given day, but certainly on holidays.

Located on Lenox between 140th and 141st streets in Harlem, Roarke, Roxy, and I arrived at The Savoy together, planning to meet up with Finn and our other friends there. The place was already hopping. Chick Webb's house band was playing with Ella

Fitzgerald. The floor teemed with swing dancers, dressed in a dazzling array of colors, the air crackling with energy. The beat of the bass and drums quickened my pulse, and between the bandleader's smile and the crowd's shared joy, the place beckoned like a grandma opening her arms to a great hoard of grand-children.

Roxy had already found someone to dance with, and just as Roarke glanced at the bar and opened his mouth to speak, I cut him off and said, "Let's go!" I grabbed his hand and pulled him onto the dance floor.

Roarke was such a good dancer that anyone he danced with felt like they did every move perfectly. I only stepped on his toe once. He looked great, as always. His sandy hair and golden-brown eyes were a charming combination. For a man who loathed his dimples, he sure wore them well. We tended to get in some scrapes together, but we always had each other's back. I was really feeling the warmth of the room after a couple of dances and decided to get a drink to cool down. The windows were open to the fresh air, but all those bodies made it sweltering. Not nearly like August would be, but still.

With that thought, I wondered if I still looked put together. I ran a hand through my hair to smooth it, then dashed a glance back at Roarke as we headed to the bar. I rolled my eyes; as usual, he looked impeccable. As if he'd just walked in the door with a fresh suit, crisp tie and not a bit of sweat on his face. I probably looked like I ran the whole way from City Hall.

I ordered a beer, and boy, did it taste good. I felt a tap on my arm, and I turned to see Mr. Dewey. It was an odd juxtaposition, the district attorney amid swing dancers and big band music. Kind of like your parents going to the prom with you. But we had an appointment, and it looked as if we were set to go.

I introduced him to Roarke, then followed him to where a few of the guys from the next band were standing, about to go on stage. They were young and dashing, with impeccable tuxedos and shining shoes. Mr. Dewey's contact stood with them. I was really looking forward to this meeting.

Mr. Dewey caught the group's eyes, and the circle parted to let us in. "Hello," he said, "looking forward to the performance."

Greetings went around the band, and as he and his contact gave a quick nod of hello, we moved out of the group's circle.

"This is Lane Sanders, aide to the mayor. Lane, this is—"

I cut him off. "Mrs. Eunice Carter. I'm honored to meet you. I've been following your work closely."

At first, her eyes had been a touch icy, but my words softened them just a bit. Mrs. Eunice Carter was the first Black woman prosecutor. It was *her* work that took Lucky Luciano down. In fact, as he said, Dewey had been reticent at first when she argued they could get to Lucky through his prostitution racket. It had never been done. But she overwhelmed his concerns with solid evidence that couldn't be denied. And like I already knew: it worked.

"Eunice, Lane might have more to share with you about the suspect we spoke about last night." He was careful not to say the words *Uncle Louie*; his name alone could cause a panic in a place like this.

Eunice lifted her chin, assessing my face with the scrutiny of an experienced mother of several mischievous children and nothing ever got by her. "Oh, I'm familiar with your work, too, Lane Sanders," she said, with a southern accent mixed with an edge of New York.

I gulped.

She allowed a small smile. "I'm just joshing you, Miss Sanders. I know exactly how hard it is for a woman to get ahead in this city. You've made some interesting choices." My eyebrows tried to make a run for it into my bangs. "But I like your style, lady. I like your style."

I don't think I had ever been more pleased in my entire life.

"Oh dear," said Mr. Dewey as he looked between us, seeing a budding friendship begin right before his eyes. A rascally one, to be sure.

I shared a knowing look with Eunice as she gave a quick cackle. "All right. Let's have a chat," she said, getting down to business.

The three of us walked deeper into a corner that allowed for a little more privacy.

"Lane, why don't you tell me what you know."

I filled her in on finding the boys at Harlem prison and gave her a few more details about how Fio ransacked the place and laid out his expectations to the guards. Her eyes sparkled at that, clearly wishing she could've seen it. We still had the boys at our place and soon would get them to the Child Society while we figured everything out. Then I told her exactly what they saw and our concerns that it just didn't seem like Louie's usual work.

"Oh, I agree. We are looking to see if there are any other witnesses. But it got out that it was supposedly Uncle Louie, and no one will talk. We located the men that the victim was with, but honestly, they'd already broken off from Troppington and didn't see what happened. And of course, we can't find Louie. Other than the boys, we don't have any evidence, And after speaking with them, they mostly recognized the build and his bushy eyebrows. It's not enough for a judge to issue a warrant to search his place. We did get one description from a man who saw the men Louie was supposedly with. The man didn't see the shooting happen, but he heard it. He only remembered the one guy because something had caught his eye when they'd passed him, and he did a double take. It was a fat diamond ring on his pinky. But other than that, an average man with fashionable, expensive clothes. That leads me to believe it wasn't a couple of hoodlums, nor a random shooting."

"Yes, the boys said none of the men acted angry beforehand, or as if they were apprehensive about seeing each other. So it wasn't like a shakedown over an unpaid debt—that would not have been friendly at all."

We decided to make a weekly appointment to share information and any insight, then we parted ways. Dewey back to his home, Eunice to her jazz friends, and me to dance a little more.

I brought my empty beer glass back to the bar and set it down. The bartender was busy, so I turned and rested my elbows on the bar, enjoying the crowd. To my left a pretty heated conversation was happening. The proper and polite person in me wanted to edge away and give privacy where privacy was due. But we all knew that particular part of me was also bored and half-starved, so the investigative reporter in me edged closer while making a nice show of bobbing my head to the music and even giving a little wave to a fake friend on the dance floor.

I listened in for a while, then I felt his presence before he actually sidled up next to me, mirroring my stance at the bar.

"What's a nice guy like you doing in a place like this?" I quipped.

"Who says I'm nice?" Finn whispered, with a hint of a growl in my ear.

Heat flared through me as I turned my head to face him, within kissing distance. "Well, isn't that the greatest greeting ever. I like it when you growl."

"I try," he said, as he leaned in the last inch for a good kiss.

"I just finished my meeting," I said after enjoying him for a hot-buttered minute.

He kissed my temple and signaled to the bartender for two beers. "Intriguing place for a business meeting."

"A smidge better than City Hall. It was with Eunice Carter. Dewey set it up."

"Learn anything?" he asked.

"Not yet, but it's great to have more minds on this."

"I'm certainly glad to have hers on our team," he said. "She's amazing."

I smiled. "I agree. I had a hard time not fawning all over her. I wonder if history will remember her for taking down Lucky—the significant prostitution angle was her work—or if Dewey will get all the glory." Finn just gave a look that said, *I hope so, but don't bet on it.*

"I know, I know," I complained. "But anyway, there's still something off about the shooting. She feels it too. I can't put my finger on it. Something about that diamond the witness saw is niggling at me."

"You mean the one the boys said they saw on the pocket watch?"

"That one, too. But Eunice said they located one other

witness who didn't see the gun go off, but he heard it. When he dashed around the corner to see what happened, he got a glimpse of the men that were with the shooter, supposedly Uncle Louie. The guy said he remembered them as they passed him just before the incident, only because one guy had a large diamond ring on his pinky finger. It's something about a diamond."

"Say…that rings a bell with me too. I can't place it, but if I think of anything I'll let you know," he said.

"I'll do the same."

"You know, it looked like the two guys next to you when I came up were arguing a little. Anything up with that?" he asked.

"Do you honestly think I'd be eavesdropping? On innocent individuals just out for an evening?" I asked in mock indignation.

"So it wasn't very interesting?" he asked with a smirk.

"Nah, nothing good. The only thing that came up outside of girlfriend issues was they mentioned the *Hindenburg*. It should be coming in again soon, right? Early May?"

"Yes, I think about May 6th or 7th."

"I was just thinking, we should go see it when it flies around the Empire State Building, or maybe when it docks. It'd be incredible."

The dirigible from Germany was a regular sight in New York, as it always made a circle above Manhattan before landing or taking off in New Jersey. It routinely tooled across the Atlantic in style and speed. The fastest way to get across, actually. The trans-Atlantic liners were already incredibly fast, built for speed. In fact, the *Normandie* that Finn and I took back from Europe was recently outfitted with new propellers and made the crossing in just under *four days*. Unheard of!

But I still longed to take a trip on the *Hindenburg*. A friend of ours from England, Miles Havalaar, who was a contact of Finn's, had recently taken the trip and he told me all about it. Gently floating thousands of feet above the ocean and such a marvel, most people chose to not even sleep in their berths for the mere two days of travel. Instead, spending time in the lounge with the live piano and a stocked bar in the smoking room. It was even more of an expensive luxury than a super liner, but still the heart could dream…

We enjoyed our beers and listened to the music, soaking up the spectacle of the stunning dance moves all around.

We finished our beers, and Finn said, "Feel like a dance?"

"Always."

Eunice's friends, Fletcher Henderson and his band, started their set. "Smack" Henderson was a lot of fun as he enthusiastically led the numbers. I wished I could have seen them when he had Louie Armstrong playing in the band, but Armstrong had gone back to Chicago.

I loved dancing with Finn. He wasn't as up on all the new dance moves as Roarke, but he was smooth. He always moved with the graceful prowl of a panther, and it translated to dancing wonderfully. The first time we danced together, we hadn't had one single date yet. It became our favorite place in Little Italy, Da Nico's. It had a small band that, as they began to play that first night, Finn literally and figuratively swept me off my feet. The chemistry was potent, and the dance was sultry.

I enjoyed Finn's closeness and the perfect fit we had as we danced to a slower number. I glimpsed Roxy across the room with Roarke and a few others. I missed Valerie and hoped she was feeling better; I was growing more and more concerned.

Finn tipped his ear toward me as I said, "You haven't seen Val around, have you? The past week? She's missed work again, and I can't locate her. She called in with a cold but it's so unlike her, it must be a really bad one. Plus, she's been anxious and just…*odd* lately."

"No, I haven't. That doesn't sound like her. Want to stop by her place tonight?"

"I don't know. It's late. If she's sick, I don't want to wake her up, and she did call in today so it's not that she's missing. But let's try tomorrow if you're up for it."

"Sounds good. Is she still seeing Raff?" he asked, looking like he was holding back a snarl.

I laughed. "You said he worked well with you when he helped us on the last case. Admit it."

"Yeah, he did, but I don't have to like it. You don't suppose Val's *sickness* has anything to do with his line of work, do you?" His eyes grew black, and he clenched his jaw. He loved Val like a sister.

"Actually, I don't," I said. "I think it's something else. I don't know what, but I don't like it."

He shook his head, worry changing his features from anger to concern. "Let's definitely check it out tomorrow. You're right. It's not like her at all."

Chapter 11

In just one week, everything had changed. Valerie sat on the deep blue velvet couch in Raff's office inside his beautiful apartment. She'd been there a few times since they'd been dating seriously, but today it was different. Her entire world had tilted, and the very ground she walked upon felt altered.

Despite the unbelievable comfort of the squashy couch and its color that conjured dreams of the Mediterranean Sea, Val was on edge, as she was sitting directly across from the man she'd only seen once in real life. In a momentous act of courage, when her best friend Lane had been in terrible jeopardy, he was the only one who might have had the resources to save her. Val had marched right into his office—her heart still pounded when she thought of her own audacity—and asked him for help. Today? She sat across from him once again, needing his help. Infamous gangster, Louie Venetti.

They studied each other as they awaited their mutual ally. Raff came in carrying a tray with rich espresso and all the accoutrements for cappuccinos. He set the tray down, poured, added in what he knew was Venetti's and Valerie's preferences and handed the fragrant, creamy cups to them.

Valerie took a bracing sip of the rich brew and felt the heat and delicious flavor fill her with warmth. She felt Raff's eyes. She'd never realized you could discern that kind of tangible love right in mid-air. She darted her eyes to Venetti and, to her surprise, found his steely gaze had softened and melted his stony countenance. Thus, Valerie felt completely at odds. Everything she knew to be true about the world and her perspective had flip-flopped. Though shocking, the feeling wasn't negative—it was surprisingly pleasant.

Uncle Louie, mobster, broke the ice. "Where on earth does one possibly begin?"

Both she and Raff couldn't help themselves and let out completely uncouth barks of laughter. But it was just what they needed. Raff joined Valerie on the blue velvet couch and took her hand in his.

He began, "We can't thank you enough. You've done so much for me and now Val—"

"No, no. Please." Uncle Louie held up a hand in a gesture that couldn't have been more commanding—even Pope Pius XI would have looked less authoritative.

Despite the warmth flowing around the room, the power that rippled from Louie was something distinctly alarming, and Val felt an indescribable need to edge as far away as possible, yet she held firm.

Louie paused, every second of it measured and deliberate, then continued. "I've made a lot of evil choices in my life, Rafael. Some I felt justified; some I wish I had chosen differently, and I know I will face that judgment from my Maker. But I can say that, since I was a young boy on the verge of manhood, I decided that if a good person—an innocent—was in peril and I had the power to change their situation, I would do whatever I could. And that too will be judged one day by '*io credo in Dio*.'"

He turned to Raff and they began to talk about future plans. Val allowed her mind to drift to the day she told Raff her story. No one—not even Lane, her dearest friend—had known. Val had been consumed with worry for the last few years, but with leaving her home and having such a good job at City Hall, she'd made a fresh start. She was independent, strong. And she was making good money to help with her siblings.

Her story was nothing unique. One of millions where the

family had grown large with a Catholic devotion to children and the church's abhorrence of birth control. Her mother grew thinner and more exhausted every year. Her father had been a decent man in the past, but the Depression broke him. An anger that she'd only seen fleetingly in the past, made its bulky and disturbing presence known more and more frequently until it was a monster living in their own home. He *became* the monster.

Her dad took it out mostly on her brothers. She'd tried intervening in the past but that only made things worse. Her younger brothers, barely men themselves, took his wrath, telling her they knew if they didn't their father would turn on her, their sisters, and their mother. She knew it was true, without a doubt.

The shame and the anxiety had reached a climax last week when she'd brought over groceries and hand-me-down clothes. The air inside their home was thick with the static electricity that preceded a storm. As soon as she'd opened the door, she saw her mother stooped over a soup pot, for all the world looking as if she'd like nothing better than to disappear within its depths. Her sisters were nowhere to be seen, but she thought she heard a muffled sob escape her brothers' room where they most certainly locked the girls in safely.

Her eyes darted about the room as her voice faltered in its greeting. Val's father was pacing like a caged animal, her two brothers sitting on the edges of their seats, trying their best to be invisible, yet ready for anything. *God, she hated days like this*. She'd gotten a few knocks lately with his bad moods, a few bruises which she'd hidden with her long-sleeved blouses and makeup, but not the worst he'd ever been. Today, he felt dangerous. Someone must have mouthed off again at the bar, surely saying truths that her father was a scoundrel unhappy in work he felt beneath him (if he actually chose to show up), yet entitled to use the family's money on drink. He'd lost all sense of duty and goodness, having eyes only for his own misery.

Valerie carefully set the bags on the table, unsure of what to do, how to defuse the situation. But then she belatedly realized her mistake. She'd become the fuse just by showing up.

"You think you're so high and mighty now, missy? Coming in

here with your charity? Your judgment? Of your own father. It's disgusting. I'm ashamed you're mine." Her eyes darted to the boys. They were still young men, only about her size. The three of them would have a hard time physically controlling their father who was a massive man, though much of his muscle had atrophied to fat. Her mother stirred the pot.

What came next remained a blur of action, fear, and pain. It would remain so for most of her life. Her father made a lunge at her youngest brother. Suddenly filled with a rage she'd not allowed to surface, Val dove at her father along with her older brother. The first punch from her father landed on her brother's jaw, the second, third, and fourth she'd taken. As she fell to the floor, she knew the boys had gotten a couple more. Then beefy hands grabbed her from the floor and lifted her off her feet by her throat.

The most eerie, terrifying wail hit the air. A loud and drawn out, "No!" It was filled with such fury and energy Val felt the walls shake. Her mother had issued forth a battle cry. Val dropped to the floor as her father let go. She hated him, and she was instantly worried as she knew he'd begin his usual apologies to mask the devil inside. He whimpered, "What have I done?" Instead of feeling sympathy, as she had in the past, she knew there was no changing him. As her tears flowed, she realized with certainty that this hellish cycle would keep going until one of them died. She was as sure as she'd ever been about anything.

But before she passed out from pain and shock, she heard the strongest words her mother ever spoke. "Get. Out. And if you ever step a foot back in this house, I'll kill you myself!" Then one of the most reassuring sounds echoed through the room: the *chook-chook* of a shotgun being cocked. "Get out," she repeated through her teeth.

As Val's eyes fluttered, pain in her ribs and neck pulsing, she suddenly felt that maybe there was hope for change after all.

This was what she'd told Raff. Having been trained to be afraid of a man's rage, she was uncertain if Raff could take this without him making it even more difficult for her, making his anger the focal point. She thought she knew him well, but she'd loved her father once too. Would he take her father's side, diminishing her pain and her viewpoint? Or take her side but run off in a fury just as scary? Would he blame her in some way? She'd witnessed a few women who had shiners and their friends would say something inhumane like, *What did you do? Did you provoke him?*

But Raff did something that shocked her even more. As she'd been bracing herself, he quietly and kindly reassured her that he'd help in any way she wanted, that she was safe, and he was so sorry she'd had to endure this. Before, she'd had an inkling, but in that moment she knew that she loved him. Oh, she most certainly saw the anger blazing inside his eyes. In protecting her own siblings, she knew that primal anger well. But there was nothing sexier than power under control, of someone refusing to indulge their anger when it would only bring more harm to the person actually hurt. Raff had opened his arms and let her come to him, and then he gently wrapped her in his embrace.

Hearing her mother stand strong against her father was definitely the beginning of the change, but it was in the instant of trusting Raff with her story that tipped the dominos of action. Shortly after, Raff convinced her to go with him to Uncle Louie's. She wasn't even afraid. After mulling it over with Raff, she was just so fed up. The police didn't care, the law didn't care, the women and children just had to keep suffering. The world merely gave a callous shrug and said, *Whaddaya gonna do?* Or worse, the Bible thumpers made a case that controlling your woman—even with physical harm—was biblical. They were just women, y'know. She'd had it.

By the time they got to Uncle Louie's place that day, despite her pain, she fairly stomped into his office. Then the fear factor hit as she felt the power he radiated. That was, until Louie tipped his head down to peer at her over his glasses and said, "You again."

A funny hiccup of a laugh escaped her mouth. She had the weirdest circle of friends. They made a plan together to make sure Val's father wouldn't harm them ever again.

A day later, when the three of them had entered her childhood home, the eyes of all her siblings couldn't have been larger. Val's mother, however, looked like she'd had just about enough of swaggering men. She eyed Raff and Uncle Louie up and down with such undisguised acrimony, Raff took a small step backward. She shot a good angry eye toward Louie and patted the butt of the shotgun standing next to her as she leaned against the kitchen counter, heels crossed.

Louie bit back a smile and deferentially introduced himself. He'd asked her permission—which made her pop her head back in surprise—to "collect" her husband at the bar he was surely patronizing.

She said, "You gonna kill him?"

Louie pursed his lips and raised one eyebrow. "You want me to?"

Raff and Val eyed each other.

"Nah. Too messy," she said, as if she'd just said *No pickles* on her hamburger order. "No one else needs to suffer any more trouble from him. Just get him out of our lives." She took a pull from a cigarette, which Val had rarely seen her do, and let out her breath thoughtfully. Then her stony features softened. She set the cigarette down, walked toward them, and extended her hand. "Uh…I don't quite have the words to say. I'm sorry to involve you. But thank you, Mr. Venetti."

Uncle Louie took her hand in his and gently shook it. "Well. I like to be able to help my friends if I can. All right, Raff, let's go do some collecting." Raff kissed Val's forehead and followed Louie to the door.

At the threshold, Louie stopped and turned back. "And don't worry, Mrs. Pelton, I won't kill him. But uh…let me know if you change your mind." He had the charming audacity to wink at her mother, then walked out the door.

Remembering that wink, Val smirked and took another sip of cappuccino. "So what did you do with him? He didn't give you any trouble at his bar, did he?" Val asked.

Raff let out what was practically a snort of a laughter that he'd been trying to keep at bay. "Sorry, Val."

Louie said, "Let's just say he would have, but he was the last to realize that the bar had gone completely silent when we walked in. I wanted to make sure he didn't have a way to come back and haunt you. Bullies live on weaseling their way into places without the work it takes to earn a position. I also didn't want any negativity to come to your mother and all of you."

Val's gut took a dive, and she whispered, "You didn't tell the people at the bar what he'd been doing, did you?"

"No, dear girl. That's for you to share with whomever you deem worthy. It's not mine to tell. And I certainly don't want you to carry an ounce of shame that some ignorant fool might want to throw at you. The consequences of your father's actions are his alone to carry. I just let them know that he was no longer welcome in New York, and that his hardworking and generous family deserved better." He paused to finish his cappuccino. "Then Raff grabbed him, and we took him away."

"Where?"

"I'm giving him a chance to not mess up again. I took him somewhere far from here, got him a job and a small place to live. I told the local pub that in no uncertain terms could he be a patron."

"That's not all…" said Raff suggestively with his eyebrows raised in mirth.

At this, Uncle Louie finally let out a low rumble of a chuckle. "Yeah, I gotta say that was a stroke of genius. When we drove into town, I noticed a church and recognized an old priest who was a friend of the family. I made a stop. On top of his job, your father will be doing ten hours of service duties for the church every week."

"For how long?" asked Val.

"Forever. He'll be doing that as long as he's physically able. I think it might teach him a thing or two and Father Moretti is no pushover. I'll tell ya that. Arms like Popeye and I'm pretty sure your dad's work hours will begin with latrine duty."

Valerie processed this crazy turn of events as fast as she could. She couldn't wait to visit her mother and siblings again to see how they were doing.

"Well, thank you so much for your help, Mr. Venetti. I had never imagined we could get a fresh start like this."

"I would have helped Raff's friend for any reason. But that you are also Lane Sanders' best friend, it was my pleasure."

Valerie took another drink of the cappuccino, then said, "So after you made your little visit to collect my father, I just want you to know my family is doing well. I helped the boys find jobs after school. And with my father not drinking our wages, we'll be much better off now. My mother looks ten years younger. I helped her file for divorce. No matter what—even if our priest says otherwise —she'll be fighting for her family."

Val shook her head, recalling that banshee-like warrior yell her mother had let out that day. She whispered, "In that moment, I think we were all a little more frightened of her than my dad. I didn't think she could make that kind of noise, never mind cock a shotgun."

Val turned and extended her arm to set her cup down, but it was a long stretch and her broken rib sent out a stabbing pain. She let out a yelp but managed not to let the cup fall to the floor.

"Okay, Val," said Raff softly. "I think you need some rest. Do you want to go home? Lay down for a while?"

"Yes, I think the past couple days have been a lot. Which sounds ridiculous to say out loud. Thank you, Raff."

Louie raised a gentle hand. "Oh Val, one more thing before you go. Like I said, I'm happy to help a friend of both Rafael and Lane. And to be honest, the first time we met when you marched into my office to secure help for Lane, I admired you greatly."

Val felt her face flame at the praise.

"But I need to ask something of you. I find pleasure in helping people who are innocent and who have been victimized. I have great power and I suppose there is a sense of penance in me as I age. But this time I'm in a different position."

Raff and Val turned to each other, exchanging a look of concern.

"In this rare case, it is I who must ask for *your* help."

Chapter 12

At the City Hall office the next day, my mind kept repeating the conversations from The Savoy with Finn, about Val who hadn't shown up for work again today, insisting her cold was lingering, and with Eunice Carter teaming up with them to find out what was going down with the gangsters.

The shooting allegedly involving Louie Venetti just didn't sit well with me. It was too perfect in some ways, meaning a setup, and then imperfect in that it wasn't his style at all. Not to mention just plain stupid for a hit to happen midday outside the Chrysler Building, directly across from bustling Grand Central Station. Hundreds of people filled those sidewalks at any given moment, and had it been anyone not as outrageously dangerous as Uncle Louie, we'd have had at least several witnesses come forward—plus, a hundred false calls and probably a few aspiring artists sending in hand-drawn renditions of what they thought happened. New Yorkers loved to tell a good story. But for this one? Nothing. Only the one guy who heard the pop of the gun.

Just as I craned my neck to look at the secretary pool in the silly hope that Val might have turned up after all, a knock sounded, and in strode Eunice.

"Well, this is a nice surprise, Mrs. Carter," I said, standing to shake her hand. "Are you here to see the mayor?"

"Actually, Lane, I'm here to see you. Just a quick visit, so I'll keep my coat," she said.

"Please, have a seat." I gestured to the chairs on the opposite side of my desk. She took a seat and looked over at Fio's office. His door was open, but he was deep in thought, working on a speech, so he didn't notice her arrival. He was pacing his office floor, carefully stepping over the tiger skin rug as he went back and forth.

"Is that a tiger skin rug?" she asked incredulously.

I nodded, smiling.

"He's not a hunter, is he?" She wrinkled her nose in distaste.

"Oh no. It's a…" I had a to clear my throat to hold back a laugh. "It represents the Tammany Tiger." Our adversaries and corrupt powerbrokers for over a hundred years were the leaders of Tammany Hall. Since taking office, Fio had been working to rid the police force of the politicians, and even some judges who let greed and corruption guide their work. He hated Tammany Hall—the feeling was quite mutual—and was always looking for a chance to give his adversaries a good dig. The Tammany Hall mascot was the tiger, and Fio took great pleasure tromping over that rug every day, all day.

Eunice shook her head and allowed what I presumed to be a rare laugh. "He gets more outrageous the longer I know him."

"Tell me about it," I said in solidarity. "Don't even get me started on the chairs in his office."

"What did he do to them?"

"Oh, I'll let you figure that out on your own," I said with a satisfied grin.

She rifled through her handbag and pulled out a pad and pencil, murmuring to herself, "She's as bad as he is…" Then she jotted a quick note and handed it to me.

"What brings you here this morning?" I asked.

"Here you go. Here's the name of a friend you met briefly the other night. He has a gig tonight at a smaller club where he's heard rumblings about what's been happening in the world of organized crime. Not really any of the major players, mind you, so it won't be a dangerous situation tonight, but he said there's something happening lately. No one can get any answers, but they feel it. Ever since the NYPD officer's murder and that grab for control by the gangster called the Crusher, then Daphne Franco… nothing has settled down."

I took the slip of paper and thought back to the power struggle a couple months ago, the case that sent Finn and me to London. At least two major gangs started a free-for-all war within organized crime. Daphne Franco ended up in the middle of it. With the threat of war in Europe on the horizon, the world was rife with instability, and gangs always took advantage of instability. Prohibition had set the gangs up in power, and then thugs like the Crusher wanted to wrangle control for themselves in this new and unsettled climate. Then there were the once-in-a-lifetime crime bosses like Capone. And Daphne Franco.

But try as I might, I couldn't relegate her to even that kind of infamous status. It was too normative to what I'd read in newspapers. Daphne was so much more. I recently learned that she had been a part of my life for years. As I began the work of uncovering what my parents had been involved in during the war and tracking down their killer, memories started surfacing like grease swirling in water. The hit that took out my parents almost killed me too. And I remembered Daphne leaning over me, leering at me in the hospital ward. She'd tried to kill me more than once.

Could she be at the root of this? Did Daphne create a setup to frame Venetti? Or was it some other upstart gangster? I had been waiting for her to make a move. But I didn't want to start seeing her hiding around every corner—it was the way of obsession, and easy to do for cops who'd been tracking the same career criminal for years. But still…my intuition kept pulling at me that she was there. Waiting in the dark.

I looked at the slip from Eunice and said, "Fletcher Henderson? They call him Smack, right? Smacks his lips a lot? Yeah, I remember him. I've always liked his playing. Please tell me he's not at the Cotton Club. I don't like that place."

She tilted her head in surprise at my directness and replied, "No, he'll be at Café Society tonight."

The Cotton Club had fantastic performers, including Henderson, Louis Armstrong, and Fats Waller, but they served a "white only" clientele, and the name alone should give an indication to the decorative themes within. Aunt Evelyn and I steered clear of attending. I hadn't been to Café Society yet. It was in Greenwich Village and was the first jazz club intended for an integrated crowd.

"Fletcher knows the man who runs the place, Barney Josephson. He'll make sure you're seated in a good spot. But don't expect to hear anything while the bands are playing, it's a strict listening-only type place. No dancing, no talking during the show. High priority on the music, but plenty of chit chat between sets."

"I love it already. So, we've been thinking that this murder might be a setup to frame Louie. There seems to be no motive and we all know it wasn't Louie's style, not to mention he'd just have his men take care of any dirty work."

"That's definitely a possibility. There's an awful lot of power to be had if Louie was taken out," she said with an impressed whistle. "So do your thing tonight. Listen in to conversations, be subtle, don't ask for trouble."

I nodded, mentally moving more puzzle pieces around, thinking about Daphne or who else would have the guts—or the stupidity—to mess with Louie.

"But uh…how do I put this? I wouldn't take your boyfriend," she said with a grimace.

I knew what she meant. "Oh, I know. His look screams 'cop' from a mile away. I'll take my partner."

"You have a partner?" she asked.

"My friend Roarke and I work all of our cases together."

"*Cases*? Never mind, I don't want to know. You do what you need to do," she said.

"Always," I said. Roarke and I had taken to calling all our intriguing mysteries "cases." We got a lot of guff from people, namely Finn, but that was no skin off my nose.

"Let me know if you find out anything useful."

"I will. Thanks for your help, Mrs. Carter."

"You're welcome. Just be careful, Lane. Tonight shouldn't be dangerous, but these players sure are. Watch yourself."

As she purposefully strode out the door, I picked up the phone and dialed the number for Roarke's press room. After a crackly few seconds of someone fetching Roarke to the phone, he answered.

"Hey Roarke. How do you feel about a jazzy night in the Village? We've got a mission."

Chapter 13

On the way to Café Society, Roarke and I stopped at Valerie's first to see if she was home. From the office, I'd let Finn know that Roarke and I were going downtown and that we'd check on her. No luck and no answer yet again. If I couldn't reach her in another day, I'd find her address somehow and go over to her mother's in person.

Roarke and I took the subway downtown. Despite being early spring, they already started the ceiling fans in each car; the tall guys had to duck underneath, otherwise they'd get a little off the top. It was that in-between time of year when winter could still strike, but we were used to cold, and the balmier days could feel downright hot in places like the subways or buildings with steam heat. They were meant to keep a place warm even with the windows cracked in the severest of cold winter days, helping to freshen the air inside of our tightly packed city. Once that government implemented the policy of increasing steam heat and keeping windows open, we saw a pronounced decrease in winter illnesses. But later springtime could be a bugger. Even with the windows wide open, the outside air wasn't cold enough to bring down the inside temperature.

Fanning my face with my clutch, Roarke and I discussed the evening ahead. I anticipated a great night of jazz and hopefully some sleuthing that did not end up with me dangling from a bridge or dodging a bomb. One could hope.

"Do you know who's playing tonight?" he asked as he adjusted his dashing fedora with a pinstripe ribbon around the crown.

"I think it's the house band with Benny Goodman. Say, you never told me what you've been so secretive about when we were at Evelyn's the other night," I said elbowing him in jest.

"Well, I heard that you had an escapade at the Cloud Club that you haven't told me about," he said in a sassy voice, elbowing me in return.

"Touché. I'll tell you the fun details later, but it's how I got that meeting with Dewey and Eunice Carter at The Savoy." Roarke would have absolutely loved watching me traipse into the Cloud Club, decked out like a man.

"Ooh, I can't wait to hear what the clientele of the Cloud Club thought of you!" He chuckled merrily. "My secrets, so to speak, aren't that formed yet. But I might have an idea about who the men were that shot Troppington. It's just an idea because of some chatter I overheard at work with the other reporters."

The train pulled in, so we decided we'd save our revelations until later, then we exited and climbed up the metal stairs. The club wasn't too far away, the feel of Greenwich Village enveloping us immediately with its unique warmth of colorful, universal welcome. The buildings were shorter in this part of the city. The grid system of the streets in Manhattan began north of Greenwich, so the streets were not as easy to navigate, yet I liked how it made you meander along and look around instead of racing to your next stop.

Once inside the club and seated at a table, our drinks ordered, the band took the stage. Just as Eunice had said, the crowd naturally became quiet, attentive. The plucks from the upright bass and the tinkling notes of the piano raised the energy of the place, anticipation heightening. The saxophonist took up the tenor and dazzled the keys, the trumpet player tested out a few notes. I picked up my drink, a Bees Knees, and clinked glasses with Roarke's Lime Ricky. Then we settled in to thoroughly enjoy and soak up the ambiance.

After the last notes of the set reverberated through the room, the applause and conversation began. Everything ticked up in energy after an hour of artistry and the velvety haze of a smoky, jazz-filled room. It was magic.

I leaned over to whisper in Roarke's ear, "I guess we have to get to work. Let's see what's been going on in town."

His dimples came out with a grin; he enjoyed our escapades as much as I did.

He struck up a conversation with the ladies at the table next to him, offering a light. I decided I'd rather eavesdrop. The table behind and to my right held a group of men I didn't recognize, but they had the right look.

There was a nuance to figuring out people. I once was near two men in a café who weren't doing anything wrong, merely speaking to each other. But they were *off*. There was something about them that was tightly encased; their bearing such that they were on edge yet trying not to be. They neither looked around in angst nor did much of anything but talk. But I couldn't shake the feeling that something wasn't right. When I discussed it with Finn, he had immediately said, "Opium. It's a weird thing. I know what you're saying. It makes people seem intense and not quite right, something about their eyes. Just like you said."

The men behind me didn't give that kind of aura, but there was something seeking in them, something that said they weren't there just for the music. Not to mention, they looked tough, the kind who could give and take a punch. They were all Black men, nicely dressed, a high-end ring on one, a gold bracelet on another, but also a certain *essence* to their powerful bearings. They kind of reminded me of Uncle Louie. *That's it.* I'd bet a hundred bucks they were Black Mafia. Perfect. Just what I was looking for.

I leaned back and lit a cigarette, the motion making a great cover for expanding my personal space but still looking casual. I listened as I watched Roarke lean closer to one of the gals to his right. He then made his way to the bar and worked toward the far end.

I inhaled, tilting my face to the ceiling to exhale and listened to the conversations flowing around me. After a few minutes, a sentence made my ears perk up.

"Bumpy says he's worried. I never heard him say nothing like that before. I'm telling you, everyone's got eyes on the streets and what we're hearing don't make any sense."

Another voice, concerned and lowered replied, "What are you saying, Mo?"

"I'm saying, I don't like it. Bumpy don't like it. Normal gang shit going down is one thing, this is another. And I don't want no part of it." Then he mumbled something, and I caught only two words. Two words that made my blood run cold.

The group started to get up and Roarke ambled back to our table carrying two martinis.

"No luck. Nothing going on at the bar more than people cheating on spouses, lipsticks being swapped, and drunk talk that was scintillating only to themselves. Any luck here?"

"Hand me my drink and then I'll tell you."

"Oh dear," he replied.

I nodded, took a sip, and ate an olive, my mind running in circles about what this could mean.

"Okay. Did you get a look at those guys?" I motioned to the table behind me, currently being reset for a new group.

"Sure." He mouthed *Black Mafia*. I nodded, eyes wide.

We both leaned closer across the small table, almost forehead to forehead. I said quietly, "The only names I caught were Mo and Bumpy. They were talking about stuff on the streets not being the usual gangster stuff. Mo didn't like it one bit."

"Did he say what?"

"No. But then they started talking lower, kind of like we are now and I couldn't catch much. I know all the gangs are still reeling after Daphne Franco's coup attempt and everyone is jockeying for position. Then add in our dear mayor who's gone after all the slot machines and pinball machines, costing them all tens of millions."

"Yeah, I get all that, Lane. But why do you look so pale? What else did you hear?"

"I only heard two words clearly, and they don't make sense."

"What did they say?"

"They all got up abruptly as the guy said it and they left."

I took another sip of vodka as Roarke said, "Well lay it on me. What did you hear?"

"Something about the gangster wars, something about 'that scary woman' which I think must mean Daphne, because you know she scares the daylights out of everyone, then... Well..." I took one more sip, then said, "I heard two words that scare me even more than Daphne."

"What, Lane?" whispered Roarke.

"*Hindenburg* hit."

Chapter 14

Before I could even get my cup of coffee at work the next morning, my mind exploding from the tidbit of information from Café Society, Valerie called.

I answered my phone and was shocked to hear her voice. "Valerie! Are you all right? We've been so worried about you!"

"Hi, Lane. I know. I'm okay, I'm so sorry to worry you. I have a lot to explain. Can you all meet tonight at your place?" She was basically asking for what we affectionately called a council of war. I agreed to help arrange everything and made a few calls to all of our friends. Roxy and I debated all day what this might mean but came up with nothing.

So around seven o'clock, we descended upon Aunt Evelyn's. We gathered around the parlor, Mr. Kirkland and Evelyn, Roarke and Fiorello, and Roxy and me. Only Finn was left to arrive—and, of course, Valerie herself.

"How are Frank and Patrick doing?" asked Roarke.

Aunt Evelyn said, "Quite well. I think they'll be here just another night or two. I know the Child Society will handle things, but honestly, I do love having them around. I'm going to miss them."

"Where are they now?" I asked.

"Oh, we trained them how to walk Ripley around the neighborhood. We figured it would be good exercise for them and they're very good at it. We wondered if maybe they could start a little business with walking dogs. And it would give us time to talk by ourselves for a while tonight."

I was about to say "great idea" but the doorbell rang, and then the sound of Finn entering, interrupted me. "Hi, everyone, Val is just a minute behind me. Hey, real quick, before they get here. Just a heads up. Uh…we have an interesting development on our hands. Fio? You're going to want to sit down. Lane, you too."

"Oh, boy." Well, didn't that charge the room with a certain kind of electricity? Just as Evelyn reached for her restorative tot of bourbon—a comfort she favored in trying times—and just as I was about to ask who was coming with Val, since Finn had said "they"…the doorbell rang again.

Curious and concerned glances were shared about the room as Mr. Kirkland answered the door. He was apparently struck dumb as he shot Evelyn a petrified look, then stepped back as he opened the door wide. Valerie strode in, followed by her boyfriend, Raff, and Uncle Louie Venetti—in all his glory.

Fiorello gave one burst of outrage, but Finn shot him a stern eye and calmly said, "Mr. LaGuardia, please sit down." Fio didn't look too pleased, but he did sit back down.

The shocked silence pulsed with a tangle of emotions—confusion, anger, fear, and what I can only describe as a premonition of doom. But I only had eyes for my best friend and the concern rippling out from her.

I jumped up and ran to hug her, but before I could get to Val, both Raff and Finn gently held me back with a hand.

"What's wrong? Why can't I hug her?"

Val looked at me with tears shining. "It's okay, Lane, you can hug me. But it has to be very gently."

"Oh no! Are you okay?" I asked, going slowly to my dear friend. She wrapped one arm around me slowly and brought me to her side. Her head bowed to touch the side of mine as she said, "I'm better now. But it will take some explaining. I'm sorry I waited so long. It's just very complicated."

We all sat. Raff and Valerie held hands, sitting side by side on the loveseat. Finn perched on the arm of the couch next to me, his hand resting on my shoulder. The emotion between Val and Raff reminded me of what I had with Finn. That feeling that you had a partner, the one in the room who would have your back no matter what; the bond you shared that no one else quite understood. It was a powerful and sweet feeling, and I was pleased to see it between them. Plus, it also meant that whoever must have done harm to my Valerie wasn't him—which meant I didn't have to kill him. Which was great.

But someone had hurt her, and I was seething at the thought.

Valerie got right to it, explaining how her father had been sinking further and further into his depressed, abusive self. Then how it had progressed to violence with her brothers. How she'd intervened before but hadn't gotten more than a smack. At which I was so angry I wanted to throw something through the window. I felt Finn's whispered breath upon my ear as he leaned over and gently kissed my temple and said, "It'll be okay."

Then it all quickly devolved into what happened the other night, how her father had punched her three times and strangled her. I could practically see steam rising off all our heads. It was like beating up a kitten or a puppy. Filthy and reprehensible.

"I didn't know what to do. Legally, what recourse do we have? And I knew he'd only get worse." But then she told us about her mother's banshee cry, the shotgun, and lastly her visit with Louie.

Louie had stayed completely silent until now. All eyes found their way to him. Like Fiorello, he was not averse to a good audience. He took a breath, expanding his already large frame, and nodded. "I have great admiration for your mother, dear Valerie. Has she…changed her mind?" he asked with a smile not unlike a lion about to devour an antelope.

Valerie couldn't help herself and laughed, then winced at the pain. "Don't make me laugh, Louie. It hurts. No. She hasn't changed her mind." *Louie*? They sure seemed on familiar terms.

Evelyn said, "Changed her mind about what?"

Uncle Louie said, "Her mother asked me if I was going to kill him. And I asked her, 'Do you want me to?'"

Kirkland blurted out, "Hell, yes!"

"She said no, but I told her to let me know if she changed her mind." Uncle Louie went on to explain his plan and how their father was well and truly out of their hair and under the watchful eye of a tough priest.

After a pause, Fiorello said, "So it seems you were with Finn before this meeting. I feel like there's another part to this story."

Finn nodded gravely. "Oh, there sure is," he said.

But at this point, Frank, Patrick, and Ripley arrived back from their walk. No one knew what to do. The ruckus they made at the front door with Ripley's claws clacking on the floor, coats and hats being torn off in the usual frenzy of boyhood, and the laughter and loud talking, made all of the adults in the room look wildly around, because Venetti—sitting right here in this very room—was the man they'd fingered for murder. Once again, we were woefully shocked into silence. What on earth would their response be?

The boys, newly heartened and confident in this house, came right in, and Frank said, "Hello! Who's this? Sorry we interrupted your meeting." We watched in total fascination as both the boys looked carefully around the room, especially at Val, Raff, and Louie, lingered an extra moment, then Patrick nonchalantly said, "We're going to go get some cookies! Come on!"

After they left, I said, "Hold on. What the heck just happened here?"

Finn said enthusiastically, "I think this fully corroborates what I was about to tell you. The day that Louie and Raff went with Val to her family home, the same day that they went to the bar and scared the daylights out of Val's father and took him to a little town about two hours out of the city…was Tuesday. The same day that Venetti supposedly shot and killed a man. I verified everything already and it's airtight. Valerie is Uncle Louie's alibi."

Chapter 15

Well, the room simply erupted. Not unhappily, odd as that might seem. But then again, we all were quite used to strange situations bringing people together. It was deemed necessary for some drinks and maybe some of the cookies the boys mentioned. We all convened and filed toward the kitchen, where most of life's best conversations happened.

I looked at Roarke, and he was jotting down a few quick notes. He leaned over and said quietly to me, "This is what I've been working on that I couldn't disclose. Not one of my sources knew of Louie's whereabouts. Not one! I've been hunting down an alibi or a witness who did see Louie because it was like he simply disappeared that day."

Finn went and talked more closely with the boys, and I saw him point at Louie Venetti. I saw the boys shake their heads and animatedly tell Finn more details. They then got their cookies and took Ripley upstairs to Evelyn's loft to do some painting.

The adults reconvened around the kitchen table with cookies, wine, and bourbon. And two aspirin for Valerie. Finn picked up the story again. "So Valerie and Raff came into the precinct and told me everything. The pub verifies the story too. I already called and, seeing as Mr. Venetti here makes quite an entrance...*ahem*... he's very memorable. And of course I spoke with Valerie's mom, so truly, his alibi is solid."

I asked what had been on my mind since I heard of the alibi. "Then who looks like him and either set him up—or happens to look like him, which I just don't buy that coincidence. At all."

"I thought the same thing," said Finn. "So I was talking with the boys just now and it's interesting. Louie here is even taller than you'd think from the newspapers. The boys noticed that difference. But they also noted that his eyebrows were not the same, either."

We all took a good look at Louie, and he rolled his eyes at the attention and took a big glug of his bourbon. His salt-and-pepper brows were very much his signature look. But you couldn't fake power.

Finn said as much, "Yeah, they were impressed, Mr. Venetti. You are a much more imposing figure than whoever the murderer was, which is why they didn't recognize you just now. And they said his eyebrows were bushier." Venetti grunted with an amused half grin as he took another cookie.

As he took a bite, he said, "Mr. Kirkland, I'm going to need your recipe. These have to be the best sugar cookies I've ever had."

Kirkland, whose face had held a tapestry of barely concealed emotions the entire night, suddenly got all sheepish and delighted. He was not a fan of Venetti's, but I guessed when someone liked your cooking, all bets were off. "The secret is brown butter."

Evelyn—just as amused as I was at this exchange—rested her elbow on the table near Louie and put her chin in that hand, unabashedly getting a closer look at the two powerful men bonding over cookies.

Roarke, who was next to me, whispered, "Oh, good Lord. I need to write this down."

I laughed, then tapped the table to regain their attention. "So, do we have any leads on who set this up? Because this means that we have some big problems on our hands. It takes a lot of bravado to take on Uncle Louie. Any theories?"

Of course I was thinking of Daphne. I wondered who else would bring her up. Ever since Eunice said that there was a lot of power to be had if Louie was taken out one way or another,

Daphne came to mind. She had taken over for Rex, as the heir to his gang. However, things were changing with the repeal of Prohibition. Power didn't come from the same avenues. And Daphne was untried. She was new and she was a woman. Perhaps she was finding that she needed to prove herself to continue ruling this powerful gang, and taking out Louie would do that. But if that failed…

Louie and Raff exchanged a glance.

Raff, silent except to speak in a low voice with Valerie up to this point, said, "The gangs are definitely at war since Daphne's grab for power last year, and they're all trying to out-maneuver each other. I'd say it has to be another gang with that kind of *oomph* to back this up. It's not a new one; it's either an established gang or *possibly* someone new, but they'd have to have a lot of power behind them."

"What about Daphne?" I finally asked.

Louie's eyes darkened. I took my glass and clinked his. "Yeah, I don't like her either. Cheers." Which made him shake his head, like you did with a puppy who wouldn't behave but was adorable nonetheless.

Finn said, "Let's all use our resources to see what we can find. I'll clear this with the DA, Mr. Venetti."

It felt a little bit like things were wrapping up, but I still had my little bombshell.

"Actually, before we all head home, I have more information."

I swear a few uttered curses went around the table.

"Roarke and I went to Café Society last night on the directive of Eunice Carter. To just be around, listen in. Her friend Henderson at The Savoy says that he's been hearing some rumblings around town that don't bode well. And that trip to The Savoy was on the directive from DA Dewey from when I went to the Cloud Club."

They must've been getting used to my escapades, because not a single person asked how I got in to the Cloud Club. Which was a little disappointing. But the concern I had over what I'd over-head at the café outweighed the fun of that.

"So I heard a couple of Black Mafia fellas talking. A Mo and

Bumpy. But given that it sounds like a gangster is going to have to do something big to prove he—or she—is capable of a massive takeover of power, what I heard is even more alarming."

Fiorello asked, "Was it about the murder or the setup, Lane? Did they mention Venetti?"

"No, but they were talking about takeovers and the gangs vying for power, like we've all been hearing. These two looked very nervous and lowered their voices even further. But then I heard them say something about a hit and they wanted no part of it. They were scared. I think there's an assassination attempt coming. They said the words: *Hindenburg* hit."

Chapter 16

The following day, Valerie finally came to work. It was like the sun came out on a cloudy day. She was such a dear friend, and I had missed her more than I thought possible. Roxy and I had become very close, despite a difficult beginning to our friendship. Even more so with all of Valerie's drama—and, of course, her new love interest, Raff—which took a lot of her time.

Roxy and I greeted her at the door and gave her a gentle hug. We'd explained to the office that she had been in a small car accident but was now feeling better. We needed to explain her injuries but also tried to keep her privacy.

In the breakroom, the three of us clinked our coffee mugs in a toast, happy to be back together again. It was there that we realized Val's presence was missed by far more than just us. Ralph, our incorrigible office flirt, who really was a very nice guy, came in with a cake. As usual, he spoke in one breathless rush of one long sentence, barely pausing for air.

"Valerie! We're so glad you're back —we all chipped in on this Welcome Back cake—your favorite, strawberry with lemon frosting—and you look amazing, is that a new dress, we should all go dancing again soon—I mean as soon as you feel like it, and I think I hear my phone ringing, so I'm going to put this down— Lane and Roxy, you look great too, don't eat the cake until after lunch, and don't let Harry have any because he'll eat the whole thing if we let him. Okay, that's great, have a wonderful day!"

And he left the room with a *whoosh* of air, practically running out.

"Wow. Has he been practicing? Because that was a lot even for him," said Valerie. "I think I need a nap."

We all laughed. The cake was adorable with little light green polka dots around it, Val's favorite color and her most-favored pattern for her dresses. We made plans for lunch together and quickly got back to work.

Fio was working hard on a speech, and since he was throwing out the first pitch for the Yankees soon, he was simultaneously practicing his wind up. As he pitched imaginary baseballs, he'd asked me to come in to take some notes.

I pulled in my own chair, the ones in his office having been doctored by him. He loathed long meetings, so he had our handyman cut off an inch of the front legs of all the chairs, making his guests slide forward the entire time. In the winter, he rarely let his commissioners even take their coats off, sure to make everyone as speedy as possible because of their total discomfort.

I took dictation for several letters, made some notes on confirming some of his plans, and then we came back to the many revelations from the night before.

"Lane," he said, taking a moment to roll his sleeves. "Any thoughts on what we covered last night? Anyone come to mind who might be behind Louie's setup?"

"There's something still nagging at me about the boys' description of the shooting, but I just can't figure it out. And while overhearing the conversation about the *Hindenburg*, I remembered something I heard at The Savoy the night I met with Eunice. I didn't hear much, but they, too, mentioned the *Hindenburg*. They'd been in a heated discussion, not mad at each other, but they were anxious. Just like the guys at Café Society. Information is going around, and people are nervous."

"Maybe I'll give Eunice a call today and see what she thinks. I can give her the lowdown on anything she hasn't heard yet."

"Do you want me to get her on the phone for you?"

"No, you're going out to lunch with the gals today, right? For Val's first day back?"

"Yes!" I said happily. "We are treating her to the little Italian place just north of here. It's not Da Nico's in Little Italy, but it'll be great for a special lunch today."

"Wonderful. I've missed seeing her around the place. I can make the call to Eunice myself. You go have fun."

"Thanks, Fio. I'll see you after lunch."

I rounded up Valerie and Roxy and we headed over to the restaurant.

Roxy said delightedly, "Oh today is really starting to feel like spring!"

We walked through City Hall Park and pointed out all the daffodils to each other. Val walked a bit slower than usual, trying not to jostle around too much. But she looked great; a wonderful color hit her cheeks and her smile was wide.

"You look fabulous, Val. Are you feeling better? How's everything going with your family?"

"You know? Sometimes I think you don't even realize the heaviness of all that's been loaded on top of you until someone helps take it off. My father's decline has been going on for years. I guess it's the proverbial frog in the pot. It's been a long time of slowly turning up the heat for all of us. My sisters look taller and lighter. My brothers seem more confident, and I even caught one of them twirling a neighborhood girl around in the street. Without any music playing!"

Roxy asked, "How's your mom?"

"Oh, she's lighter too. And driven. That day, it hit her like a ton of bricks that there was no way out except to fight her way out. Something snapped into place, and she knew it would fall to her. She's pleased with how Louie handled things with discretion and a thoroughness she never guessed we could enjoy, but she's the one who made the start. I'm so proud of her."

"I'm so glad," I said with a breath of relief. "Let me know how we can help."

"Oh! I already have a request from my mom. She wants you

and Kirkland to teach my sisters some self-defense," she said with a wink.

We all cracked up. "I would be pleased as punch to do that." I also took a second to touch my favored pearl dagger at the back of my belt. I'd grown up with my own father and mother teaching me self-defense, logic, and critical thinking. I was naturally talented at knife throwing and I continued working on it. I had also been taking shooting lessons from Kirkland.

I thought of the secrets of the dagger that my father had left me. Its backstory was all about beauty out of ashes. It gave me hope that maybe Val and her family would come to find beauty out of tragedy too. Not that anyone is ever thankful for adversity, nor should they be when they've been maliciously harmed. But I hoped they'd discover how to survive and thrive once again.

We got to the restaurant and found our table. We were going to try to get our favorite, the one in the window, but a group of businessmen had come in and taken it just before we arrived. It didn't matter to us; we got the one closer to the fireplace, which was loaded with flowers instead of flames on this balmy day.

It was a wonderful time of reliving our favorite stories and funny moments Valerie had missed the past weeks. She told us just how in love she was with Raff, and I had to say, I liked how their relationship was so solid and sweet. They'd met when Valerie had slipped on the shiny floor of Penn Station, and he'd caught her. She'd even knocked his hat askew and was mortified. But then he carefully set her back upright, and then she fixed his hat. Suddenly the fire of the romance had been lit.

We ordered all our favorites: a whole dish of olives, parmigiana cheese, crisped prosciutto, and fried artichoke hearts drizzled with lemon. Afterward, we shared two big plates of chicken marsala and eggplant parmigiana.

I was full, but I think it's a culinary law that you have to get cannoli. We ordered cappuccinos and cannoli, then I excused myself to freshen up. On the way back from the ladies' room, I was passing the bar when the manager of the restaurant waved me over to the phone he held in his hand.

Curious. I had never once gotten a call at a restaurant, but I'd bet a hundred bucks it was Fio. In fact, I was so convinced it was my boss checking in on how much fun we were having, that I answered it saying, "Hi Fio! Just checking up on us?"

It was not Fio.

"Lane! This is Eunice. Get out of that restaurant! The gang that tried to frame Louie is coming after his alibi. They're coming after Val. Right now!"

In that charged second, I dropped the phone and swiveled to my best friends at the table. They watched me with perplexed expressions as I turned deadly white. In my peripheral vision, I caught the sight of two men in long black coats and fedoras slowly walking to the center of the wide front window. Holding Tommy guns.

I ran.

"Get down! Everyone down!"

I threw myself at Val and Roxy, knocking them to the ground, toward the cavernous fireplace. The restaurant had been shocked for a moment of grisly silence before the peril swept in like a tornado. Gun fire erupted as I yanked over the table we'd just been sitting at in front of us like a giant shield. The guns cut through the place with the shriek of a locomotive.

Plates and napkins and pieces of shredded wood flew through the air. Glass exploded. Screams. The scent of blood mixed with spilled wine and gun powder.

The table shielding us was being hit repeatedly, it wouldn't last long.

"Get as far into the fireplace as you can!" I yelled.

Just as the edge of the table broke off from a bullet right near my hand, I got a glimpse of the front window. One guy was reloading, the other had stopped to look around. He caught my eye. He leveled the gun at us.

A black car came roaring in. It rammed so hard and fast into the two gunmen that they were knocked clear off their feet into the air like bowling pins with the ferocious strike of a ball. With a great *crash!* everything came to a stop, and sirens rent the air, approaching fast.

I still crouched behind the table, mouth agape at the close call and the heart-pounding ending to the shooting. The driver's door opened, and Uncle Louie raced out. Raff opened the passenger side, following in Venetti's wake, making a quick scope of the area, securing the perimeter. I watched as he signaled to others not visible to me. They'd brought backup. Venetti ran toward me and picked me up by the elbows, then crushed me to his chest. "Oh my God. You're okay? Val! Roxy!"

He let me go and we both bent over, threw the table to the side, and located the girls. They were both bleeding, but not shot. I was probably covered in cuts too. But it could have been much, much worse.

Raff came over to Val, his gaze full of storm clouds and raw love. He carefully put his hand to the side of her face, and she clutched his forearm with both hands, then slowly lowered her head to his chest.

Venetti and I got Roxy to her feet, and I pulled her in for a powerful embrace. "You're okay, Rox?" I gasped.

"I think so," she said, clutching my waist.

"Dear God," I said breathlessly. We released each other, but I took her hand in one of mine, and Venetti's with the other. We three turned and slowly our gazes raked over the carnage.

Roxy and I shared one more glance, then we looked toward the men who had taken the table we'd been aiming for that day for our celebratory lunch. They were all dead. One was still at the table, his hand around his glass of wine, the white tablecloth slowly turning blood red.

Chapter 17

Fiorello and Finn arrived just as the ambulances came roaring in. By then, Venetti and Raff had taken Valerie to a safe place.

The gruesome sight of the restaurant brought Fio's usual blustering bellows to naught. Finn only had eyes for me. I'd been searching for him before I even recognized the fact. He ran over and gently but firmly wrapped me in his arms. Then, spotting Roxy beside me, he wrapped an arm around her and brought her in too. He uttered, "Bloody hell, that was close."

I quickly relayed what Eunice had told me. Finn had the same realization just as one of the tails they'd placed on Val radioed in about some suspicious activity. Venetti and Raff had gotten there in the nick of time; we wouldn't have survived another round. God bless that gigantic car and Venetti's lead foot.

After endless interviews with the police and medics, Roxy and I were fine and free to go. With just abrasions and some bruises, we were allowed to go home as long as we kept on eye on the injuries to make sure nothing got infected. I insisted she come home with me, and Finn would be staying over too. With him and Kirkland in the house, we'd be safe. Plus, I had no doubt Finn *and* Venetti would be placing extra backup all around the house and neighborhood.

As often happened, the sight of my home with the warm windows shining in the darkness brought me a sense of well-being, even smack in the midst of this chaos. It probably had something to do with the man, woman, German Shepherd, and two young boys all gawking out the front door in anticipation of our arrival.

"Are you ready for this, love?" asked Finn, a gentle hand on my lower back.

"Nothing like coming home."

I took Roxy's hand, and we climbed up the steps to hugs, some dog kisses, and lots of love. After Roxy and I got cleaned up and changed into comfortable clothes—we had stopped at her place for her bag—we met in the kitchen with the adults. Kirkland prepped a simple supper of leftover soup and sandwiches. It already seemed like days ago that the attack happened, or like another world at least.

At the table, I rubbed my forehead with both hands, then stretched my stiff and sore neck from side to side. "So, what's going on down at headquarters, Finn? What's the word on the street about what happened? When Eunice called the restaurant in a panic, she said she found out that the gang responsible for framing Louie was out to finish off his alibi. Valerie."

"Yeah, thank God Eunice had been with Fio when she'd figured it out from one of her many contacts," said Finn. "Word had gotten out that Louie had an alibi and who it was. Plus, the gangsters all know about Valerie and Raff, so her name was familiar to them. Fio knew where you were having lunch and even knew the phone number. He ran to his car, calling the cavalry while she called you. I spoke with the medical examiner, and I think I might know who these guys are. Do you remember anything about what happened? What they looked like?"

I thought back to those terrifying seconds between hearing Eunice's voice and turning toward the window to see those men in the long coats. "Let me think about it for a minute, maybe something will hit me."

"Okay, let's get some sandwiches, shall we?" said Aunt Evelyn. Kirkland and Roxy helped her arrange some things while Finn came behind me, kissed my head with his hands on my shoulders, then proceeded to open a couple bottles of wine. *Bless that guy.*

I let my mind drift back to the restaurant. I'd learned from several incidents over the years that making myself go over them mentally step by step actually helped me feel less afraid of them, or as traumatized. It wasn't easy, but it worked.

I thought about the heavy black phone receiver in my hand, Eunice's urgent voice, my glance back to the girls, happily unaware and enjoying what was supposed to be a friendly lunch. I forced my mind to remember the front window. I tried not to look too closely at the three men who'd been at the table that we had hoped to get. I focused on the window, the glare of the afternoon sun. The awning out front fluttered in the breeze. The first of the two men came from the right, a silhouette of black with a long trench coat, a fedora with a light-colored band that must have had a silver thread or something because the sun caught the light on it. The second guy was right behind him. The sun glistened off the jet-black Tommy guns as they both started to raise them. A wave of revulsion went through me at the sight of those glossy, deadly weapons. And one more thing was lit up bright and shining like a small piece of fire.

"I got it," I declared decisively.

"What did you remember?" asked Finn, sitting quickly beside me.

"It's not a gang here. It's a Chicago gang. Trying to frame Louie, making a takeover move."

Everyone resumed their seats at the table, excited to have something solid to go on. I drank a quick sip of the red wine Finn placed before me, getting my thoughts straight.

"You mean like in 1930, when Capone had Paul Ricca come here during the peace talks to end the war between the Italian gangs? You think it was Ricca?" asked Kirkland.

"Not exactly. Ever since we heard that Troppington had a big diamond watch and then that other witness saying that one of the men had a fat diamond ring, something about it kept ringing a bell. And when the boys thought they heard the shooter say something like, 'I'll do it my way—or this way...' I kept getting this feeling that the saying was a clue."

"I see where you're going with this, Lane," said Finn. "That diamond they saw must have triggered a thought, because it was

Diamond Joe back in Chicago who originally saw the talent of Ricca. Capone loves Ricca; everyone says even though Frank Nitti got the head honcho role after Capone was put in the slammer, it's really Ricca who has all the control. And now that I think about it, I think Ricca wears a big diamond pinky ring—like that other witness said he noticed."

Evelyn added, "You know, Frank said that the shooters talked funny. Chicagoans have a very different accent. He's probably never heard that twang before. I think you're right, Lane."

"Yeah, but I don't think it's Ricca himself, it just seems below him to frame Louie and, honestly, in such a messy, unprofessional way," I said. "You're right, that diamond made me think of Ricca and because the guy *did* say he'd do it his way, which is Ricca's catchphrase. It's someone from Chicago and probably someone who is trying hard to sound tough like Ricca.

"But I think these guys are just lackeys for someone else. Someone wanting to make a big move, who's just pulling the strings. Someone who wants to gain control over Uncle Louie's territory, maybe prove she is powerful enough. Who is someone who is losing patience, getting desperate because we've thwarted her earlier moves, and needs to make something happen *now?*"

It clicked with Roxy first. "It's Daphne. It's absolutely Daphne who's pulling the strings."

I nodded.

"Oh goodness," said Evelyn. "That does make sense."

"Sure does," said Finn. "I'll start looking into it."

I darted a look to Mr. Kirkland. The old spy was a wise, savvy man and I knew he was thinking through all the possibilities. What shocked me was what he said next: "We need to send word to Louie Venetti. He's got to know who might be behind this."

Chapter 18

Louie took a long, fond look at Raff and Valerie sitting on the lush sofa opposite Louie once again. Raff kissed Val's hand, his sincere face speaking volumes of his love. They had just told Louie their plans to get Valerie out of New York for the time being.

Louie could practically feel the love between the two of them, like the Aga in his grandmother's kitchen radiated heat and comfort. The vivid sweetness of that memory sent a pang of homesickness right through him. Homesickness for his grandmother's, but also another feeling. Wistfulness? Envy perhaps? He'd loved many women, but only one woman did he love the way he could see in Raff's love for Valerie.

"Well, my dears, I like the sound of that plan. In fact, I—"

But he was cut off by his butler announcing two *special* visitors. The particular way he comically held his eyes wide open in surprise told Louie exactly who had come to visit.

Before she even got fully through the door, he said, "Lane Sanders. Always a delight."

The look on Lane's face was just as amusing as the look on the face of the person right behind her.

"And Mr. Kirkland," Louie greeted. "A pleasure."

Kirkland sputtered, "You knew? How—"

Lane interrupted him with a genial hand outstretched to

Louie. "Thanks for seeing us with no notice, Mr. Venetti." She had a good handshake. Warm and strong, just like her mother.

She continued, "I apologize for the inconvenience, but we have information you need."

Valerie uttered, "Oh boy."

Louie sat in his favorite cognac-colored leather chair with the grace of an old lion. When he heard Lane had news for him, he suddenly craved a brandy and signaled his butler to offer beverages. Lane greeted Valerie. Their bruises and scrapes from the close call that afternoon rankled him. He should have seen this coming. They had a lovely friendship, the two gals. They were going to miss each other.

Lane's keen eyes took in everything as she sat in the second-most-lordly chair he had. She watched Val and Raff closely, then scanned the room and ended by locking eyes with him. Neither flinched. They had an odd understanding with one another. Would he ever tell her about his past, why he had an interest in her? Would there be any upside to telling her?

The butler finished passing around drinks, then departed. They were free to get down to business.

Lane filled them in on her hypothesis that the gunmen were thugs from Chicago. He'd figured out from his own contacts that they'd been hoping to hit Valerie, thus their plan to get Val the heck out of Dodge. But the Chicago gang made sense with the copycat strategy and even the parlance of Paul Ricca.

Raff said, "I can't see Ricca being that foolish. He might dare to do it, but he'd have been a lot cleaner. Smarter. I don't think he's behind it."

Lane said, "Neither do we. But someone's pulling the strings. And it has to be someone impatient, needing a change in power… Someone whose own power has been slipping lately. Someone who wouldn't mind killing my best friends—not to mention yours truly. Especially since I saw her murder her own husband, the one who *should* have been the heir to the gang's legacy." Lane was nodding encouragingly, looking right at Louie.

He whispered with the hint of a growl, "Daphne."

They all took a moment to let that sink in. Lane swirled her glass of red wine, deep in thought.

"Did you think of something else, Lane?" asked Louie.

She looked out the window for another silent moment, then said, "I just… I'm surprised I didn't *feel* her coming for us. I know her so well. I even know her perfume. It's like I can sense her presence."

He shared a look with Raff.

"Well, that's an interesting segue, Lane. I was actually going to request a meeting with you all. It's fortuitous that you came today."

He heard an audible gulp from Kirkland, which made his lips twitch.

"We've been keeping tabs on Daphne, of course, but this part of her plan had slipped past us, which also suggests that framing me was an impetuous act. It leads me to believe that her next move is something big. Something never attempted even by her. Perhaps this attack at the restaurant was a Hail Mary, a way to gain the power she desires without taking the risk that would be required for her final move."

Mr. Kirkland said, "That all makes sense, Louie. What have you learned that you haven't told us yet?"

He finished the last ounce of his brandy, feeling the warm and spicy energy flow through his body. "My sources followed Daphne, and through a series of cat-and-mouse chases through the city, recently witnessed her boarding the *SS Bremen*."

Lane's gaze pierced his once again. "She went to Germany? She went to Germany!" she exclaimed.

Lane looked from person to person as the enormity and complexity of that information settled upon them. She finished her glass of wine and firmly set it down, then stated, "So it's Daphne for sure who's involved with a hit on the *Hindenburg*. We have to stop her."

Mr. Kirkland surprised them all when he said, "No, Lane. *You* have to stop her. You're the only one who has a chance."

"What?" exclaimed Lane.

Valerie, silent up until this point, bravely said, "He's right,

Lane. You know her moves, you would know her even in disguise, and as you said, you even know her scent. You are the one who can outsmart her just like you did on our other cases. You think outside the box in ways that she can't anticipate. For Pete's sake, no one can anticipate!" She ended with a small laugh, holding herself steady, trying not to jostle her sore ribs.

Kirkland added, "You were the first one to figure out the Chicago gang ties with Louie's setup and the attack at the restaurant. There's no one like you for this job. And with the unrest in Europe, this may be our only chance."

Raff took Val's hand and kissed it, giving her an encouraging nod.

Then Val smiled mischievously and with a wink, said, "And we have a great way to get you to Europe."

Chapter 19

I was still practically stumbling in shock. Louie's driver took Kirkland and I back home. On the cold sidewalk, under warm lights looking down on us with the promise of belonging, we exchanged a look and drew a deep, bracing breath. Then we climbed the steps to our beloved home in silence. Ripley met us at the door, the first sentry.

"My good boy," said Kirkland gruffly with an affectionate pat to Ripley's head.

Roxy and Finn rushed to the door, Evelyn just a step behind.

"Well?" asked Finn.

"I… I better sit down."

"Oh dear," said Evelyn.

Roxy blurted, "Well, that can't be good. I've never heard you at a loss for words, Lane." Which broke the spell of shock and worry that had weighed me down for the whole ride home. Finn snorted in a way that said *You got that right!* Which made me laugh, the final shreds of shock lifting from my shoulders.

We made our way back to the kitchen to the table that hosted all our councils of war. I should have known—he had a sixth sense for when and where to show up for the best dramatic effect —Fiorello was waiting for us, hands clasped on the scrubbed pine table, fully smirking at my stunned look. Kirkland brought me brownies, and I gave him a grateful glance. Chocolate helped everything.

Before I could organize my thoughts properly, Fiorello piped in, saying, "I have some big news."

Kirkland growled, "Can't be bigger than ours."

Fully expecting to be the only one with a bombshell to share, Fio's shoulders sagged just a bit. But his black eyes gleamed, sending sparks of energy around the room. He said, "Well… I just got off the phone with Winston Churchill. Did you?"

Evelyn made a squawk of surprise and sat down hard.

"Well, Fiorello," I said, "it seems you have the floor."

He wore a smug look, but then shot a glance at Finn, which made me wonder just what Churchill had up his sleeve.

"Well, things in Europe are heating up, as we all know. But beyond the political climate, as we saw with Lane and Finn's trip to England a couple of months ago, the organized crime world is evolving in new ways every day. They're gaining power, but the authorities are more concerned with Germany and Hitler's power plays. Churchill's source says Daphne is on the move again. And Lane? He's asking you to come to Europe once more. Based on the update I'd given him—how you tracked Daphne's movements in England and especially here—he knows you've seen her in ways no one else has. You're essential to stopping her."

"Well, that actually fits well with what we learned from Venetti," I said. "We told him the details of our Chicago gang theory, and he agreed—it made sense to him. In fact, he was just about to pay us a visit himself."

The tension thickened around the table. I'd been part of many plans with these dear friends. Being with the team felt like being home. But a pang of anxiety hit me—my next assignment would likely be entirely on my own.

I continued, "Venetti understands our logic—someone else is behind this. Combine that with the things we've overheard about the *Hindenburg*, and the last puzzle piece falls into place: one of his men recently saw Daphne board an ocean liner, the *SS Bremen*. We believe she's planning on assassinating someone on the *Hindenburg*.

He thinks our best chance is for me to follow her, get on the *Hindenburg*, and uncover what's really going on."

Fio said, "I better let Churchill know. He said he had a feeling that she might be trying to rub shoulders with the Nazis."

I said disgustedly, "Yeah, it's not like she's ever shown discriminating taste with her relationships."

"Bah!" laughed Kirkland. "That's my girl."

Finn turned to me and set his hand on mine. "How do you feel about this, Lane?"

I caught Evelyn eyeing him keenly as she said, "You're not going to forbid Lane to do this, Finn?"

He made a *pfft* sort of noise and said, "Well, two things: Firstly, *please*, as if I could tell her to do anything. Secondly, Lane has shown us that she can handle this kind of mission."

As I traced my hand along his jaw, his five o'clock shadow scratched my hand, and his mouth twitched into a smile.

It reminded me of one final spicy detail. "Oh! And I will have travel companions on the way to Europe. Louie and Raff are getting Valerie out of New York, so Raff is taking her to Italy to visit his hometown. Louie booked us passage on the *SS Normandie*. They'll travel on to Italy from France, and I'll meet up with our previous contacts from London in Paris."

I stood up, having come to terms with it all quite suddenly, like clipping the final latch on my suitcase closed. My life was never typical, and for a long time I wrestled with why. But it was part and parcel for a child who was brought up by spies, and I was Charlotte and Matthew's daughter through and through. Plus, I was surrounded by the best group of friends and family I could ever hope for. It made sense with my curiosity, my peculiar-and-not-always-feminine talents, and my love for justice. I would see this through to the end.

"Then I'll take a train to Germany. I'm going to get on the *Hindenburg* and I'm going to stop Daphne."

Chapter 20

I only had one week to prepare for the voyage. Between wrapping up some office work, advising my replacements for my absence, and packing, I didn't have a lot of time. But I would make time—any time—for an invitation from Finn to go on a date.

We ate a quick dinner at a local pub near my place then headed toward Midtown. We were going to Swing Street. I had walked the block on 52nd between Fifth and Sixth a lot, just north of Rockefeller Center. But I tended to frequent The Savoy, so I hadn't explored the jazz scene on 52nd.

"I heard someone special is playing tonight. Just had to take you, love."

We walked over to Fifth Avenue and caught the bus down, then walked along, enjoying the bright lights of 3 Deuces, Club Carousel, Jimmy Ryan's, and Onyx.

"I loved coming here during Prohibition," said Finn.

"You little devil! They let you in with all your presence that screams police?" I asked, teasing.

"Yeah well...I tried to tone it down. The Onyx Club is all about new tunes. It's legal now, but when it was a speakeasy, you'd get to number 35 on 52nd Street, go down a few steps to a basement door. Follow the long dark hallway then go up a flight of stairs..."

"I've lost you already," I said, laughing.

"It's in an old walk-up apartment, started up about ten years ago. You then find a silver-painted door and knock; a guy would look out through a peep hole. You'd have to tell him you're from 802. Which was the number of New York Musicians Union, and then they'd let you in. And I'm tellin' ya, the main act tonight is really good."

We got to the main door and stepped into a flood of artistry and joy—a jazz band played at full volume while the crowd nodded, stamped, and shimmied along, utterly captivated. Smoke curled into the air, mingling with the scents of liquor, sweat, and perfume, the sizzle of jazz all around us. We grabbed a small table for two, and Finn went to the bar to get an Old Fashioned for me and a lager for himself.

We listened to a couple of songs, then the opener wrapped up and the next band set up. Finn regaled me with tales about the place. "I know the owner, Joe Helbock. He's the guy who made 52nd what it is." He laughed, eyes shining. "In Prohibition, he was a bootlegger, and he told me he counted Teddy Roosevelt as his best customer for home delivery services. He used to deliver the booze in a briefcase instead of a paper bag. I asked him why and he tells me, 'We're polite bootleggers!'" I laughed and made a mental note to ask Fio if he'd ever met Teddy Roosevelt. I would love to have seen that meeting!

As I sipped my bourbon and bitters, I took in the ambiance. The walls were silver and black, with a large black marble bar at the back—hence the name *Onyx*. The air was electric and had a darker, sultrier feel than Café Society. I loved it. The main act took the stage.

"Oh my God, it's Billie Holiday," I gasped.

Finn, smiling widely, clinked my glass with his bottle. "I knew you'd love it."

I sat back in awe that I'd finally get to hear her. She was going to be big—you could just tell. There was something magnetic and determined about her. Like she'd overcome a lot, and she was going to be damn sure she got to wherever she wanted to go.

Through "Symphony in Black," "Fine and Mellow," and "Big City Blues," I listened to her unique voice, the way she tenderly syncopated her vocals and cherished the music as she sang. When her instrumentalists had solos, she was just as involved, like she was tasting the very music they played. I stroked Finn's hand on the table and drew my chair even closer to him, so we were pressed against each other.

The whole evening heated up every inch of my body. Then Billie began "It Had to Be You." Something about her tunes drew people together, and Finn and I weren't the only ones sitting closely, whispering to each other, stealing kisses. Then several of us decided to dance, even though there wasn't a proper dance floor. It was a tight place, but that didn't stop those of us who felt the music in our souls.

Finn and I held each other close, swaying gently to the soft piano, swishing drums, and saxophone. There's this funny, strange current of energy in New York City. It runs along like a swift river and if you're lucky enough to jump in, it awakens the senses. You see the coils of smoke that play with the sparkling lights, you hear the glasses tinkling and the passionate music, you feel your partner's warmth and his hands drifting downward.

I thought of our first meeting, our first sultry dance before we even knew each other's names. And I thought of leaving shortly on a mission alone. I adored that he trusted me and had faith in me. But this wasn't the first time that our plan both invigorated and terrified me in equal measure.

A look of love and concern etched his face as we danced.

"I wish I could go with you," he said, putting his hand on the side of my face, rubbing my cheek gently with his thumb.

"I want you to come, too."

"But I know the fewer of us, the better."

"We have a slight chance of trying to disguise my presence, but if any more of us go on the trip, the greater the chance she'd recognize us immediately. With just me, she might be less threatened even if she does recognize me. We definitely don't want her feeling cornered on an airship," I said with a grimace.

He shivered. "No. We don't." He looked intently into my eyes. "Lane, I… I don't think I ever thought I'd find you. And now that I have, I'm worried I'll lose you."

"You can't," I whispered. "It's impossible." I raised up on my toes and circled my hands around his neck, pressing my lips to his as if trying to say through our kiss everything my heart felt, in the dark and smoky room with jazz in our hearts.

Cheek to cheek, I whispered in his ear, "Thanks for tonight, Finn. It's a dream."

"I knew you'd love it." We swayed closely, our hearts pressed together, as Billie Holiday went right into her next tune, "Solitude."

"I love you, Finn Brodie."

"I love you, Lane. Always."

Then he gave me one more knee-wobbling kiss, and we danced for hours.

When Finn and I left the club hand-in-hand, we were both starving.

"Hey, I've got an idea. I've got a buddy who has a small place uptown, but it's worth the quick train ride. Not officially opened up, yet. You have *got* to try the best late night snack known to man. *Especially* after a good jazz session."

"I love it already, lead the way!"

We took the train then walked only a couple blocks down and sure enough, a few tables were set on the sidewalk outside a big brownstone. Several people were eating. They were obviously musicians with various instrument cases lying at their feet.

Two of them saw us approach and lifted unsure eyes to us. When they recognized Finn, broad grins spread across their faces before they tucked back into fried chicken.

"Wait, is that a waffle? Are you eating a waffle and fried chicken?" I yelled by way of greeting.

Finn chuckled and said, "Joseph Wells, this is Lane Sanders, my girlfriend. I'm pretty sure you're going to have another lifelong customer."

The men scooted over as I grabbed a chair and quickly sat right next to them, eyeing their food.

"Hey little lady, get your own," said a tall, lanky man holding his chicken leg away from my greedy expression as he laughed.

I gave a hopeful look to Joseph and he said, "Coming right up!"

I laughed and patted the guy's arm and said, "I'm just kidding with ya. Unless Joseph runs out, of course, then all bets are off."

The guys laughed and we made introductions. Most of them were coming from or on their way to a jazz gig. Joseph came running out and set a large plate between Finn and me filled with a giant waffle and a crispy chicken leg and thigh. It looked like it was drizzled with honey, and the scent of creole spices wafted to me.

"Goodness gracious, that's incredible," I whispered, making the men chuckle in appreciation.

Joseph, incredibly pleased to see Finn and I respond with such delight from his food, set his hands on his hips as he tipped back and forth on his toes. "Yep! I'm thinking that I can make this work. See now, I got the idea from a bunch of us that left a club late, headed here and it was too late for dinner, too early for breakfast. I had some leftover fried chicken and I had just made some waffles earlier that morning. I got to thinkin'…why not try to put them together? We all love chicken and biscuits, maybe this would be pretty damn good! And it was! I'm thinking I'll feature the chicken and waffles, and call my place Joe's Club."

"How about Wells Club?" chimed in Hank, my lanky friend, as he wiped his mouth with a napkin.

Joseph said, "I like that. But it sounds more like a music place. Which I'd love, too. But I'm thinking a restaurant."

"Club sounds fancier, though," I said. "How about Wells Dinner Club?"

"Wells Supper Club! How's that? Kind of between dinner and breakfast, right? Wells Supper Club. I like it!"

After we all finished eating and said our goodbyes, we walked toward the subway. I tried to hold back a yawn, but it was late and I was stuffed. We waited at the corner with several other late night partiers, a tall, golden haired gal on my left.

"You love her red shoes, don't you?" asked Finn.

"I sure do! Was just admiring them—"

A loud screech of tires cut off my sentence as a car careened right toward us. Finn and I locked eyes. With a growl, he shoved several us from the edge of the curb with his incredible might. "Get back!"

People leaped out of the way, screams pierced the air. The tall girl and I fell backward as the rear end of the car crashed into the crowd, throwing a few people in front of us right off the curb.

Chapter 21

I turned back and saw Finn drag the driver out of his seat when the car came to a stop. As the guy went to grab a pistol from his holster, Finn punched him, a spray of blood and at least a couple of teeth went flying. Another guy with a gun jumped out the passenger side.

"Finn! Get down!" I yelled.

He hit the pavement. The *crack* of three gunshots sounded and I covered the lady next to me, wrapping my arms over her as I forced her to the ground. I looked up and the shooter ran down the block, making a sharp turn around the first corner.

I looked over at Finn, relieved to see he was moving. But then I glimpsed a red stain oozing through his shirt.

"No!"

I ran to him, slamming my knees down on the street next to him, careless of the pain. He groaned as I put my hand over the red patch of blood, but then said in a gruff whisper, "It's okay, Lane. Just grazed me. I think my jacket caught most of it. Just nipped my side."

"Oh thank God, oh thank God," I kept saying. I couldn't say anything else. My heart raced and even with the relief of his words, my hands wouldn't stop shaking.

"Here," he said, taking my hands abruptly into one of his, and lifting his shirt so I could see the damage for myself. "See? It's okay, Lane, it's okay."

I looked at the deep cut that must have hurt like hell, then I looked at my own bloody finger tips. I was suddenly freezing and light-headed. He searched my face then wrapped his arms around me and brought me onto his lap, holding me tight, slowly rubbing the side of my head. He gently rocked and said softly, "Keep breathing. Try to slow your breaths in and out, here do it with me."

He inhaled and I tried to mimic him. The trembling began to slowly subside. Up until this point, I'd been the one who had been in the most dangerous and deadly situations. The very real threat of losing Finn hit home.

I took one more jittery breath and said, "I think I'm good now."

"Just one more minute," he said, not moving to release his grip around me.

"That lady next to me looked like Valerie, didn't she?"

"Yeah. She did," he said, holding me close.

Sirens approached, people were running everywhere, a clamor of yelling and cars screeching surrounded the area, but I was only aware of the two of us. Finn and I had shared many romantic, passionate moments. And we'd also enjoyed sweet dances, laughter that made my sides ache, and even the fun of flying a kite together. But it was this moment that was the most earth-shaking for me, an inch farther and the bullet could have killed him. There are moments when your feelings and ideas and philosophies are put to the test, and you realize in a flash your deepest gratitude and passion.

I looked up at him within his embrace, and with a finger turned his chin to face me. "One more time, promise me you're okay."

His eyes crinkled with a smile and yearning as he searched my face. Then his countenance became intense and serious. "Yes, Lane. I promise."

"I wish you could go with me on the mission."

"I do too," he whispered gruffly. "Tell me you'll come back to me, Lane."

"Always."

He brought his lips to mine as a swell of love rose up and through me as we held on tightly to each other. I'd never felt such passion for someone. But even with the love I felt, its light couldn't quite dispel a frightening kernel of truth: There was a good possibility that I might not make it out alive from this mission.

Chapter 22

Valerie and I waved furiously to our friends and family from high above the Hudson River aboard the *Normandie*. I had to hold on to my red pillbox hat so it didn't fly away in the stiff wind. Though I was excited for the trip and for my mission, it was a difficult goodbye with Evelyn and Kirkland, but most of all with Finn.

We'd managed to work together on so many of our prior cases and investigations. There was something sinister hanging over us with this and made me edgy, perhaps it was the monumental nature of the mission. Or maybe it was because I'd be on my own, in mid-air above the ocean, surrounded by flammable gas and a mad woman.

"Yep, that'd do it," I sarcastically whispered to myself.

With Daphne, anything could happen, and I could never depend on typical motivation with her, even predictable self-preservation. I'd seen the mask she wore slip a couple of times. There was a monster lurking beneath that beauty.

"Here, sweety," said Val as she handed me her handkerchief.

"Thanks. I know it's silly." I dabbed my eyes, careful not to muss my eyeliner.

"No, it's not. Never say you're sorry for feeling," she said as she leaned over and rested her crossed arms on the railing, looking intently at the hundreds of people milling around the harbor. Her honey-brown hair shone bright in the sunshine, her navy hat contrasting with it and bringing out her light green eyes.

"Thanks, Val," I said as I leaned forward, pushing up next to her, enjoying the togetherness of the warmth and the friendship. There was nothing like girlfriends.

Finally, my eyes found Finn's across the distance. I felt him as if he were right next to me. He'd been supportive and not hesitant at all about this journey. Yet I knew his concern ran deep, and he'd be itching to be able to help just as I would if it had been him going alone.

I raised my hand and gave a small wave, then placed it on my heart. He nodded and put his hand on his heart. We were even on the *Normandie*, the same ship Finn and I sailed on recently on our way home from Europe. I was already missing him dearly and I suddenly, urgently, wanted to do something, say something that covered everything he meant to me.

Overcome with emotion, I felt a tear hit my eye. He'd become my closest friend, confidant, lover, partner… I wasn't sure if he could see my face closely, but in an instant I knew what I wanted to say. I mouthed slowly, *Will you marry me?*

His hand patted his heart as a smile spread across his face and he nodded. Then he mouthed, *I love you. Be safe.*

After the ship left the harbor and we passed by the Statue of Liberty, Valerie took a deep breath and said, "Come on, let's go check out our room. If Louie made the reservations, it's going to be divine!"

I hadn't thought of that. We looked at each other, our grins growing with understanding of *just what that meant.* "Oh my gosh," I whispered.

When Finn and I traveled on this ship, we certainly didn't have the first-class options that Louie did. Val and I took off running, trying and absolutely failing to maintain our dignity because we kept laughing and pushing each other playfully out of the way.

We located our room and looked at each other, still giddy with expectation. I nodded for her to open the door.

"Oh my…" she said with a seductive tone that made me snort.

Louie had booked us a suite. A *suite*. I was excited just to have my own bed and not have to share with Valerie—let alone this.

"Holy cow," was all I could say. The entry room had a large sitting area with a floor-to-ceiling window as the centerpiece. Four leather club chairs sat in a regal circle, surrounded by white walls with elegant moldings and light blue murals. Art Deco furniture graced the space on one side of the dining room, on the other: two bedrooms with large beds. And we even had our own bathroom. A bottle of champagne rested on ice in the middle of the main sitting room table beside a large bouquet of flowers in light blues, whites, and a few magenta roses that added spark and spice to the arrangement. Valerie went right to the bottle of champagne and popped it open.

"God, I love you," I said, which made her laugh even harder than she had yet.

She poured us two coupes. We clinked our glasses, then sipped and took a closer look at the place.

"Louie went all out," Val said thoughtfully. "He's really got an interest in you, Lane. You said he knew your mom. What else ties him to you? Louie keeps turning up when we need him, yet he's a gangster and we know he's done really awful things. It doesn't make sense. Raff too. But I love him."

"I know. It's a puzzle. I'm kind of hoping that maybe I'll have some time with him on this trip to figure it out. I've seen people change, so he could be turning over a new leaf. But I agree with you. There's more to his past with my mom than he's telling me. You know her name was Charlotte, nickname Charlie. But when he says *Charlie*, he says it with meaning. In this earnest, raw way."

Valerie nodded. "Yeah, and there's power in a name. When someone says your name with a certain tone…boy-oh-boy. It can pack a punch."

Just then, a knock sounded at the door.

I let in a porter pushing a cart with a tray covered in a large silver dome. Alongside it sat a second bottle of champagne and a large pot of coffee. The porter set the tray down in the sitting room and, with a practiced gesture, removed the cover from the glittering tray with a flourish. "Voilà!"

He quickly departed, and we descended upon the tray laden with a French high tea. Or in our case, a high coffee, as we preferred coffee. Small sandwiches of cucumber and salmon; savory choux pastry filled with crab, herbs, and crème fraiche; then petit fours and fruit tarts… I might have drooled. I had never seen such an array of incredible bite-sized food.

"Oh look!" said Valerie. She handed me a slender box as she eagerly reached to open her matching one.

I lifted the lid and nestled inside was the most gorgeous Art Deco diamond bracelet. I immediately thought of my mother's earrings that I had brought and was absolutely certain matched this bracelet. Finn was capable of this kind of over-the-top creative generosity—he gave very thoughtful gifts—but I knew it wasn't from him.

"Oh, it's lovely!" gushed Valerie. Her box contained a beautiful pearl necklace from Raff. I helped her put it on, and it matched the glow of her skin perfectly. We happily spent an hour eating and reminiscing.

"Did your bracelet come with a note?" asked Valerie. "Maybe Raff didn't want you to miss out since he was getting me this necklace."

"Oh, I know who it's from and no, it's not Raff," I said with a smirk.

Tired, but too giddy to nap, Val and I spent the afternoon leisurely exploring the ship.

Later, we gathered at the formal dinner, enjoying a large group at the Captain's table. We'd first peeked in at the children's dining room, which was adorable with the walls covered in prints of Babar the elephant. The main dining hall was unbelievably beautiful and enormous. At a staggering three-hundred-feet long, the size was unheard of, but the *Normandie* architects designed the funnel uptakes to split and go along the outside of the ship instead of through the interior, allowing for this uninterrupted hall. The pamphlets onboard said it was longer than the Hall of Mirrors at Versailles. Twelve long Art Deco chandeliers of Lalique glass with

38 matching columns along the sides gave the room a luxurious glow, and you didn't miss having exterior windows at all. This incredible lighting inspired the *Normandie* to be nicknamed the Ship of Light.

After a sumptuous dinner of the finest French cuisine, I sipped the final bit of a frothy cappuccino and let my thoughts settle around me like the gentle swaying of the ship as we eased farther into the Atlantic. The day had been utterly amazing with the glamour of the ship, enjoying Valerie's company, and the adventure of all adventures at hand.

The only thing that had distracted me from the joy of the day was the realization that I had been subconsciously scanning my surroundings. Constantly searching and looking closer at individuals who had the same arch of the neck, the same sauntering walk, the same look of a predator as my nemesis, Daphne Franco. She was supposed to have been on the *SS Bremen*, but I still couldn't stop watching for her. Being followed provoked a cruel, primal fear—like a mouse stalked by a cat, waiting for an opening to crush it. It had been a cold realization when I discovered she'd been watching me since I was a child. How many times had I been in peril and hadn't even noticed?

I needed to write this stuff down, maybe take up writing a novel like Roarke. There was little justice in the real world, maybe it would be healing to create my own in a fictional world.

The days passed in a dream of lazy hours of reading and walking the deck with Valerie. The afternoons were full of lunches and games on board, we took a few swims in the indoor pool and saw a film at the cinema. We even played a game of tennis since the ship was the only ocean liner to have a regulation sized tennis court on deck. The evenings were filled with more delicious food and dancing in the café grill that was transformed into a nightclub after the dinner service. The final night was the biggest banquet yet, and there would be a dance and long nighttime hours soaking in the last moments on the gorgeous *SS Normandie*.

The dancing was in full swing in the nightclub, and I caught the eyes of Uncle Louie on me. He had worked the room all night with the charm of Fred Astaire and the aplomb of our president,

FDR. Now he was off to the side, elbow upon the bar, smoking a cigar while calmly watching me.

Despite the power and strength that seemed to create an aura around him, his eyes weren't currently those of a predator, but of a bushy-browed friend. Yes, he was certainly quite the puzzle.

I walked over to him. He had a dirty martini waiting for me, just how I liked it: with three olives. I wordlessly took the glass as he picked up his drink and we clinked glasses. I mirrored him with my elbow on the bar as we surveyed the happy, clamorous room that just started showing signs of slowing down. Sweeter, slower songs brought out the romantic dancers and invited intimate conversations around the room. It made me miss Finn even more, as I remembered our long dances in this very room. Small groups of two and three broke off to little tables glittering with candles burning low. The scent of coffee, cigars, and brandy filled the air.

"Well done, Louie. This has been a wonderful voyage. Thank you for making so many beautiful arrangements like the high tea our first day and the theater and even signing us up for a spot to play tennis."

"Lane, dear, I wouldn't have it any other way," he said, in his rumbling voice.

"And…thank you. For the bracelet. I love it more than you know." That got him.

He muttered, shaking his head, "I shouldn't be surprised you knew it was from me."

I laughed as I gently fingered the Art Deco drop earrings I was wearing, the ones of my mother's that suited us both to a tee. "You gave my mom these, too, didn't you." It wasn't a question. "I've always loved them. I had assumed they were from my dad, but then again, he was never a connoisseur of jewelry. And these are exquisite."

Louie would never offer information of any kind until he was ready. So I knew I couldn't pry about the story of his shared past with my mom. The most important stories came from the heart and you just couldn't force that. We watched each other thoughtfully, and his shoulders relaxed. He looked around the room and gave a contented sigh, as one does when surveying a gentle sunset over a calm lake.

After several moments, he turned to look at me and said, "I did. I gave them to her a long time ago. I had a lengthy past with your mother."

"I can tell," I said with a soft smile. "Tell me whenever you're ready."

The band started "Sentimental Mood" by Duke Ellington. I stood up. "Well, Uncle Louie? How about a dance with your honorary niece?" I held out my hand. His brow crinkled as a genuine smile spread across his face.

"I…" He cleared his throat, then started again, "I would love that."

I'd had a short dance with him once; he had to get a message to me when Finn and I were at the El Morocco. He was an excellent dancer, but that time it was like dancing with a controlled thunderstorm. This time…it was like dancing with a beloved uncle or grandfather.

After the dance ended, we went to a small table in the lounge and ordered cappuccinos. More and more people were leaving the room—Raff and Val had disappeared long ago. Louie's men were still nearby, keeping a sure but discreet eye on both of us.

After a couple sips of the creamy coffee, though I wouldn't pry about my mother, I did have a lot of other questions. "So exactly how long have you been keeping an eye on me?" I asked with a raised eyebrow. He gave a low laugh that made me think of an old grizzly bear.

"You know I like to keep you on your toes," I said, knowing he'd understand my blunt question.

"That you do, Lane." He cut the cap of a fresh cigar with careful pleasure. Once he puffed a couple of times, he said, "Well, my story with your mom goes back a long way, so I started keeping tabs on you ever since we lost Charlie. You see, I owed it to her. Your mom and I grew up in the same part of the city a long time ago. I think I need to tell you from the beginning. So you understand."

"Okay," I said softly. I sat back and crossed my legs, ready to hear a good tale. "I'm all ears. Start from the beginning."

Chapter 23
A LONG TIME AGO...

Louie sat up in his tree—the only place that felt like home. His black hair fell into his eyes as he looked down at the little wooden dog he carved with his army knife. He had big hands, but they were capable and gentle. The features of the hound had come to life with soulful eyes and long ears.

He was alone. Gut-wrenchingly lonely. He lifted his shirt to see the bruises and winced. He hoped none of his ribs had been broken this time. At least his face had been untouched. He'd go back home once his uncle—who wasn't his uncle at all—had passed out. He'd have to wait until after dark which made for a long day. His stomach was already rumbling from hunger.

A flash of red caught his eye, and he looked over to see a girl, a few years younger than him—maybe eleven or so—taking long strides from the meadow into the woods. They were in Prospect Park, but this area was densely wooded, with no sight or sound of city life.

The girl had auburn hair wound into a thick braid over her shoulder. She was lovely, but the most striking thing was that she carried a bow and arrow, and a dead rabbit slung over her back.

She walked along, unaware of anyone's eyes upon her. He'd never seen anything so earnest. Her walk was confident, but not cocky. Her head was held high, but not in arrogance, just all the better to see everything. She radiated curiosity.

She looked his way so suddenly, it was almost as if she'd heard his thoughts. A blush crept up his neck. She tilted her head to the side in consideration, then she came over to him.

"Hello," she said. "Great spot."

"Yeah. I like it," he said, wanting to sound calm, cool, and collected but feeling anything but.

"I caught a rabbit," she said.

"I noticed. Do you, uh, shoot very often? You seem to be pretty good."

She nodded sagely. "Yes, I do. My mother makes very good stew. I haven't been able to catch any squirrels yet, though. Too fast."

He'd never been able to talk to a girl like this before. It was easy. And very pleasant. "There's room up here if you want to have a look around," he offered.

"Okay." She put her bow and rabbit down, then climbed up and sat right next to him on the thick tree branch, her shoulder touching his. Two things he'd never done were already checked off his list that day: he spoke with a girl easily, and now she was pressed against his shoulder.

She smelled like the meadow, summertime sweat, and something vaguely sweet like vanilla or cinnamon.

"I like that dog. You're really good." She looked down at his hands and ran a little finger over the hound's snout.

He was pleased like never before. No one had ever given him a compliment—except for when he'd behaved well while sitting motionless in church.

"What else can you carve?" she asked.

"Well, mostly dogs. I've done a few different kinds. Little ones and big ones." *Aw jeez*, now he sounded stupid. But he felt much better when she didn't seem to mind.

"I love dogs. I'd carve them too, if I could."

"What else would you carve?" he asked.

"Oh, I'd carve a little cat! Not a lion or anything, but a little cat with sweet eyes and good stripes," she said definitively, as if she'd been thinking of this answer for years.

He smiled and she smiled back. He asked, "Why a little cat?"

He knew she had a story, a face like hers had a lot of stories and dreams in it.

"Well, cats symbolize wisdom, magic, and mystery. And those little ginger ones are also just very cute." She looked at him frankly. Her green eyes were the most sincere eyes he'd ever seen. He determined then and there that he'd carve her the best little cat he could possibly make.

"What's your name?" she asked.

"Louie. What's yours?"

"Charlotte. But you can call me Charlie."

Chapter 24

"You met her when she was hunting rabbit?" I asked. "With a *bow and arrow?*"

He chuckled. "Well, squirrels too. The city was much more open and wild back then. Especially out in Brooklyn. It wasn't exactly legal, but some of the poorer people would occasionally hunt for rabbit and whatnot. I mean, at that time even Central Park had a lot of wildlife and some of the park was used for farming. The city has grown so much the past forty years."

I nodded, thinking of the two of them so young, so new to the world. But then again, Louie had already known evil within his own home.

"So, I'm guessing your childhood was what led you to take justice into your own hands at times. Like with Valerie's father?"

He nodded solemnly and puffed his cigar. His anger was palpable, rooted in decades of hardship. "Yes. My father abandoned my mom and me when I was too little to remember. We floated around from friend to friend, her own family wanted nothing to do with us. I think they were religious, so they were ashamed."

"That's one helluva religion to turn out a daughter and her child."

"You can say that again," he said. *Puff puff.*

I thought about that little cat he wanted to carve. "You know…she kept that carving of a cat you made for her."

His eyes pierced mine. He whispered, "She did?" His deep brown eyes broke my heart with their earnest hopefulness. The little cat was on my dresser with her other favorite things. I hadn't known where she'd gotten it, but the feline face was so sweet and so adorable, it looked as if it could stand up and walk across the surface at any moment. He had put a lot of love and care into creating it. I looked at him with new understanding. And he recognized it.

With a self-deprecating nod, he tapped his cigar, the ash falling to the crystal tray as his dark brown eyes glistened with heartache.

"Yes, Lane," he said softly. "I loved her. More than any woman in my life."

My heart gave a thud of shock at his words, but then again, they also made perfect sense.

"Do you have many memories of her?" he asked.

"Some. I wish I had more. I was so young when she and my father died. But once in a while memories come back, and even though it's tragic, those memories are a gift. In fact, that's why I keep things like this on my person. Not just for safety." I pulled out the pearl dagger I carried with me most days. I balanced it by the hilt on the pad of my middle finger, then flicked it up and over until the point just touched the table, where I continued to balance it precisely. When I'd found that dagger, my muscle memory kicked in and I was able to do that trick like it was nothing. I kept up my dagger routine as I continued, many of the eyes of Louie's men focused on my handiwork.

"Last time I went to Michigan I had to wrestle with that loss, not just losing my folks but also feeling like they'd lied to me about their work. And because of that, I felt like I couldn't even trust *myself*, my own intuition and judgment. I'd taken great pride in my instincts and judge of character. But if I had such great intuition, how could I have been so thoroughly duped by my own parents? Then Tucker too. So I'd started to wonder if I'd even read Finn wrong…"

"Tucker Henslowe? Daphne's son?" His eyes turned a dangerous black. I held the dagger point against the table, my eyes snapping to his.

Tucker. At first, he'd been a potential boyfriend I'd met at work, but then he got pushy. He arranged what I thought had been a business trip to Michigan that happened to overlap with mine. He showed up when I was at my lowest—reeling from my parents' lies, doubting my own feelings and intuition, blindsided by the revelation that they weren't just ordinary bookshop owners but spies in the Great War.

I'd only just started dating Finn, but I already had deep feelings for him. Even so, I almost fell for Tucker—who, as it turned out, was only trying to get at the information I had from my parents' takedown of gang leader, Rex Ruby. And still, that wasn't the whole story.

Tucker was a sublime actor, but there was real emotion in his eyes as he'd tried to seduce me. I didn't think he'd been bluffing. Then his own mother, Daphne, turned on him too. He sent me a note afterward, admitting his role in my parents' deaths. He insisted he hadn't known I'd be involved—and that what he thought was only a scare tactic had, in truth, been a hit. His letter was the first step toward a new start. It seemed he did not want to go the way of his mother, who had turned completely and wholeheartedly toward the darkness. Now it controlled her.

Louie watched me closely as those thoughts flew through my mind in a few seconds.

"Have you ever read Robert Louis Stevenson's *Jekyll and Hyde*, Louie?" I asked, setting the dagger down.

"Oh yes, I have," he said with a look of understanding. "It's always been something I've pondered."

"Monsters?"

"Exactly. The human kind. And how they—*we*—are created, nurtured…"

"And when there's no turning back," I said with a snap of my fingers. "I'd been reading that book while I was in Michigan. At one point, Tucker got his hands on it, and I think it had a big effect. I think he's seen the real Mr. Hyde, his own mother, and he's rightly afraid of that loss of control. More people should be. We'll see about him. Time will tell."

He looked at me with a searching gaze. "I knew Tucker had been involved, but it seems like you're saying he was more involved with you than I realized." The last few words were more of a growl than actual words. Not loud in the least, but I felt them in my chest. Two of his men tensed and stepped a foot closer, but with a casual flick of his left hand, they settled back into place.

Before I knew it, I'd mimicked him with a flutter of my hand and said, "God I wish I had that kind of power."

His eyes pierced mine once more, but a spark of amusement floated in those black depths. He started to chuckle, then it turned into a laugh, the likes of which I'd never heard from him. He wiped a tear of mirth from his eyes. I was delighted to watch what would happen next.

He turned to his men and said, "My God, gentlemen. Do you believe her? Isn't she just her spitting image?" They'd smiled more broadly than I thought they ever would and one of them shook his head, expecting nothing less than mischief.

I turned to Louie. "Spitting image?"

"Of your mother. Charlie. No one else could take me completely off guard—especially with her rascally wit—like she could. Except you." Still shaking with laughter, he muttered, "My God, she and Matthew created a monster."

"I heard that!" I said, but then started laughing too.

One of his men standing at the bar, Marco, said, "Well, as soon as we witnessed the whole junk cart getaway, I knew we'd have our hands full."

"You saw that?" I exclaimed. All of them were laughing but not making fun of me. I could tell that I'd given them more fun than they'd ever expected.

Louie ran a hand over his face, and Marco said, "Yeah! We were just about to jump in to rescue you and Fiorello when you were kidnapped at the New Years party, but then that Morgan gal swept in with her crew. Then the petrol bombs started flying. The guys and I all looked at each other, unsure of what the hell we'd just walked in on. Next thing we see is you running toward the street and jumping onto a junk cart."

I'd started laughing, too, because it had been one of my most spectacular moments. I took up the story. "Well, Daphne and Rex's gang had abducted Fiorello, and I'd caught them in the act, so they threw me in the van too. We'd been at the party, all decked out in our finery. I had on a red ball gown, and by the time I'd jumped onto the back of the cart with Morgan's team, my hair had all fallen down from its updo, and I was carrying my dagger in one hand and my high heels in the other."

"Tell us the rest!" asked Louie of Marco with a laugh. "It's so good."

Marco was happy to oblige. "Well, everything about the damn thing was so unexpected, we decided to follow you to see what would happen. The cart driver raced those horses through the streets like a maniac to police headquarters—it took a lot to follow him, too, I can tell ya—and finally he came to a sudden stop right in front."

I took it from there. "Right where Finn was standing with his hands on his hips, jaw clenched. Then a big pot broke free from the giant piles of junk and bounced down the street, banging as it went along. Everyone was dead silent."

Another guy wanted in on the story and said, "Then that littlest kid with Finn says—he was so right, it's hilarious—we'd all been looking at you with your big red dress, hair flying, holding your dagger…and he says, 'She looks like a pirate!'"

The next hour went on like this. They brought out some Drambuie, and I can definitely say I had too much of it. I hadn't laughed like that in a long time. Later, I told Louie more about Tucker and what happened in Michigan. He listened well. I could tell by the cynical tilt to one of his bushy eyebrows that he doubted if Tucker had really changed, that it was probably just a passing moment. I couldn't deny I felt the same. I'd seen people change, make a new start. I'd also witnessed firsthand Daphne's kind of violence where the darkness now controlled her. But if anything *could* change Tucker, it'd be that. He was terrified of losing control.

I learned a lot that night full of Drambuie and memories. Louie had changed over the past decade, and he'd been keeping an eye on me for quite a while. I hadn't noticed his men during the junk cart getaway. That was rather shocking. And most of all, I believed I discovered why he held such an interest in me, watching out, rescuing, or sending in his men if I needed help: He still loved my mother with every ounce of his heart.

Chapter 25

Louie

In the morning, nearing the final miles of the journey to France, Louie stood at the deck railing, looking toward the first sight of land. He'd been giving a lot of thought to the night before, when he, his cronies, and Lane shared stories and memories and laughs. And heartbreak. He blamed the Drambuie for making him freer with his words than he'd planned. Freer with his own emotions which leant him a vulnerability to which he wasn't accustomed. He came out on deck early so he could get his thoughts straight. He let his mind drift back once again to his childhood and the years after.

When he'd decided to get into organized crime, it wasn't one big decision. It was a hundred little ones. Unable to find enough food for his family, he first stole not a loaf of bread, but a small candy from the deli counter. When he got outside with his stolen treasure, it was his first candy—a rare morsel of goodness in a dangerous but monotonous life—that was his alone. He didn't need to share it. He didn't need to hand it over to his loathsome "uncle" who ruled the family with a cruel hand. He didn't owe anyone anything. That cherry candy tasted sweeter than anything in his life.

There were so many things in his way to finding employment, security.

Your pants or sleeves had ragged cuffs? Your shoes had cardboard in the bottom to fill the holes? You looked poor? Meant you looked untrustworthy. No job.

You looked hungry? They figured you'd steal. No job.

You looked tired? They figured you were up all night doing bad deeds. No job.

You looked Italian, Chinese, Black, any color other than English European White? No way. No job.

How did you get out of that? Everything about your condition of life was given to you without your will—there was no way out, then they blamed you for it. It made it easy to slip into a job taking messages to a "businessman" that he'd met while trying to steal a loaf of bread, having made the jump to more substantial theft from candy. After years of hardship, the brutality of his home life, the people he worked with at least seemed to take care of him as long as he did what they told him to do. He liked that. It was secure in its own messed up way. Dangerous, he quickly came to realize, but dependable. He climbed that ugly ladder and made more money than he'd ever dreamed.

But then he lost something priceless. He lost Charlie.

He'd loved her from the very moment he met her; it took her until she graduated high school to realize it. They were always together, and they planned to marry. But as he leaned into his life of running underground crime, she despised that he went down that dark path. Because of it, he lost her.

Louie took on the leadership of the organization after the boss died. The boss's own son had passed in childhood, so he'd given it all to Louie. Despite the despicable things he did, Charlie remained his conscience. Though he didn't seem to have a problem with certain crimes, he took the business out of prostitution. It was pretty easy to do, actually, because with Prohibition, he made millions in illegal liquor sales from Canada and distribution up and down the east coast. It was smarter to concentrate those efforts, plus, there was something loathsome in the sale of human flesh. Not to mention, the more people involved, the more people to keep quiet. So it made good business sense. Focusing on liquor and the slot machines and pinball machines doubled his business, and he gained control over several smaller gangs. Prohibition was an absolute boon to organized crime.

After many years and hearing about some of those changes, Charlie and Matthew came to him for help with a few issues in their work in Intelligence when the Great War started. He was happy to have Charlie in his life in any way he could. He would always love her. Her heart belonged to Matthew, but he hoped she'd always save a small part that she would share with him as his friend.

Louie gazed from the deck at the continent drawing closer. He took out a cigar in preparation for the worst memory. It was so bittersweet he rarely lingered on it, certain his heart might stop from the weight of heartbreak if he did.

It was January of 1923. Matthew and Charlie had come to New York for their work. He hadn't known what they'd been dealing with, but he read the fatigue and the worry in the shadows under their eyes, and occasionally, a keen look of distress that made Charlie's brow pucker.

One late night, she came to see him at his home office after they'd all met up earlier that evening. She wore a white satin dress that clung to her body and a white fur around her shoulders. The same dress, in fact, that Lane had worn recently to the El Morocco. Charlie's visit surprised him, as they'd said their good-byes earlier. He'd just been about to pour a scotch when his butler let her in then closed the door silently behind her.

His heart lurched with the love he still felt, but just as strong was the sense of alarm he read in her eyes. It quickly cleared, as if she just remembered herself, and she strode gracefully toward him. He'd know that stride anywhere, the same she used when she had the bow and arrow in her hands all those years ago.

She came close to him, and he put his scotch down. "Are you okay, Charlie?"

"I have something to ask of you."

"Anything," he said softly.

"First, Matthew and Lane mean everything to me, I know you know that. But there is part of me that will always love you, Louie." She looked deeply into his eyes and whispered sweetly, "You were my first true friend, my first true love." She leaned in and gave him a tender, small wisp of a kiss upon his lips. One he would hold on to for all time. A sudden look of urgent intensity swept across her countenance.

"What's wrong, Charlie?" he asked, his voice husky with emotion, wrapping his hand gently around her arm.

"I can't shake a certain feeling lately." She looked frightened, a rarity with her. His concern instantly tripled. He slid his hand down to hers then brought her soft knuckles to his lips.

"How can I help?" he asked, his eyes searching hers.

Charlie turned fully toward him, inches away. The heat and years of longing palpable between them. "Promise me, Louie. Always keep an eye on Lane for me. Please."

He began to ask why, but she shook her head as if trying to forget. "I'm sure I'm just tense because of our work. Don't worry, I'm not going anywhere. But Louie, look me in the eyes and tell me you promise. I know you can't guarantee her safety, but please promise you'll try to protect her."

His heart plummeted. This was a side he'd never seen of Charlie. Her intuition was razor sharp, and if he ever bet on someone's intuition or sixth sense—whatever you wanted to call it —he'd bet on hers. Which scared him to death. Charlie's green eyes were shining with unshed tears and grave anxiety. His heart pounded, his own emotions flowing strong. "My God, Charlie. Of course I promise. *Anything* for you."

An expression of total relief came over her. She took three deep breaths as if she'd been holding them in for an hour. "Oh Louie," she whispered as she let one tear fall. She came into his arms, and they kissed with the sweet, intense passion that he'd only ever known with her. Then he held her tightly, stroking her head as it rested against his chest. She drew away and with her thumb, wiped the tear that had appeared at the corner of his eye. "Thank you. Goodbye, my dear Louie."

For the life of him, he couldn't have realized it would be their last kiss, their last goodbye. But somewhere deep in his soul he felt it.

Chapter 26

I took a walk around the deck early on our last morning and saw Louie deep in thought at the railing. I walked up to him, and he flinched in surprise.

"I'm sorry I startled you," I said. "I was just taking a walk to clear my mind. It's been quite a trip, hasn't it."

He took a deep breath, then *puff puffed* his cigar. "Indeed, it has, Lane."

I stood next to him, placing my hands on the railing, thinking of the moment Valerie and I boarded and stood there waving farewell to New York at the beginning of this adventure.

"Last night was fun. Honestly, I haven't laughed that hard in a long time," I said.

"Well, you certainly don't disappoint with your stories. My men have enjoyed your capers. To say the least." He bent over and set his elbows on the railing, looking far into the distance.

If I read him correctly, he'd probably shared more than he expected to last night. His business was built on invulnerability. To share those moments of mirth—even with his men just watching and enjoying my antics—could be read as weakness. I had spotted a couple of his men who hadn't been too keen on the friendliness that was happening. Throughout the night I had given some thought about the long years that he'd been keeping track of me.

"So… I'd like to propose a wager."

"A bet?" he asked. His bushy brows rose in askance, a one-sided smile pulling at his mouth as he straightened.

"Yes. I bet you a hundred dollars that my mom made you promise to keep an eye on me all these years."

His face was unused to surprise. A look of acute blankness came over him. His hand slowly went into this suitcoat pocket, assumedly to locate the money he had just lost.

I set my elbows upon the railing just as his had been. "*Aw* keep it, Louie. Don't be ridiculous."

I felt his chuckle as he set his elbows into place back against mine on the railing. I took a deep breath of the briny air and listened to the sea gulls circling above as we approached the southern tip of Ireland and England, glimpsing Spain and France in the distance. We'd go into the English Channel and finally north to Le Havre, France. I was wishing the *Normandie* docked in Monaco so we could take the southern route to catch a glimpse of Casablanca and Tangier. I'd always dreamed of going through the straits of Gibraltar into the Mediterranean.

"Yes, Lane, Charlie made me to promise to watch out for you. She knew I couldn't guarantee your safety, but indeed, I promised to try. Let's just say you haven't exactly made it easy," he said with a droll tone.

"Yeah, well the apple doesn't fall far from the tree," I said barely under my breath.

"That white dress of hers that you wore to the El Morocco—she wore that the last time I saw her."

His voice was tinged with the kind of heavy sadness that came from years of grief.

"I have a photograph of that night. With her, my dad, and you."

He gasped. "I remember a photographer now. I never thought a photograph would have survived after all this time."

"It was in an album my parents made for me with our photographs and mementos from those ten years we had together and some from before I was born. That was the last night you saw her? She must have had a premonition or something."

"Yes, it was January, the month before they were killed. Could I see that photograph some day?" he asked gently.

"Of course. Could you tell me more about her? I don't have many memories. I *feel* her more than I actually remember her."

He turned a thoughtful eye toward me, but before he could respond, something caught the corner of my eye. I turned quickly and Louie instantly had a revolver in his hand.

"Man or woman?" he asked.

"Couldn't tell, a fedora and a flash of black. Could be either. Come on."

We rushed toward the door the person had been peering around, but it was easy to disappear, as ships had hundreds of little doors, hallways, alcoves, and stairways. Someone had been eavesdropping and, in Louie's world, that was never an innocent coincidence.

"There!" said Louie under his breath. We took off down the starboard hallway; he was fleet of foot for such a large man. Frankly, I was surprised none of his men were around. They usually kept a close eye on him. And for heaven's sake, me too.

I spotted a figure in a pant suit, which could have been a man or a woman, running like mad, then dashing to the left down another hall. As he or she turned up a stairway, the fedora fell off and they left it behind. I picked it up, letting Louie continue on. It wasn't Daphne's scent of expensive, too flowery sweet perfume. It was a musky, cedarwood cologne mixed with Brylcreem. Most likely a man then. Or someone in disguise. It wouldn't be the first time someone had been watching me while hiding in plain sight.

Louie came back, the eavesdropper obviously not in his grip.

He straightened his tie and said, "Have you had any other incidents onboard the ship, Lane?"

"No. And I definitely would have told you if I had. In fact, I haven't even had the hairs on my neck raise with that feeling of someone watching me. Now that I think about it, that's quite a long time without it happening."

He rolled his eyes. "So, no signs of Daphne? Tucker? Anyone else?"

"Nope. And this hat smells of a man's cheap cologne. In

disguise, that person could have been a man or woman, I never got a close enough look. But I don't think it's Daphne."

"I agree. But someone definitely has us in their sights. And that's not good."

Just as I was about to suggest we head back to the main dining room for breakfast, one of Louie's men came racing up. He quickly leaned into Louie and whispered urgently.

"Okay, stay with us. Lane? Let's go to breakfast. Two of my men are down—"

"Dead?" I yelped.

"No, no. But we think they may have been drugged last night. It's not like them to be this out of it. But it doesn't look like anything that will cause them serious harm. My men, however, never oversleep and we have redundancies for illness. So this is highly unusual."

"Unusual enough for our eavesdropper to not be coincidental," I said.

"Yes, exactly. Someone is keeping an eye on us and hadn't gotten close enough for most of the cruise. So he or she had to make a more drastic move. And you know what that means?"

"Nothing good."

Chapter 27

The disembarking process went smoother than any other travel I'd ever done. Even when Finn and I took the *Queen Mary* to England—and it was sublime and elegant—*this* was exceptional. No lines, no luggage touched my hands; it was as if I'd sauntered off the ship with my purse and everything magically appeared when I needed it. I ribbed Louie about starting up a travel business, he was so good at all of it, but then he shut me up quick when he drily suggested that perhaps he already had.

It was hard saying goodbye to Valerie, but I knew it wasn't forever, and she'd be endlessly safer in Italy. And seeing the love between her and Raff made it even easier. She was looking forward to meeting his family and seeing his hometown.

After we all said a fond farewell, I made my way to Paris. Louie's men checked out the train for me before I got on board, and I assured them that I was fine. Our intelligence contact, Miles Havalaar, would meet me at the Gare d'Orsay. After a last hug from Uncle Louie, I was really on my own.

The train ride through the Normandy countryside to Paris was peaceful, with the early spring colors of trees softly rolling by the windows. It gave me time to think and prepare myself for the next leg of the journey.

We pulled into the station, where Miles waited for me. From there, we took a taxi to the Hotel Lutetia on the Left Bank. He told me it was a dearly loved hotel and the only grand one on the Left Bank.

The porter brought my luggage to my room, and after I freshened up, I met Miles in the main lounge off of the dining room. The pungent scent of Gauloises cigarettes left a permanent impression on my mind, mingling with the vision of the incredible two-story Art Deco lounge of the Salon Borghèse. This was where the journey pivoted, where everything had been leading these last few weeks of figuring out Daphne's moves and motives. It was sobering yet invigorating.

I expected a certain bigger-than-life personality to meet us. After I tore my eyes away from the thousands of sparkling bottles on the second floor of the lounge—like a boozy library—and the soaring ceiling with pastel frescoes adorning the marble walls, I spotted them right away. Already started on his famous, vermouth-less martinis.

"Mr. Churchill, delightful to see you again, sir," I exclaimed.

Both men stood to greet me, Mr. Winston Churchill clasping my hand in his. "I trust you had no problems traveling with the certain…travel group that accompanied you on the *Normandie*?" he said.

He always reminded me of Sherlock Holmes's older brother, Mycroft, the way he seemed to be omniscient—or at the least the holder of many secrets and connections. He was like Fiorello in that way. I took a good look at Churchill. He was still in his self-proclaimed *political wilderness*, not yet having attained the position and power he sought, but he was well on his way.

"Indeed. No trouble at all," I answered with an appreciative chuckle. "In fact, even leaving the ship was seamless. And such a quick trip across."

I ordered a martini with olives and quickly picked up the discussion about my mission.

"So, Miss Sanders—"

"Please, call me Lane," I cut in.

"Lane. Taking into consideration the rather public place where we're meeting, tell me how you're feeling about this *trip* you'll be taking."

He clearly meant the mission but certainly didn't want to use that word, nor the word *Hindenburg*. Germany was well and truly making everyone nervous. The *Hindenburg* was synonymous with the Nazis, and I suspected that espionage of all kinds had been ramping up. Not only with regard to organized crime, such as Daphne's coup, but also with Hitler making more moves that were not in accordance with the Treaty of Versailles. The British government was currently taking the peace-at-all-costs stance. No one wanted a repeat of the Great War. In fact, Hitler didn't either.

As long as the world gave him whatever he wanted, that was.

The charismatic man was scary to watch on the news reels played before every movie. He had a way of winning over his audiences with wild promises. I hated his screaming and there was a sinister feel to the way his soldiers marched and saluted him. They certainly did not carry an attitude of peace, but of building toward war. It had all the momentum of an upswing, not something rebuilding for their country's sake, but an insatiable desire for *more*, always more.

"This *trip*, Mr. Churchill, will be undeniably exciting. I know our Miles Havalaar sure had a wonderful time on it on his way to the US last fall."

Usually taciturn, Miles was overtaken by a big grin, his speech pattern becoming more cockney. "Yeah, I sure did, Lane. It was really something. I have to say, though, it was a bit strange, yeah?" He lowered his voice, and we automatically leaned in a bit more. "To be in it flying high and looking down on Germany and France and England…when really not that long ago at all, we'd been dashing around on those same lands." Then his voice cut to a whisper. "Dodging bombs lobbed from contraptions just like it in the war."

Mr. Churchill nodded sagely. "Indeed, Miles. And you bring up the more unsavory aspect of Lane's trip. You know, the ones in charge of the ship." Obviously meaning the Nazis, but that word had a menacing effect on a room. And you never knew who was listening. "I will have a man on board with you, Lane. You hopefully won't need any assistance, but he'll keep an eye out if there's trouble."

"Thank you. Should I contact him?" I asked.

"No, no. He'll find you. But you may never know who he is, if there isn't a need."

He took a couple of puffs from a cigar, not unlike Uncle Louie, and took a moment to contemplate. We all did. A lot was at stake, and I was putting my life on the line more than I had even through all my escapades this past year. Given that I'd been in a couple of explosions, kidnapped, forced to run from bad guys on several occasions, was perched outside on a window ledge at Grand Central, dangling off both a bridge and a roadway at one point, among many…that was really saying something.

I turned to Miles and said, "Can you help me with some disguise options?"

"Of course, Lane. Happy to."

Aunt Evelyn would probably be dying of envy since she truly enjoyed a good disguise. But I supposed I needed to be a lot more subtle than she preferred.

"How about Scarlett as a name?" I asked, unable to be *that* subtle.

Churchill coughed and Miles looked at me with the fondness saved for a wayward puppy, very similar, in fact, to the way Uncle Louie was apt to gaze upon me. "Lane, love, you positively sparkle when you choose a route that is, oh let's say *bigger than life*. And no matter what garb you're wearing, anyone can recognize that in you. So to blend in, you must choose a bland option and behave accordingly."

My face must have looked mutinous, because Churchill took a rare moment of levity and patted my hand as he bit back a smile.

"Fine," I complied. "Nothing outrageous. I'll go for a look that is natural and something that anyone who knows me decently well would have trouble recognizing."

"I can help you do that, love," said Miles. "It's a specialty. In fact, let's head to my place and we can take a gander at what I have and some possibilities. Then I have another friend I think you'll enjoy meeting."

"Well, Lane. You have my highest regard for taking on this… trip." Churchill's eyes pierced mine. His bulldog appearance with eyes full of challenge, fortitude, and I had to say a bit of envy and humor, gave me a burst of resolve. I always loved a challenge, and he must have seen my inner response because a small smirk pulled at his mouth.

Both Churchill and Miles were fantastic conversationalists. But what I'd remember most from that time with them was a notable difference in the atmosphere between that of Europe and the States. In any given lounge or bar, there was a kind camaraderie and *joie de vivre* to be had. But there was also a wary note mixed with a rash devil-may-care, almost violent need to enjoy. A feeling of static electricity that was waiting for something to pounce and an uncertainty of what it meant.

It could just be a wariness because the Great War felt like it was last week. My own parents had been in the thick of it and I was born out of it. Was it really possible that the world would be thrown into that hell again? Was the current prime minister being the proverbial ostrich with his head in the sand? Would the new king, being crowned in about ten days, be a help or a hindrance? So far no one was standing up to Hitler, and I couldn't see his appetite being assuaged one bit.

At one point, Churchill said something I'd never forget, and I continued to mull over it all evening. It strengthened my resolve for the task ahead. "Lane, dear. Your assignment is crucial, and yet I know how much we are asking of you. The danger involved. Keep remembering who you're doing this for. What is the use of living, if not to strive for noble causes and to make this muddled world a better place for those in it to live after we are gone?"

"Think creatively. The Germans are. Daphne will not play by the rules, neither should you! This is one of the reasons we thought you were perfect for this role. How do we not simply survive but get *ahead*? How do we outsmart? I trust you'll do quite well, my girl. And if things look bleak, you know my motto: Never give up. Never give in."

Chapter 28

After Churchill left and Miles and I had a long discussion on tips for my disguise, Miles said that I needed to change into something for an elegant nightclub and that it wasn't possible to overdress for this place. The more over-the-top, the better.

Happy to oblige and mentally rubbing my hands together in great expectation, I chose a sequin gown with cap sleeves, beaded strands dripping from the edges. A deep scoop neckline crowned the design, its color shifting from a deep peacock blue-green at the bodice to midnight blue at the hips, before flaring into radiant fuchsia at the hem. The gown hugged my hips, its lines drawing into the waist, then rippling outward like a pond stirred by a pebble.

When I came down from my room to meet up with Miles, he gave a low whistle and said, "Oh, she'll love that."

"She?" I asked.

"Mm-hmm. All right! Allons-y!"

In fluent French, Miles directed the driver to take us around the highlights, then to a club. He'd spoken so rapidly I didn't catch the name. Given the smirk on both the cabby and Miles, it was going to be a good one.

We drove through the Left Bank as he directed my eyes to more sights than I could keep up with, including the apartments of James Joyce, Gertrude Stein, and at least three different residences of Hemmingway.

Miles took on the tone of an experienced tour guide. "The Left Bank, Lane, is where the artists gather. It's a bit more quiet and definitely more romantic than the Right Bank. But you, of course, must see all the famous places too. This is your only night; we will make the most of it."

We drove lazily by the glorious Eiffel Tower and the Champs-Élysées, soaking it all in. Miles was silent for the most part, letting me enjoy every moment of the city of lights. We drove past the Moulin Rouge with its red windmill on top, then over to Montmartre with the good and gentle Sacré-Coeur beautifully perched at the top. It was another artistic area where the artists lived and breathed, smoked and drank, and created freely. So many had fled the United States when Prohibition began. After living through the Great War, the last thing the scarred survivors needed was another limitation on a simple joy. The Temperance Movement had good intentions, mostly, because there was so much loss and destruction that alcohol fueled. However, it was also about control. Artists despised that. As did I.

The car went down numerous one-way streets through the 9th Arondissement, the cobblestones jostling us about. The age of the charming buildings and the streets shining from the gas lights brought to life the ghosts of many eras before us. I could easily imagine the spectral figures of the Belle Époque winding their way in and out of these same establishments. I longed to join in.

The car suddenly came to a stop at 39 rue Fontaine.

My breath caught. It was Chez Josephine. Josephine Baker's elegant, most-desired of all Parisian clubs.

After exiting the car, I took Miles's arm, and we entered. The club was a triumph of elegance and sophistication mixed with Josephine's outlandish exuberance. Just last year, Josephine had ended a year-long stint in New York City working with the Ziegfield Follies. Her reception had not gone well, and she was disgusted by the racial inequality, so she went back to her beloved Paris where she was adored.

Led to our table by a hostess, I drank in every detail, committing it to memory. The club featured a large band area for a full orchestra—a rarity, as most Parisian clubs had space for only a few musicians. The dance floor was enormous. I'd heard that all the occupants of the entire club could fit on it at one time, so Josephine could dance with everyone. Cut glass mirrors flanked the stage, and a mirrored back wall made the space seem even more expansive. A colorful mural of Josephine dancing had been painted on one wall. The other white walls and pillars were edged in gold, adding to the generous elegance. Blue chandeliers gave the atmosphere a cool and mystical feel, one that whispered of other worlds and mystery.

After we dined on a late-night dish of sumptuous oysters and fresh baguettes, caviar and several delectable cheeses, I was just about to suggest we head to the dance floor when a loud ruckus began that could only mean one thing: Josephine had arrived.

I had never experienced such a flamboyant and joyous entrance. People, wild colors, and *animals*. Josephine donned an incredible gown of blue snakeskin and tulle, radiant in her thousand reflections bouncing off the plentiful mirrors. She was followed by all her servants, one who delicately picked up her wrap as it slipped from her shoulders, then took the leash from Josephine's fingertips and led the potbellied pig toward the kitchen. Following was another servant leading an enormous white dog.

"Is that a Great Pyrenees?"

"Yes, that's Miss Blanche. The pig is Arnold."

"Ah. I see."

Josephine quickly greeted the adoring crowd and went into the song "La Conga Blicoti."

Miles and I danced, but I could barely keep my eyes off her. At one point, I caught a nod between Miles and Josephine. If I wasn't mistaken, her eyes grew more luminous as they crept up and down my sparkling gown. Then she went back to eyeing herself in all those mirrors. Who could blame her?

Heading back to our little table among the many surrounding the dance floor, I asked Miles, "So you're actually friends with the Josephine Baker? Are we going to get to meet her?"

"I'm friends with her, yes. But even if I wasn't, by the look on her face when she saw you…" he said with a devilish look. "She'll definitely be wanting an introduction."

Before I could utter any reply, Josephine breezed over.

"Miles, my darling!" she exclaimed. They exchanged *la bise*, the three kisses on cheeks. Josephine leveled her gaze at me with the wattage of a lighthouse. "Is this the friend you wanted me to meet? You did not tell me she'd be so delectable."

You couldn't tell from the blue lighting, but I blushed from head to toe. She'd had many lovers, both male and female, and I could see why. She carried this *heat* with her, as if her internal temperature ran much higher than the rest of us mere mortals. Her gaze lingered on the high slit along my leg, then slowly drifted upward meeting mine with a smoldering intensity.

I stood to greet her; we were about the same height, around 5'7". Before Miles could finish the full introduction, she leaned in to give me *la bise*. With each delicate kiss to my cheeks, gravity shifted and centered upon her. She drew people in with a charisma that was like the sun sweeping the planets around her in a cosmic dance.

Staying close and sliding her fingertips down my arm, she grasped my hand and whispered in my ear, "Come, let us dance."

She pulled me to the dance floor, all the eyes in the club pivoting toward us. Between her blue snakeskin dress and my peacock splendor, we became something of a sensation. I thought we would be dancing in a group setting, but once we were in the very middle of the mirrored, sparkling club full of curling smoke, she pulled me in closely. She was an excellent dance partner, leading with confident, smooth moves.

After a few classic swing steps, she drew me back in and said, "*Ma chère*, we have much to discuss. Here no one can listen in. But first, you must tell me where you got that pearl dagger I saw so seductively lying against your thigh. I need to get one of those."

I was indeed wearing my dagger, but my mouth went dry, and I didn't know how to respond. I struggled to come to my senses and said, "A dagger like it would suit you. Inscribed inside the handle is *pulchritudo ex cinere*. Latin for—"

"Beauty out of ashes," she supplied. "*Oui*, a powerful theme of my life. I think you and I have much in common, Lane." She smiled at me bewitchingly and said, "Miles has filled me in on your trip across the ocean."

She looked at me with a knowing gleam in her eye. "I see you are wondering why he would bring me in?"

I wrangled with my ability to speak; she made it difficult. "Well, actually, yes. Do you have information on the flight?" I asked, curious as to how she would be of help.

"Not as such. I am aware of Daphne, but I don't know her. But I know people. And I am a very aware kind of person. Do you like my staffing choices?"

I smiled wickedly and said, "Yes, I noticed they all have certain similarities."

"They are all white!" she exclaimed delightedly. "Me. A great-grandchild of two slaves in America. And look at my mostly white clientele." She laughed, her accent American yet slanting toward Parisian. "This is why I returned to Paris. In America, they would string me up for having the audacity to be the star, to own my elegant club, and to have white servants. White Americans are afraid of Black people having power, afraid that we might make them our slaves. That is telling, yes? Their fear comes from their own guilt. I love my country, but I cannot stand the hate. Hate is the downfall of any race or nation. This is why Hitler cannot continue. I believe he will take us all to hell on earth, but I believe he will ultimately fail because of this hate. More is achieved by love."

There was great valor in her eyes. I liked her, I loved her. I bet most of the world would feel that way.

"Miles tells me you have a difficult task ahead of you. He also tells me that Churchill feels you will need to think creatively and get ahead of this Daphne. As you can see, I am an expert at thinking this way. Don't go by the rules. *Make* the rules. There is no limit to what we can achieve if we believe in ourselves. Life is a dance, and we must keep moving to the rhythm."

She spun me in a twirl then brought me back in. She bit her lip thoughtfully as she looked into my eyes, searching.

"Have you ever danced with a woman before?"

"No. Not like this."

"I dance with men and women alike. I am not immoral, I am natural. Lane, *ma chère*, I dress to kill, but not to conquer. I was born to entertain, and I will continue to do so until the day I die. This is my advice to you, never forget it: Don't wait for the world to change, be the change you want to see."

Just then the song ended. She gave me a lingering kiss on the lips, then lightly spun away and walked back on stage to finish her set.

I wobbled back to my table, breathless. I sat down inelegantly and faced a smirking Miles, elbow on the table, chin in hand.

"All right, mate?" he asked, eyes glinting.

"A lot happened out there," I said weakly, beginning to laugh at myself. I took a long drink of water, needing to cool down a bit.

Miles gave in to his amusement and chuckled. "You should see her banana costume. *Wow*. She has that effect on everyone. But she definitely has a shine for you, love. Did she give you good bit of advice as well?"

"She did, in fact," I said, nodding. "Very good advice indeed."

Chapter 29

Back at the hotel, it was difficult to sleep. From my time with Josephine to my class on disguises from Miles, my mind was energized, and I felt as prepared as I could be. The most successful disguises were subtle, ones that could be carried easily without too much complication. They actually had little to do with fabricated noses or severe makeup. The best kind were one of character.

So I became a student of my own mannerisms. And when I gave up on trying to sleep, I worked on holding myself with a different posture than usual. I practiced walking with a slower gait and using fewer, smaller gestures and even speech patterns. One in particular I hated: forcing my voice to go upward in pitch at the end of sentences as if everything was a perpetual question. I kept my New York accent, exaggerating it a little but not as far as the extreme mid-Atlantic accent of the movies.

I also chose clothing more casual and bland than what I usually wore. I went to a local shop and bought a beige cardigan and a few items that I would never typically choose. I tended to like jewel tones, so I went with earthy colors like browns and drab green. I wore my hair in a dowdy updo and Miles gave me a set of wide framed glasses to increase the look of the size of my eyes. Instead of black mascara, I used only a little petroleum jelly on my eyelashes as well as a little brown eyeliner.

Miles showed me how to add a few crow's feet to the corners

of my eyes and a few at my smile lines with shaded streaks of brown eyeliner. I worked on smiling with lips closed and what I can only describe as simpering. I went for a personality that did not want to be an independent woman, a spinster who needed a man or a protector and wasn't very comfortable with the idea of traveling on her own on the *Hindenburg*.

My cover story was that the wealthy woman I was to accompany became ill and decided to stay with relatives, then take an ocean liner for the return trip. But since my ticket had already been purchased, she decided I should use it and then set up the household before she arrived.

Though I despised the shoes that were plainer and more clunky than I'd have chosen, I did love the lower heel. But once I got home, I would never wear drab brown ever again. Having shipped most of my luggage back so that I didn't have to carry it all with me, I only had my purse and a suitcase with overnight necessities plus two simple changes of clothes and one extra outfit for emergencies. I didn't expect to sleep much, most people chose to stay up for the short trip so they didn't miss out on anything.

For the entire afternoon aboard the train that would take me to Frankfurt, I continued to work on my new persona as I watched the German countryside flow by. The next time I'd see it, I'd be up a thousand feet high above it. It gave me chills of excitement just thinking about it. The few hours passed rather quickly despite my growing enthusiasm which usually slows time down. I got a cab from the train station and finally—at last—arrived at the airfield. Stepping out of the car, I looked in awe at the wide-open field and the massive hangar that housed the *Hindenburg*.

The *Hindenburg* was a technological marvel crossing the Atlantic in only 48 hours, give or take about ten hours depending on the winds. It was less than half the time of crossing on an ocean liner. Ever since hearing about Miles's trip last fall, I had been enthralled by it. Supposedly, even people who suffer from a fear of heights didn't have trouble in dirigibles because it was such a gentle lift-off from the ground.

Holding my pocketbook, I walked to the gathering area and kept an eye out for anyone who remotely caught my interest. The passengers were all waiting to board. Some were getting in their last easily accessible cigarettes. The *Hindenburg* had a smoking room that was vacuum sealed as to not allow any sparks to get out anywhere near the extremely flammable bags of hydrogen that kept us aloft. We were carefully warned about no matches allowed. Matches and lit cigarettes would only be available in the smoking room, and we'd be monitored by a security guard ensuring that we did not leave the smoking room with either.

Suddenly, the call to board came across the loudspeakers and we all began to walk across the large field toward the hangar. Humongous doors were pulled open and we got our first glimpse of the *Hindenburg* as the men below it led it out via the guide ropes not unlike the Thanksgiving parade balloons in New York. Multiplied by a thousand.

A band played patriotic German music, and banners and flags flew from a large crowd that had gathered to watch. People and soldiers milled about all over the hangar and grounds. The *Hindenburg* proudly displayed Germany's Nazi swastikas. My enthusiasm took a hit to the gut, filled with sobering animosity whenever I glimpsed those symbols.

I once asked a librarian friend about the swastika that Hitler chose for Nazi Germany, because I had only known it to be an ancient symbol up until then and didn't know what it stood for. She told me that for millennia it represented good luck, infinity, even the sun for many groups and religions especially in the far east. But a German excavator began a search for the lost city of Troy and made a big find off the coast of Turkey. Besides silver and gold, he found over 1800 symbols of the swastika. After that, throughout Germany, the swastika was all over sports teams and advertisements, anywhere that wanted good luck. It eventually began to metamorphosize into a representation of the Germans who felt that they were descendants of the Aryan race. Chosen ones. Hitler loved that idea and embraced the swastika for his new regime.

This Aryan race ideology was dangerous. Anything that said one race, gender, or religion was better than another made it easy to start seeing other humans as animals, degenerates, property, disposable. When my train had crossed over the border into Germany, I was torn. On one hand was this beautiful land, and I knew many wonderful German people, yet on the other, it was revolting crossing over into a country that used nationalism to harm people, including its own.

I'd heard that the German government began programs that were, on the face of things, supposed to help with healthcare for those who were blind, deaf, mentally ill, had a chromosomal anomaly or genetic disability... They were taken from families and told they'd be treated. So far, I hadn't heard of any who were returned. I'd also heard of camps for political prisoners, which began peppering the German landscape as soon as Hitler took over in '33, four years ago. And now there were bigger ones and many of us in politics knew these were not just for those opposing the Nazi regime, but anyone the Nazis deemed dangerous or unworthy. For four years, they had been boycotting Jewish businesses, burning books by Jewish authors and political dissidents, and stripped Jews of German citizenship. And it had already been two years since the Nuremburg Laws were enacted, taking legal citizenship away from anyone Jewish and forbidding Germans to marry Jews.

So the Jews were definitely in mortal peril. And the Romani, the Jehovah's Witnesses, and also a lot of Catholics. Homosexuals. Anyone who spoke against the government or even just looked like they might speak against the government. And then add in the Germans who weren't physically fit. Deaf, blind, mentally ill, chronically ill.

And yet. I looked around this clamoring field of patriots. The crowds cheered and applauded and cried for this regime. For Hitler. For the splendor he promised. The music began to feel abrasive, chafing my ears. The exclamations of pride sounded a sour note.

The way Germany brought in law after law, one little thing at a time that chipped away at its own citizens, then bigger and crueler laws, but now the people couldn't envision him a monster, they believed his lies. And in the aftermath and poverty of the Great War, a quiet, ugly, secret part of them felt the same way.

Hitler's fervor emboldened them, fanning into flame their own hatred. The way this plan cunningly emerged had all been obvious to Fiorello. He'd called out Hitler early on and he'd gotten backlash for it.

I wondered if time would show the monstrosity of it all. Or if people would make excuses. In my job with the mayor, I saw first-hand the ability of people to delude themselves that things weren't that bad, it couldn't have happened that way, or my *favorite*: but the taxes are better. It never failed to amaze me what people could be persuaded to do and believe and eventually sacrifice…for the promise of just a little more money.

As I walked toward the large airship with the black swastikas that no longer meant luck and goodness, I suddenly knew deep in my soul one thing. In that moment of celebrated grandeur in complete contrast to my internal disgust and raging fear: the world was going to go to war again. And this time it would be even bigger.

Every step I took closer, I keenly felt the gravity of what I was doing. There were moments in life when you starkly realized there was no going back. There was no returning to what you used to know, what you used to believe. I knew that if I was able to do anything for my family and friends, for my city, and for people who cared about justice, I would fight for goodness and rightness.

Churchill's words came to me again. *What is the use of living, if not to strive for noble causes and to make this muddled world a better place for those in it to live after we are gone?*

Just then, a cold breeze came to me across the field, ruffling the flags, carrying a certain scent that I'd known for years. Daphne was here.

The *Hindenburg* loomed over me as I walked closer, following the line of passengers. I went to the steps that folded down from the airship and, taking hold of the railing, I knew this was a moment I'd look back on. This was the instant where I could still turn back. With a deep breath full of resolve, I scanned the crowd one more time for Daphne. Then I boarded the airship.

Chapter 30

"I've got a bad feeling about this," said Evelyn, her teacup rattling as it slipped from her fingers onto the saucer.

Kirkland's eyes snapped to hers.

"Do you now," he said. He'd learned a long time ago to pay attention to her intuition. He used to make light fun of it; a friend of Evelyn's from England had been very dramatic about omens and portents of the future, and he felt it had rubbed off on Evelyn. However, the accuracy of imminent danger following closely on the heels of such moments shut him up quickly.

"Indeed, I do. Something is nagging at me about it."

"Well, let's go over what we know," he suggested. He had to admit, his old spy intuition hadn't felt quite right about things either. He liked a plan. He liked having a clear mission and this was anything but clear.

Evelyn stood and put her hands behind her back, pacing with the authority and pomposity of a general. He bit back a smile and reclined, readying himself to listen to her ruminations.

"All right, then. We know that Daphne organized the setup to frame Louie and the car that almost crashed into the woman they thought must be Valerie, as well as the shooting at the restaurant."

"Yes. Check."

"We know that there have been rumblings about a *Hindenburg* hit and that Daphne will be on board to make that hit happen."

"Check."

"We know she's capable of murder, in spades."

"Sure is," he said with a growl.

"And we know she has power and panache. She had her offices in a lunatic asylum, once escaped a building by jumping out a window onto a fireman's safety net as Lane and Finn closed in, and years ago deceived all of us into thinking she wasn't the mastermind of organized crime behind the façade of a flighty housewife…"

"Definitely," he said with a *harumph*.

"So we know that she's more than capable of creatively executing a hit without using a gun, which would detonate the entire ship. And she's capable of pulling off a complicated scheme. She has resources and has marshaled an entire network of criminals."

Evelyn walked toward the drink cart but paused at the French doors leading out to the small backyard. The large maple twinkled and glowed with lights, lanterns, and delicate chandeliers that Kirkland had hung with love. The space that Lane loved dearly and had brought her not only comfort, but joy for all her years with them since she was ten.

Kirkland stood and joined her, placing his hands on her shoulders, rubbing them softly.

"Worried about her, Ev?" he asked in his gruff voice.

She let out a long sigh and set her hand atop his on her shoulder. "I hate to admit it, but yes, I am. I thought it was a smart idea, and she certainly can handle the mission. But I can't get this feeling of dread to go away, Kirk. There's something more that we need to know. To help her."

Her voice quivered at those last three words. This was costing her more than he'd expected. Kirkland knew what to do.

"All right, my girl. Let's get ourselves a little *medicinal* help and then do what we do best."

He gently took her by the shoulders and walked her back toward the couch, then he got them both a generous pour of bourbon. The amber liquid shone through the cut glass, glittering from all the lights off the maple tree.

He handed her the drink and sat next to her, their knees touching. They clinked glasses and took a deep draft. Already, the spark was coming back to her eyes. She just needed a little push in dealing with that emotion.

"So, what do we do best, Kirk?"

"Action. We can't just sit around here worrying. We need to do something."

"You're absolutely right," she said with a thump of her hand on his knee.

She put her empty glass down with a *thunk* and got back up to proceed with her pacing. "Action. We need action…" she said, ruminating. "You're right. We don't have to sit here helpless. In fact, that would be a disservice to Lane and whatever is happening."

"That's my girl," he said proudly.

"We need to do more than just put Lane on that airship. I think we need to gather our own resources here and figure out what exactly is going on, why the *Hindenburg* is the chosen moment for this hit, who the hell is on that aircraft, and how we can help our girl!" she said vehemently.

"Language, Evelyn!" he said in mock offense. "I agree whole-heartedly. So what do you propose we do first?"

"We need to call a council war."

Chapter 31

Daphne's scent still lingered in the air, yet I hadn't seen her, perhaps she'd gotten an early boarding. I worked at my slower, moderated pace and made sure my shoulders curved inward unlike my usual posture of shoulders-back, chin-up.

I watched a gentleman lead his German Shepherd up the stairs and onto the ship, reminding me of Ripley. I would've given a lot of money to have Finn or Roarke or Aunt Evelyn with me at that moment. Home felt so far away.

I was feeling homesick and mourning the state of the party leading Germany, but my curiosity about the ship overcame my nerves. I made my way past Deck B, with its kitchen, bathrooms, smoking room, and lounge, then went up to Deck A, home to the dining room, entertainment lounge, writing room, and staterooms.

The lilting notes of a piano floated through the hall. *Jazz.* Shocked that the Germans would allow it—they weren't exactly known for their love of jazz—I followed the notes into the lounge. Sure enough, a steward was speaking to the pianist, telling him to cease playing. But a wealthy, powerful woman *shushed* him away and motioned to the young gentleman to continue. The soft jazz spoke to my soul, making home seem not quite so distant.

The piano was made of aluminum alloy and hollow tubing. It

sounded pretty good, maybe a little brassier than usual, but that was to be expected. I read that it weighed about 350 pounds, compared to the typical grand piano, which could be closer to 1,000 pounds.

But there was no time to dally, everyone gathered at the slanted windows that looked out over the airfield. There were viewing areas on both Level A and B on both sides of the ship and we all flocked to the windows. The crew on the ground carried ropes to pull us fully out of the hangar, and then before we knew what happened, the German Queen of the Skies gently floated upward. I'd heard that people sometimes missed take-off completely because it was such a peaceful process. We lifted off, and I watched the ground slip away from us as we quickly ascended.

The music shifted from jazz to Wagner, as another pianist sat down. With the change of music, the sensations of homesickness and trepidation returned. Even crossing the Atlantic with a known mobster felt more comforting and familiar than how I was feeling right then. I was well and truly alone, on a difficult mission. The thrill of the journey ahead had been tainted by the macabre foreboding that I witnessed with the complacency toward the Nazi regime and their gross Nuremburg laws. How were we allowing this?

Then I thought back to my recent read of Dr. Jekyll and Mr. Hyde by Robert Louis Stevenson. People rarely believed in monsters. Cynicism overrode their concern about Hitler. The threat of war was real, but I believed that the greater problem was deciding not to face it head-on. Mr. Kirkland was outraged that France did nothing when Hitler took the Rhineland. I understood how France was severely wounded, having the war fought mostly on their land, but I agreed with Mr. Kirkland. I'd never known a bully to stand down of his own accord. Until someone stood up to him. I wiped a pesky tear from the corner of my eye.

Just then, a hand set gently on my lower back. "You still look lovely, but dull brown and frumpy is definitely not you, Lane."

I whipped around as if I'd been stung by a bee. He gave a dashing grin and disappeared down a hall.

Gobsmacked, I whispered to the space he left behind, "Tucker."

Chapter 32

Good heavens. Another nemesis.

Tucker had played on my emotions when I doubted myself the most, just as I learned that my parents had betrayed me, hiding the truth about their roles in the war all my life. Placing high value on my sense of judgment, then to be wrong about them, had taken a sad, heavy toll on me.

Despite Tucker's lies to get me to give him the information he craved, I had glimpsed more in his eyes than I suspected he even knew. In the end, he saw—and felt—the cruel side of his own mother, Daphne. We both almost perished, but he survived, then disappeared. He now painfully understood just how evil his mother's choices were.

And yet, here he was.

To trust or not to trust? *Pfft*. I absolutely did not trust him. But it was a strange comfort to see his familiar face. He was someone I knew from my life in New York, which was feeling like a different world. One from which I was horribly separated.

I stood, gazing out at the spectacular view as we passed over Cologne. The sun had set in gorgeous purples and amber, and now the heathery twilight rolled over the countryside before the black of night crept in. The Hohenzollern Bridge, with its tower gatehouses, spanned the gleaming Rhine, leading to the Cologne

Cathedral in all its ancient glory. I gave a contented sigh at the beauty as another passenger sidled up next to me.

"What a view," he murmured in awe. "Takes one's breath away, yes?"

"Indeed, it does," I said, turning to him. "Oh, I saw you bringing your German Shepherd on board," I said, then greeting him, telling him my name was Penny Adams—my assumed name, of course.

"I am Joseph Spah. Pleased to meet you. Yes, my Ulla is doing well down there in the hold, but I worry. I'm taking her to my family for a gift," he said with a heavy German accent. "She's been part of my act, but I'm taking her home now."

"Oh, that's lovely, Mr. Spah. What kind of act do you do?" I asked.

"Please, call me Joseph. I'm an acrobat and a comedian. Ulla was my assistant," he said, with a proud grin.

"Do you have more shows coming up in New York? I'd love to see one," I said, still working on my voice raising at the end of sentences, slower paced just like my steps. He and I exchanged more niceties, and I made a mental note to attend his show. I hoped to go visit Ulla in the hold at some point too.

On the lookout for the man that Churchill planted, I made a point to speak with as many passengers and crew members as possible. Knowing him, however, I wouldn't know who it was until he was needed. Maybe it was Mr. Spah. The manifest for this flight was only about half full. I was told there were 36 passengers and 61 officers and crew members.

"Mind if I take your photograph, ma'am?" said a man behind me. I greeted him and he said further, "I'm the airship photographer. Karl Clemens."

"Of course," I replied. He took a few photographs of me next to the windows and directed me to place my hands on the ledge and keep looking outward at the scenery.

"Do you fly on all the trips?" I asked.

"Most of them. It's a wonderful job. This ship is a delight," he said, bouncing happily on his toes.

"I've been doing some research on the ship because she is

truly spectacular. I have to say, the *Hindenburg* exceeds my expectations." Appealing to his national pride, I hoped he'd become helpful in getting to know the ship. "Do you think it would be possible to have a tour? Do you know whom I could ask?"

"Look no further, *fräulein*," he said, chest puffing in pride just as I wanted. "I'd be delighted. Let us wait until we fly over England. After that we will mostly be over the ocean the rest of the way, outside of seeing the southern tip of Greenland. I'd hate for you to miss any of the sights tonight. Even after the sun sets, the lights in the towns and cities are incredible. I believe the captain said we'd pass Beachy Head in south England late tonight, around two in the morning. So perhaps after we all get a little rest, we could meet in the morning tomorrow?"

I told him that sounded grand, and we'd have daylight to be able to see better anyway. I wasn't sure I'd be able to actually sleep with not only my duty to find and keep an eye on Daphne on my mind, but also the sheer thrill of being onboard this ship.

It was time for dinner, so Karl and I headed to the dining room. It was a small enough group that we could all eat together instead of in two seatings. I noticed Joseph Spah entering the dining room, too, with an air of trying too hard to be inconspicuous. I guessed that he might have made a surreptitious trip to visit his dog Ulla.

I was dying to see the inner workings of the ship. It was far bigger onboard than I expected. I'd only ever seen the *Hindenburg* as it floated over Manhattan. I couldn't imagine how vast the catwalks and infrastructure would look.

I motioned to Joseph to join Karl and me at our table, its white linen tablecloths contrasting nicely with the red upholstered dining chairs. Vases of fresh flowers adorned the tables with fine china and crystal that had been crafted especially for the *Hindenburg*. I introduced the men and took a look at the menu. The evening meal consisted of broth with baked dumplings, rack of veal, steamed chicory, spinach soufflé, carrots in butter, new potatoes, Charlotte pudding á la *Hindenburg*, and mocha.

Just as a steward came to pour us wine, the air in the jaunty dining room shifted. That scent that I knew so well of florals and a musky, sweet spice came to me. I had to make considerable efforts not to look in her direction and continue to talk in my slower drawl, shoulders curved meekly as if I hadn't noticed anything.

I sported my frumpy brown disguise. But Daphne? She was all out there, all Daphne. She swept in with the outrageous panache of Mae West. Wearing a cherry red gown worthy of Hollywood, her platinum hair gleaming, diamonds sparking in the light, Daphne made *an entrance*. But she also had the aura of a predator, highlighted by her blood-red lipstick and a hungry expression that was all teeth and want.

"Guten Abend, darlings!" she greeted, with the voracious, greedy expression of a wolf looking at a group of delectable little lambs. She set herself in her chair. With the flamboyant air of the best stage magician, she flicked out her napkin and set it upon her lap. "Well! I think it's safe to say we're all in for the ride of our lives, aren't we?"

No one answered, cowed by her masterful presence. She eyed a couple of the crew members and men at the table who were particularly fine specimens of the male persuasion. She swept her tongue across her front teeth, and said, "Bon appétit!"

Chapter 33

If I'd questioned the possibility of Daphne rubbing elbows with the Nazis before, I no longer did so. She was in deep with them. The crew treated her like a queen. Well-known, revered, and they seemed slightly unnerved to be in her presence. The other passengers didn't bother to hide their gawking to see if they recognized her from high society or perhaps Hollywood.

Tucker was nowhere to be seen. And I wasn't the only one not making eye contact with the sharklike diva. Joseph Spah turned decidedly white and briskly made comments on the dumplings being served and the wine, yet he was merely brusque, not nervous. Well, that made sense, he *was* a stage comedian familiar with working a crowd and the ability to hide behind a façade. But that was the problem: he *looked* like he was acting. What was he hiding concerning Daphne?

After the meal, most of us took in the sights from the great windows once again. Daphne made her way to the piano lounge, declaring all of her wishes loudly to the crew. It took great pains not to roll my eyes, but she'd surely recognize my kind of sass.

We were now flying over the Netherlands. The sun having gone down long ago, the Royal Palace of Amsterdam—once known as the eighth wonder of the world due to its mammoth proportions—shined like a beacon under the midnight blue sky and twinkling stars. It was a stunning view. I yearned to share it with Finn. There is something of wholeness that happens when you get to share an experience with someone dear to you, or when you introduce them to a place you love. But this thought brought home the feeling of being alone once again, on a dangerous mission. I wasn't cowed by Daphne, but I had this strange feeling that everything we were doing, we were doing for the last time. It was the same dark premonition that had triggered my panic when that bullet grazed Finn. I shook my head, willing the foreboding thoughts to clear, and focused on the beauty surrounding me.

The romance of this height that was aerial yet close enough to see the details of the cities and countryside, the peaceful yet swift trip across Europe and the ocean was a graceful dream that I'd never imagined possible. However, I wondered how long it would be before the *Hindenburg* and her sister airship the *Graf Zeppelin* were outdated. Pan American World Airways was already technically able to make the trans-Atlantic flight with their Clipper III, if only England would allow it on their end. They'd been waiting until their own flight program caught up to America, so it was just a matter of time. But if it became outdated because of desiring higher speeds and quicker service, what a shame it would be to lose this journey of beauty.

Just as I was fully enjoying the view, I spotted Joseph Spah slip out of the lounge, looking shifty and slightly proud of himself. He was surely going to check on Ulla again, which was certainly not allowed at this time of night.

So of course I followed him.

He clearly was an acrobat. Not that he did flips or anything, but the stealth and smooth way that he glided down the stairs to the B level was elegant and silent. He also had a way of blending in and looking like he was confidently not just allowed, but *supposed* to be entering the Crew Members Only area.

It reminded me of Aunt Evelyn and Mr. Kirkland's Three C's principle. Well, actually it was all New Yorkers' Three C's principle. Confidence, Confusion, then Compliance. Act confident and you can gain access almost anywhere. Someone challenges you? Act confused because *of course you're supposed to be here*, unless of course you're not. Then if all else fails, go with compliance. *Absolutely! My mistake, I don't know how that happened!*

So I followed suit. In fact, I got out my notebook and pen and pretended to be taking careful notes as if I was some kind of ship's compliance officer.

Past the crew member rooms, a walkway extended toward the rear of the ship. I held back at the corner and peeked around to see where Spah was going. He slipped through the door, closing it quietly behind him. About to follow, I abruptly stopped and held my breath. Daphne walked out of a crew room and went through the door after him.

Heart pounding, sweat pricking at my forehead, I couldn't risk going through the door. But it was a circular handle, so I thought I might be able to slowly twist it without someone seeing it move and if I opened it a crack, I might be able to hear something.

I counted to ten, eyeing the doors along the hallway and the staircase, making careful mental plans should I need to run. I gripped the handle and began to slowly twist, willing there not to be a loud *click* and making sure to keep my grip strong, not allowing an ounce of slippage. When the knob would go no further, I gently pushed, opening it a millimeter at a time. I bent forward to get my ear as close to the crack in the door as possible and waited.

Sweat trickled down the back of my shirt, making me shiver. I grasped the handle harder. At first all I heard was Spah talking to Ulla and Ulla's gentle yips and little puffs of air, clearly pleased to see him. Then I heard some crunches as he must have given her some treats.

Worried that my hand might begin to slip, as my palm was dampening, I tried not to flinch when I heard Daphne's clear voice ring down the pathway.

"Well, Joseph. Name your price."

He gasped. "*Fräulein*, I do not have a price. I have told you this."

"Oh Joseph. Have you not heard about me?" Dead silence. "You must realize I will not take no for an answer. This is my time.

I feel as if it's been ordained. So you *will* do as I ask. You know I can make it so that your family lives in comfort forever."

"No. I said no."

It took all I had not to gasp. Daphne didn't *do* "no." He would've been safer to string her along. He made a strangled sort of noise, and I knew her façade of humanity was slipping. I'd seen it before. Like a mask dropped and a glimpse of the monster was allowed to peek through.

Her voiced pitched lower, a prickly heat hit my chest as I felt the tone of her voice take on a slithering, menacing note. "You don't say no to me."

He made an audible *gulp*. Then Daphne's mask was tightly back in place once again, having achieved the reaction she desired, as evidenced by her words now in her normal voice. "Good boy."

Time for me to go.

I slowly, painfully closed the door and eased the knob back again. Then I ran up the stairs and to my room, slamming the door behind me, trying to shut out the monster I'd just seen.

Chapter 34

I stood back against the door, panting and slowing my breath one moment at a time. Anxiety and panic licked at my heels. Unlike any other mission or adventure, I felt the peril drain my usual reserves of moxie, like a vampire siphoning blood. I had to fight off the claustrophobia of being trapped in a flammable contraption, hunted by a lunatic killer, thousands of feet above the ocean, no backup.

I had to get my panic under control, so I counted things: the furniture, the berths upper and lower with a ladder attached, the pull-down miniature aluminum desk, the washstand with two handles hot and cold, closet, the foldable stool for the desk, the pull chain for service. Most of the rooms were in the interior, but this year they added nine rooms with windows. However, I wasn't so lucky as to have one of those. I slowed my breath further and focused on one thing at a time. I counted the holes on each side of the aluminum ladder. Seventeen on each side.

All right, all right. Enough. I splashed some water on my face and reapplied the peach lipstick that I hated. I took down my hair and revamped the boring hairdo. For one moment, I straightened my stature and placed both hands on my hips, shoulders back, chin up, defiantly choosing Lane. Not wimpy Penny Adams.

I didn't have anyone to talk to, so I quietly whispered to myself, working it out. "Okay, Daphne needs Joseph Spah to do something she either can't do herself or won't do. Let's see, he's German but lives in America. Does he have access to someone she doesn't? Someone on board? Or maybe he has something that she wants? Could she need Ulla for something? Security rarely looked at the dogs; it'd be an easy way to get something into the country. It would explain his reticence to allow whatever she was asking— he clearly adored the dog. Maybe he had an audience with someone important in the US or back in Germany. Maybe he was friends with Hitler or close to him somehow. She's been hobnobbing with the Nazis, but maybe she needs an in with Hitler himself."

The only thing to do was to keep an eye on her. A big yawn came over me, I realized I was exhausted. But I had a job to do, and I thought I'd go back down to the bar and have a nightcap. I wanted to at least see the last view of England before the long hours of black ahead of us until Greenland.

I assumed my demure Penny stature, reminded myself of her mannerisms and that I should not even have my favorite drinks at the bar, a martini with olives or an Old Fashioned.

Outside my room, I took a quick view of the lounge. There were still some stragglers, but the families had gone to bed. I walked down the set of stairs to B Deck and over to the bar adjacent to the smoking room.

Entering the smoking room through the vacuum-locked door, I saw that the father of a sweet family with three kids I'd noticed at dinner was just finishing a drink. They'd had an animated meal with the girl of fourteen or fifteen cheerily sharing her excitement, while the younger brothers talked about the trip and their plans in New York.

"I'll have a Sidecar, please."

The Sidecar was still a strong drink, but not as masculine or sophisticated as some I often order. So I thought Penny could get away with it and the bourbon, orange liquor, and lemon hit just right. The father I'd noted from earlier came toward the bar and ordered a scotch, neat. I gave an uptilt of my chin in greeting. He smiled in return and after he got his drink, aimed to sit back down at one of the groupings of chairs and tables.

"Mind if I join you?" I asked.

"But of course," he replied and held an arm out toward his table.

I greeted a few other people. This was certainly the most popular room on the ship. Here, troubles were set down, smoking enjoyment embraced, drinks made merry. None of us knew one another prior, but being a small group on an adventure together connected us. Two men sat talking intently, their backs to the rest of the room. The photographer I'd met, Karl Clemens, was at another table with Joseph Spah. Without Daphne in the room, Joseph looked at ease, shoulders relaxed. I couldn't blame him.

I sat with Mr. Hermann Doehner and he offered a cigarette. I paused for a moment, thinking of the massive hydrogen cells that kept us aloft.

"It is a fascinating gesture of faith, is it not?" asked Hermann, with a twinkle in his eye.

"Oh, it sure is," I said with a here-goes-nuthin' grin. I leaned into the light he offered and inhaled. Strangest cigarette of my life. The steward at the door caught my eye. He was responsible to guard each and every person who left the smoking room, making sure no one had any lit cigarettes or matches on their person.

Seeing my glance, Hermann said, "Most important man onboard, yes? Max Schulze."

I nodded with a chuckle. "I heard you and your family speaking Spanish at dinner, you have a bit of a German accent as well, and your English is wonderful. Where are you from?" I asked.

"Mexico originally. We moved to Germany after we married. Now we are headed to New York for business. This trip is the chance of a lifetime, so I brought the whole family. The boys are ecstatic. Could barely get them to go to bed. Walter and Werner are just eight- and ten-years-old, so everything is an adventure," he said.

"I can imagine! Your daughter is lovely. Is she having fun?" I asked.

"Ah yes. Irene. She is a little nervous, but she is enjoying herself. She and my wife were not as excited about the journey.

They prefer the ocean liners. But I think I might have them convinced that this is the way to go. Germany is exceptional at air travel. This is the height of innovation, and there is a big future for our airships."

As I sipped my drink, I noticed the beautiful panels all along the walls with paintings of air balloon travel through the years. The chairs were aluminum with leather cushioned seats and backs. The aluminum was for the light weight, but it also had the flair of modern design. It was an eclectic mix of comfort and sleek, futuristic lines.

A man at the table next to ours, who'd been in deep conversation, turned around to face us and said, "Well hello. It's Penny Adams, right?" He reached across to shake my hand with a cheeky grin and then introduced himself to Hermann. "Hello there. My name is Tucker. Tucker Henslowe."

Chapter 35

"Nice to see you again, Mr. Henslowe. So, what brings you on board this splendid airship?" I asked nonchalantly, trying to dim my usual "sparkle," as Miles had put it. But maybe I could have a little fun, knowing that Tucker knew who I was anyway.

"Are you still into gambling? Or was it surreal art? I can't quite remember. Did you finally get your Aryan certificate for it?" I was goading him to see what he'd do in front of Mr. Doehner. In 1933, the Nazis passed the Reich Chamber Culture Law that compelled artists to get an Aryan Certificate for their art, and if artists worked in Surrealism, Expressionism, Cubism, Dadaism— almost any *ism*—it was considered degenerate. Therefore, one would not receive a certificate and could no longer create art. The government believed that art they didn't approve of would taint and corrupt society, therefore it was not allowed. Not to mention, it put a target on your back.

Tucker's eyes went satisfyingly wide as he choked on a sip of his martini. I excelled at the well-place bombshell statements. Mr. Doehner's eyes squinted in disapproval of Tucker.

Tucker collected himself and pierced my eyes with a flash of humor. *Challenge accepted.*

"Oh, you must have me confused with someone else, Miss Adams. I just finished a business assignment in Berlin and am returning to the States. I am a representative for Ford Motor Company, and we have plants in Berlin and Cologne."

Then he cemented his acceptance of my challenge by turning to Mr. Doehner and began to converse in respectable German. Apparently, Mr. Doehner was pleased with whatever Tucker said, because he abruptly got up from the table and brought back three ice-cold glasses containing a dark brown liquor.

"A friend of mine, Curt Mast, just developed this a few years ago. It is sweet, herbaceous, and quite strong. It is called Jäger-meister. Prost, my new friends!"

We clinked our glasses amicably. Tucker had the gall to send me a wink. Despite not knowing if I was clinking glasses with an enemy or two, I felt a surprising release, having allowed myself to be more "me." At least for a few moments.

But I needed to stay hidden and bland to see if I could follow Daphne and prevent or ascertain whatever she was planning. The words *Hindenburg hit* haunted my thoughts and dreams. Who, why, and how? If she was taking someone out, it would be someone whose killing would prove she was important and useful to the power brokers, or it would be someone she wanted to usurp. And what on earth was Tucker doing here? Exactly?

The liquor was indeed sweet with tastes of licorice, clove and cinnamon, and stone fruits. A little went a long way, and I let the complex taste linger as I contemplated my next question.

"Mr. Doehner—"

"Please. Hermann."

"Hermann," I said with a soft smile meant to inspire confidences, secrets, information. He wasn't a man of arrogance, but Hermann did possess an attitude of a proud German; a look in his eye that said class mattered, as if it reflected true character. He most certainly had looked affronted with my suggestion that Tucker might not have followed the government protocol for obtaining an artist's license. So I decided to try to appeal to his masculine pride in business and connections. "It seems like there are several important businessmen onboard, such as yourself. I work for a firm in New York that is interested in making connec-tions with German businesses. Do you have any suggestions?"

Hermann eyed me carefully as did Tucker. "What type of business firm exactly, Miss Adams?" Ah. I'd gone down in estimation from Penny to Miss Adams.

I replied, "I'm afraid anonymity is of the essence, Mr. Doehner. However, I can say that it involves the public sector more than some know. Let's just say that not all parties in New York City were fans of the way the 1919 Treaty unfolded for Germany. And we are looking for new partners. Have you heard of Tammany Hall?" I asked, referencing the powerful political party that had a hold on all of New York until my boss took office as mayor right after Prohibition ended. He'd cleaned house of the dirty cops and lawyers, as well as the organized crime that had taken root in Tammany during Prohibition. One crime boss alone —Ciro Terranova—had made $34 million annually from the slot machines and pinball machines in the delis. Fiorello rounded them up and threw thousands of the machines onto a garbage barge. He even did a press release photograph with him on top of the mountain of confiscated goods, smashing them with his own sledgehammer. Fio loved a good photographic opportunity. I, of course, kept quiet about my allegiance to the mayor for the time being.

For just this type of situation, I took my pocketbook in hand and pulled out three long cigars. As hoped, Hermann's eyes grew round, and his lips twitched in anticipation.

"Cuban?" he asked.

"Is there any better? *Romeo y Julieta.*" Churchill had given me these, his favorites ever since his time in Havanna. I'd heard that he smoked a whopping eight to ten cigars per day. In his country house in Kent, he supposedly stocked between three and four *thousand.*

Another steward came and offered to cut the cigars for us. Hermann was fairly bouncing in his chair, newly energized to speak with me. Tucker took a moment to sniff the long cigar.

He purred, "Mmm, very nice L—. Miss Adams."

I bit back a smile at his misstep, as well as the look of sheer pleasure on his face.

"Do you need a moment alone, Tucker?" I said with a droll

tone, which earned a hard-won chuckle from Hermann. Okay. Things were warming up. I mentally rubbed my hands together, aiming to get some good information.

I thought I'd start with what mattered most to me. I gave an inner nod to Uncle Louie and took a thoughtful *puff puff* on the cigar, crossing my legs. "So, Hermann. What do you make of..." I lowered my voice and leaned a little more forward, inviting good gossip, "...*that woman.*"

I shot my eyes to Tucker, his eyes dilating, then we both intently gave Hermann our utter attention. Daphne had made a significant impression. There was no way a single soul onboard wouldn't know who I meant by *that woman*. In fact, I'd been hearing those two words used frequently since her first appearance.

Hermann leaned forward with a look of disapproval fighting with the fact that he was enticed by a delectable morsel of gossip. "Yes, who exactly is she? I've heard..." he began and paused leaning further in, Tucker and I following suit. "That she is a major investor in Eastman-Kodak. I hear she is an ambassador of sorts. But she's not the typical German professional, no?" he added quizzically.

No. No, she is not. There was not one "typical" bone in Daphne's body.

I glanced at Tucker to see what he was thinking. A look of dawning understanding ran across his features in an instant, then his usual nonchalance was quickly back in hand.

"Is she working with, or trying to work with anyone here onboard?" I asked.

"Not that I know of," replied Hermann.

Tucker asked, "Have either of you seen her being friendly with anyone in particular?"

I did not want to share my information about Spah. I could feel Tucker's eyes on me, ready to pounce on any piece of information or the slightest change in my demeanor. *Puff puff.* The cigar really came in handy to smoothly divert attention away from myself.

Hermann shook his head. "I've seen her with many people, as

if she's the hostess of this journey. Which, I have to admit, the crew is certainly acting as if she is," he said with a mix of disgust and admiration. "I heard her demanding in her sultry way a tour of the ship tomorrow. The crew seemed eager to oblige. Except that fellow Max who checks us at the door of the smoking room. He did not seem as pleased," he said with a nod behind us.

Just then, before we could dig further, the bartender made the announcement that we would be seeing the last view of the coast of England. It was two o'clock in the morning and those of us still awake did not want to miss out.

We collectively went to the windows. Though it was the black of night—darker than when we flew over Amsterdam and the English Channel with their sparkling urban lights—the village lights shone up at us. We hovered over them with the ease of Peter Pan in a whisper of wind.

The moment was full of the spice of Jägermeister and the earthy smokiness of the Cuban cigars as I stood admiring the last bits of countryside we'd see for a while, flanked by Hermann on one side and Tucker on the other. A man who'd been an almost-lover not to mention a villain, possibly reformed—time would tell. It was a strange moment I'd never forget. Eerie, dangerous, tantalizing to all the senses. It was the thrilling edge of adventure. The doldrums of working alone had vanished momentarily, and I was full of the energy of making a difference in the world.

Tucker's elbow touched mine. "You're smiling, Lane," he whispered. "Are you finally having fun, my dear?"

Then Hermann brought me back to reality and the essential nature of my mission. His tongue had considerably loosened from when we first began conversing. His shoulders were more relaxed than his usual state of military attention. He gazed east and I wondered if he was thinking of his homeland.

"I dreamt of this moment for so long. Flying over Europe, departing to the open sky and water between our two worlds. But I somehow feel a sense of loss or sadness. I miss my Germany. *Bah.* I am showing my age," he said with a self-deprecating shrug and a little chortle. "Forgive me."

"Nothing to forgive," said Tucker with a supportive pat upon Hermann's back.

I added, "This is the kind of adventure that makes the emotions run high. How could you not have deeper feelings about it all?"

Hermann smiled at me and nodded slowly. "True. True. Perhaps that is why I feel so contrary to *that woman*. She does not seem to have the same seriousness as I do. She is boisterous, but there is a more worrisome quality as well."

"You could say that again," muttered Tucker near my ear so that only I could hear.

"How do you mean, Hermann?" I asked.

"She was drinking the Jägermeister earlier in the evening. Without the reverence that it deserves, mind you. But there is also an intensity about her. She is after something, yes?"

Tucker and I both nodded, apprehension taking a more profound hold on me.

"I think that is why the Jägermeister in her hand triggered such a reaction from me," he said, warming to his subject, having come to a conclusion.

"Why is that?" I asked.

"Well, it is why the makers chose the green bottle. To signify its roots and what it symbolizes. Yes, yes. That is why she looked so driven. I am sure of it. It all makes sense."

"How so?" asked Tucker.

"Well. She is driven as if she is on the hunt. So it fits with that liquor."

I had a sinking feeling about this, as if a bad omen was about to be declared, and I wanted to block it so very badly. But as all omens were, it was unstoppable. I shot a look to Tucker to stop talking, one last effort to stall the omen from being said out loud. But he missed it.

"What does Jägermeister mean?" asked Tucker.

Hermann replied with great relish, "Master hunter."

Chapter 36

Having received Aunt Evelyn's messages, the usual participants gathered at her home to have—as she thoroughly enjoyed calling it—a council of war. That was, all but one important player.

Roarke missed Lane and their friendship over the past weeks she'd been gone. He hadn't realized how much he'd come to enjoy —and count on—their working relationship. The fellow-reporters in his world were pals to banter with, but at the core, they were competitors. Which didn't inspire deep friendship. If he were honest, Lane was his best friend. She really hadn't been gone all that long on this journey, but there was something about this trip that had him more worried than usual.

Maybe it was because she was on her own versus with the team of people who were gathering, and usually, they all worked together. Maybe it was because he wished he could've gone. Maybe it was because there was something just *off* about the mission. He couldn't put his finger on it yet, but he found himself anxiously processing the details of the mission and what happened in New York running up to Lane's departure. Frankly, he was glad Evelyn had called this meeting. Maybe he wasn't the only one feeling this way.

Kirkland welcomed them in, Morgan and Finn arriving at the same time.

"Hello, Mr. Kirkland. Hey, Ripley! How's the good boy?" he

said as he gave a back rub to the excited German Shepherd. All of Ripley's favorite people were arriving, and he was clearly in his glory. "Hey Morgan, Finn. How are ya?"

Finn was obviously on duty, not noticeable because of his attire, but because of his all-business stance. Not a smidgeon of a smile, his movements careful and quick, with the ease of a panther. Clearly distracted, he barely nodded at Roarke.

Morgan gave a quick glance toward Finn, then back to Roarke and raised an eyebrow. Roarke just raised his shoulders, saying without words *I have no idea what's going on with him.*

She greeted him, "Hello, Roarke. Great to see you."

"Come on, come on, let's go back to the kitchen," said Mr. Kirkland gruffly. "I made us all pork chops for dinner. Think better on a full stomach."

Evelyn was seated on a couch just off the kitchen, sipping a glass of wine with Fiorello seated next to her. Their voices were low as they leaned toward one another in deliberation.

"Come in, everyone," Evelyn declared, standing to attend to the drinks. "I took the liberty of getting some wine prepped for everyone. I dare say we are all in need of a little?"

Ah, Roarke thought to himself. *I guess we are all feeling a bit nervous about the situation.*

After Evelyn poured a glass of red wine for everyone, they got down to business. They looked to her for direction, even Fio. He was certainly the leader of the city, but in their own little group of sleuths, spies, cops, reporters, and misfits of all kinds, Evelyn was the clear director.

She looked at the group carefully, took one more sip of her wine, and set her glass down firmly. "So. Given the uncertainty written upon your faces, I feel confident that none of us are feeling too…*eh*…confident with our inability to help or to even know how Lane's assignment is going."

Finn ran a hand through his dark hair, leaving it rumpled in a way that he never usually allowed. "Yes. Definitely yes," he declared openly. "I wish one of us could have gone with her."

"She's completely up to the task, Finn," said Evelyn with a certain edge to her voice.

"Oh, I know that," he said frankly. "More so than any of us, with her ability to think on the fly with everything regarding Daphne, and changing tactics when necessary. But being suspended in the air like that with Daphne on board... Not to mention, alone."

With a grin, Morgan added, "You know? That's very observant. I couldn't figure out why I've been more concerned than usual, and yes, I know it's because it's incredibly dangerous, but for heaven's sake, Lane's whole life has been dangerous lately. Nothing new there. But I think you hit the bull's eye. I've been worried about her being alone."

Finn nodded and both Evelyn and Kirkland smiled with the golden look of pleased parents.

Evelyn sat forward and said, "You know, I hadn't thought about it with this trip on the *Hindenburg*, and I regret that I didn't. But I've noticed that Lane has a great dislike of anything that has a hint of being trapped."

"I haven't ever seen her claustrophobic," said Roarke, thinking through their capers.

"No, not that exactly," said Evelyn, thoughtfully. "Although she might be if she was in an enclosed space for too long. I mean in ways that limit her options or obstacles that would hinder her control."

"I see what you mean," said Morgan. "She once told me that a drug like opium was something she would never try, not even laudanum to help with sleep. She hated the idea of not being in control."

"Exactly. So it's dawning on me that I wish we'd given her more counsel on that aspect of her mission."

Roarke said, "Because she's flying around in a flammable ship, surrounded by at least one enemy, and perhaps a disguise that hems her in, so to speak."

Finn rubbed his forehead, as if staving off a rising headache.

Fio barked out a little too loudly, but in a way that everyone had grown to expect, "We need action. We need to focus on what we can do to help her. I'd like to go over everything leading up to the *Hindenburg* mission. I want to be sure we understand every detail and see if we can think of anything we missed. I can get a radiogram to the *Hindenburg*. So we can help strategize with Lane on board, or at the least tell her that we are able to help somewhat. It might allay some of the anxiety we're all feeling as well as send her our support."

"Excellent idea, Fiorello!" exclaimed Evelyn.

While Kirkland put the dinner on hold, they began to outline the details of the crime that was a set up to frame Uncle Louie, to Daphne being behind it vying for a big power grab, to overhearing the threats of the *Hindenburg* hit around town.

"One thing that keeps bothering me," said Finn. "Why the *Hindenburg*? Exactly? It has to have a point. Otherwise, why would you take a gamble of assassinating someone on board when you can just as easily take them out before they board? Or after they debark?"

"Well, Daphne does like the show," said Morgan.

"The show?" asked Kirkland.

Finn and Roarke both nodded. Finn said, "Just think about our last escapade at the Majestic Theater after the *Voodoo Macbeth* production. She wants power, she'll do whatever it takes to get it, but above all else, she loves spectacle."

"I'll never forget walking up to her office in the lunatic asylum. Jesus, Mary, and Joseph," said Roarke, rubbing his temple. "Who thinks of that? She knew it not only was a perfect hidden gem, but it was also entirely creepy. And she relished that aspect. I remember watching her face when Lane and I interviewed her. The story was that we were interviewing her for a magazine, a kind of They Should Have Been Discovered article. Daphne had hoped to be a Hollywood star at one point."

"Until she realized power and murder were more her strong suit," murmured Morgan sarcastically.

"Bah!" laughed Kirkland gruffly.

Roarke continued, "The interview went fine, predictable for a while. And then Lane said something innocuous, but whether it was her tone or that Daphne finally realized exactly who Lane was, she got this...*look*. It felt like she was metamorphosizing into something else. Something inhuman. I swear to God, the room dropped in temperature." They stilled with his words, all of them feeling that moment with him as he recalled the details.

"Her face changed, like her mask had slipped. It was suddenly asymmetrical and no longer beautiful but disturbing. Daphne loved the effect it had on us. Lane had become almost paralyzed, like stone. Daphne licked her lips at Lane's revulsion. Then she started laughing."

"Dear God," said Kirkland, repulsed.

"She hates Lane, I mean really hates her," said Roarke.

"I don't know about that…" said Finn reflectively.

Everyone's attention snapped to him in disbelief.

"You see," he continued. "I think it started that way, but there's something in her that respects Lane. And since Daphne loves spectacle, I think she likes Lane's style. Think about it. Who else has given her the kind of adventure and panache with the hunt that we've given her these last months? Especially Lane."

"You're right," said Morgan. "It's a game to her. And people who enjoy the game don't want easy, boring wins."

"Maybe we can work with that," said Finn. "I've heard back from Miles, and they've instructed Lane to be as bland and unassuming as she can be, to blend in. Her disguise is everything that Lane is not, I hear."

Mr. Kirkland made rude noise. "She's going to hate that!" he exclaimed with a laugh.

Roarke chimed in, "I give Lane… Let's see…" He theatrically checked his watch and said, "About twenty-four hours before she ditches that idea and comes up with some sort of wild plan."

"Why are you smirking, Evelyn?" asked Finn.

"Well, I think you're right. I popped into her room when she was packing her smaller bag for the *Hindenburg*. You all know she'd no doubt bring a set of trousers."

"Just in case!" said Roark and Morgan in unison, mimicking Lane.

Evelyn laughed. "Exactly. And also…a new dark purple, velvet dress trimmed with silver studs and crystal beads."

"A cocktail dress?" asked Kirkland.

Finn smiled, shaking his head. "If Miles made her matronly or boring or fuddy duddy, she's not going to be happy at all. And I guarantee that dress will be worn. For certain."

Evelyn said, "So let's get back to the *Hindenburg*."

Finn said, "Well, it's definitely got spectacle and power. But the Nazi question should also be at the center. It's one of their biggest propaganda tools, not to mention their pride and joy. It's the largest aircraft ever made."

Kirkland added, "I agree. Daphne is not beneath working with the Nazis. She'd work with anyone who could offer her more power."

Morgan was taking it all in, then her head popped up like she'd gotten an idea. "We need to find out who Daphne's been working with here in New York. Who are the groups ready to side with her, to have her lead them? Because framing Louie was a serious power move."

"But she already had that kind of power, didn't she? She only had to take control of a couple more gangs," said Roarke.

"Well, Roarke," said Evelyn. "Women can't just take the power, we have to do double that to prove we not only can take it, but that we deserve it and can keep it. Daphne *needs* spectacle. It's about fear tactics, showing her lack of concern that she'd be challenged, displaying her power."

"Okay," said Finn. "So let's find out more on who she's been colluding with and what's the word on the street. Fio, can you get a manifest for this *Hindenburg* trip?"

"Sure. I'll get on it," said Fio.

"Great," said Finn. "The rest of us, let's see what else we can find out. Fio, I'll get a radiogram to Lane. I know what to say. Let's remind her she's not alone. Then we need to be ready to stake out Lakehurst, New Jersey when the *Hindenburg* lands. The hit could happen after they disembark. It's possible the whole journey was just about information that leads up to a hit. Either way, we need to be there to help. I just... I still don't have a good feeling about this."

Roarke agreed. On one hand, he felt relieved that the group had all gotten together and they had a plan to help. But on the other, the questions they raised were valid. There was a lot at play, and the power brokers were serious, deadly people. All of the plans of the council of war, the radiograms, and stake outs felt flimsy and insubstantial here on the ground. Lane was a thousand feet in the sky, locked in with a madwoman who'd repeatedly tried to kill her. So yes, *the other hand* was simply lousy. Finn was right. Roarke didn't have a good feeling about this either.

Chapter 37

Jägermeister. Master hunter. *Good grief.* On that happy note, I decided to turn in for the night.

I thanked Hermann and Tucker for the conversation and headed toward the stairs to A Deck and my room. But before I took the first step up, I spotted Joseph Spah slip through the same doorway that he'd used earlier toward the cage where Ulla was kept. Without Daphne around, I decided to follow him again.

He walked through the hallway with the crew's quarters and went straight back without hesitation. I quietly followed him, and he quickly stopped, unlocked the crate and eased Ulla out. She immediately spotted me.

I was delighted.

"Ulla, how are you, girl?" I asked quietly, crouching down to beckon to her. She clearly knew I was a dog lover and most likely smelled the bits of chicken that I'd saved in a napkin in my pocketbook for her.

At first, Joseph looked stricken but quickly realized I was a fan of Ulla's with a snack to boot, so he relaxed. He allowed Ulla to come over, and after my offering of chicken, she let me quietly give her pats and rub her big ears—just the way Ripley liked.

"Oh, you're beautiful, aren't you?" I cooed.

"Dog lover?" Joseph asked with the gentle look shared by all dog lovers who adored their companions.

"Absolutely," I replied, keeping my voice down. I'd rather not be found in the hold, wanting to continue my anonymity. "We actually have a German Shepherd at home. A little bigger than Ulla, but similar markings. Such an incredible breed."

"She's not too happy being here on this ride. At least it's a gentle journey and much faster than the ocean liners. I try to take her for walks and bring her treats as much as possible. The crew isn't too pleased."

We exchanged a few more quiet pleasantries, and I said good-night to them both. I walked along the hall but just as I was nearing the end of the pathway toward the public stairs, a crew member's door popped open, and I ducked into a closet.

In an instant, shivers ran up my spine, as I heard Daphne's voice ring down the hall. Then a warm hand came around my mouth and a voice breathed into my ear, "Don't scream."

I was a mere second away from screaming, biting his hand and kicking back into his knees, when my brain realized it was Tucker. He abruptly let go of me in the *don't shoot* manner one did when a gun was pointed at them and urgently whispered in a hiss, "Please." He remained close, he didn't have a choice since we were wedged into the tiny broom closet together.

I had a lot of questions. But most of all, I wanted to hear what Daphne was up to, and I sure didn't want her attention on me. I sharply nodded to acquiesce.

Her voice carried to us despite her quiet tones, just as a whiff of her perfume arrived. I breathed it in, using it to bolster my confidence. "You know I have the connections at Kodak, Spah. This timing will be perfect. I need you to do as you're told," she purred. "You'll receive what was promised. With your dog, you have the perfect excuse to be down here. I won't ask nicely again."

Ulla growled.

"*Shhhh*, it's okay Ulla, it's okay," he said, trying to calm the shepherd who did not appreciate Daphne.

"Keep her quiet, Spah. Or I will," said Daphne. Then her shoes began to click on the floor, coming closer.

Neither of us breathed. Once again, grateful I didn't wear perfume as Penny Adams, I stood perfectly still, willing my heart not to beat too loudly. Tucker's hand briefly pressed against my wrist in a *hold steady* gesture. She went by, not pausing for an instant, and the soft snicks of the stairway door opening and closing came to us before we allowed a breath.

I wanted to get out of there, but I waited a few extra moments. Tucker's hand inched down my wrist toward my fingertips. I placed my hand on the doorknob.

I opened it gently but before I could bolt, Tucker said just barely above a whisper, "Lane. Please be careful. I know Daphne had a man on board the *Normandie* who was trying—at best—to see what you and Louie were up to, at worst, finish you both off."

"So it was her man after all," I whispered. "Louie's men were drugged the last night of our trip and we saw a man listening in to our conversation. Yeah. I'll be careful."

"But what are you doing—" I cut off my question. Because I knew I wouldn't get a truthful answer anyway. "Never mind. You be careful too."

I quickly went out the door and had to try to stay calm to keep from all-out running to my room. When I got there, I locked myself in and stood breathing hard from the nerves, hands on my hips.

I whispered to the room, "So, Daphne is definitely working with Kodak and needs Spah to do her dirty work of some kind. And what the hell is Tucker doing?"

I paced back and forth with my hands locked behind me in thought, turning about every three strides. Tucker could be watching out for Daphne as her security, or he could be tracking her movements just like I was. Or he was doing his own dirty work and making sure she didn't mess it up. What if he was the one behind the *Hindenburg* hit?

Chapter 38

The next morning, I woke rather late, given my usual routine of waking around six, but I had been up until after three o'clock in the morning. I suspected most of us traveling would keep strange hours, leaning more toward the nocturnal side.

I dressed in my next dowdy outfit, looking in the mirror in disgust. This one was a dull brownish-peach color, my most hated of all colors. It sapped the pink tones from my skin and made me pasty, not to mention grouchy. I put the dagger in my purse, choosing not to wear it to make sure that I completed the boring image of Penny.

I said to the mirror, "All for the cause. You're still Lane or Scarlett underneath the drabness." I shook my shoulders lower, dipped my head, and let myself slouch. *Blech.*

I went up to breakfast in the dining room. We were allowed an extended time, most of us entering into the room slowly with fatigue pulling at our heels. The families had already eaten if the tables being cleared of extra crumbs and dirty dishes were any indication. I spotted Mrs. Doehner and decided to make her acquaintance.

"Hello, I believe I met your husband last night, and I've been admiring your lovely family, Mrs. Doehner," I said.

She greeted me kindly and offered me a seat at her table. "Are you sure?" I asked. "I don't want to disturb what looks like a very peaceful moment to yourself," I said with an understanding smile.

"Not at all, Miss Adams. Please, sit. It will give me an excuse to stay a bit longer and enjoy a cup of coffee with you as you have your breakfast. My daughter Irene has the boys in hand while my husband is still asleep, and I get a bit of time to myself."

I chuckled. "Yes, the smoking room was full of people who stayed up late, wishing to get the last glimpse of England before the long ocean voyage today."

We would go over the southern tip of Greenland later that day, and then it was all dark water until we hovered over North America. The sun was shining, the sky was cerulean, and the Atlantic was vast. I always marveled at the deep royal blue waters tipped in white froth here and there. Seeing it above sea level was magnificent. The curvature of the earth was noticeable as we floated above, gently pushed along in the wind currents. It was utterly different than traveling on the water, calm and weightless. Swift but not careening over the earth as I did on the Pan Am flight between Detroit and New York. There was something other-worldly about this sort of travel, conjuring the nostalgia of fairy tales and Jules Verne adventures.

We chitchatted as I ate my breakfast, and she enjoyed another cup of coffee. The boys and Irene were in the reading room. "So Mr. Doehner said you prefer the ocean liners. Are you enjoying the flight anyway?"

"Oh, yes. It's quite lovely. But it's a little unnerving as well. This height, the extra care you must take for smoking and what-not… We'd actually thought about leaving Germany earlier in the winter, then returning by way of the *Hindenburg*. It would have been better for some of our family plans, but the return flight of this route was booked completely. So we decided to rearrange accordingly."

A man I had yet to meet approached our table and in a British accent asked, "I'm sorry to interrupt, Penny Adams?"

"Yes," I said, immediately intrigued that he was one of very few British people onboard. Perhaps he was Churchill's man?

"I was just sending a radiogram when this came in. Since I was coming to the dining room and thought I had seen you here as I finished my breakfast, I offered to bring it to you. Good day."

"Thank you," I replied, as he quickly turned away.

I asked Mrs. Doehner, "Have you met him before?"

"Ah…yes, we met him briefly in the writing room. I think he's an agent with a shipping firm, I believe William H. Müller & Company, he said. I only remember because he and Mr. Doehner carried on and on about shipping statistics for so long." She rolled her eyes and grinned.

I smiled as I opened the radiogram. "That's odd," I murmured.

"What's odd, dear?" she asked, leaning forward.

"Oh…" I had to make sure I stayed in character. "It's from my boss, nothing important. But it's not what I expected." It was a short message from Fio's office. It didn't give any directive other than to keep an eye on the very person who delivered me the message, George Grant. Was he of interest because he is in fact Churchill's man? Or was it his industry connections that perhaps made him a possible target for Daphne?

Just then, the ship's photographer, Karl, came to the table. After introductions, he said, "Would you care to take that tour now, Miss Adams? I have secured permission from the captain."

"Absolutely! I'd be delighted," I replied.

Mrs. Doehner and I said our goodbyes, and Karl led the way down to B Deck where we'd begin. In silence, he went down the long hallway past the galley and the crew's quarters, past Ulla who sat quietly watching us, to the door at the end. He opened it, then with a proud smile and a wide gesture of welcome, said, "Here we are. The underbelly of the beautiful beast."

I walked in, then let him lead the way. A narrow catwalk extended toward the rear of the ship. The immense proportions of the largest air ship ever built was difficult to put into words that properly described the awesome qualities. I'd been to the top of the Empire State Building, down into the depths of the subways in New York City, I'd walked across the Brooklyn Bridge. Hell, I'd dangled off the edge of the Queensboro Bridge, leaping to the catwalk on one of its massive pillars. None of that prepared me for this.

The inside of the ship was not filled with the hydrogen cells, but they were far above us. The ribs of the ship spanned away from us in a cylindrical arc to the top. I could not stress enough the narrowness of the catwalk. I was not afraid of heights, but this was unreal. The aluminum rails on either side seemed like mere twigs. I carefully followed Karl's lead as he rattled off interesting facts about the materials used, how helium would've been better —not flammable—but too expensive, the oil tanks on either side, the special cotton fabric sprayed silver and red in places to reflect the sun's heat, the special flame-resistant qualities, etc.

He stopped and waved with a flourish to another insubstantial railing. I peeked over the edge, and there was a flimsy ladder leading to the control gondola where the captain piloted the ship. *Good God.*

Thankful once again for my low heels, I followed him closely as we crept down the ladder into a small room with a 360-degree view of the world. *Breathtaking* didn't do it justice.

Captain Pruss was the commander for this flight, but several other captains were onboard as observers or additional crewmen, and he introduced us to two of them, Captains Sammt and Lehmann. Captain Pruss was proud of his craft, and I was in awe of the simplicity of the machinery, yet the careful planning it took to maneuver the airship. He explained the dials and the wheel that turned the rudders. We were at times at 1,000 feet, others 10,000. Most of the time around 6,000.

"We strategically plan where the gentlest, yet swiftest winds prevail. And of course, we can take liberties with what views we prefer," he said, puffing out his chest and smiling as he surveyed his kingdom.

"I especially loved the view of the route you took over Amsterdam," I said. "What a gorgeous night."

He nodded, receiving his praise like an emperor.

"We will be going over Greenland today. The winds once we approach North America might prove a bit difficult to make our original 7 a.m. landing. So I believe as of right now, we will go over Newfoundland tomorrow early morning, then make our way south to New York and New Jersey. The good thing about going over Newfoundland in the daylight is that we shall see the brilliant icebergs in full display. It is exquisite."

After that, we went to the Radio Room, and I sent a radiogram to Finn. I wanted to get across a message, but of course I couldn't be sure who would see it, so I had to be careful.

The Radio Operator, Willy Speck, was on duty and happily took my message.

HELLO ALL! I AM ON COURSE AND WILL SEE YOU TOMORROW. HAVING FUN MAKING FRIENDS. SAW TWO OLD ONES. THINK ABOUT MY QUESTION FINN. LOVE FOREVER, PENNY

I had to sign it Penny, of course, and sent it not to City Hall or police headquarters, but a local TransUnion near Aunt Evelyn. I hoped "on course" would let them know I got Fio's message and would be working with that, and the "two old" friends meant Daphne and Tucker. I tried to play it off as a bit ditsier than Penny or I usually carried ourselves, but I figured it would seem less suspicious if I acted like an excitable female with the crew. It was disgusting.

After that, we headed back along the catwalk. I looked up, having gotten my nerves and footing under more control than when we first began.

"Is that another catwalk up there?" I asked, pointing far above us.

"Yes, that is for the crew to check on the hydrogen cells and perform our regulations. You can see there are a few different ladders to access those upper catwalks."

I did indeed see all those insubstantial ladders. Everything had to be weight conscious in an airship. The narrow ladders were but wispy stems, holding up a behemoth. Karl and I grew quiet again, just as we'd been at the beginning of his tour. It was a lot to take in.

As we strolled along, I ruminated on the exciting and almost mystical aspect to this fairy tale trip in the clouds. It should have been the adventure of a lifetime. But the mission I was carrying out was the most dangerous of my career.

An uneasy truth coiled within me, akin to the foreboding notion that struck me last night while drinking Jägermeister— spicy and sweet, yet bearing a name that inspired great hunts and death: there was always a dark side to fairy tales.

Chapter 39

Lunch was another divine affair: turtle soup, veal cutlet English style with spring vegetables, followed by ice cream and mocha. I sat with a new group of people, a variety of ages and backgrounds. We all chatted about our day; I told them about sending the radiogram, and one of the men said he got to go out onto one of the engine gondolas. He tried to look nonchalant, but he paled as he described stepping outside of the main hull of the ship onto a narrow bridge to the little gondola.

We spent a wonderful hour in our group. But as we finished, an unwelcome presence made itself known, her scent of flowers and sweet musk preceding her.

"Oh dear," I murmured, the eyes of the guests shifting toward me and my unusual comment.

But then they all turned to where I'd been looking and their faces exhibited the same feeling, complete with sighs of long-suffering. Clearly having been in *that woman's* presence at some point earlier, they'd come to similar conclusions. If they only knew.

Daphne swept in, wearing a pale blue, diaphanous gown—more suitable for the El Morocco in Manhattan and a night on the town. She was nothing if not too big for any room she entered. She sucked the air out and made everything feel too close, too unnatural, too tight. This was predictable, however. What she did next was not.

"Lane Sanders, how divine to have you on this most majestic of voyages."

Dammit.

"Oh, don't look so sullen, it ages you," she said, regally pointing to a steward to pull out a chair for her next to the British gentleman, George Grant. Well, now I was mad.

She whispered something flirty or suggestive to George, his face turning red with pleasure. Then she leaned into the small table separating us and laced her fingers, placing her chin atop them. "I see you're shocked. But please, give me a little credit. Just as you know me so well, I know you just as well, my dear. Even without your usual perfume and clothing...*choices.*" She said *choices* with the derision this awful color I was wearing deserved. Couldn't fault her there.

I decided to go for a clear strike. With a fatigued and bored kind of voice, I asked, "What are you doing here, Daphne?"

"Am I not making this exciting enough for you?" she replied, the spark in her eyes clearly up for the challenge. "I truly thought having Tucker here would make this *exceptionally* interesting for you."

That got me. I felt myself blanch, my heart pounding. She knew I'd be here and that Tucker's presence would make me more vulnerable?

"I mean, it'd be better if your lover—that divine policeman of yours—could have been here instead. He's always been a distraction for you, but I figured Tucker might lend himself to your baser instincts. You do have a base side, Lane. Even if you won't admit it to your goody-goody self."

She was landing blow after blow to my ego, my scruples, and the man I loved. I had to work hard not to remain paralyzed with my jaw on the floor.

But before I could utter one rebuttal, she took more shots. "Well, now I'm disappointed. Are you going to just sit there gaping? Really, I thought you were made of stiffer stuff. Perhaps your brain was more addled than I anticipated with the demise of your parents all those years ago."

The table made a collective gasp at her cruel words. But that blow exposed that she wasn't as in control as she thought; she was trying too hard to throw me off course. Which meant that I was on track, and she was not happy about it. I took a deep breath, willing myself to give the satisfied smirk of a cat, a nonchalant predator with a mouse in sight.

"Oh Daphne, how I love to see you lose your cool," I purred, as I set my elbow upon the table. Then I whispered, mimicking her tone, "After all these years."

One time, when I first met her in her "office" in a lunatic asylum, she'd let her mask of controlled beauty and power slip. Just a tiny, grotesque bit. And I got a glimpse of the deranged monster beneath. The monster she'd cultivated over the years that caused me to truly wonder if she controlled her madness or if it controlled her.

Well. If I'd seen her mask slip that first time, this was something else entirely. In an instant, the mask got a full-fledged crack down the middle.

Her left eye twitched and the side of her mouth pulled downward almost as if she had a palsy. The asymmetry of her expression made everything feel off kilter, like a train about to derail. Of the many times she'd chased me, stalked me, teased me with her power, chided me, angrily yelled, leered at me right before her effort to kill me was thwarted…this moment was by far the most terrifying. The entire room felt it, even if they couldn't see it. Like a shift in the air the moment before a lightning strike, or when a car accident was just about to happen.

But then, she masterfully pulled it together again. Nice and tight. She licked her lips.

"Ooh, Lane. You should be more careful," she said slowly, taking lipstick from her reticule and applying a fresh coat of blood red.

Cutting her short, the steward abruptly called to the room that Greenland was now visible, and in the excitement, most people quickly got up from the lunch tables and raced to the windows. In the rush, Daphne stood and swirled out the door in a flurry of icy blue puffs.

Chapter 40

Despite the incredible view of Greenland—a once-in-a-lifetime event—I couldn't get those moments with Daphne out of my mind. She'd won that match in our game of chess, that was for sure. She hadn't been fooled by my disguise, whether through her own knowing or someone had told her. Tucker? Another spy of some sort? And she'd used Tucker to get to me, whether he knew about it remained to be seen.

She was unpredictable, even for me, someone who knew her quite well. However, I'd noticed two important points that I could hopefully use against her.

One, her madness was having a greater effect on her than I'd seen in the recent past. She was losing control. I wondered if she felt it nipping at her heels. She was getting desperate; I'd been consistently thwarting her since I was ten years old. Even the setup against Louie didn't work. Her options to take hold of power were running out.

And two, I got a glimpse of something that made my blood run cold. As she rushed from the room all ruffles and anger, the slit of her dress up one thigh revealed a flash of black metal. Not only something capable of taking a life, but just about the scariest damn thing one could see onboard an airship. A pistol in Daphne's hand was never a good thing, but here? It could take all our lives in a flash.

"*Fräulein?* This just came for you," said a steward, holding out a thick, expensive folder with the crest of the *Hindenburg* on top.

"Thank you," I said distractedly as I opened it. It was a radiogram from Finn, this time.

WE ARE WORKING HERE CAREFULLY WATCHING THE SKIES. FOLLOWING LEADS. I LOVED YOUR QUESTION. YOU KNOW MY ANSWER. LASTLY, NEVER FORGET WHO YOU ARE. WEAR THE DRESS.

A laugh released within me at his last words. I wondered how he figured out I had packed the new dress. Aunt Evelyn, to be sure. That meant they'd had at least one council of war, which made me feel immediately more at peace. I might be alone up in the sky, but I was never truly alone with that crew of family and friends.

Back in my room, after reflecting on the luncheon and Finn's telegram, I felt like a new person. I knew a disguise was necessary at the beginning, but to choose one so contrary to who I was at my core felt claustrophobic and hindered my ability to think clearly. I realized I had been yearning to be set free from the boring façade I'd been carrying around. And now that Daphne was no longer fooled, or perhaps never had been, I could be myself.

First, I decided to take a break by enjoying a small nap. Second, a plan had been forming at the back of my mind ever since I heard those most-loved strains of jazz music when I boarded. It brought back thoughts of Josephine and her sense of drama, adventure, and justice. And of Winston's confession that they chose me for this job because I was well-suited to outsmart Daphne.

I jotted a few ideas in my notebook, then took a chance and wrote two messages on *Hindenburg* notecards. Before I got ready for the evening, I left my room and headed to the smoking lounge in search of the smoking-room guard, Max. I spoke a few soft words in his ear and palmed him a large tip. I quickly proceeded to the doorways he directed me toward and slipped the notes beneath each one, ready to bring this game of chess to fruition later that night.

I freshened up in the bathroom and the surprisingly spacious showers. I wanted to wash off the leftover Penny Adams feeling and begin anew. I applied some fresh eyeliner, mascara, and dark red lipstick. I gave myself a better, more modern look with curls and a few suggestive finger curls near my temples. Then the dress. And I absolutely wore the dagger.

This evening I would also be keeping an eye on that George Grant. Anyone in power would be a successful hit for Daphne, especially with the panache of an attack disembarking from the *Hindenburg*. He was in shipping, and that was one of the largest global industries. With war possibly on the horizon, it would become even more important to the world economy.

It was almost time for dinner, but the first step in my plan required a visit to someone.

I went quickly toward the hallway that held Ulla and made sure to bring the snack I'd been keeping for her, some cheese leftover from lunch. Before I got there, I met the recipient of the first note I'd slipped under the door.

"Mr. Spah. Thank you for meeting me. I brought a treat for Ulla, is that all right?" I inquired. His facial features had been edged with suspicious sharp lines, but at the mention of Ulla's treat, they softened.

"She does love cheese. Thank you," he said with a little bow.

After a few moments of fawning over Ulla, and Mr. Spah trotting her up and down the hallway quickly and lightly so as not to attract attention, I eased into the purpose of my requested meeting.

"So have you been acquainted with Daphne Franco for long, Mr. Spah?" Usually when I brought up Daphne, the response was either immediate fear or disgust. His face exhibited both.

With a shake of his head, he replied, "*Nein*. Not long. A fellow entertainer introduced us at my last show. I thought she was an admirer of my work. I do not understand her request, but I do not like it."

"What did she request?"

Suddenly aware that the fear outweighed his disgust, Mr. Spah shut his mouth tight with a snap. He uttered a string of German that I couldn't understand, but the hand he held up in the universal sign of *stop and desist* was clear.

I looked around, remembering that Daphne had been in one of the crew's rooms that lined the hallway the last time I'd been down here. So I leaned in and whispered quickly, "Did she want you to get her close to someone in the States? Or on the ship?"

He shook his head violently and made loud conversation about Ulla as if I'd asked a question about her. "Yes, a thorough-bred German Shepherd. Famous in my act. We've had many, many hours of training together." Then he whispered closely, "She said she wants to hire me for my skills as an entertainer." Loudly again, "So now that she's had a little refreshment, I am now heading to dinner. Wonderful to share a love of dogs. *Auf Wiedersehen.*"

"I'm heading to dinner as well. Thank you so much for letting me see Ulla. What a wonderful friend she is."

He stopped mid-stride, turned to me, and said sincerely, "Yes. She truly is." He cleared his throat and led the way to the upper deck for dinner. Spah's mannerisms were always slightly suspicious with the feel of over-acting. Though his dislike of Daphne was certainly genuine, I wondered if he was telling the truth about her hiring him. Or maybe she was putting him on entirely to draw closer to him. Spah was pretty famous, and just like George was a possible target because of the power within the shipping industry, a celebrity murder might make an even bigger newsworthy event. An international celebrity, to boot.

The passengers were so few in number onboard that all the faces were now familiar, and I'd generally conversed with most of them. However, only as Penny Adams. We arrived fashionably late, as I'd hoped, and as I swept into the dining room, I ordered a martini with extra olives from the nearest steward. If Daphne had made a big entrance earlier with her swirling light blue skirts, I arrived with my own brand of spectacle and panache, feeling more alive than I had in a while.

Martini in hand, wearing a vibrant purple velvet cocktail dress that clung to all the right places and sparkled with crystal gems like little stars. I, too, was well-versed in making an entrance.

Churchill said to outwit, to not play by the rules. Josephine said not to wait for change, but to make change happen. This was my game now.

The recipient of my second note—Tucker—had been fore-warned of my entrance and my new plans. Eyes popping with my transformation, Tucker had to hide a laugh of genuine pleasure behind his fist as his eyes shifted between me and Daphne.

I had the room's attention, especially that of my gawking nemesis in a glittering black cocktail dress of her own. Oh my, did it feel good to make a move that shocked her.

I gave a big smile that was more wolf than mirth and said, "Ladies and gentlemen, let the games begin."

Chapter 41

Well, now I needed to weave a good story, didn't I? I had to figure out an entertaining way to explain why I was suddenly going by a different name and how I could be myself now. I chose a casual route and just went with the confidence of a New Yorker. That until I knew the passengers a bit better, as the mayor of New York's aide, I needed to be a bit cautious since he often has adversarial difficulties. Which was a vast understatement. Regardless, it opened up a whole new line of conversation with people. Not to mention, Daphne had made quite a few people nervous with her domineering presence and since she was obviously shocked and silenced by my entrance, it brought a lot of cheer to those same people.

Including Mr. Spah. He looked happier than I'd seen him this entire journey. This was going to be our final night onboard. Delayed by winds, we were to land at around seven in the morning in Lakehurst, New Jersey, so I would need to make these final hours count.

Mr. Spah and I joined a table that held a few people I had yet to talk with at length, in an effort to make sure I hadn't missed anyone of interest. There was one person who wasn't coming out of their room; I'd heard they weren't feeling well. Churchill's "man" was still a mystery, but I really didn't think I'd know that person until they wanted to be known. It could be anyone, even the most unassuming crew member or passenger.

I looked over at the Doehner family, eating together happily. It would be hard to be a spy within a family unit, but then again, I'd seen stranger things. I had a feeling I would be up most of the night once again.

The dinner of queen soup, flatfish cooked with salt potatoes and hollandaise sauce, loin cut a la Baltimore with fresh peas, and lemon souffle…was delightful and passed with no exciting interlude. However, gauging by both Daphne's and Tucker's glances throughout the meal—one full of mischief and one full of malice—I was in for a treat after dinner.

So after the dessert had been served and coffee enjoyed rather quickly, we were practically vibrating with readiness for the next round of games. The families headed to bed and the adults who'd been keeping track of Daphne and me all followed along downstairs to the smoking room.

Just as I'd hoped—courtesy of an exorbitant tip to Max—a phonograph was playing some jazz. Surprisingly, "Love and Kisses" by Ella Fitzgerald was on, taking my mind right back to New York City. I'd seen Ella perform at The Savoy, and though this particular recording got just a mediocre response, she was something special. Her voice had this warm, rich tone that stilled a room and wrapped us all up in her arms. Anyone who heard her live knew she'd go places.

Around the room, patrons were sitting at a variety of tables with after-dinner drinks in hand. The board was set and ready for play. Daphne and I sat across the room from each other, talking with our own groups. Tucker, as a kind of referee perhaps, sat at the table between us with Mr. Spah. I wondered if this seating was of Daphne's choosing, still unsure of Tucker's loyalty. He didn't seem to be at odds with Daphne, I'd even caught them whispering to each other during meals or at the windows enjoying the view. Once, he'd seen me watching them and quickly turned away, stepping slightly further from his mother. He was a consummate actor. Whatever his motive, he'd proven to be a dangerous adversary no matter how charming. Just like his mother.

Mr. Doehner was serving more Jägermeister at his table. I sat with Karl and a couple whom he seemed to be friends with. I met with them, and we all chitchatted, but the way one did before a movie began.

A song by Benny Goodman came on, and I eyed the man working the phonograph, then gave him an appreciative nod. In this room full of smoke, the scents of expensive alcohol and perfume wafting about, satisfied patrons full of an excellent meal and heady with adventure, there was a space of camaraderie with no swastikas, no religion or politics. Many times, I had found these in-between places of being not here or there fully, places where new friendships were fleeting and possibly never found again, fostered a feeling of an alternate universe. This thought was infinitely enhanced by the DaVinci-like contraption we inhabited these couple days, floating beneath the stars and over the vast ocean.

I considered Daphne; I had a long history with her. It was novel and strange to sit across from her in a civil environment. She was a study in contrasts. Each flick of her hair, every sip of her champagne, every word she spoke was considered and well-crafted to gain the response she desired.

And yet, I realized I had unsettled her more than I expected. With each gesture under immense control, there was a counter movement that was not. A shifty, restless eye toward me. A nervous tap of her foot. One extra blink with her left eye, like a wink except directed at no one. *Oh, to be ahead of her for once*, it was sublime. Churchill was right, there was no playing nice with Daphne.

But I still had no idea who her target was. Daphne desired control over all else. The money was important of course, but it was mostly about being at the top. Being God over the kings and pawns of men. Making the world around her curve and bend to her desire. That was why she killed my parents: they got in her way. Everyone on board was relatively wealthy, so they could be the target. But of all the businessmen I'd spoken with, George Grant was the most powerful and Spah was the most well-known.

I'd have to stay near her and use my wits to try to get her to crack. That was what I did best.

A couple got up and began to dance near the phonograph in the corner. The next tune picked up in pace with a sultry energy that brought the already alive place humming. Another couple joined the first on the floor, dancing with a magnetic tension, then another made their way to the middle. The jazz song was almost a tango, pulling at us to partner and to devour its notes. Daphne rose from her seat to head toward the bar to get a drink.

I needed to make a move. *What would Josephine do?*

Chapter 42

I sashayed to her side in an instant. I took Daphne's right hand in my left, the other on her waist and swept her toward the center the of the room, joining the dance. I had to give her credit, she didn't hesitate or balk at this sudden turn of events.

I had never been this close to the overpowering floral and musk scent of my nightmares. Oh, this woman had a range of conniving efforts that affected me over the years, but now I was leading the dance. "Hello, Daphne."

"Hello, Lane. Nice dress."

I swung her toward the phonograph, her feet matching mine step for step. "Thank you. Much preferred over the brown one I'd been sporting, yes?"

"Most definitely."

"Come here often?" I asked, trying to crack the beautiful mask that was inches from my face. Because she was indeed beautiful. Dangerous, mad, unpredictable. But beautiful.

One side of her mouth pulled into a smile as she replied, "What are you up to, Lane?"

"That didn't sound like a question."

"No, with you it's more of a typical greeting," she said.

"Fair point."

"I suppose you're about to warn me not to try any nefarious schemes."

"Should I?" I asked. "What would those be exactly? Who is in your sights, Daphne?"

She gave me careful consideration, her mask of lucidity not flinching or dropping. I marveled at being this close. If Finn could see this, he'd about have a heart attack. He once witnessed me dancing with Uncle Louie, but this would be an all-new high. Or low, whichever the case may be.

"You know, this isn't my first time on a floating airship of sorts."

"Oh, really?" I said, conversationally.

"Yes. My grandfather once took me up in an air balloon, much smaller of course. Just as gentle. It's quite amazing how soft the flight is, isn't it? Not jarring like trains or automobiles. But as we floated toward our little town, I was so excited that the towns-people would get to see us. And most of them did. It was quite a sight to see.

"But what always shocked me, Lane, were the people who didn't take notice. There was the farmer who'd been plowing behind a horse. A woman racing to the town's general store, looking fiercely at the list in her hand. We were that close, I could see the piece of paper. The only ones who spotted us easily and unequivocally were the children. The adults were much too busy to see something so original and unexpected."

Stunned with her openness, I forgot the game for a moment and asked, "Is that the inspiration for your...*creative* ideas? Your original and unexpected style?"

She gave a soft laugh. "Yes. I didn't want to fade away in the midst of ordinary life."

I felt that sentiment deeply. But then her eyes went dark, and she added, "And it gave me power. I realized if I could see what others couldn't, I could *take* what others had. In a way they couldn't see coming. It is often right in front of their eyes. And I could do the unthinkable, because no one thought I could. Or would."

We made a couple of turns, the swirls of smoke wafting with our revolutions. Tucker's eyes never leaving us.

She carried on, "We women are given very few choices.

Having to deal with the power of men over us, even the most measly and weak men are still men. They've always just taken what they want from us. I wanted a turn."

"So, what exactly do you want to take with Mr. Spah's help?" That brought her up short. The light and easy, almost fun rapport that we'd never enjoyed ceased suddenly. Her face drained of color, the moment brought to a head. Her eyes darted to a man in the corner I hadn't seen before, and it occurred to me he was the one person unaccounted for as yet. He was the picture of Aryan perfection with blond hair, blue eyes; I supposed he was German. The more intriguing thing was why was she looking to him? Approval? Fear? Plain and simple awareness? Or was *he* the man who Churchill said he'd have onboard, and she knew this?

I swung her back toward the bar area, checking on Tucker as we turned. He was in discussion with his table mates but was clearly keeping an eye on us. Most of the room was.

"I do not have any plans for Mr. Spah, Lane. What makes you think I do?"

"I saw you two in the hold where he keeps his dog."

She swallowed and leveled her eyes at me with a tinge more respect. "Ah. I had gone for a walk and noticed his lovely shepherd. Nothing more. What could I possibly have need for in a comedian?"

"Working on being more likeable?" I parried.

She sneered delicately, but slight amusement flickered at the side of her mouth. "Lane, darling. *You* most certainly do not require comedic lessons. It's a shame we've been adversaries. We could do wonders together, you know."

Another turn toward Tucker and the phonograph.

"Oh, you know we'd never play well together, Daphne."

"But this dance is much more my style than yours," she said.

The tempo slightly picked up pace, swinging deeper into its groove and its own desires like tangos did. I pulled her tighter to me. We were almost the same height, both with crimson lips, swirling skirts, our hair opposite counterpoints of light and dark.

"Why? Are you uncomfortable with it?" I asked in a low tone with an edge of challenge.

Another turn, the bass thumping, the saxophone and trumpet charging the song with electricity. The blond man's seat in the corner was suddenly empty. I looked at Tucker, his eyes on the door where the man must have just exited. Daphne's face looked more natural again, less stricken and pale. Desire and intrigue written on her features.

I'd feared Daphne for most of my life. I hated her for the evil she'd done and—as hate often did—it turned to ravenous fear. I'd become exhausted with it. Fed up. So there was something exhilarating about what I was doing. In facing the monster, in doing the unexpected in a brash, emotional, mad way… I faced the monster head-on—and found it wanting. By taking it in my arms and drawing it close, I discovered I had an anger that had been simmering just beneath the surface for years. It was licking its chops to be let out. I could. I truly could let it out.

But instead, I'd use it.

"I thought you'd be more predictably couth, Lane. This is a rather unladylike surprise."

"Well, you should know by now when it comes to you… I'm no lady."

I dipped her, then set her back upright. I came up close to her, close enough to kiss her and whispered, "I'm watching you, Daphne."

Chapter 43

Gathered around Evelyn's room off the back of the house once again, Morgan gazed outside at her favorite chandelier strung beneath the maple tree in the back yard. This one had more color than most chandeliers. It was diminutive, yet more radiant than the others. It spoke to her with its luminous glow and the sparks it threw all around, adding spots of color everywhere as it danced in the breeze.

All day she had scoured the streets, meeting with her informants, the invisible street urchins that made up her own little army. A lot had changed in the past year. Lane and Evelyn, Roarke and Finn. She'd never trusted older people before, none had been trustworthy, plain and simple. She learned that one had to be discerning and not to blanket an entire group of people from the bad experiences of a few. Or even many. People could still surprise her.

And then there was Dead Shot Mary who surprised her more than anyone. One of the city's first women detectives who sported a matronly guise that was truly invincible against the pickpocket gangs. She was a crack shot—infuriating the more insecure men on the force for besting their abilities—and she was on track for making over a thousand arrests before her eventual retirement. She'd taken Morgan under her wing, and Morgan never felt so powerful.

But looking around at the concerned faces surrounding her at this moment, the feeling fled like a mouse before a hound. It was Lane's presence that had created this group and bound them together in hard work for the city, pushing boundaries of the unexpected, and her own special brand of levity. Lane brought color and unity to this incongruous crew.

Evelyn called them to order, Fiorello would be joining them shortly.

"All right, everyone. What have we found?" asked Evelyn. Evelyn must have been truly feeling apprehensive because she hadn't even offered the group her usual *medicinal* drinks before their chat.

Morgan shared a quick nod with Roarke that said *okay then, let's get down to business.*

Everyone was ready to share important details, but Roarke spoke up first. "I checked with my informants and there is definitely movement in the gangs. They've been told—I'm assuming by Daphne's people—that in the week ahead there will be a display of sorts that will prove she should not be challenged in any way to lead her own organization, but that she's also the best to lead the currently headless gang of Uncle Louie as well as any other groups who'd like to join."

Morgan nodded and added, "That's what I've heard too. Even the ones who didn't have much interest in her before, now do. Hey, we're New Yorkers. We all like our wisecracks and a good show." She shrugged and pulled her lips into a moue of agreement. "It's what we do. We can't help it." Kirkland and Finn both laughed. Everyone knew this was an accurate statement.

Kirkland decided to share his hand next. "I talked with a few of my old cronies, you know, see what they're hearing, and it's much of the same. But they have ties in Europe, and what's interesting is the European gangs are all ears too. So I think we're on the right track. Daphne isn't just going for a power move; it's The Power Move to unify a larger underground network of criminals than we've seen before. Both in Europe and here."

Finn added, "And with Hitler aiming for another war it seems, that could play nicely into their hands."

Kirkland said, "Well it certainly did in the Great War. Anything that brings chaos and distraction to law and order, makes a great playground for the criminal element."

Just then, a commotion at the front door erupted with a loud bang and bellowing that echoed through the house.

"Ah. Fio's here," said Evelyn with a dry tone. "I'll pour the wine."

Morgan smiled in relief; Evelyn hadn't been very talkative, and having forgotten to pour the wine or offer drinks ahead of time, Morgan worried about her, concerned that something even more dire was at hand. To have her go through her normal motions brought an ounce of reassurance. The way Roarke and Finn took their wine with grateful smiles as they tried to read Evelyn, she was sure they felt it too.

After Ripley's barking calmed down, the storm that was the mayor burst into the room.

"Great! I'm glad we've begun. You all know Mrs. Eunice Carter, prosecutor extraordinaire. Oh, I am ready for that wine, Evelyn. Thank you," said Fiorello with a heartfelt sigh of pleasure as he took his first large gulp.

Morgan, Kirkland, Finn, and Roarke all stood to shake hands with Eunice, the men out of good manners, Morgan out of adoration. She swallowed the girlish hero-worship that wanted to come rushing out of her mouth.

She couldn't stem it entirely and gushed, "Mrs. Carter. It's an honor. I've been reading about your work, and I am… I really admire all you've done."

Eunice smiled and thanked her with genuine interest. After Morgan sat back down, Roarke turned to her and said so only she could hear, "Do you want me to get her autograph for you, Morgan?"

"Shut up, Roarke," said Morgan quietly in a playful tone.

Finn brought Fio and Eunice up to speed and Eunice said, "That all makes sense on my end. I think we should put some extra hands around at the landing, Mr. LaGuardia."

"Here it's just Fio or Fiorello, Eunice. And yes, I agree. I'll get on it," said Fio.

"I also think we need to consider unexpected possibilities," said Eunice. "Surprises. From what I can gather from your prior cases, this Daphne Franco is only predictable in her unpredictability. She's artful, conniving, and psychologically unstable. I believe this could be her last hurrah and when it comes down to it, that is always the most dangerous position. A friend of mine in the jazz world told me his son—a music aficionado—said that the key to jazz is that it's not about the notes you play, it's the notes you don't play. There's something about this that just isn't adding up, and we need to look at the notes Daphne isn't playing if we want to outsmart her."

The group sat in silent agreement, nodding and contemplating. Kirkland was still watching Evelyn, as was Morgan. She seemed like a shadow of her usual self. Distracted and a bit flustered.

"Aunt Evelyn," said Morgan. "Are you feeling all right? You look a little pale."

Evelyn took a deep breath and came to a decision. "Thank you, Morgan. I do feel a little off. Not ill, but Kirkland, dear, do you remember the day that Archduke Ferdinand was assassinated and it launched the war? We were together that day."

He sat up on the edge of his seat. "I do, Evelyn. I do."

"I know it sounds odd, but I knew in my soul that the assassination was setting off a legion of harm and destruction. I felt off that entire day and even cried that night. I never cry about politics! But I knew deep down that it was going to unleash something terrible. Since our last council of war, I've had the same feeling. I know you've all made fun of my friend in England who often gets premonitions and bad omens, but I can't shake this. I think it's serious and I am very, very worried."

Eunice spoke up again and added, "Oh Fio, I have the manifest for you. Maybe there's something here. I didn't recognize any major names. A few businessmen, an actor, the usual. But maybe you can see something I can't."

She handed the few pages of the manifest to Fio, and as he turned to the second page, he raised his eyes at the group with a stricken look on his face.

Finn snatched the papers out of his hands before Fiorello could gather himself.

"Dear God," uttered Finn, his face blanching just as much as Fio's as they shared a knowing look.

"What? Who?" exclaimed Aunt Evelyn. "Spit it out for God's sake!"

"Tucker's on board," said Finn in hushed tones. "Daphne's son. That's what Lane meant in her radiogram by seeing two old friends. They're both on the *Hindenburg*. Last time she saw him, Tucker almost killed her."

Chapter 44

After our dance, Daphne glided away to her stateroom. Or so she said. I too left the smoking room and went to the lounge windows on A Deck. In the small hours between late night and early morning, we were just coming to the coast of Newfoundland. The sky began to barely lighten as my eyes searched for any lights of small towns. One of the crew members said we were between 600 and 1000 feet above the ocean. The waters had been stormy, but we were calmly above it for the journey.

Just then, I spotted a field of white blotches beneath us in the graying dawn, outlined by the black water.

"Icebergs!" exclaimed an excited passenger beside me.

I wasn't as enthusiastic. Even from the air, icebergs read as portents of danger to me. The idea that the largest and most dangerous aspects were beneath the surface of the icy waters. The Titanic certainly had been taken down by one, though it was hubris that steered it toward its fate, in declaring that even God himself couldn't sink it.

A shiver went through me, and I decided I needed a couple hours of rest. We had faced head winds getting to Newfoundland and expected more that would slow our progress to Lakehurst. We were supposed to be landing in a few hours, but it was looking like we might be six to twelve hours late, depending on the winds once we were over land. Most of the airship passengers were exhausted from the excitement, and being that we'd have a long day ahead, many were heading to their staterooms.

With a yawn, I turned away from the window and ordered a hot tea. Something warm sounded comforting, then I'd go relax in my room. Just as the server was bringing me a tray with the tea service, Mr. Spah rounded the corner, and the server ran right into him.

His instincts took over as he twirled under the tray at the right moment, catching it—and the elbow of the server—to keep everything upright. It was such a suave show of stylish grace, those of us in the lounge all spontaneously applauded.

Grinning at the server, Mr. Spah winked, and they both took a bow. They filed over to my table, and Mr. Spah poured, then handed me a steaming cup. "Sugar?" he asked.

"Two, please, and milk."

"Ah. You've been in England a while, yes?" he said, a charming sparkle in his eye.

"Well, I was raised by people who preferred the English tea service. So indeed, yes."

"I'd stay but I need to head to bed. Lovely running into you." He nodded a farewell as he turned on his heel.

I finished my cup quickly and yawned again. The stress and the excitement had gotten to me, the exhaustion starting to really hit. I left and just as I turned the corner to the hallway, I almost ran into the light blond German who'd been watching Daphne and me from the corner of the smoking room.

"Excuse me," I said. I hadn't heard footsteps or any conversation, so he must have been just standing there. "Are you waiting for someone?" I asked.

He gave me a considered look, his eyes then shifted toward the end of the hallway but no one was there. "*Nein.* I was waiting for a colleague, but perhaps I will look for him in the lounge."

The man abruptly left, pushing past me, clearly not wanting any further questions.

I paused for a moment, and then, not too far away, I heard what I thought might be his voice, joined by someone else speaking in urgent whispers. I edged toward the end of the hall, hoping I could safely eavesdrop from around the corner. I gently walked on the toes of my high heels.

Daphne hissed, "I told you, Schäfer, I am friends with the Reich."

"Yes, as you have said. Repeatedly. However, after our rejection of your proposition, we felt it quite necessary to keep our eye on you. Especially on our most-honored airship."

Rejection? Well, well, well. Daphne was too much even for the Nazis.

After a disappointed click of his tongue, he asked, "And as for that other concern onboard—"

She quickly interrupted him. "I have it under control. You can count on me."

"Fine. We shall see. For now, we have a few extra hours before anything can be attended to because of the delay in our landing. You are certain we don't need to worry about any other problems? I haven't been fond of your garish displays, Fräulein."

"It's been taken care of," she said in clipped tones.

"Very good."

Two sets of footsteps faded away from me.

I ran to my room and shut myself in, heart pounding. I paced back and forth, trying to think. Trying to make sense of everything I knew and had heard. Daphne's hit reminded me of the assassination of Archduke Franz Ferdinand that sparked the Great War. Who was that important or that connected that it would stoke the flames of greater power for her?

Another yawn came over me. Well, I could get a couple hours of rest if Daphne could; I was more fatigued than I expected. I changed into my most athletic attire, feeling like I wanted to be as prepared as possible. Just like my cocktail dress, I always brought one pair of trousers just in case. I brushed my teeth, ran a brush through my hair and laid down on my bed to rest my eyes.

Before I let myself fully embrace a good sleep, I ran through the moments with Daphne like scenes from a movie. I tried to look at them with a different perspective, hunting for any new notion or idea about what it meant and who was the target. Another possibility occurred to me. Could the Nazi who was disappointed with Daphne be her target? Schäfer wasn't just a Nazi, he sounded like he was with Hitler's SS, or even the intelligence arm, the SD. She was definitely unnerved by him, the way she always darted her eyes in his direction and seemed twitchy when he was in the room. She was playing nice and submissive, which had to have been very hard for her. If she killed someone in Hitler's service, she certainly would prove that she was powerful and gutsy. It would probably be a death-wish, but gutsy nonetheless.

I felt I was on to something, but my speculations didn't last long, my eyes burned with fatigue and mental stress. I sighed and turned over onto my side, arm under the plush pillow. Comfortable and warm, I gave in to sleep.

⊏⊐

I AWOKE WITH A GREAT GASP. I sat up in bed, sweat breaking out on my brow. The sky was lighter than I expected—I'd slept longer than a couple hours.

Anxiety and dread sat heavy on my chest. Groggy from deep sleep, I couldn't think straight. I sat up and slid to the edge of the bed. I usually woke up with a lot of energy, but my eyes felt heavy, and I longed to lay back down. I shook my head, trying to clear my thoughts.

Subconsciously, something had jogged a memory or an idea because I woke up frightened, pulse racing despite feeling so exhausted. Maybe I was coming down with something. I stretched my neck then washed my face and brushed my hair. I forced myself to run through the last hours of the prior night. Dancing with Daphne. The cup of tea and the comedian's perfect trick with the tea tray.

The perfect trick. I grabbed my watch from the nightstand. Holy hell it was almost three in the afternoon! I stood, heart racing. Mr. Spah put something in my tea. Beyond a doubt, that was it. Mr. Spah. Daphne. The blond SS agent I ran into. *Shit, shit, shit.*

Another moment of that night was toying with my brain,

trying to get noticed. I was close to understanding something. Something important.

"Okay, okay," I said out loud as I paced, then went to the sink to brush my teeth and splash cold water on my face, trying to get my brain working and fully awake. I finished and put on my shoes. "What do I remember?" The whole conversation I overheard with Schäfer was crystal clear, but there was something else teasing at my thoughts. Something I missed.

I paced and tried to get the moments of last night to fit together. I'd been dancing with Daphne. We'd been playing a game of words. What had she said when she waxed philosophical about that balloon ride with her grandfather? Looking at those people who couldn't take their eyes off the ordinary, the everyday mundane things of life. She'd said, "I realized if I could see what others couldn't, I could *take* what others had. In a way they couldn't see coming. It is often right in front of their eyes. And I could do the unthinkable."

She could do the unthinkable.

Chapter 45

I raced out of my room, darting down the hall to find Tucker. I didn't know if he was really on my side, but the idea that just dawned on me was something he couldn't be in on. Not because of any altruism on his part, either. I ran to the lounge and the dining room—nothing. I flew down the steps to the smoking room and skittered to a stop.

"Thank God," I said, making Tucker and the two men who were with him grin cheekily, as if I was thanking God for their presence. "Funny," I replied drolly. "Tucker, we have to talk."

Finally reading the desperate look on my face, he stood and quickly took my elbow, ushering me out of the room. Outside the door, he looked around and bent close. In a low voice, he said, "What's going on? Are you all right?"

"Someone drugged my tea last night. It was Joseph Spah."

He felt my forehead for fever and said, "I was wondering why I hadn't seen you all day. But a couple people said they saw you at lunch. Wait. That was Spah who said that. *Shit.*"

I nodded. "Yeah, that's what I said too. I didn't think he was working with Daphne—I thought he might be the target—but it looks like he is. And I overheard Daphne talking with that blond Nazi. His name is Schäfer and he's got to be SS. It sounded like Daphne proposed something to Hitler and they turned her down.

Once they found out she was going to be on the *Hindenburg*, he was sent to keep an eye on her."

Tucker crossed his arms and tapped his chin. "Daphne would've loved the kind of power that goes with working hand in hand with Hitler. And she would not take the rejection well, to put it mildly. Maybe she proposed working together along with Kodak. I'd heard that she was in league with that company, too, for some reason. That's why I brought it up when you challenged me to a lovely game of wits with Mr. Doehner."

Kodak? Why the photography company?

"But why drug you?" he asked, his eyes snapping to mine. "Are you sure you're all right? Any heart palpitations, migraine, anything more serious? Was…was it just a sleeping medication or…"

My stomach dropped. I whispered weakly, "I hadn't thought of that."

Daphne had whispered, "It's been taken care of," when Schäfer asked about the other potential problem onboard. And he said he hadn't liked her garish displays. He certainly didn't look pleased when she and I had our dance. Maybe he felt I was too much of a provocateur for her; and she knew I would only be a nuisance to her plans. *I was the potential problem.*

My knees buckled with the weight of realizing I could've been killed, and he quickly put an arm around my waist. "Whoa, Lane. It's okay, you're okay. They wouldn't want to make a scene like that; a death onboard would cause a commotion, and I guarantee they don't want that."

I appreciated a more analytical approach to my horror. "Thanks. Yeah, I'll be fine. I just… I hate the thought that someone gave me something to tamper with my mind." I despised being out of control. I hated, *hated* being trapped, and being drugged was just like that. But worse. Nothing scared me more, it was a kind of smothering claustrophobia with me.

"I can't stand the thought of being out of control. But that's not all," I said.

"There's more?" he groaned.

"When I was dancing with Daphne, we were playing chess with our words. This whole thing is a game, Tucker."

"Oh, I know."

I took a moment to gather my wits about Tucker. I had a feeling that by the end of the trip, all our secrets would be out in the open. One way or another. I would be a fool to completely trust him, but this whole conversation made me think he wasn't working with Daphne. But I had trusted him before. The most cunning monsters are charming and polite. I'd thought he was my friend several months ago right up until he held me at gunpoint. I'd be stupid to assume these fun little conversations were purely innocent.

What was he after? And why would she want him on board if he wasn't working with her? Then again, she did say she liked the idea of having him around if I might show up. For diversion and distraction. With her, the more chaos, the better. I couldn't trust him, but I could at least trust him with this information. I had one more piece of the puzzle that scared me more than anything.

"Daphne told me a story about how she realized if she could see what others couldn't, she could *take* what others had. In a way they couldn't see coming. She said, and I quote, 'I could do the unthinkable.'"

"But what does that mean?" he asked.

I didn't know why Tucker was here and I knew he could be a threat, but our situation was getting more desperate by the minute, I could feel it nipping at my heels. "I'm onboard the *Hindenburg* because there was a threat of a hit happening."

"I'm aware." *Interesting.*

"Well, listen. We know Daphne loves a show. She loves spectacle."

"Right."

"You know that we've been thwarting her moves the past year, and she's getting desperate to prove herself. She needs something big to prove that she should not only be leading her gang, but Uncle Louie's, and possibly even gangs in Europe."

"Right again."

"I came here to try to stop her because I thought she was

going to take out someone big, someone important. Spah's a renowned celebrity, so he could be the target, but it looks like he's with her. There's the shipping magnate, George Grant, and he's got the power and wealth behind that industry, so he, too, would be a good target. Then, there's Schäfer. It would be the power move of all power moves to take out an SS agent on their own *Hindenburg*."

"I can agree with that, Lane. But what aren't you saying?"

Was I really thinking this? Could she really do this?

"Okay, let me think, let me think. I'm still a little cobwebby from the drugs. So maybe a hit was her first plan and any one of those men would fit the bill." I ticked off my fingers as I said, "But now, one: she's a woman scorned by the Nazis. Two: she needs to prove she's a power player. And three: she loves a big spectacle…"

He pulled his head back with a look of dawning revelation, his face draining of color.

"Tucker. When she said, 'I can do the unthinkable,' she meant a hit isn't happening on the *Hindenburg*. It *is* the *Hindenburg*."

"Dear God," he whispered.

"Where is she now?" I urgently asked Tucker.

Before he could reply, a crewmen announced, "Ladies and gentlemen, we are now approaching New York City."

Chapter 46

We ran to the dining room, where many people had already been at the windows enjoying the scenery of the east coast. But New York City was coming up, and this was something everyone had to see. We found a space at the windows.

"There's *The House That Ruth Built*," I whispered, half-happy to see my city, half-terrified to be drawing near. "Yankee Stadium."

A woman next to me asked, "Ruth?"

"Babe Ruth," I said. "The Bambino."

We were floating over the Bronx, the spire of the Empire State Building in the distance. Tucker and I shared a look of dread. This was my city. This was my home. Our history, our story, my job, my family, everyone I loved.

"We have to stop her," I said to Tucker.

He clenched his jaw and nodded. "Come on. Let's check the lower level."

We went back down—and nothing. She wasn't anywhere in sight in the regular rooms for the passengers to congregate.

"She could be in her stateroom, I suppose," he said weakly.

I shook my head. "Let's check the radio room and the control car."

We went down the long hallway along the tour route. We passed Ulla and came to the door that led to the catwalk. I opened the door and Tucker gasped.

"Haven't been out here yet?" I asked.

"I have. I just don't like it," he said.

I looked far above me at the hydrogen cells, the upper catwalk parallel to the track we walked. God, it was massive.

We carefully made our way across the narrow passageway to the radio room. I opened the door and stepped into the small space. The radioman was busy working the radio and twisting several other dials, a set of headphones on his head. He held up one finger while he jotted down a note then looked up cheerfully.

"Would you like to send another radiogram?" asked the eager Willy Speck, radio operator.

I looked at Tucker and then turned back to Mr. Speck and said, "Yes, thank you."

I thought for a minute about what to write. I wanted to send a warning of some kind, but I also didn't want to throw oil on the fire, making things worse. When I was ready, I wrote out the messages and the corresponding destinations.

Tucker and I watched as Speck sent them. When he was done, he made notes in the record book, and we stepped back out. Closing the door behind me, I took a deep breath, willing that the words I had just sent wouldn't be the last I'd send to City Hall— and to Finn.

Chapter 47

Tucker was with Lane. *Jesus, Mary, and Joseph*, thought Finn as he made his way to City Hall to meet with Fiorello.

He'd almost lost Lane to him, both her love and her life, at one point. What sent dread snaking down his body was not jealousy that Lane could be persuaded toward Tucker, but that Tucker was so goddamn dangerous. Finn wanted to believe that Tucker reached a point where he would no longer harm Lane and realized just how evil his own mother was, how she'd raised him with manipulation and depravity. But it was like Russian roulette. If you miscalculated with him, it could mean your life.

The cherry blossoms were in bloom in New York, surrounding the Georgian building that housed the mayor's offices. The blush blossoms and the bright greenery of early spring were usually on full display. But on this dreary afternoon, despite the light pink petals, the air was thick with oncoming rain and a heaviness in the air. It was humid with threatening storms drumming up in the distance, and the dark clouds looked more like late fall, invoking a desire to hunker down in front of a fireplace with a hot chocolate.

It was these split and opposing feelings that pulled at Finn like a sore tooth. Things that should feel one way but felt another. The look that should speak of lightness and springtime newness, spoke of the dying autumn. It was off, it wasn't right.

He went through the large doors of City Hall, nodding to the security team, and ran up the stairs flanking the entrance hall. Every time he did this, he recalled his first glimpses of Lane and all the tantalizing emotions of those early days. He had a desperate urge to be across the intimate table at Da Nico's in Little Italy. With the three-piece band that occasionally played after dinner service and the patrons having pushed the tables to the edges, everyone danced with abandon to the sultry music and candlelight. *God*, he missed her.

The large room full of the secretaries and aides and messengers was a buzz of activity like any other afternoon. It felt odd without Valerie, but Finn's eyes landed on the light blonde curls of Roxy almost immediately. She'd been on the lookout and ran over to greet him.

"Hey there, Finn. You okay? You look a little uneasy," she said, with her own worry pulling her brow into a furrowed crunch.

"Hi, Roxy. Yeah well, I can tell you feel it too. I'm anxious about this mess with Daphne," he said. "I don't like it. Lane can handle it, but there's something not right, and I'm worried we aren't seeing the whole picture. I keep asking why the *Hindenburg*? Wouldn't it be easier to nab someone as they're getting on or off or anywhere else besides a floating airship?"

"I agree," said Roxy. "If there's motive, there's motive regardless of the venue. So you pick the best, the most strategic place. What makes the *Hindenburg* strategic?"

That feeling of dread suddenly tripled as a thought hit Finn. But before he could voice it, Fiorello came bursting out of his office.

"Finn! Glad you're here. We just received a telegram from Lane onboard…uh…you know where." His arms flapped with impatience as his bellow increased in volume and pitch. "But what does she mean by *think bigger…perhaps the whole store?*"

Finn yanked the message out of Fio's hand. He read the message quietly, "She says hello like nothing big is going on, sounds flighty, clearly has to be careful with what she writes of course. Okay, then she says, 'The original idea that I was looking for on my shopping trip just isn't the right thing, darling. I think we should think bigger. Maybe it's not about the perfect item, but bigger. Perhaps the whole store! Haha - Love and miss you. See you soon.'"

Roxy urgently set her hand on his arm. "Wait! Does that mean—"

"*Shh*," Finn interjected. "Don't say it." His gaze darted around and took in all the people surreptitiously watching them. "Quick. In Fio's office."

Roxy and Finn rapidly followed after Fio as he headed to his office in a jog. Finn closed the door, having a hard time not seeing Lane's ghost all over that office. Walking gingerly over the tiger skin rug, bringing in her own chair, taking copious notes, making that gesture when she brings a stray hair around her ear and crinkling her nose when she's deep in thought…

Fio exclaimed, "Okay, so enlighten me. What does Lane mean?"

Finn cleared his throat and said, "She's saying that our first plan, that the hit happening onboard the *Hindenburg* isn't the actual target. It's not Daphne's plan."

Fio said, "All right. But what does that second part mean?"

"It means the hit isn't *just* a person, we have to think bigger," said Roxy, her color rising in terror.

Finn said, "The hit isn't going to happen on the *Hindenburg*, it's the whole thing. The hit *is* the *Hindenburg*."

Fio sat down hard into his chair, looking as sick as Finn felt. "Okay. How do we help? Lane is the only one who can handle everything up there; how can we help down here? And where the hell is the *Hindenburg* now? It's over ten hours late, I heard it hovered over Manhattan just a bit ago, after 3 p.m."

"Yes," said Finn. "So at the very least, we can assume that if the idea was to do something over Manhattan, Lane either thwarted it or it's a plan for later."

"Which is good news," exclaimed Roxy.

"Very," emphasized Fiorello. "Because that could have meant thousands of lives. All right, we need to get out to Lakehurst."

"I'll call in extra hands with the NYPD," said Finn.

"I'll have a few extra fire trucks available with New Jersey," said Fio. "I'll make it sound like it's just an overabundance of caution since it's been raining."

"Right. Let's go. Roxy, can you stay here and be on radio communications? If Lane sends another message, we *have* to know. Then you can radio us," said Finn.

"Got it! I won't leave," said Roxy, determination making her voice harsh.

"Come on, Finn. I'll have my driver get us there. Let's go!" said Fio, off like a shot out the door and down the stairs at a run.

Fiorello's driver missed his true calling.

"Goddammit, Ray, it's not the Grand Prix! Get us there alive, mate!" shouted Finn, holding onto the door handle while Ray careened around a corner toward the Holland Tunnel. Fio simply urged him on, fearless. Then again, the drive could take a few hours. If they were lucky. "Scratch that. Push it, Ray."

Chapter 48

Tucker and I made our way from the radio room to the control car, then climbed down the ladder.

"I don't like this even more," grumbled Tucker, making my heart lurch, missing Roarke, my usual sleuthing partner.

Every mile closer to Lakehurst, fear gripped me tighter. I cared so much. I had to force myself to stay level-headed. I was the queen of getting us out of tricky predicaments, I could do it again.

Daphne was not in the control car, but we thought to ask Captain Pruss about her, since he and his crew had been obvious fans of hers.

"Ah yes! She is with Crewman Schnitz getting a tour with Mr. Spah." His face that had been delighted when discussing Daphne, then grew disgruntled with the mention of Mr. Spah.

"Has Mr. Spah been a problem for the crew?" I asked.

"That dog of his. He has been sneaking around to give her treats and walks. We are under strict orders to not allow unchaperoned passengers anywhere on the ship." I tried not to give Tucker a guilty look, since we were completely not chaperoned at this very moment.

The captain chuckled, "*Ach*, not you two. You have been given clearance."

I figured my clearance came courtesy of a man who drank

martinis and smoked several cigars daily, finagling some kind of German permission.

Before we left, we took a good look around at the unbelievable view from the gondola. You'd think flying above the ocean or the flat lands of England I'd feel the sensation of the height more, but it was desperately more frightening over big cities. The soaring nature of the buildings—where we flew just a bit higher than the tallest spires—gave a dizzying perspective.

We crawled back up the ladder and went down the catwalk. We'd just passed through the hallway of the crew's quarters when we heard Daphne's voice. We both leaped into the broom closet we'd occupied on another occasion.

Tucker was behind me again and I backed into him closer as Daphne's voice became louder. A door opened and shut, and the musky sweet floral scent was right there on the other side of the door. The walls in the ship were thin due to weight constraints, so we heard every word clearly. But I worried they could hear our breathing or my heartbeat, it was so loud.

"All right, all right, Ms. Franco," said Mr. Spah in a belea-guered voice. "I will do it. Let us go now."

"Excellent," said Daphne with a little more zeal than control. She must've been worried he wouldn't comply. I rarely heard any sound of concern or worry from her, which meant she was near her limits.

Okay. I could work with that.

Their voices trailed off as they went back the way we came, toward the control car. I turned around, staying up against Tucker, our faces just inches apart. The light from the crack in the door illuminated his eyes.

There was that thing that I'd seen in them back in Michigan, when he'd tried to seduce me. When I almost let him. I'd been so shattered by the double life my parents had lived. I'd doubted myself and I'd felt so alone.

I set a hand on his chest and gently pressed him away. "Let's go," I said.

We carefully exited and strode in the direction Daphne had gone: back to the catwalk. I softly, slowly opened the door that led back to the cavernous insides of the monster aircraft. When we were almost to the edge of the radio room, we stopped and listened.

Voices echoed to us, but they were distorted, farther away than I expected. I peeked around the corner.

"Oh my God," I said quietly. Daphne and Mr. Spah were up on the higher catwalk. Where the narrowest ladder I'd ever seen reached far up from the lower passageway. The insubstantial nature of it was nauseating.

Then Spah did the unthinkable and climbed up even higher above that catwalk where there was no ladder, scaling the light-weight metal rigging like it was the easiest thing in the world. Something bulged upon his back, and at the top, the highest he could go, he reached behind and retrieved the pack from a strap around his middle.

It was silver, about the size of a large jewelry box, and he care-fully set it into a corner crevice. It was of similar color and sheen as the aluminum walkways and from where we were, it was invisi-ble. It must've been sticky on the bottom, because he pressed it down, then tried to rock it back and forth, but it stuck firm. Satis-fied it was secure, Spah backed quickly down, as simply as if he climbed up and down a tree. Tucker and I both leaned back behind the wall so we couldn't be seen.

"Finally. If you'd just done this yesterday, we could've had a much more enjoyable journey, Spah." She gave him a light double smack on the cheek. *Good boy. Sit. Stay.*

Just then, an officer came out of the radio room.

Tucker and I winced, not moving a muscle. The officer saw us but decided he wanted his break more than trying to figure out why we were standing there silently.

Daphne and Spah remained on the upper catwalk and proceeded toward the front of the ship. After they were out of sight, Tucker and I carefully prowled toward the ladder that would lead to the upper level. Then we stood there, debating. My nerves told me to stay put, but my courage said get up that ladder.

I shook my head and angrily muttered, "It's always about dangling over something terrible. A bridge? Sure. A speeding highway? Of course! Now a stupid airship." I crept up the narrow ladder as Tucker chuckled beneath me. Well, at least that was similar to what Roarke and Finn would do. I cracked a smile, thinking, *If Finn could see me now, good heavens.*

I got all the way up and landed my feet on the upper catwalk. It was better than being on a ladder with nothing to catch my fall, however…change that…it was suddenly far worse. A sound that no one wants to hear in an airship rumbled through the air.

"*Shit*, was that thunder?" exclaimed Tucker, almost to the top.

He was at a precarious spot on the ladder. I bent down and said gently, "It's in the far distance. Be careful, Tucker. Just a couple more steps."

Just as he was about to make the final rung of the ladder, the ship rocked a bit. Down lower, it was hardly noticeable, but up here…

Tucker's foot slipped. Goddamn slippery dress shoes.

I fell to the floor and grabbed the one hand of his still clasping the ladder rung with all his might. "I've got you. Take one foot and put it back on the ladder. You can do this. Breathe and concentrate," I said sternly but quietly.

He forced his flailing arm back toward the ladder with a massive effort and got his feet back upon the thin rungs. He let out a string of expletives as he shakily made his way up, while I kept my hand outstretched toward him as he clambered to the top.

He got to the platform, wiping the sweat from his brow with his arm as we both sat there stunned and breathing heavily. I said in mock-outrage, "Language, Tucker."

Humor had gotten me through a lot of scrapes, but before we could enjoy a moment of levity, we spotted Daphne at the other end of the ship on the lower catwalk. As one, we both looked up at the corner where that silver box had been hidden. I'm a good tree-climber and I thought when I got to the highest level, I'd find a way to grip the rigging like Spah had.

"Oh bugger," I said.

"How the hell did he do that?" exclaimed Tucker quietly. I tried to grasp the rail and levered myself up a little, but Spah must've had special, grippy shoes to scale the slippery metal.

Tucker gave it a go, too, but neither of us had the skills necessary to climb up there. No wonder Daphne had worked so hard to get Spah.

"So let's think," I said, crossing my arms and tapping my foot. "It has to be a timer and a bomb, right? What else could be worth all this trouble?"

"It's not a gift basket," he said with black humor. "And I'm certain there's a timer, Daphne would never commit suicide for a mission. She needs to show off. She's not going down with the ship."

"For sure. We can notify the crew once we've landed, but I'm worried that if we tell them now, she could find out and do something desperate. She's losing her control," I said, worry furrowing my brow, tightening my shoulder blades.

"We have to keep an eye on her; we can't be certain that she won't do something drastic. But if we're around, maybe we can stop her if she does."

I felt that way too. But what exactly was going on here with him? "So, for God's sake, Tucker, what are you doing here?" I asked, putting my hands on my hips. I hadn't come right out and asked him because I didn't think I'd get an honest answer, but I had to try.

A serious, deadly look came over him, and he said, "Jekyll and Hyde, Lane. Jekyll and Hyde."

He instantly crept away, leaving me no choice but to follow him. I looked down; the height below us was amplified by the surrounding airship's enormous frame and the knowledge that we were floating high above New York and New Jersey.

Suddenly, I felt her gaze. I looked down and Daphne locked eyes with me. She ran.

Chapter 49

We sped toward the ladder at the front of the ship where we'd seen her and climbed down carefully. We raced to the center stairways and first checked the smoking room. Nothing. We ran up to the dining room, and I caught her scent. I glimpsed the Chrysler Building's spire far in the distance. *Thank God.* We were already past the most densely populated area of the boroughs and heading to our landing at Lakehurst, New Jersey.

Doors slammed as I caught a glimpse of the shipping yards in New Jersey. We were nearing the landing. My mission was almost over. If I could get to Daphne to stop whatever move she was going to make, I could instruct the landing crew in Jersey to inspect that silver box before they switched crews and set off for Europe. The crew had been complaining about our late arrival; they were on a tight turnaround with a full manifest for that flight back across the Atlantic, as Mrs. Doehner had said. They'd have a lot of people getting miffed with the delay. But we were going to make them even later.

The flight back across the Atlantic. Full manifest. Because people were flocking from all over the world for the major Royal event: The coronation.

"Tucker! I think I know what she's trying to do. We can't let it happen. We have to watch her, but not spook her. We just have to land and get everyone off."

The next few hours were the most infuriating of my life. We checked every inch of the ship and it was as if Daphne had vanished. We scoured the kitchen, the lounges, the bathrooms… Of course, we couldn't search every stateroom, so it was possible she was hiding there or a crew member's quarters. We couldn't get a crew member to retrieve that silver box until we landed, in case it was something that could detonate, not to mention it would draw Daphne's attention, and who knew if she had a device to set it off early.

"Look, let's get a drink," said Tucker, clearly as exasperated as I was. "Honestly, this might be a good thing. The closer we get to Lakehurst, the better. We have to get these people off the ship safely—not to mention ourselves. At the least we've gone over Manhattan and all the boroughs which if the city had been the target, we would surely know by now."

"True," I said with a grimace.

"You said earlier that you knew what she was going to do. What did you learn?" he asked, resting an elbow on the bar.

I lowered my voice. "Okay. So we both agree that Germany made an awful enemy with her, the whole woman scorned idea, right?"

"Definitely."

"Well, they're not the only ones who refused her. When I was in England with Finn a couple months ago, the English gangs ultimately rejected her when we thwarted her efforts. Plus, the PM and the head of Scotland Yard helped me out. I brought in the whole cavalry."

He gave a grim smile as he pointed to his drink, asking the bartender for a refill.

"So in one major event, she'd get everything she's every wanted. She wants to create a spectacle that proves her power, she'd love nothing more than to make a strike against something the Germans love—our airship, and in one fell swoop create mayhem and injury against England? Because you know what's happening May 12th," I said with a significant pause.

"Millions will be heading to London for the coronation," he whispered. "That's it."

Chapter 50

We let a long pause settle over us as thoughts of what the next few hours could hold for us sobered our mood even further. But the clock just wouldn't move. Trying desperately to make time pass, I said, "Did you hear about how the initial plans for the Empire State Building had the spire act as a mast to anchor the airships?"

"Ha!" laughed Tucker. "I'd have loved to see Daphne try to maneuver down that. Leave it to her imagination, she'd have tried it."

"Don't I know it. Did you hear how she escaped from our last encounter?"

He shook his head. "No, I was still recuperating. From…you know."

His sister had been tricked into gunning down who she thought was Finn and me but turned out to be her own brother. He was lucky to have made it out alive, but that recuperation must have been both mentally and physically grueling. I enlightened him about the chase at the theater that had been playing *Voodoo Macbeth* and her leap out the window when we had her cornered. Her henchmen had been lying in wait beneath with a safety net from a fire rescue crew. Unbelievable.

"I've got a question," I said. "What if she decides to parachute out? And if she starts feeling desperate, just picks New York as her target, she could do something to detonate it once she was clear. It's not as great as London, but good enough."

"We're too low for that, now. I mean, not that she wouldn't try it anyway, but the most experienced parachuters need 2-3000 feet. I think we're hovering at about 1000 or under."

We both had decided on bourbon, it didn't seem like the time for a martini or an Old Fashioned. It was medicinal, as Aunt Evelyn would say. I took a sip, trying to think of my home that seemed so far away, impossible to reach. The taste was like a physical memory of connection, and the warmth of the burn gave me a needed boost.

Tucker said thoughtfully, "You know, that whole *Voodoo Macbeth* escape is Daphne in a nutshell. On one hand she's clever and almost a—dare I say it—*fun* adversary. But then the other…" His voice dipped low and painful.

I whispered, "On the other hand…she could kill everyone you love."

He nodded without looking at me. Then added, "And your soul. I'd thought she loved me somehow. I guess I thought she wouldn't turn on me, but she did. She knew that Eliza was going to be tricked by Donagan. And Daphne could have stopped it, could have stepped in because she'd been pulling the strings all along. It almost killed me. That's when I started planning. I knew she was aiming to do something on the *Hindenburg*, but I didn't know what exactly. I wanted a reckoning. Something profound that would reach right down to her soul—if she has one. That's why I'm here."

I could see it. I could see how Daphne's charm and her beguiling manner could lull anyone into thinking she'd treat them fairly. Hell, I felt the same way as I'd danced with her. I simultaneously wanted to gain her approval as much as I wanted to take her to jail once and for all.

"We all make our choices, don't we?" I said.

"Yes. And if we aren't careful, the choices start making them for us." A clear nod to Jekyll and Hyde again. So he wasn't here to stop her, but was he here to kill her? To take over for her?

"Really, Tucker. Why are you here, clearly not working with

Daphne, but she's just happy to have you here? How did that come about?"

He took a moment to consider the question. Swirling the bourbon in his glass, he said, "The last time she almost killed me, I hadn't taken care to be absolutely certain what she was doing. I had my own goals and my own hubris got in my way. I made the mistake of taking my eyes off the wasp in the room, Lane. Thinking it wouldn't sting *me*. I will not do that again.

"As I said, I want a reckoning, and I won't underestimate her again. I simply appealed to her vanity and asked to come along. I knew she was up to something. I promised to not get in the way, and she loved the idea that my presence might give you a hard time should you show up. She knew about how I tried to get the gold pawn from you and…failed."

Before I could say anything in response, a shout and the sound of doors slamming compelled us to yet again run in search of Daphne and whatever the hell she had planned. The door through to the crew's quarters banged shut up ahead, but no one was in sight. We followed in pursuit.

"Ulla, good girl," I crooned, the German Shepherd was agitated and pacing. We ran by and slipped into the outer passage. I silently urged the ship to get to the landing quickly. And I prayed that my message had gotten through to Finn and Fiorello. Hell only knew what we'd face when we landed.

Angry voices rang out.

"I will not let you do this!" exclaimed Mr. Spah, racing back up the ladder to the upper catwalk.

"Get down, you idiot!" yelled Daphne.

"Stop! Both of you!" I commanded.

"Well, well, well, Lane. Aren't we all threatening and demanding."

Spah stopped in his tracks, having just reached the highest catwalk. His chest heaving up and down after his fast climb, he leaned toward the rigging that he'd shimmy up to get to the silver box, depending on what happened next.

I felt in my wide belt for my dagger. I'd thrown and struck her with it before, I could do it again.

"Don't move," she said in a deep voice, not sounding like her usual self at all. Tucker gasped.

She drew a Luger and cocked it. *Click.*

"No!" I whispered urgently. "You're going to kill us all?"

One side of her mouth pulled upward, that weird, creepy mask of her face slipped down and it was like I was at the lunatic asylum interviewing her all those months ago. That *something* beneath her mask was trying to crawl out. Chills ran up and down my spine, and I subconsciously stepped back an inch to feel the warmth of Tucker behind me. He didn't move away, apparently just as happy as I was for the human touch warding off the disturbing waves emanating from Daphne. His mother.

High above, Spah wanted nothing more of this. He outright ran along that upper walkway toward the front of the ship, getting as far away as possible. Daphne shook her head.

"Lane, Lane. I really thought we could have worked together after our lovely dance and all," she purred, sounding more like the Daphne I knew. Whatever happened, I needed *this* Daphne to stick around. Not the monster with the deep voice that lurked behind the mask. That needed to stay far away from me.

"What is your goal, Daphne?" asked Tucker. Ah. So he *definitely* didn't know what she was up to. He was telling the truth. At least about that.

Her glare turned to him. Her eyes went glossy like a frozen doll's.

"Tucker, dear," she said in that dark voice once again, full of disappointment and danger.

He inched closer to me and uttered, "Jesus."

"You really could have been amazing, you know? Your sister, *Eliza...*" she said, in a mocking baby voice. "As she likes to be called now, was always fickle. Dark and weird, just like I raised you both to be, but flighty too. Never could count on her fully." With every word, her vile hatred reached closer and closer to the surface. "But you, Tucker. I had high hopes for you. I can't *believe* you would turn on me like this!" She was losing control. That could either work to our advantage, or it could be devastating.

With the experience of someone who'd seen this side of

Daphne before, Tucker softened his voice and took on a more malleable stance. I could feel it from behind me as he lowered his shoulders and relaxed his muscles.

"Oh, mother. I could never really turn on you, you know that. I had to do what I had to do to get what I wanted. You know that was the number one rule you taught us above all else: You do what you have to. Take what you want." He was pretty damn convincing and that made my heart race even faster. Despite our conversation about a reckoning, was he going to inevitably turn to her?

As if she couldn't help herself, a small smile of pride pulled at Daphne's lips as her eyes softened.

"True, Tucker dear. True."

But she didn't lower her gun, and my gaze was glued to it. Daphne looked up to where Spah had been standing, then her eyes shot to the corner where the silver box was hidden.

I decided to finally reveal what I was sure would cause a reaction. She would never surrender. But I could get her talking. And if I could convince her that escape—which she was so good at—was her best way out of this, we could get everyone off the ship safely. We inched closer and closer to the landing field. I'd spotted it as we flew over it the first time, unable to land in the rain. If Daphne lived to kill again another day, it would be better than a desperate move right this moment.

"Daphne. You weren't going to assassinate Spah or Schäfer or even George Grant, were you."

"Well I was at first. So I can't fault you there. Spah was my initial choice since celebrity deaths always cause such fanfare; I'd be sure to get some good press. But after my *discussion* with the Nazis, I changed plans. And you know? Things became much more interesting then. Necessity truly is the mother of invention."

This right here was why Daphne was a diabolical opponent. She was charismatic in her own way at the same time she was talking about killing people.

"Did you like my message from your dear Fiorello?" she said with a snap to her teeth.

"You sent that?" I gasped.

"Well I had to *help* you on your mission, now, didn't I?" she said with a sarcastic lilt. "I needed to have you on the trail to protect someone and to quit bothering *moi*. And I figured a good Brit like George Grant, tied to great wealth would be a lovely target. He had been another good option, but as I said, plans changed." No wonder the short message didn't seem quite like something Fio would write.

I decided I'd go all-in. Time to make the winning wager. "So obviously, the *Hindenburg* itself became your target. But not this trip, the next one. Most importantly, it became not only the target, but the *weapon*. So what was it going to be? Detonated over London just in time for the coronation?"

Daphne looked so genuinely shocked and dismayed that I had figured out her plot, I knew beyond a doubt that my guess had been spot on.

"Well, shit. This isn't going to work, is it?" she said in a droll voice.

She lowered her gun abruptly, letting her arm slam to her side. The force of which made me jump, she was not being careful enough with that firearm in the midst of a ship that held massive bags of hydrogen. Any spark could set off a horrifying chain reaction.

"Look, you have the gun, when we land, simply escape with all the flamboyance and style you crave. Live to kill another day, Daphne."

She smiled genuinely and chuckled in a self-deprecating manner like we were all good buddies. She was a master. Every-thing about her was curated to make us want to relax, to feel like we had won, and we could let her go on her merry way. It was all just a big misunderstanding.

I knew better. This was Daphne.

Another rumble of thunder sounded from a long way away, but it was powerful enough to make Tucker and me take a surprised breath. Daphne smiled wider.

"I guess I'll have to be satisfied to just take care of you," she spat out as she abruptly leveled the gun at my heart.

Chapter 51

Fio's driver Ray charged into the airfield. The *Hindenburg* was in sight, making its ponderous way back around after a long trip south, waiting for an optimal time to land.

Finn said, "They should be landing soon, right? That trip south was the final circle?"

Fio answered, "Yes. That's how I took that radio signal. I think they've delayed as much as they feel they can. They'll be almost twelve hours overdue. The next flight will have a quick turn-around, and they hope to take off about 10 p.m. They always do, it's a round-trip flight, after all. But this time the return flight is sold out, so they must be feeling the pressure."

Fio reached forward and affectionately patted the massive police radio taking up his front seat. He'd had it installed in his car for times like this. The back seat was full of the office supplies he used to do business from his car, which was where he spent much of his time. He folded up the little desktop and arranged some of the papers he'd been trying to peruse on the journey to Lakehurst. It was the most infuriating few hours of his life! There was nothing they could do but drive and hope they could help upon arrival.

Fiorello missed Lane dearly and felt that a crucial part of the whole office had been missing since she'd been gone. He dashed a look to Finn, seeing deep lines of concern on his brow. He loved

Lane like a daughter, but Finn? There was something of his soul swept up in his love for Lane. When they looked at each other, you could tell the whole world dropped away. He couldn't imagine what he must be feeling at the moment.

He gave Finn's knee a quick pat. "We're here, old boy. We made it and we can help. I feel sure of it."

Finn gave him a smile that tried to be reassuring, but failed miserably. "I just don't know, sir. I just don't know." Fio couldn't blame him. He was pulled taught with nerves, and the bad weather wasn't helping.

Ray, covered in sweat as if he'd physically run them the whole way there, raced to a screeching halt and both Fio and Finn bolted out the doors.

Finn immediately did a perimeter check, sure-footed and stealthy as a sheep dog surrounding his flock. Fio flew to the nearest reporter on scene. A van with a crew that was going to do a live radio announcement at the landing was all in place. Photographers were scattered here and there.

Fio asked the radio reporter if he'd seen anything interesting or out of the ordinary, trying hard to ask questions but not create a panic.

In that fast radio voice that actor and radiomen alike called mid-Atlantic, he said, "No, no. Nothing out the ordinary, Mr. LaGuardia. The only troubling thing has been this crazy weather!"

Just then, a long distance away, a deep roll of thunder crept toward them, making everyone crane their necks in that direction.

The radioman continued, "Well, I hope they land this thing soon. I'm starving! Been here for hours. My wife is gonna kill me, told her I'd be home for dinner. But this kind of thing doesn't happen all the time, too exciting to pass up. I haven't seen the airship up this close before, have you, Mr. LaGuardia?"

Fio was only half listening. The thunder made a thin sheen of sweat break out over his entire body. Pilots never did like it. Lightning and storms were unpredictable beasts. His time as a fighter pilot in the Great War was the most exciting, intense, and terrifying fun he'd ever had. But storms gave him the willies. He'd once seen lightning strike sideways, hitting an aircraft nearby.

"I don't like this," he said, clenching and unclenching his fists. "I don't like this one bit."

The *Hindenburg* was flying very close now, looking like a hulking, fat caterpillar crawling through the air, releasing ballast in big gushing rivers of water over the earth. The enormous mooring mast had been dragged into position on the field. The ground crews were assembled all around, ready to grasp the ropes that would be thrown down from the aircraft.

He scanned the area and found Finn and jogged over to him. "See anything, Finn?"

"Nothing. A few gangsters I recognize, but they're all occupied and chatty. Not a care in the world. Doesn't make sense. I thought we'd find something," he said with a frustrated grunt.

"I know. Feel the same way. And I don't like this thunder. It's not too close, but it's never a good idea to land an aircraft with a storm in sight," said Fio pensively.

The ground crew was divided in Fio's eyes. Many looked just as pensive as Fiorello felt, the long wait for the overdue aircraft in the midst of a nearby storm. The rest were eager and excited, like the radioman. It was a teeter-totter of anticipation with no middle ground. It would either land perfectly, or… He stopped himself. It was too unthinkable.

Chapter 52

"Daphne no!" yelled Tucker. "You'll detonate the whole ship!"

Daphne slowly blinked.

"Oh, I have no desire to burn alive in here. I mean, you'll be coming with me, Lane Sanders. I might not be able to complete the objective I wanted, but you'll fetch a fabulous price in the underground crime scene."

"Just don't pull the trigger. I'll go, Daphne," I said. I didn't know what to do. I could tackle her or throw my dagger at her, I was a great shot, but she'd pull the trigger and the whole place would go up in flames.

Daphne looked around her, then went on tiptoes to see through the window slats, perhaps trying to get a feel for where we were. I'd been doing the same, and we were so close. We'd been descending and I could even glimpse the approaching mooring mast below us. A fine drizzle had been falling, and the ground was glossy with the airfield lights and news trucks and cars surrounding the area. I could hear the crewmen lowering the guide ropes from the outside perimeter of the ship.

She eyed the control car not too far away from us, then her eyes shot to the silver box. She shook her head in frustration. "I can't believe you ruined my plan again." My eyes went wide as I had never seen her so clearly exasperated. She breathed in and out like a bull preparing for a raging charge.

"I will never let you forget this, Lane Sanders," she seethed. "You have been in my way for too long. I should have come back to kill you as a child. But you know what? This is even better. Because I want you to know that I will *ruin* the life you planned and the lives of your loved ones!" Her voice went dark and became a growl.

The game we'd been playing came to an end. No more cat and mouse chases. No more dances. The end.

"I know where you live, I know where your friends live and what matters to them. I know that you think of Evelyn and Kirkland as your mother and father. I know that Fiorello is another father figure. I know you love Finn. Hell, I even know you value Tucker! I see you leaning into each other. I will finish you. I will take care of you both once and for all, and I want your dying thoughts to be that I will torture every one of your family and friends. And I will enjoy every minute of it," she hissed. Her body swayed back and forth, as if she were listening to some forbidden and disturbing internal music.

"Look, I'll come with you. You know I'd do anything to save the rest of the people onboard. Right? I'm a goody-goody," I said, trying to convince the madness to ebb.

A look passed over Daphne's face that I will never forget. A look of malevolence so irrevocably evil, I knew she'd fully embraced that inner monster. She licked her teeth, then bit her lower lip so hard a few droplets of blood flowed and fell. She put a finger to the blood then sucked her finger. But she hesitated. She would ultimately want to escape, and I was a fantastic trophy. It would work.

"Halt!" said a stern, deep voice behind Daphne. He ascended from the control car like a demon from the depths. Schäfer.

"I've heard enough," he said, teeth snapping at every syllable. "You will not jeopardize this ship. We will land and you can have your little friends here, but then you never again set foot in my country nor our ships! Put the gun down and come with me. Now."

"Oh no," I whispered, watching the effect his voice had on Daphne. Just seeing him sent a shiver through her and a look of revulsion crawled over her face. His words were dripping with condescension and scorn. He was treating her like a spoiled child. I could feel her wrath building with every second.

He was woefully unprepared to deal with the likes of Daphne. He had his own pistol, but neglected to pull it. As if it never entered his mind he could have a need to; that someone would actually disobey him.

"I'll come with you, Daphne," I said soothingly. "Like I said, live to kill again another day."

But she hadn't heard me. Her gaze was glued to Schäfer, she continued to sway to that internal music. Then her mask fully slipped and a look of pure, monstrous hate poured out. Schäfer's face fell as he gasped. She snapped her head toward me, her eyes full of black fire.

"Goodbye, Lane."

She raised the gun toward the silver box and pulled the trigger.

Chapter 53

The *Hindenburg* was in position near the mast.

The ropes were thrown to the ground crew, the grass shining in the lights from the earlier rain.

Finn looked up at the giant airship. Lane was near—he could feel her presence. But he wasn't at ease. That nagging, terrifying fear hadn't stopped pulling at him, tearing at his anxiety all day. He'd expected to feel relief once they got to the airfield, once the ship was in sight and they were about to land. It would only be minutes before he could see her again, hold her close.

He looked over at Fiorello, worry etched across his face.

"You feel it too, huh?" Finn asked him.

"Yes. Yes, I do, Finn."

The ground crew began preparing, the beast was almost to the mast.

Come on, Lane, come on, Lane. You can do it, he willed.

The behemoth inched closer to the ground. Almost there.

Suddenly, a bright light against the dismal gray sky broke out in a small explosion near the rear of the ship.

"Oh God. No!"

Chapter 54

Daphne pulled the trigger.

In an instant, the silver box exploded.

Tucker and I threw ourselves down to the floor of the walkway as a blast of heat and fire shot toward the front of the ship.

Daphne's demented cackle raised gooseflesh on my arms, but as I looked at her, the ship tilted, and she fell from the platform onto a cradle of fabric torn loose below.

Fire instantly began eating the entire ship like a monster devouring its prey. The rear of the ship started to fall. Tucker and I bounced up to our feet and looked over the edge. Flames tore their way toward Daphne. The ship lurched, throwing us both to the floor again. Daphne held on to a piece of metal as the material beneath her turned to ash. Burning debris fell to the earth faster and faster, the fire had a voice of its own as it tore through everything in its path. The metal crumpled and moaned.

Only seconds had passed, but we could already see the sky in parts around us.

Daphne laughed, a demon-possessed sort of sound that made me wonder if there was merit to the phrase *making a deal with the devil*. I caught her eye just as her last fingerhold was about to break.

I fell to the floor and reached out a hand, just as I had with Tucker not too long before.

"The end, Daphne. Give me your hand!"

"Looks like you win," she muttered through her teeth.

Schäfer stepped to my side. "Enough," he spat, and gave a vicious kick to the railing.

Like the tight string of a violin plucked, her last finger hold snapped. In a snarling mass of twisting arms and legs, she fell to the hard earth far below.

The ship jolted sharply. Tucker grabbed my arm and I grabbed the railing. Schäfer's foot slipped, his arms trying desperately to find purchase. Tucker punched him in the jaw sending him flying. He fell screaming through the air and finally landed on the ground with a violent crash, legs bent at the wrong angles. Poetically, right next to Daphne.

"Go, Lane!" yelled Tucker. "Go toward the dining room! We can jump from there!"

The fire chased us. The front of the ship tilted upward as the ship sank toward the ground. Holding the rails and running as fast as we could, we made our way toward the middle stairs. The smell of burning sulfur and oil filled the air; a heavy, greasy smoke weighed us down.

The ship shuddered, and my foot slipped on the uneven floor. My feet went out from under me, and suddenly I was suspended above a fiery pit, flames roaring up toward me. Tucker stood over me.

This was the moment. Would he choose the path of the monster like his mother? There was no longer any point to a façade. There was no more game. He blinked slowly just like her. I'd been at his mercy like this once before. And he'd put a gun to my head.

"Tucker!" I yelled. "Make your choice!"

He grabbed my hand and pulled me up onto the floor as it began to buckle in the heat. "I already did, Lane. I already did," he said urgently.

We ran.

Never give up. Never ever give in.

Ulla! She was barking and yelping. I yanked open the cage and Tucker grabbed her. We ran again, almost there. Up the stairs. The fire was growing hotter, I could feel and smell my hair burning—we didn't have much time.

To the windows. People were shouting and running, desperately looking for their loved ones.

Some had already begun to jump, leaping right through the celluloid windows. We were descending toward the earth in a hell of fire, smoke, and screams.

"Go! You have to jump!" I yelled. I saw Mrs. Doehner helping her two sons out the window, then, after a wild look behind her, she jumped.

Tucker and I vaulted over the edge with Ulla at the same time and plunged toward the ground.

Suspended in the air, I fell and suddenly hit the ground hard, forcing myself to roll on impact. A sharp pain twisted through my ankle, but it hardly mattered. I'd survived the jump; now the ship was pouring down a molten inferno around us.

"Run!" I yelled.

I couldn't see Tucker. I thought I heard Ulla yelp in the midst of screams and groans.

The first large section of the ship hit the earth with a shuddering crash; sparks flew through the air like fiery rain. I looked up and the next section was coming down right toward me. I ran harder. I couldn't see anything. Was I running toward safety?

Then I heard it. "Lane! Hard right!"

I pivoted and ran blindly to the right with everything I had. A monstrous explosion erupted behind me, throwing me forward. I hit the ground with a crunch.

I pushed up from the grass and saw the *Hindenburg* sprawled across the ground, glowing and screaming in red hot flames. The great behemoth had been slayed. The reporter Herbert Morrison stood at the news truck nearby and spoke the words that would scorch my memories and fuel my nightmares for the rest of my life.

In an utterly heartbreaking voice, he relayed the enormity, the gruesomeness of what we just survived to the world. Tears fell down my face as he broadcast, "This is the worst of the worst catastrophes in the world! There's smoke, and there's flames now. Oh the humanity! All the passengers screaming. I can't talk, ladies and gentlemen. It's just laying there, a mass of smoking wreckage… Honest, I can hardly breathe."

Chapter 55

"Lane!"

Finn was here. He picked me up and ran farther away from the wreckage, the heat blessedly dissipating. I felt the cool drizzling rain on my face, mixing with the hot tears and the icy shock.

"Tell me you're okay, Lane. Tell me," he said urgently, setting me down, taking my face into his hands.

"Finn," was all I could manage. We held onto each other in a grip that tried to bring sanity and goodness back. He fiercely kissed the top of my head as he stroked my back, then rested his head on top of mine. His heart raced against the side of my face, my weary arms tried to draw him closer.

After a few moments, I forced myself to pull away to look around. Men were racing into the inferno and back. I spotted Captain Pruss dragging out Willy Sparks then being restrained from going back in again. Spah and Ulla found each other. I tried to make out the rest of the friends I had made. George Grant was on a stretcher. I spotted Mrs. Doehner clutching her two boys to her heart, but Mr. Doehner and their daughter were nowhere to be seen. A sob erupted from my throat, Finn held me tighter. Then I saw one important person I'd been searching for.

"There," I said, pointing to our right.

The smoke toward the mooring mast floated by in intermittent streams. When a section cleared, Tucker's silhouette walked with purpose toward the mast. He pulled out a gun. On the ground at his feet were a man and a woman with white-blonde hair.

Over the din of the smoldering crash, I couldn't hear it, but I saw two shots fired, one to each. Just then, Tucker raised his eyes and locked onto mine. He mouthed, *Just in case*. Then he gave a small nod toward us and limped off into the mist and smoke, away from the news vans.

Chapter 56

Finn carried me to the emergency vehicles. He set me down gingerly. My ankle might have been injured, but I didn't care. I was certain I could walk home from there; I was so grateful to be on solid ground in one piece.

I looked into Finn's eyes, the face my heart and mind craved like a warm, sunny day after a harsh winter. In a flash, all of the moments we'd shared, the adventurous as well as the quietly comforting, slid through my mind. Our dances, our long walks; when he saved me on Main Street in Rochester and when I saved him in London; flying a kite, kissing slowly as we danced in my house with gentle jazz music floating around us. I placed a soot-stained hand on his cheek, and the tenderness in his eyes was almost my undoing.

"You're really here," I whispered. "You seemed so far away."

He gently stroked the side of my face as he brought his hand to the back of my head. He nodded, eyes shining. "I'm here." He folded me into his embrace. He was all things fire, tenderness, and comfort. We were each other's champion and he felt like home.

Then came the bellowing and the screeching. The other man I'd desperately hoped to see.

"Fio!" I exclaimed in a hoarse voice.

"Lane, dear! Let me have a turn, Finn. Move over." He grasped me into a hug, shoving Finn to the side. "Dear God, I thought we lost you. We lost so much," he said, a look of haunted terror deep in his eyes.

"I know. It's beyond words," I said, more tears coursing down my face.

We stood together shoulder-to-shoulder, all three of us holding hands. Unlike most tragic accidents of epic proportion, this one took bare minutes from the gun shot to utter annihilation upon the ground. That massive, beautiful airship was now but a flattened, thin layer of glowing, searing metal. Those who could be saved had been pulled out within seconds of crashing, before total destruction and scorching heat made it impossible to do anything but flood the area with fire hoses.

More fire trucks and ambulances had been called. Thank God Fiorello and Finn had thought to have more on standby ahead of time. They were taking the casualties to several of the New York and New Jersey hospitals. I began to make a move to go help, both men put a gentle hand on my shoulders.

"Lane, dear," said Fio. "Let us handle this. You have a long night ahead, and I know I won't be able to hold you back tomorrow. Rest now." His sad, kind eyes were glossy with unshed tears. He cleared his throat loudly. "All right, Finn. Take her home and I'll see you tomorrow."

Fio arranged to go back with the news crews and directed Ray to drive us back to the city. Approaching the car, I took one last look at the wreckage. I wondered if the New Yorkers and Londoners who'd been saved from the virtual bomb that this could have been would ever know. This was a disaster that would go down in the history books. But my God, the epic, global disaster it *could* have been, was too ghastly to imagine.

"Ready, Lane?" asked Finn gently. I nodded. We got in, settling back into the car that at one point I thought I'd never see again. It was a strange feeling to see and enjoy a simple daily object, after a traumatic and deadly catastrophe. It seemed familiar and comforting, yet so alien and odd that the little pleasures of life could go on. As if nothing happened.

Ray turned the car around and pointed us toward the city. I showed Finn where Fio kept the secret bottle of bourbon. None of us had any words to say, the silence was our comfort. As we pulled away, I couldn't help but look back at the smoking husk of crushed metal and dying embers on the field. The twisted girders glowed a hellish red on top of the blackened field.

I rested my head on Finn's chest, finally. The last thing I heard was Finn and Ray talking about which route to take home and Finn verifying that Ray was awake and clear-headed enough to drive back. Ray assured him he was Fio's man; he would get us home safely.

At last, I succumbed to a black and blissful dreamless sleep.

Chapter 57

I didn't wake until we were driving east across Central Park. I sat up, rubbing my stiff neck. I was going to be sore tomorrow, that was for sure. My ankle was a little swollen, but not too bad. I could put weight on it.

"How are you doing, love?" asked Finn.

I coughed a little, the smoke making my voice raspy. "The city never looked so good," I said with a grateful sigh.

The lights from the buildings surrounding the park were a three-dimensional frame hugging the trees and hills like giant protectors.

Before we reached our block, a big black car pulled out in front of us and abruptly stopped.

"I should've known," murmured Finn.

"Who's that? Oh!" I exclaimed as Uncle Louie burst out from the car and came jogging over.

"He's been calling a lot. All the time, in fact, checking if we had any word from you," said Finn, trying hard to look stern but unable to keep a small smile down.

I opened the car door and limped toward Louie. I started to ask if he was okay, but before I could get a word out, I was suddenly engulfed in his large embrace, my feet lifting off the ground. It was like being hugged by a bear.

"Dear God, Lane. You're all right," he said in an urgent,

husky voice. "I thought I might have gone back on that promise to your mom. *Jesus*, you scared me."

He set me gently back on the ground, his hands remaining on my shoulders as he looked me up and down, trying to assess any injuries I hadn't disclosed. I put my hand on his.

"I scared myself! But I survived, Louie. Some bumps and bruises but nothing serious."

"I had to see for myself. Fiorello let me know, but the news is full of fire and destruction. I had to see with my own eyes that you're all right, dear girl. Charlie would be proud of you. Now, I'll let you get home to the rest of your family. I'm sure Evelyn is beside herself." With one last hug and a tender, fragile smile, he heaved a big sigh and walked back to his car.

I turned around and Finn stood a little ways away, arms crossed, watching. "So, he's been calling you?"

"All of us. Fio, me, Evelyn and Kirkland."

"I learned a lot about him and my mom on the *Normandie*. He makes a lot more sense now."

"I had a feeling about that, I'll be excited to hear more. He's had a stronger link with you than anyone has understood. Let's get going, if I don't have you home in a few minutes, Kirkland will be sending out a search party for us."

I nodded and got in the car. Touched with Louie's concern, I felt a surprising link with my mom. Evelyn and Kirkland loved her, of course. But getting to know a new and different person who loved her gave me fresh glimpses into who she was. It was breadcrumbs, but I'd take it.

The car hadn't even come to a complete stop at our place before the front door flew open and everyone I loved poured out and down the steps. I was suddenly in the arms of Kirkland, then Morgan, then Roxy, then Roarke. I was set carefully down on the sidewalk, hands steadying me after all the grateful exclamations had ceased. And my eyes at last rested upon her. Aunt Evelyn.

"Oh, my dear Lane," she said tearfully.

Slightly taller than me, she was so comforting to hug. She smelled of coffee, bourbon, cookies, and paint; and felt delight-fully solid and warm. Aunt, inspiration, friend, mother…home.

Finn helped me up the stairs, the adrenaline of being home made my ankle almost painless. We gathered in the back of the house. After, of course, I wrapped my arms around the delighted Ripley and pet his silky ears and rubbed his back heartily.

Mr. Kirkland gave us a small bowl of chicken soup, figuring we'd need some strength still getting over the shock. The sleep in the car had also helped, not to mention the sheer relief of being on solid ground with all my loved ones.

Morgan sat in front of me, leaning against the couch. I bent down and wrapped my arms around her shoulders. She rested her head on my arms and gave a contented sigh. I kissed the side of her head and sat back. "My God, it's good to see you all. I missed you so much," I exclaimed. "I do not like working all alone."

"Ha!" said Roarke. "Told ya!"

"Hey! Were you taking bets?" I asked hoarsely.

"We should have," mumbled Roarke, obviously disappointed with a missed opportunity.

The adrenaline rush was waning, so I quickly told them about the trip from the beginning in Paris with Miles and meeting with Josephine, then as Penny Adams boarding the *Hindenburg*—my disdain of the frumpy disguise making them howl with laughter and I-told-you-sos—meeting the passengers and trying to figure out Daphne's target.

"I knew it would be someone with power or wealth—anyone whose death would create an uproar. I thought it was George Grant, a shipping magnate, or Joseph Spah."

"The comedian?" asked Roarke.

"Yes!" I filled them in on Daphne's radiogram, trying to get me to think her target was George, then considering Spah and overhearing those conversations. Tucker's appearance and not knowing why he was there, with or against Daphne. Then the dreaded SS agent, Schäfer.

"Well killing a Nazi would certainly have brought her some fame, that's for sure," said Kirkland.

"But then I overheard them talking and he made it clear that the Nazis did not want in on a project she'd proposed, and they were so concerned about her, that they decided she needed following since she would be flying back to the U.S. on their beloved *Hindenburg*."

"I wager…" said Roarke, eyes glinting. "That his presence did not go over well with Daphne."

"Hell hath no fury…" said Evelyn as she clicked her tongue and took another sip of her medicinal bourbon.

"You got that right," I said.

I told them about Spah spiking my tea to get me out of the way, and the final moments of catching him scurrying back up to the silver box, the showdown with Daphne, then Schäfer appearing.

I took a long drink of water, readying myself, then relayed the last perilous moments after Schäfer practically goaded Daphne to take drastic measures and she pulled the trigger, the maw of the fiery beast all around us, racing to survive, and leaping out of the flaming disaster.

"It takes longer to tell you what happened from the moment Daphne pulled the trigger than it did in actual time. It was so fast. If we hadn't known that exact route from going back and forth so many times during the trip…if we had dallied one second more with Daphne…or if that staircase to the dining lounge had been in flames…" I stuttered to a stop, knowing Tucker and I dodged death by a second or two.

Finn gathered me into his arms and brought me back to him from the edge of the couch as I'd told the tale. He kissed the side of my head, and Morgan, still sitting at my feet, rubbed my knee, then laid her head there. Evelyn and Roxy unabashedly wiped their tears, Kirkland surreptitiously dabbed at a couple. Roarke caught my eye and shared a tender look. I'd missed them all so much. I still couldn't believe I was really home.

"What's clear is that you were the right one for the job," said Roarke.

"Agreed," growled Kirkland. "No one else was able to catch her in the act, but you did. The Nazis had Schäfer watching her, and don't forget Churchill had his man too. You did what he wanted and didn't just follow her, but outsmarted her. Only you have those instincts."

A cheeky grin pulled at my lips. "That reminds me, I wore the dress, Finn. Thanks for the message. I did lose it in the crash, though," I said with a sigh. "At least I had that dance with Daphne in it."

Finn almost spit out his drink. "You what?" Morgan and Roarke both laughed, and Kirkland smacked his forehead. I'd forgotten to tell them that part.

"Oh, yes. You heard me right. I needed to throw her off balance. I'd lost a round of our little chess game of words earlier that day. You see, Josephine Baker gave me the idea. *Hoo boy*," I said, fanning myself exaggeratedly. "She gave me quite the dance around the floor of Chez Josephine."

Kirkland murmured in awe, "Danced with Josephine Baker. Good Lord."

"Plus, not only were you right for the job because of your intuition, but I think Daphne admired you, in a way," said Morgan, thoughtfully. "I think she enjoyed your chases, so you had the best chance of getting close to her. And Schäfer sounds like he was like a bull in a china shop, most men would never know how to handle Daphne."

I nodded. "Tucker thought that, too. And he hadn't caught her in the act either. He was a puzzle. I'd caught him whispering with Daphne, but it was impossible to know if they were conspiring together or not. And of course I couldn't believe what he said even if he'd denied working with her. When we finally faced off with her, he was clearly not in-the-know about what she'd planned. Especially that she adapted her scheme after the Nazis rejected her offer, from a single hit to burning it all down. But I never found Churchill's man." I sat forward to pick up my glass of wine. "Unless…" I whispered to myself. *No. It couldn't be.*

Only Finn heard my whisper and he looked at me askance. I just shook my head, a notion that was too ludicrous to fathom had popped into mind. But it was ridiculous, so I dismissed it for the time being.

I quickly filled them in on a few more juicy details like the meals, the smoking room, and what it was like floating over Europe and Greenland, then at last told them I was very ready for bed. I glanced at my tattered outfit, scorched in places with mud and grass stains. I'd had a chance to wash my face but hadn't changed yet. I looked over toward Roarke and despite the late hour, he was yet again immaculate. He wore caramel-colored dress pants and a stark white dress shirt with a perfectly pressed chocolate-colored silk tie. Not a hair out of place.

He saw me glaring at him and gave me a perfectly wicked sneer, knowing what I was thinking. "Shut up, Roarke."

Morgan let out a snort of laughter that triggered the release of all our stress and fear. The tension we'd been feeling for weeks lifted, and I allowed myself a peaceful look around at the home I loved so much. The soft velvet green chair, the candles and colorful decorations scattered about from Evelyn's travels. The maple tree outside donned with tiny chandeliers and glowing lanterns. The friends who had become family. The enormous German Shepherd resting his head on my foot. The hand I was holding of the man I loved.

"Finn, take me to Little Italy tomorrow?" I asked, a yawn breaking over me.

He chuckled. "Won't you want to rest?" he asked.

"Okay. How about Saturday?"

"Yes. Always, yes."

Chapter 58

I wouldn't let Finn leave that night. Something desperate in me needed him near, and he felt the same. Ripley stood guard at my bedroom door. After a hot bath where I soaked my muscles, tended to a few abrasions, and washed the soot away, Finn and I fell into bed exhausted.

Despite the bone-weary fatigue, the raw and horrifying memories came back to me in the middle of the night. The searing flames, the clawing fear, the moaning ship as it was eaten alive by fire.

"No!" I suddenly yelled out with a scream, about to race out of the bed.

Strong arms wrapped around me and nestled me back into the warm and safe bed.

"It's okay, love. You're safe. I've got you," Finn whispered.

My heart pounded, my eyes strained to see my room and not the devastation that was burned into my vision. I finally focused on my books, then the soft blue walls just becoming visible in the early morning, gray dawn. Finn curled around me. I pulled one of his arms over me and placed his hand against my heart.

He nuzzled my hair and kissed my head. "I'm right here, I'm not letting go. Just rest. Think of me, think of Ripley just outside the door, think of Kirkland and Evelyn, the kitchen you love with the scrubbed pine table and brownies baking in the oven. Think of the beautiful colors when the trees sway in the wind on the patio…" He softly murmured good things to rest my whirling, tormented mind upon. After that, I could finally rest with the good and wholesome visions outweighing the evil.

When I awoke the next morning, I was deliriously happy to be in my own blue and white room with Finn still wrapped around me.

Still drowsy with the in-between time of sleep and full wakefulness, my body warmed and craved Finn fiercely. All that fear and separation, worry that I'd never see him again, then the utter joy of coming home and embracing each other. I wanted more, needed to be closer, yearned to release all that passion and energy and love.

I pulled his hand from my heart to my breast and reached the other up and around his head, curling his hair around my fingertips, shimmying even closer into his embrace. His body responded immediately, surely needing everything I did. He nuzzled and kissed the side of my neck, caressed my breast making my back arch, our bodies already moving in a slow rhythm. We somehow slipped off our nightclothes without stopping our kiss, heating up to a fevered pitch, longing to be together.

We lay in each other's arms, sated and happy. I'd never felt such contentment and pleasure, wound up together as we were. I caressed the side of his face next to mine. He ran his knuckles against the outside of my breast, making me sigh happily.

After a few more minutes of rest, we both needed to get to work. We got ready and at the door of my room, I took his face in my hands and gave him a kiss that brought out a good moan from him. Reluctantly, we left and went downstairs to get a quick bite to eat before we left for a long day ahead.

⸺

THE CASUALTIES from the *Hindenburg* were taken to a few hospitals, and I wanted to make sure they had what they needed. Fio would be busy comforting the survivors and handling the press and the authorities on the cause of the crash.

I met Fio at the New York Presbyterian hospital at East 68th Street, located in my neighborhood. We visited several of the injured, including one of several captains onboard, Captain Albert Sammt, then worked our way downtown from there. Funeral services for the public would be Tuesday, May 11 at the Hamburg-American Line pier 86.

The photographer Karl Clemens survived unscathed and met up with us during the day, to continue his photojournalistic duties. I gave him a big hug and arranged a photo with Fiorello. Neither of us had hardly any words, it was all so horrible. He'd quietly whispered to me, his voice trembling, "We had *just* walked those hallways together, marveling at the engineering, Lane. And then, suddenly, it was all gone. Vanished into ash and fire." I gave him our number at City Hall and told him to contact me any time if he needed anything.

The explosion had been so utterly devastating, it was shocking to me that there were more of us who survived than perished. But the number of deaths was still crushing. Several of the new acquaintances and friends I'd met had died including Max Schulze, the smoking room steward; Willy Sparks, the radio operator, whom Captain Pruss had pulled from the wreckage alive, but his burns were too great; and many other crewmen I'd come to recognize if not by name, by a nod or a smile. Captain Pruss, the commander for the flight, survived though he was burned badly after desperately trying to rescue his crew. George Grant survived, but a fellow passenger landed hard on him after he jumped and he was seriously injured. Joseph Spah survived, but it was confirmed that Mr. Hermann Doehner and his daughter Irene both didn't make it. She'd insisted on going back to their room to find their dad when Mrs. Doehner and the boys made the leap to safety.

I found a moment with Spah during the day and I had a few important questions for him. After telling me he'd drugged me on Daphne's orders and in the hope of also protecting me, he said, "Kodak gave Daphne the timer. It's a simple device, and they certainly couldn't have had any idea what she'd intended for its use. I'm sorry, Lane. I wish I'd never taken that trip," he said woefully. He also filled me in on details about the silver box and that he did in fact have special shoes as well as incredible grip-strength to climb impossible heights. I decided to forgive him, and I did not tell him that he had narrowly escaped being her assassination target at one point. He'd have enough trouble sleeping as things were.

After a long workday filled with shock, grief, and gratitude to those who helped save lives, Finn met us at our office. Calls had been made, and that evening we were to have a council of war like no other.

Chapter 59

Deep in the underbelly of New York, there were secret rooms. Rooms that held the power to change the course of history. I had never been there before even though I'd heard about them. Not wanting to be followed, we left separately from a side door outside City Hall. Finn and I met up with Fiorello who sported some shoes with higher heels than he was used to and a fancy coat and hat borrowed from Roarke to try to hide his very recognizable self from the public.

Fio looked quite pleased with his dapper look if the rise and fall on his tiptoes was any indication. I doubted Roarke would be getting that ensemble back. Finn waved over a cab. We all piled in and made our way to the Waldorf Astoria.

Within the famous hotel, Fiorello knew his way and we followed him through a maze of hallways and security points, an elevator down to a subfloor, finally arriving at a wide steel door. We walked into a subterranean, secret train station below the Waldorf Astoria and just ahead was a large railway car. Giving each other a knowing look, Finn and I stepped aboard.

Surrounding a center table in the midst of maroon velvet and brass luxury was Aunt Evelyn, Mr. Kirkland, Uncle Louie…and the President of the United States. Franklin Delano Roosevelt.

Candlelight sparked against the glass of his pince-nez, a cigar in one hand, mouth pursed in consideration.

"Welcome. Please, have a seat," said our Commander in Chief.

Words left me high and dry as I tried to take in every detail of what I'd only heard rumors. This train had been commissioned by our venerable president a few years ago to enable him to travel between D.C. and New York with ease. FDR's train car was big enough to house his limousine, so it could exit the train car below ground and pop out of the hotel via an inconspicuous exit.

It wasn't only useful for security reasons, but it also helped keep his polio diagnosis a secret from the public. Any image of weakness—being seen in a wheelchair—was not to be allowed in any leaders, but unequivocally of the President of the United States. Fio and I loathed the idea that leaders weren't allowed to be human, only superhuman. Fio faced ramifications of that notion because his diminutive height had stupidly been a hard selling point when he ran for office.

"I'm glad to see you relatively unscathed, Miss Sanders. Though I suspect the mental wounds run deep," said the president, after a thoughtful puff of his cigar. It seemed as if most of the leadership types in my life preferred cigars, and of course Churchill instantly came to mind. I recalled with an inner smirk the couple of occasions where he scoffed at our president's *awful taste in cocktails*, meaning the audacity to create a martini with the offending vermouth included.

My gaze settled upon Louie Venetti, and I gave a significant blink in salute, more than slightly surprised to see him in attendance.

Fio was a buzz of energy, ready for battle. I caught Aunt Evelyn eyeing our Commander in Chief, obviously debating whether she could seize control of the meeting. Kirkland, also spotting these thoughts most assuredly running through her mind, set a calming two fingers on her forearm, pleading subtle restraint in the presence of the leader of the free world. *Bless him for his optimism.*

"Thank you for having our meeting in such estimable quarters, Franklin. We do appreciate your time," said Aunt Evelyn in flagrant disregard of subtlety.

I mouthed *nice try* to Kirkland.

"Yes!" shouted Fiorello. "Thank you, this saves me from having to run to the White House again—"

Clearing his throat to cut in, the president interrupted quickly at full volume, "Ah, you're most welcome, Evelyn. Eleanor sends her love." Then, in the only strategy that worked to tamp down Evelyn and Fiorello who both looked as if they were about to barge into action and begin directing, the president rushed forward with his speech in a clear tone that suggested he was not going to offer any further pauses.

"Thank you for assembling on such short notice. As you are all aware, we have a situation of epic proportions. Despite having made 62 successful flights including 17 already this year—10 between Germany and the US, 7 between Brazil and Germany—the *Hindenburg* went down *here* in catastrophic fashion. We have had worse airship accidents with many more fatalities, but none that have been caught on the news cameras, thus the fiery demise will be up close and personal to our public. Overall, we lost 36 people. 13 of the 36 passengers, 22 of the 61 crewmembers and one member of the ground crew."

Finn took my hand, watching me closely. About one-in-three hadn't survived, the statistics were staggering. Those who died were farther from windows when the explosion hit or those who hesitated to jump immediately. It was a matter of less than a minute from when the explosion hit and total destruction upon the ground.

"Miss Sanders," said the president. "I have been briefed about your mission, but I would like to hear it from you personally. The exact details from what led to the trip and onboard the *Hindenburg*. You may begin."

I took a deep breath, then carefully laid out the beginning of the story with the murder framing Louie outside the Chrysler Building. His solid alibi from helping Valerie with the problem of her violent father, then the shooters in the car up in Harlem and the attack at the restaurant aimed at silencing her. How we heard that a hit that was to take place on the *Hindenburg*, realizing Daphne was making her move and I was the obvious person to infiltrate and thwart her scheme. I filled him in on most of the events onboard the *Hindenburg* (I skipped the dance with Daphne).

"Well, Miss Sanders. That is a doozie of a story," said the president.

The room had been spellbound. I'd heard authors muse, usually over coffee or brandy, that the true meaning of the story didn't reveal itself until the words "The End" were finally written. I felt the same way, now that I had told the story again from beginning to end. I could see the themes and the players within the game more clearly than I had in the middle. Thus that weird little notion that I had the night before when I reached for my wineglass made a tad more sense. The ridiculous one. The one that *couldn't be true*. I rolled my eyes at the sheer absurdity of what I was thinking. I quickly ran through a few more thoughts about the trip, who was there, who showed themselves as actors in the play, who had motive, and who helped me versus who worked against me…

"I've spoken with Mr. Churchill. I assume his man onboard was a bit of a mystery, yes?" said the president nonchalantly.

"Oh, maybe not," I said in complete counterpoint to his assumption.

"He made an appearance? I thought his orders were to remain hidden," he said with a disgruntled tone.

"Oh, he never revealed he was with MI6," I said. I caught Mr. Kirkland's eye just at the moment he put it together too, his eyes widening with realization. The old spy still had a quick mind.

"Well, then, how can you be—" began the president.

"It was Tucker Henslowe."

Chapter 60

The president let out an exasperated breath just as Fiorello gasped with the theatrics of a film star.

I hadn't seen it until that small niggling the night before. Even then—even now!—I wasn't wholly convinced, but there just weren't that many possibilities left. You either had an MI6 agent who should have been very visible with all the crazy antics that had been going on all over that ship, therefore his absence proving him to be a lousy agent. Or…he had to be hiding in plain sight. And I always loved a good bombshell-declaration. If I was wrong, so be it. It'd be worth the risk if I got to witness the shock around the room—and I'd been right.

"To be honest, I wasn't absolutely certain. I figured it had to be someone hiding in plain sight. But also, there's this…I finally put it together just now as I thought through the journey beginning to end, seeing the full picture. When I spoke with Tucker and asked him outright what he was doing onboard, he said that, ultimately, he was there because he wanted a reckoning with Daphne. *Something profound.*"

Impressed, Aunt Evelyn declared, "Well, that certainly would be a reckoning against Daphne."

Finn nodded, his eyebrows raised in significance. "Definitely. To not only turn away from her, but to *change sides.*"

"So where does this leave us regarding the public?" I asked.

"Right now," said Fiorello, "everyone is of course putting together various boards of inquiry. Captain Lehmann, not the acting captain, as you know, Lane, but one of the few who were onboard to observe, died today. He felt it was lightning—his final words urged the crew to jump, insisting lightning had struck. Some think it was static electricity that caused the hydrogen to explode."

The president added, "The Nazis are going with Act of God. The Air Minister, Hermann Göring, put that one forth. Not sure he sees the irony in that the *Hindenburg* was the Nazi pride, after all…" This made Kirkland chuckle.

Finn said, "Another is that the guide ropes created enough friction to cause a spark. And honestly, landing an airship in a thunderstorm is never a good idea, right, Fio?" Fio nodded wholeheartedly.

I added, "I think we leave it at that and not notify the public about Daphne's actions. Although Captain Pruss is talking vociferously about sabotage. We'll see. It's very hard to find evidence after an event of such proportions. I spoke with Mr. Spah today, and I learned a couple of important things."

"Yes, why did he drug your tea, Lane?" asked Aunt Evelyn. "If he wasn't already working with Daphne, why was that necessary?"

"That was the million-dollar question I posed to him," I said with a growl, still unnerved that he'd done that to me. "He said that it was Daphne's idea to keep me out of the way. Which seems likely because her man onboard the *Normandie* drugged two of Louie's men the final night to try to get to Louie, or maybe just to eavesdrop to hear about our plans in Europe and try to follow us. Spah says that he went along with the idea because he felt that it would protect me. I'd been challenging Daphne, and he was worried she might snap. Not to mention, he didn't like the looks of Schäfer and realized he was out of his league with those two, so it was best to comply. He felt that if we could just land and get off the ship, he'd have time to notify the authorities.

"We won't find much evidence of that timer and box. Spah told me that the silver container was made of a light-weight wood that had been painted, so that will have disintegrated. And the only mechanism inside was a glorified alarm clock with a small lever attached to what would look like any cigarette lighter, so that's probably melted as well. In fact, it was Kodak who gave her that timer, but they did not know what she meant to use it on. He was certain of that. But it exposes why she was interested in the Kodak company."

"The authorities will be speaking with Mr. Spah more fully, and I'm certain conspiracy theorists will be all over this for years," said the president. "Since he wasn't involved with Daphne prior to this and acted under duress with you as an eyewitness, Lane, not to mention it was detonated before the ship landed and he never had a chance to notify the authorities before lift-off, we will be sure that his name is cleared. It may take some time, and he might have to suffer through some interviews, but we can't clear him outright without more speculation.

"Despite this being as horrific as it was, it would have been inordinately worse if the ship had been detonated at any point on the next trip. Not only could we have lost the entire ship full, but the roster was at capacity with many powerful people."

I added, "With a sophisticated timer, I suppose she could have aimed to have it explode when it circled New York City before trekking across the Atlantic, but my thinking is that she hoped to detonate it over London."

I took a drink of water, then said, "England was the target. Because of the heightened state of the nation with the coronation for King George VI. We know the Crown had planned on King Edward VIII having his coronation May 12th, then when he abdicated, they already had so many events planned, they just kept them in place for George. England was in pandemonium from all of that, plus the losses from the Great War still affecting them deeply… The *Hindenburg* crashing anywhere near England would have been catastrophic.

"And don't forget, she was refused by England gangs on my last trip to London when we'd thwarted her plans. Not to mention that I got to be chummy with the prime minister and head of Scotland Yard," I said with a smug smile. "So she held no affection for them on any level. If she had succeeded, it would have been a master stroke. Causing embarrassment and pain for Germany, chaos and casualties for England right at the time they're crowning a new king, and most importantly, a massive display of power. All orchestrated by her own hand."

Evelyn said gravely, "It also could've started another war."

"I'm not sure that we won't have another war regardless, the way Hitler is ramping up," said Fiorello. "But yes, it would have caused untold devastation with all the masses in London for the coronation."

An important question occurred to me. "I witnessed Daphne hit the ground and then later Finn and I saw Tucker shoot her, to be certain she was dead. Same with Schäfer. Were their bodies recovered?"

"On public record? Absolutely not. Well, not with her real name at least. Schäfer we can just say the body was incinerated in the wreckage and send Germany some...parts," said Fio, with a murmured *ew* under his breath. "But, yes. We collected their remains," said Fio.

It was truly over.

At one point—I was almost embarrassed to admit it even to myself—I'd hoped that Daphne would somehow change her ways. She'd killed my parents, stalked me for years, harmed many others...but I couldn't deny a strange connection as I momentarily glimpsed her humanity here and there. Not that I ever thought she'd become a saint, there was part of me that admired her strength and clever contingency plans. In the end, though, I had witnessed the tortured power that she continued to lust after. And what happened when she lost the ability to choose?

FDR set his martini down and said, "Thank you for all you've done, Lane. I've been briefed on the reports, and I had the footage of the crash sent to me directly." Fio, Finn, and I all shared knowing looks. "All of the reports were *nothing* in comparison to the film. *Dear God.* I don't think that scene will ever be erased from my mind."

It was a disaster that no one had ever witnessed the likes of on film. The theaters that had those news reels were going to have a lot of terrified people on their hands. We let several seconds pass, a kind of moment of silence for those lost and those of us who just barely escaped alive.

"I think I might enjoy another drink," said Evelyn.

Her words broke the tension in the room, and the steward prepared another round. One person had been strangely silent. He looked at me just as I turned my head to catch his eye.

"May I ask about Uncle Louie's presence?" I said, an eyebrow cocked.

Mr. Kirkland growled and I swore he mumbled, "Talk about making his choices."

"Ah!" exclaimed the president. "Fiorello and I have been in cahoots on a special project. It will *involve* Mr. Venetti at some point in the future. And I wanted him at this table as we finish this mission properly."

"Why is that?" asked the supremely suspicious detective next to me. I reached under the table and patted Finn's knee. Mr. Kirkland wiped his face with his hand in exaggerated long-suffering.

"Well, we've made an…oh…let's call it an arrangement," said Fiorello with a mischievous glint in his dark eyes.

"An arrangement?" growled Kirkland.

"So you're back in business, Louie," I said with a knowing grin.

A respectful smile crept across the large, powerful man's face. "Yes, Lane. I will not retire, and I will remain in charge of my organization. I have agreed to help with certain *efforts* in the future."

I added, "Naturally, having a known leader in charge of your organization is better for us than a wildcard—and definitely better than a turf war now that Daphne's out of the picture."

"Precisely, Lane," said Fiorello.

Uncle Louie's salt-and-pepper eyebrows lowered as he sat forward, making us all take a quick breath of apprehension as the power he easily wielded rippled outward. "I also want you to know that I will keep an eye on Valerie's father. Furthermore, I have taken care of those involved in the car crash and shooting in

Harlem, and those who shot up the restaurant, Lane. They will no longer be a problem."

I gulped. The president smirked, then he took a long puff of his cigar. He waved at his steward to go ahead and serve the next round, and I bit back a smile as he indeed made martinis with far too much vermouth. Churchill would've given his left arm to be able to be part of this meeting, I'd wager. But he'd have been outrageously offended at those martinis.

Chapter 61

It would be a couple of weeks before we could get everyone down to Little Italy for a celebration of being reunited after such a hard mission. A plethora of arrangements needed to be handled, and it took a week after the funeral for everything to settle down. The myriad emotions—from the grief and the trauma we experienced as well as the gratitude and relief for those saved—were complicated. The nightmares began to loosen their grip on me, and City Hall was returning to its normal rhythm.

Finally, on a Saturday night, Da Nico's restaurant glowed and shimmered in light and camaraderie. Our long table was full of boisterous gaiety and food aplenty. I ordered a veritable banquet ahead of time, overflowing with gratitude and joy to have these friends and family with me. To be home again and safe. To be loved and to love fiercely. Amidst the platters of salad, pastas, veal piccata, penne a la vodka, chicken marsala, bread, and bowls of olives and cheeses, many of the people I loved gathered together.

Morgan and Roarke laughed loudly as they shared a joke and scooped more pesto fettuccini onto their plates.

Evelyn and Kirkland helped dear Frank and Patrick while Mrs. Zhao looked on with approval. Both boys unfolded their napkins onto their laps and used their forks and knives like gentlemen.

Eunice and Fiorello talked shop happily with two of her jazz musician friends from The Savoy, including Smack Henderson.

Roxy and her latest boyfriend chatted with Finn as I sipped my delicious red wine. Valerie was still in Italy, and I found myself wishing Uncle Louie could have enjoyed the time with us. But he was a busy man at the moment, not to mention his presence tended to make people nervous.

I had traveled far, and though it hadn't been for an extended time, it felt like I'd been away for a year. I'd missed them all, but I also missed my city. I loved London and a precious part of my heart now adored Paris. But the thrum, the energy, the glowing surprise of New York held my soul.

Here in Little Italy, this was where the heartbeat centered. Surrounded by people I loved from a wide variety of backgrounds and experiences. The glow of candles, the scent of garlic, tomatoes, wine, and pasta.

Finn caught my eye as I happily reflected. He leaned over and slung his arm around my shoulders. He moved in close and whispered, "Happy, love?"

I turned my face to his, an inch away, and said, "Very." His eyes darkened and flashed in the way that made my insides sizzle. I closed the inch between us and kissed his soft lips.

Just then, the musicians filed out from a back room, making those little *plucks* and *taps* of tuning their instruments that signal the concert is about to begin. The entire restaurant knew what to do. Evelyn clapped her hands happily and then leaned over to the young boys to explain what was going on. Huge smiles overtook them both as they energetically stood to help.

Everyone quickly scooted the tables to the sides of the restaurant as the first strains of their own Italian take on "Cheek to Cheek" began to play. Everyone grabbed a partner and began dancing. The music brought the whole place together as we swayed and turned and dipped the night away.

Much later and after Mrs. Zhao decided it was time for the young boys to go home, I sat down to drink some water and cool off a bit. Finn was dancing with Roxy, and Evelyn was showing

Kirkland a new dance step. I enjoyed a few moments of rest, then the song ended, and Smack Henderson and his friends joined the musicians onstage with their trumpet and saxophone. The Italian musicians were clearly excited to play a collaborative number, and they began a smoky, sultry love song that was less Italian dance, more hip-swinging rumba. Finn caught my eye, and I put down my glass of water.

He pulled me in as the notes of the song began to energize the room in a new way. Hips sank lower, waists were pulled closer. Our cheeks touched as we swayed together to that mesmerizing song.

Without pulling away, I whispered into his ear, "So the day my ship to France departed...did you give my question some thought?"

He moved his hand down my back. "Oh yes, love. Every day, every hour." The heat of his hand now farther south than my waist raised my own temperature. I put both hands behind his neck as we swayed our hips together in sync.

Placing my forehead against his, I asked, "So is that a yes?"

"Always. Forever," he murmured. He brought his lips to mine.

Later, back uptown, we walked hand in hand around my neighborhood, not quite ready to end the night. As we slowly neared my place, Finn said, "Want to get a last glass of wine? We could look at the stars from the patio."

"Sounds wonderful, let's go."

We quietly walked into the house, patting Ripley in hopes that he wouldn't bark and wake up everyone. I got glasses and a bottle of wine, then headed out back with Finn.

We didn't have a lot of stars that could outshine the city lights, but a few did, and of course the beautiful maple was glowing and gently tinkling in a light breeze. It was a cooler night, so I brought out a large blanket to put over us, reminding me of when we did this onboard the *Queen Mary* not too long ago.

Tucked into the outdoor couch, cozy in a blanket, I poured us a glass of wine.

"So you said yes," I said.

"I sure did. If I could have yelled yes loud enough for you to hear from aboard the ship, I would have. Now it's my turn!"

"What?"

He pulled out a box from his suit coat lying next to him and said, "Lane Sanders. You are the best friend I've ever had, the most beguiling person I've ever met, and I love you more than I could ever express. You're a wonderful partner in life and I want to be yours forever. Will *you* marry *me*?"

I had already known that we were semi-engaged from our talk of my "question" that I'd mouthed from the *Normandie*—and I knew he meant his answer was *yes* with all of his heart—but the ceremony of him on bended knee, his moving words, and a box with a ring surely inside…it took my breath away. I'd never felt that kind of warmth and love flood my heart so completely.

He opened the little black box, and nestled inside was a ring with an emerald-cut sapphire, surrounded by diamonds in a delicate art deco setting. He was a master giver of gifts. He thought carefully about them and picked them with a lot of thought. This couldn't have been more "me" if I'd set out to design it.

"Oh, Finn. It's beautiful," I whispered. I wiped a tear that ran down my face as he put the ring on my finger. "You knew I'd rather have this moment just you and I?"

"Of course, love. Our friends and family would love to be in on it, but I thought we might want this time to ourselves. We have always loved our times just the two of us."

"It's perfect." I put both hands on either side of his face and said, "Yes, I'll marry you. I'll love you forever, Finn Brodie."

Long into the night, under the stars, we talked about our future together and even shared another slow dance beneath the glowing maple tree —we didn't even notice that there wasn't any music playing. We talked about the things we loved, the things we were afraid of, the things we wanted to share. It had only been a year since I met him, but we'd faced a multitude of obstacles, joys, sorrows, and excitement. We'd seen each other at our best and our worst. I'd never been sure I wanted to get married, because I'd never found someone I truly wanted to share my life with.

Someone who would never ask me to dim my passion for my work or my city, but instead someone who would magnify it—and whose life I could enrich in return. Now, I didn't want a future without Finn. I knew ours would be filled with love and adventure, but also calm and peaceful whenever we wished it.

Chapter 62

I had some questions.

Yes, yes, yes, I woke up Sunday morning deliriously happy thinking about the future with Finn. But those questions pestered me. So just like I did on the *Hindenburg*, I sent two messages.

Later that afternoon, I went for a long walk, then sat on the bench overlooking the East River near Carl Schurz Park. After only a few minutes, a man sat at the other end of the bench.

"You're okay? You didn't suffer any lasting injuries, Lane?" asked Tucker.

Touched at his concern, I turned and said more warmly than I expected, "Thank you, Tucker. For asking." I took a deep breath. "Yes, I'm all right. How are you?"

He nodded, keeping his eyes focused on the barge sweeping slowly toward the Queensboro Bridge. "Yes, I'll be fine. I won't be getting the fiery nightmares to go away for a long time, but I'll be fine. So when exactly did you become aware of my...official position?"

I'd written what I'd discovered about his role in the note I sent, making certain he'd show up to talk. Tucker sounded like he was concentrating hard on the facts, but the hint of disgruntlement in his voice made me want to laugh.

I volleyed back with challenge in my voice, "Ooh, you're mad I figured it out." This was going to be more fun than I expected.

He finally met my eyes, all exasperation, humor, and guilty-as-charged. "You're joshing me. How on earth could you have figured it out?"

"To be honest, it wasn't until after I got back home. I kept wavering between certainty you were on one side, then certainty on no side but your own. In the end—"

"In the end, I'd made my choice," he cut in.

I said quietly, "Daphne really scarred you, didn't she?"

Lost in his own thoughts, he nodded. "I truly thought she understood me, that she was weird and passionate but that my mother loved me in her own way. And maybe she had, but her monster always won out. Over me. Over everyone."

So the son did what the mother could not. He'd accomplished what some people thought was impossible: he changed.

"So how did it all come about?" I asked.

"I approached MI6 directly, the Secret Intelligence Service started about 25 years ago and I knew they were aware of Daphne's long history. I figured they'd be open to hearing what I had to say. And I'd gotten wind that she might be planning something for the *Hindenburg*. I gave them the relevant information, then took a ride on the *Hindenburg* myself to check things out in early April, get some ideas. But I see you probably figured that out already."

I smiled with more than an ounce of smugness. Which was what most likely made him say, "But I'm betting you didn't know I was the one on the *Normandie* that you and Louie chased."

I gasped. *Dammit.* I hated to give him any satisfaction.

"Hah! I knew it. At least I have some surprises left up my sleeve," he said with an acceptable amount of aplomb.

"Bah. We thought since Louie's men had been drugged, that it was someone trying to finish him off or eavesdrop on our plans."

"Oh, there was a guy doing that. In fact, that was who I'd been tailing and lost when I was trying to listen in on your talk with Louie. Until you caught me. But Daphne was probably only keeping tabs on you. I believe it was more about information and his men were getting in the way of following you off the ship, so he slowed them down. Either way, I stopped the guy after he disembarked and happened to push him into the water near the gangplank." He snickered. "It was very satisfying. I made it look like I just happened to run into him. And he could swim so he'd be fine, but definitely unable to follow any of us." He abruptly stood, and with a smirk turned to me.

"Hey wait! Where are you going? I have more questions!" I said.

"No, that's enough for now. I think I need to hit the road. I see your next appointment and he's picking up the pace. Bye, Lane." His eyes snapped to mine, then he added, "For now."

"Well, hey! *Oh.*" My second appointment was making his way down the boardwalk with powerful intention. His formidable entourage scattered slowly outward.

Chapter 63

"Hello, Lane," rumbled Uncle Louie as he took a seat in the place Tucker had just vacated.

"Well, hello." I said as I crossed my legs with a little flair. I was really enjoying this situation I'd set up.

"I'm beginning to understand Fiorello and Kirkland's exasperation with the company you choose to keep, my dear." He shook his head and took out a cigar.

"Not a fan of the excitement yet?"

He grunted and puffed his cigar. "I was surprised you wanted to meet. But then again, I know you must have questions."

"Mind reader, huh?"

He smiled around the butt of the cigar. "Charlie would've too."

"So what's this agreement or plan you made with Fiorello and FDR?"

"I can't give the full details, but we all happen to agree that within the next five years the world will most likely go to war again. We need to plan now. War isn't so great for organized crime. Not on this scale. Rations, a draft, scarcity... Fio appreciated my efforts with Val's father, and he knows we have vast waterfront capabilities from our setup during Prohibition."

"Oh, so let's see. You'd perhaps make good lookouts on our

many waterways on the eastern seaboard. Especially for those U-boats, I bet."

"Jesus, Lane. Yes, that's the idea. You're even faster than Charlie." He shook his head, probably figuring he'd have to be even more careful if he truly wanted to keep his secrets.

I looked out at the flowing East River, enjoying its unique scent of both salt and fresh water. The current frolicked, looking like it was going in both directions at once. Chewing my lip, I wrestled with my thoughts.

Puff puff. "You've had quite the adventure. How have you been holding up as things begin to calm down? It's a lot to make sense of. I can't get rid of those images of the ship going down, to be honest. And to think you were on that inferno."

"The nightmares are slowing down, but still punchy when they happen." I took a big breath. "I keep running the scenarios through my mind, how things could've been different."

He sighed thoughtfully. "For the sake of learning, it's always helpful to think about our choices. But we can only look forward. We are human and can only make the best decisions that we can in the moment."

I nodded. "In the moment. Yes, that's what I'm chewing on. I was so close to stopping her, disarming the entire situation. Then Schäfer was a fool. He blundered in and effectively threw gasoline on the fire that was Daphne. It's heartbreaking to know how close I'd gotten to saving everyone. I know we stopped it from being much, much worse, saving countless more lives. But I still feel the guilt."

He gave a solemn nod. "Truly, Lane, you're not alone. I have felt that weight many times, the worst being that I couldn't save Matthew and Charlie. I would've done anything for them. For you. But there is only so much we can control. We can only do the best we can. Never underestimate the tyranny of the moment. We can have twenty-twenty vision in hindsight, but in the moment, it's impossible."

"Yes. That's exactly what I've been thinking about."

"If we could change history, we always think things would be better. So we kick ourselves even when we know we did the best we could. But there's no guarantee. There are dozens of possible scenarios and none guarantee that things couldn't have been even worse. So, we learn. And we grieve. And then we look forward." He looked out to the river, his gaze following a sailboat floating serenely along.

"I've also been angry at my parents," I admitted. "For getting us involved in all of this, for keeping their secrets from me for so long by making Evelyn and Kirkland wait until I was an adult to reveal the truth of their past. And if I'm honest, I'm even angry at them for getting killed. It doesn't make sense, I know."

I turned at the *snick* of a Zippo lighter being struck and took the cigarette Louie held out to me. "Thanks."

"Sometimes it helps one think."

"But then again," I continued as I blew out a sigh of smoke, "I love my life. I enjoy the adventure, and I crave making a difference in the world. I think it's complicated, and I can't say I wouldn't have made the same decisions in their shoes."

"Life is rarely straightforward, Lane. The older I get, the more I appreciate the complexity, the gray parts." His voice grew wistful. He spoke a little slower, the pauses full of emotion and speculation.

"The gray?"

"The parts that aren't easily understood, the nuance. That it's not a formula. I used to think everything was right or wrong, black or white, truth or lies. But it's rarely that easy. Tucker, for instance. He was bad, now he's changed. I've changed. Hell, now I'm even helping our government. Go figure."

I gave a small chuckle. "Yeah, go figure. I understand that. I had complicated feelings, even about Daphne. I will never forgive her for what she took from me and how much harm she brought to so many, but I glimpsed her humanity at times. She had a strange mix of enjoying life—especially our creative, cat-and-mouse pursuits—but she was also obsessed with control and just when I'd think maybe she could change, her inner demons won her over."

I thought about the conversation we had during our dance about her first balloon flight and her realization that people were missing out on the joy. But then an internal switch had flipped, and instead of the lesson-learned being *wonder*, her takeaway was that it was a powerful tool for distraction and could be weaponized for her own brand of predatory greed.

"We appreciated each other's skills," I continued. "Remind me to tell you about our dance one day." He gave a cough of genuine surprise. "I despised what she did and who she was, but I admired parts of her."

He said thoughtfully, "People are a complicated grief. Always."

"Yes, a lot of muddled choices and a lot of gray parts indeed." I sat forward and put a hand on his arm. "You know, Louie, my mom would be proud of you. She must have understood some of your hard choices in life. She certainly made a lot of difficult ones herself. But in the end, she tried to do right for our family, for our country. And you've done a lot for me and our family."

I pulled out a leather folder in my bag. "I actually have something for you. One of Aunt Evelyn's friends who is a consummate artist copied it so I could give it to you."

He set his cigar down on the bench as I handed him the folder. "Oh my word. This is incredible. Thank you, this means more to me than I can express."

It was an enlarged copy of the photograph of him with my parents. The artist specialized in realistic charcoal drawings, and it was almost identical to the photograph. Even the white fur around my mother's shoulders was gently blowing in the wind, the lively energy of all three of them radiated off the page.

"Maybe we can have more conversations about my mom in the future. I'd love to know her better, know more about the little things in her life."

"I'd like that. Getting to know you has made her loss feel not quite as heavy. I thank you for that." He put the folder under his arm, picked the cigar back up, and stood. "I should be going. If I stick around here too long, I'll start to get noticed," he said, waggling his bushy brows twice.

I laughed and stood. "You best be off then! Thanks for meeting. It's helped a lot."

"Well, it's quite a coincidence that you gave me such a sweet gift as I just sent one to your home as well. It's something that your mother loved, so I know you will, too. Better start heading home, it should arrive in about twenty minutes."

Before I could say thank you, he pulled me into an embrace. I hugged him back. "Thank you, Louie. For all these years of watching over me."

In my ear he said in gruff whisper, "My pleasure, Lane. I feel a little closer to Charlie when I'm around you. I'm forever grateful."

He pulled away, keeping his hands on my shoulders. Eyes twinkling, he added, "Also, I saw your ring. My sincere congratulations, dear girl." With a last gentle pat to my shoulder, he was off, his entourage coming in behind him to walk down the boardwalk along the East River.

Chapter 64

I looked out at the slate blue river, shining in the sun and gave a contented sigh as I stubbed out my cigarette with my foot. I spotted Finn hovering nearby and I gave a big laugh as I waved him over. "Not quite ready to have me out of your sight?" I asked, lightly jabbing him in the ribs with my elbow, then kissing his cheek.

"Not in the slightest, love." Finn slung an arm around my shoulder as we began to walk along the river.

"Good. I don't mind one bit. Had a couple of intriguing appointments."

"I'll say. Busy day. Learn anything?"

"A lot, actually." I filled him in on what both Tucker and Louie had revealed. Then I said quickly, "Oh hey, we'd better start heading toward my place because Louie just told me that he has a gift arriving there in the next twenty minutes. He also noticed my ring." I gave him a significant glance.

"Jesus, Mary, and Joseph. Evelyn will kill us if she finds out Louie knew we were engaged before her!"

"We better pick up the pace, buddy."

Chapter 65

We arrived home before any package and raced up the front steps. Together we told Kirkland and Evelyn of our engagement, and were met with much merriment, hugs, and congratulations. Fio arrived suddenly, unannounced, guided by his typical intuition that something important was happening. He'd barreled in, joined the celebration, and even shed a couple tears. He was such a romantic.

Life was complicated, Louie was right about that. I felt lighter after sharing those emotions and concerns with him, and later with Finn on the way home. I thought back over the last weeks when it all started and our race to Harlem Prison, meeting Frank and Patrick… In fact, I was thinking we might be seeing a lot more of them. I overheard a few conversations with Kirkland and Evelyn. I wouldn't be surprised if we had a couple more additions to the family. Then Valerie's troubles and her heroic mother, the shooting at the restaurant, then the trip across the Atlantic on the *Normandie*, the dance with the electric Josephine Baker, and everything that led to becoming the *Hindenburg* spy. I learned a lot about myself, the complicated nature of people, the endless support of the family that Aunt Evelyn and I created with our friends, and the fact that I not only prefer to be myself, but I also worked best that way.

I thought once again about the overarching theme of my life

that was etched into the dagger I carried from my parents: *pulchritudo ex cinere*. Beauty out of ashes. I saw that theme worked out every day in my city. Despite the hardship of the day, the beauty and the art of Right Now was so yearning and reaching, it begged to give us life. So, I would survive the fire and the despair of disaster, and I would focus on the goodness, the hard-won beauty. Josephine would be proud of me. I needed to write that fantastic, spicy woman a letter of thanks.

Finn had been whispering to Evelyn, and she ran over to the phonograph, selected an album, and set the arm to play at a specific point. "It Had to be You" came lilting off the album into our wonderful home that overflowed with love. I was well and truly grateful. I fell into Finn's arms, laughing, and dabbed a tear from the corner of my eye. I could feel all their happy eyes on us. Evelyn, with her hands clasped beneath her chin, beaming and crying.

"Come on! Join the dance!" I said. Kirkland and Fiorello took turns with Evelyn while Ripley tried hard to tippy tap with whoever was odd-man-out.

At the end of the song, Finn gave me a sweet kiss. Looking into his eyes full of joy, warmth, and spice, I said, "I'll love you forever, Finn Brodie."

"I'll love you for all time, Lane Sanders."

"I'll take it! Now dip me," I said, and he did, then added one more good kiss.

Just as Kirkland was opening a bottle of champagne to celebrate, a knock came at the door. Ripley, instead of barking his head off as usual, started yipping and whining in a peculiar manner.

Kirkland ran to the door, and Ripley was calming down, but still seemed rather excited. Kirkland came sauntering back with a goofy grin on his face and handed me an envelope. "Something arrived for you, Lane. Better open it up."

Ripley was circling Kirkland oddly, and I quickly opened the letter and read it out loud. "Dear Lane. Your mother always wanted one of these since we were kids. She said throughout history they had a heart of wisdom, magic, and mystery. There is no one I know who deserves that wonderful magic and love more than you, my dear. All the best and thank you again for reminding me of my sweet Charlie. Love, Louie."

"That's so sweet, but what does he mean?" I asked.

Ripley was nosing Kirkland's hip and finally I saw his sweater pocket move.

"What is in your pocket?"

With a great grin and more of that simpering, sappy face he always got around animals, Kirkland drew out a fluffy ginger kitten with blue eyes.

"Oh my gosh, he's adorable!" I exclaimed, taking him into my hands and nuzzling his fur. "Look at his great stripes! And white paws and little tail tip!" Everyone cooed and tickled his little chin and cheeks. He ate it up, instantly a part of the family.

Kirkland and I weren't the only ones enamored; Ripley was already deeply besotted with the little guy. Kirkland said, "No worries, I've trained Rip to be around other dogs and cats since he was a pup, he's good with them all."

He rolled his eyes just as Ripley dropped to the floor with all four paws in the air, tongue lolling out of his mouth. "And as you can see," he continued in a droll tone, "sometimes he falls in love at first sight. Good heavens, Ripley, have some dignity."

"There is no limit to what we can achieve if we believe in ourselves. Life is a dance and we must keep moving to the rhythm."

—Josephine Baker

Author's Note

To this date, the *Hindenburg* remains one of the largest aircraft ever made. It was the length of more than three 747s.

Chicken and waffles really was created in Harlem at what would become Bells Supper Club.

Fiorello did have a tiger skin rug mocking the Tammany Tiger, an office in his car with folding desk and secret cabinet for bourbon, and he did in fact have the chairs in his office doctored to keep meetings short.

Eunice Carter was the first Black woman prosecutor in NYC and she is given credit for taking down Lucky Luciano in real life. Thank you to my friend, David Hammer, for telling me about her amazing history. A plaque hangs at 100 Centre Street in her honor.

I did a lot of research on the *Hindenburg*. I tried to include many of the actual names and backgrounds of some of the people onboard including the Doehner family, Karl Clemens, George Grant, Willy Speck, Max Schulze, and Captains Pruss, Sammt and Lehmann. Joseph Spah was an acrobat and comedian in real life who did bring his German Shepherd, Ulla, on the trip. Spah survived but had to endure many interviews after the crash because he had been seen below with Ulla a few times and because of that, was a person of interest.

Thanks to my husband, Bryan, who is a wonderful research

assistant and found some amazing books with the menus that I included from the Hindenburg, photos of the rooms and berths, as well as insights into what it was like to be onboard.

Hopefully after reading this novel, you'll have an even greater understanding of how and why there have been such wild conspiracy theories about the *Hindenburg* crash. There was plenty of empirical, scientific, and weather-related evidence that it was an accident. But that pesky, real life manifest of the next flight heading to the coronation! It was a lot of fun to play with. And in some reports, including a documentary on the History Channel, Captain Pruss had received intel that sabotage might be an issue on the flight. They chose to disregard it.

As in most of my books, the founding crime or incident happened in real life. Fiorello did in fact discover two children being held in Harlem prison for witnessing a crime. He had an absolute fit and the scene played out pretty much as I wrote it. It was a normal practice to "hold" witnesses back then, but children were another thing entirely. He got the two kids out of there and to the Children's Society right away. But this is why I love historical fiction: you get to be an eyewitness and really feel what it was like to be around famous people, wild historic events, and incredible eras. And what began this whole mystery was that I read about this account of Fiorello's, but the history books don't say *what those kids had witnessed*. So that's where the fun of fiction begins! What was a big enough crime to not only hold children in custody, but to place such an enormous bail on them…?

Many, many thanks to my dear friend Helen Brien for helping me extensively with Josephine Baker, her quotes and her style. And thank you for enjoying this adventure with me, Helen! You have been a delight. Merci beaucoup, ma chère amie.

Josephine. *Good Lord*. I wanted a spicy scene with her and man, I tried to do her justice. She gave me a lot of material. The more I read about her, the more I loved her. I tried to give her the words she actually said herself throughout history. Her club, Chez Josephine, was exactly as I described including the mirrors, the wait staff, her blue snakeskin dress, and the animals. She became a powerful spy in the French Resistance of WWII, which is what gave me the idea to have Lane meet up with her. And if anyone possesses the overarching theme of this novel—the ability to live a big life, to be your true self, and hold on to the beauty within our gritty lives—it's Josephine. I highly recommend *Agent Josephine: American Beauty, French Hero, British Spy* by Damien Lewis. Other fun facts about her: in *Zou Zou*, a 1934 film, Josephine was the first African American woman to star in a major motion picture. She received the French military honor, the Croix de Guerre—the first American-born woman to receive the honor. Josephine continued to fight for racial equality and even spoke at the March on Washington in 1963.

The Hotel Lutetia later renamed their famous bar Salon Borghèse—featured in the scene where Lane meets up with Churchill and Miles—Bar Josephine in honor of Josephine Baker. It is scrumptious! Truly a gorgeous library of liquor bottles.

All mentions of Evelyn's friend from England with dramatic omens, premonitions, stout boots, and a love for councils of war are Easter Eggs of Amelia Peabody by Elizabeth Peters. She was the author of the first historical mystery series that captured my imagination so much, I began to imagine my own world that I could create.

Acknowledgments

So much love and heartfelt thanks to my husband, Bryan, and my two sons, Jack and Logan. The past several years have had high highs, and low lows. You were always supportive, loving, funny, and the best family I could have ever wanted. Thank you for believing in me and enjoying the journey with me. Thanks to Bryan for being an amazing research assistant and for creating the New Yorker's Three C's Principle—Confidence, Confusion, Compliance. LOL. Thanks to Jack for giving me wonderful books and material on the jazz world, it was incredibly helpful and energizing. And thanks to Logan for being my adventure buddy all over New York City.

Special thanks to Tanya Crosby-Straley for the publishing love for these books that mean so much to me. Thanks to Kim Killion for the fabulous and spicy cover. And thanks to the whole Oliver Heber Books team. You made this project beautiful inside and out. Special thanks to Sally O'Keefe, Jill Stadler, and Pamela Oviatt for the hard work taking over a series midway and making the book shine.

The crime-writing world is amazing. Big thanks to Colleen Gleason (Cambridge) for your willingness to be a sounding board and to go above and beyond to help your fellow Michigander. Thanks James D.F. Hannah for geeking out with me about beautiful words and commiserating with the harder parts of writing. Thanks to Jess Lourey for your wisdom and encouragement. Loads of love to Deanna Fowler for wandering NYC with me and sending the mutual and almost daily laughs on IG. And endless thanks for the inspiration and love to Wanda Morris, Greg

Herron, Susan Elia MacNeal, Kellye Garrett, Kristopher Zgorski, Vivien Chien, Gabriel Valjean, Susie Calkins, Cheryl Head, John Copenhaver, and Catriona McPherson.

And a special thank you to my wonderful agent, Michelle Richter and the whole team at Fuse Literary, especially presidents Laurie McLean and Gordon Warnock. I have appreciated not only your professional excellence, but your kindness, your integrity, and your encouragement.

Discussion Questions

1. Who are some of your favorite characters and why? Which characters were most relatable or intriguing to you?

2. What are some of your favorite scenes and why did they stand out to you?

3. An overarching theme of the series is beauty out of ashes. What scenes come to mind when you think of that theme? What aspects of Lane make that apparent?

4. What aspects of the Hindenburg airship were surprising to you?

5. Another theme of this series is chosen family. What are your favorite parts of the chosen family in this series?

6. There is always a backdrop of art in each of these books that comes alongside Lane and other characters to help them in their pursuit of not only solving the mystery, but also working out their own issues in life. In this one, the art form is jazz. Talk about the scenes

where jazz was important and why. What performer or club would you love to go back in time to see in person?

7. Was there anything about the era that was surprising to you?

8. How would you adapt this book into a movie? Who would you choose for casting?

9. How did the book make you feel?

10. If you could ask the author one question about the book, what would it be?

Also by L. A. Chandlar

Art Deco Mystery Series

The Silver Gun

The Gold Pawn

The Pearl Dagger

The Hindenburg Spy

About the Author

L.A. Chandlar is the award-winning author of the ART DECO MYSTERY SERIES. She's been nominated for the Agatha, Lefty, Macavity and Anthony Awards; and winner of Suspense Magazine's Crimson Scribe. She's been living and writing in New York City for over 20 years and has been speaking for a wide variety of audiences including a women's group with the United Nations. Laurie has also worked in PR for General Motors, is the mother of two boys, and has toured the nation managing a rock band. She is a fierce advocate for women's rights. She loves coffee and bourbon; and hates thwarted love and raisins.

OLIVERHEBERBOOKS

A small press bound by the belief that every voice matters.

Sign up for our newsletter to learn about new releases and more.
https://oliver-heberbooks.com/subscribe/

Follow us on social media:

facebook.com/oliverheberbooks

instagram.com/oliverheberbooks

amazon.com/oliverheberbooks

youtube.com/@OliverHeberBooksPublisher

www.ingramcontent.com/pod-product-compliance
Lightning Source LLC
LaVergne TN
LVHW090841111225
827354LV00003B/14